I'LL PAINT YOU A SUNSET SOMEDAY

BEX ALEXANDER

*For anyone who feels deeply and anyone
still learning to let the light in—hold the line.
You are not alone.*

- playlist -

....

Invisible String | Taylor Swift

Belong Together | Mark Ambor

Us | James Bay

You Are In Love (Taylor's Version) | Taylor Swift

Wild Love | James Bay

Feels Like | Gracie Abrams

evermore (feat. Bon Iver) | Taylor Swift, Bon Iver

This Love (Taylor's Version) | Taylor Swift

past life | Elijah Woods

you were in my dream | Laur Elle

2% | Jenna Raine

The Architect | Kacey Musgraves

Innocence and Sadness | Dermot Kennedy

Call Your Mom | Noah Kahan

dead the day ur gone | Matt Hansen

Forever | Lewis Capaldi

Little Bit Better | Caleb Hearn, ROSIE

Love Like This | Ben Rector

Wildest Dreams (Taylor's Version) | Taylor Swift

I Don't Wanna Leave Just Yet | Thomas Day

Falling | Harry Styles

Ghost | Justin Bieber

Coping | Rosie Darling

Memories | Dean Lewis

Begin Again (Taylor's Version) | Taylor Swift

Timeless (Taylor's Version) (From The Vault) | Taylor Swift

- prologue -

Hallee (December 31, 2041)

Note to self—manifestation requires diligent attention to detail. It seems I've willed into existence ending the year with a bang. Unfortunately, said "bang" is my face landing a bullseye on the corner of a barstool as I mosey over to my friends huddled in the corner of the club.

Well, *friends* is a relative term, at least in these circumstances. A more appropriate title would be forced acquaintances or predestined companions. The truth is, I can't remember the last time someone called me a friend.

I can't remember much at all.

Because it's New Year's Eve, we've cast our votes for the final labels to define us, celebrating the memories we made and the personalities we grew into. *Least Coordinated*—that was the superlative awarded to me this year. With only ten minutes left, I'm properly fulfilling the given title. However, I can't say I'm sad to see it go. Surely it can't be my best.

Embarrassment welcomed me in a warm embrace but did nothing to slow my fall, and judgmental eyes laughed as the cold smack of the concrete floor rattled my hollow bones. Well, they aren't actually hollow, are they? I'll have to research it tomorrow if I remember. Which, I won't. In a mere few minutes, this spotlight moment will be forgotten. Hopefully the secret of my clumsy past won't be revealed by a purple and blue shiner highlighting my cheekbone in the morning.

Air—the ultimate opponent. Who knew?

Attempting to reclaim my final ounce of dignity, my hand grabs the end of the barstool. It was rude of it to assault me, so the least it can do is help me up. Too bad I can't sue it for emotional and physical damages. The crowd's lingering, mocking stares would close the case in my favor.

"What the fu—"

"Oh my gosh!" I gasp, suddenly drenched in the nauseating smell of a freshly mixed whiskey sour. "*Really*, it couldn't have been vodka?"

"Excuse *you*, whiskey is a perfectly respectable drink for a man," the extension of the drink grumbles, steadying me with his hands.

Tears lock and load in my eyes, preparing to send streams of self-consciousness down my face, but my laughter soaks them up before they can ruin my makeup. What an unplanned, messy end to the year.

Least Coordinated, indeed.

One glance into *Whiskey Sour's* eyes burns my cheeks more than whiskey burns to drink, and the smug little smirk on his face only raises the stakes. I hate that he knows I'm embarrassed, but at least he doesn't look like he wants to fight anymore. As his hands unclenched, he must've inhaled a shred of empathy for me. Or maybe he's hoping I'll buy him another drink.

Using his beverage as my evening shower surely warrants an apology, but *Least Coordinated* seems to have forgotten how to hold a conversation. How typical of me. After a year of trying, I still haven't won the battle against my timidity. Will I ever?

"If you wanted to shower with me," he slurs, taking a single step forward, "you could've just asked."

Verbal denial isn't my strong suit, so a shy smirk and a quick shrug will have to suffice. Of course I don't want to shower with him. But maybe I would, if I could? I mean, look at him.

In a half-hearted attempt to end the year on a good note, he reaches out. It wouldn't matter if it ended poorly, but it wouldn't kill me to shake his hand either, and I might as well put the icing on the cake with my winning smile. It's the sweetest one I have, but like anything these days, it's forgettable at best.

"Hallee," I blurt, "but my friends call me Hal. So either one works, I guess."

Time slows as my name sails away in the sea of his hazel eyes. Criminally attractive, that's what he is, and my cheeks heat as his sparkling gaze crashes over me, flowing from head to toe. Someone arrest him for looking this good on a night we won't remember.

Those eyes of his are the kind you can't say no to. They're a momentary escape to an infinite galaxy, speckled with an immeasurable amount of shooting stars to wish for all of your dreams to come true. Clearly, my red bralette was the right choice, because his wish-granters are fixated on my chest, and his jaw might actually cut me if I get too close. It's a compliment, I think, but does he have to stare like that?

Like he'd never get enough of me.

There's something endearing about him, innocent almost, although that's highly unlikely. Those eyes, that smirk—he's checked out plenty of girls in his lifetime. I wonder if any of them were worth remembering.

Am I worth remembering?

"Hi, Hallee, I'm—"

Strong hands grip his shoulders, hauling him away before his name's grand reveal. They must be his roommates. It's common to end the year with the only people we truly have forever.

I blink three times, my heart palpitating as the three musketeers run off to make a memory they will only forget. That is the one guarantee we have these days—the endless fulfilled promise that, on New Year's Day, everything will be forgotten.

It's my favorite gift I've ever been given.

Dean (December 31, 2040)

My hands tremble, pulling up the suspenders on my uniform as a faint yell urges me to get to the truck.

"We are ten minutes out. Let's go, Dean!"

This is my first year as a firefighter. At least, I think it is. Honestly, I can't remember. This is just the job that was assigned to me, no doubt because of my muscular build. It's as enjoyable as it can be, I guess. I can't recall what I wanted to be before this.

The drive to the house seems endless, as it always does when someone is relying on us. Keeping it together during the anticipation of disaster is the most challenging aspect of firefighting. The silence before the scene almost tears me apart, every single time.

We don't discuss it as a team, the horrors we walk out of together. It's not our job to be each other's therapists. That role is reserved for government officials. The keepers of our minds also being the keepers of our hearts seems dangerous, but in these circumstances, there's nothing to be done. The government occupies all of the jobs that require extensive training. Somehow, firefighting didn't fall into the *extensive* category, and they settled for relying on one week of practice to protect the city. That fairly risky gamble is their choice, so the casualties should rest on their shoulders.

Should, but . . .

Well, the memories won't haunt us for too long anyway. There's a time limit on our trauma because of The Gift.

A house fire on New Year's Eve is a horrible end to the year, especially when the scene looks like *this*. We got here fast, but it doesn't take long for our government-assigned housing to burn, so the flames have already reached the outer perimeter of the residence. This is unsalvageable. Nothing, and no one, walks away from tragedies like this one. Regardless, the mission remains the same. Save the civilians, stop the spread, and extinguish the fire.

My gear weighs heavily on my shoulders as my feet sprint toward the unstable structure. I have minutes, if I'm lucky, before the bones of this house give in, obliterating everything left inside. No pressure, but I better not be inside.

"Fire department!" I yell as I walk into a completely decimated home, and my initial assessment rings true. There are no remaining survivors here. My hands are of better use outside, but as I turn to leave, my feet lock into place.

The crackling of burning wood, accompanied by the pitter-patter of splitting boards starting to fall, is the sounding alarm that I need to flee the scene, but as I try to run, my feet protest. What do they know that my mind doesn't?

The neighbors' mournful cries coat the air outside as they witness the tragedy we're desperately trying to contain—the tragedy I'm about to be.

Then, like a whisper in the wind, I hear it. A faint and hopeless cry.

Every thread that binds my panic burns apart as the whimper echoes through my head. Surely I imagined it. Surely my mind is betraying my heart with the hope of a soul to save.

I'll wait thirteen more seconds. One for each of the lives I have personally carried out this year.

Thirteen stories that got to continue.

Thirteen faces that I will soon forget.

Popping wood counts the seconds as they pass, and my foot finally lifts off of the melting ground at second fourteen. As if I've stepped on a trigger, an unmistakable desperate plea rings out in a last-ditch effort for salvation.

"I hear you! I'm here!" I scream as adrenaline surges through me, stealing the remainder of my active consciousness and propelling me to the back of the house.

There on the kitchen floor is my fourteenth life to save, covered in the rubble of the home that once protected her. Debris rains piece by piece as I lift her into my arms.

"You are a *very brave,* clever girl," I affirm, turning to make our escape.

She covered herself in wet towels, which could've just saved her life, but as I race against time, her fragile body leaves me hoping that her desperate plea was not a cry of death.

The universe cuts the final tether holding up the house as we clear the skeleton of the front door. Collapsing to the ground, I shelter her body with my own and absorb the brunt of the debris. She's so limp, so unresponsive. Was I too late to save her?

Don't let it be too late.

Please, let her be alive.

Fear medicates my adrenaline, lowering it enough to draw attention to the shrapnel impaling my left side. A sound I've only heard from victims escapes my body. Scares me a bit. Scares me more that she didn't flinch at my scream. It must've scared them too because within seconds, helping hands surround us both.

Reassurance and comforting words are drowned out by the ringing in my head as I look around for the other survivors—some proof that this precious fourteenth life will not be alone, but no civilians step forward in concern for the angel on earth that might leave too soon. The punch to my heart hurts almost as much as my injury, and reality sets in.

She's alone.

We all are.

During these final moments of the year, her unconsciousness is the only gift that this universe can give her. As pain blurs my vision, the only peace for my soul is that our memory of this will be wiped clean in an hour.

- 1 -

January 1, 2045

Hallee

As my eyes crack open, I blink a cream-colored cover into focus. The fabric is soft, lightweight, and somehow fluffy. I can't quite think of a name for it, other than unfamiliar.

This bed is unfamiliar.

This room is not my own.

A chill snakes up my spine, shocking my heart to thud faster as I try to recall the events from last night.

Or the night before last.

Or the night before that.

It's not a hangover. There's no pounding in my head or overwhelming nausea. Just underwhelming nausea, but that's probably because it's getting harder to breathe.

What mess did I get myself into last night?

Why can't I remember any of it?

Tossing the covers aside, I roll to plant my feet firmly on the floor. The cold hardwood shocks them, but my shoulders relax as if the squeak of the creaky floorboard is familiar to me.

Maybe this place is mine? Surely I have a home, but the further I reach for the memory, the more lost I become.

If this place isn't mine, then where has its owner gone off to?

"Hello?" I call out.

"Hello?" I insist, but no response answers my question.

Who does this room belong to? The boxy furniture is as white as the unsettlingly blank walls, and it's all so hollow it's making me feel hollow, too. Even just *one* small pop of color would bandage the sting of the doctor's office ambiance, but apparently appearing welcoming isn't on the owner's list of priorities. It would be on mine. Wouldn't it?

Does anyone even live here?

"Hello?"

Is the air thinning? I swear it's thinning. Has to be because the room is swaying through my blurred vision, intensified by the bone-chilling silence. What is going *on?*

Why can't I remember anything?

My lungs fight against my emotions for a deep breath. Running through the doorway on my left, I crash directly into a bathroom vanity. The counter slams into my gut like my growing questions slam into my brain.

My name . . . what is my name . . . ?

Like the rest of the place, this bathroom reveals nothing about the owner. It's neat, clean, and seemingly untouched. The gold-rimmed mirror is practically glowing on the wall, ready to reflect and unveil the mystery of my appearance. Do I have to look into it? I guess I should know what I look like . . .

Bravery lifts my gaze, only for a moment, before fear stomps it back down. The brief glance was enough to notice long blonde hair framing a soft, timid face, but not enough to note any other details about my appearance, and shame punches me in my gut. What a coward.

Yellow sticky notes stuck to the side of the mirror catch my eye as I release a heavy sigh. To read them would be an invasion of privacy for whoever this cold, sad apartment belongs to. I shouldn't, really. Shouldn't, but—curiosity gets the best of me. The first one is written to Hallee, whoever that is. She must own the place.

Good Morning, Hallee. Happy New Year . . . it begins, and the handwriting hits me with a second pang of both comforting and alarming familiarity.

You are probably feeling fairly panicked right now. It's not the first time you've felt this, but I know you can't remember. What a rough way to start the year, am I right?

The first note concludes, and I don't hesitate to read the second.

It is January 1st, 2045. You've been given a Gift by the government to free you of your anxieties, regrets, and mistakes.

Panic is correct. This pounding in my chest is pure, undiluted panic, yet through welling tears, I dare to continue.

Everything else you need to know is bound together and sitting on the coffee table in the living room, written in the story of your life.

Oh, and Hallee? You have roommates.

A loud crash sucks the breath from my lungs, and my hands instinctively raise to shield my face seconds before I'm dragged out of the bathroom by my hair. My assailant is spewing words so quickly it's impossible to make them out, but fear and confusion are powering her. I'm less alone than I feel.

"Hallee!" I blurt. It's the only name I can remember. She freezes at the admission, left hand mid-air and wound up for a slap.

It's hard to understand someone's expressions when you don't know them, but I'd swear there's a desperation behind the overpowering disdain in her eyes. A brief blink of confusion, and then a plea to connect with another pair of eyes stuck in this quicksand of fear. She's less alone than she feels, too. Doesn't know it though, so she's a coiled python ready to strike.

"My name is Hallee! Please don't hurt me!"

Tears water the seed of realization that I know nothing about myself. I have nothing to soothe her restless hunger for understanding.

I have nothing to soothe my own.

As her face shifts into contemplation, my stomach sinks. The thought didn't cross my mind before I foolishly claimed the name of a stranger, but the sticky notes said Hallee had roommates. Those roommates would *definitely* know what she looks like, which must be why the firecracker in front of me has turned into a mute. She sees right through me.

"Hi, Hallee. It's good to meet you," she whispers, replacing the fight in her voice with a breathy gentleness.

"You're kidding me." I chuckle, hysterically. My sanity must've found the exit because it's running out the door. "Who did I almost lose my head to this morning?"

My question hangs in the air for longer than it should before she replies, "I wish I could tell you, but I can't remember."

The sticky notes weren't a joke then; we must be living in a gift.

"Hallee isn't my name. Well, I guess it might be? I can't remember, but I didn't want you to hurt me."

The shock on her face rattles any shred of peace I've started to feel in the realization that I'm not alone.

"I wouldn't have actually hurt you," she mumbles, crossing her arms to maintain her tough exterior. "At least, I don't think I would have."

"Okay, good, because I need to show you something."

Hesitantly, she accepts my outstretched hand.

The sunlight dances off of the pristine marble countertops as we creep back into the bathroom. Our reflections may be strangers staring back at us, but we are united and prepared to take on whatever comes next. My heart skips in hope, ignited by the glimmer of connection binding us as two individuals who have experienced a life-altering circumstance, together.

As she reads the sticky notes, her muscles tense, tightening her grip on my hand, and without a word, her retreating footsteps expand the space between us. There's probably a bathroom attached to the room she woke up in, but I don't follow. She should get to learn her name alone. It's the only piece of autonomy that I can offer her, my newest and only acquaintance.

Seconds could be hours and hours could be days, but when I finally tip-toe into her doorway she's frozen, white-knuckle gripping the edge of the counter. Tears gleam in her wild eyes as they rip from her sticky notes to me.

"I'm Marlowe," she says, trying out her name like she's trying on a new sweater.

A gentle smile raises my cheeks as my mind begins construction on a new castle of characteristics that will now be addressed as *distinctly Marlowe*. Long, auburn hair falling just above her waist, eyes as blue as the ocean. Model height, and porcelain doll skin that's peppered with freckles.

"Hi, Marlowe."

Not an acquaintance, but my first friend.

Dean

The translucent curtains in this room are absolutely useless. The sun may be silent, but it's still a brutal alarm, beaming through my closed eyelids and demanding I rise. *Not yet,* I groan, forcing my heavy limbs to roll me to my stomach. Burying my face in the pillows is the only escape from this existence. But where exactly am I? This stranger's bed must've been the destination of a wild night—why can't I remember her?

Or me?

Or her under me?

My sleepy eyes rise before the rest of me, searching for pictures of my conquest, but there are only bookshelves filled from floor to ceiling. Probably the kind of books where the girl takes off her glasses and the guy finally realizes the masterpiece that's been standing in front of him all along. Except if a man is so inept that he can't recognize beauty when it's standing right in front of him, his man card needs to be confiscated.

A neon red cover requests to be read, but it's clearly mistaken me for someone else. My priority is to get the hell out of here before running into the mystery lady. There's no need for the uncomfortable exchanging of details. I'm not relationship material.

At least, I don't think I am.

Who have I become?

Shoes are nowhere to be found as I stumble into the gray sweatpants and white T-shirt from the floor, but time is not of the plenty. This walk of shame will be taken barefoot, and alone.

Tip-toeing to the door, every expletive known to man sounds off in my head as I open it. Just my luck that the loudest door in the world is in this apartment and has turned my stealthy exit into an opening set at a concert. Hopefully I'm not here to see the main show, although I am a little curious about what she looks like.

Laughter pierces through the door's echo as I slam it shut. Damn, it's super lightweight. Startles me enough that I almost let my calm facade slip, but don't. Never let 'em see you sweat.

To my surprise, it's not my mystery lady behind me, but two men. They must be boyfriends of the women who live here, taunting the new guy escaping from his one-night mistake.

"The front door is that way," the one with the buzz cut says, sounding oddly entertained. Nodding a silent *thank you,* I speed walk my homestretch to freedom.

"Read the note on it before you go," his friend says with a chuckle.

Do you remember your name?

Must be a joke, except—my sanity slips through my sweaty palms. It's, um . . . well . . . my name . . .

What the hell is my name?!

Their smug grins transform into empathetic glances.

"Keep going," they mutter, like two annoyed brothers waiting for their little one to catch up.

Right, you don't remember your name. Actually, you don't remember anything.

Here's what you do now: go to the refrigerator, grab a drink, and sit on the couch until there are three of you. The answers to your questions are in the books on the table. When you are all together, you can start. Most importantly, you did not have a one-night stand. This apartment is yours.

Replacing fear with composure, I press my shaky hands over my eyes and start to believe I'm in a dream, until the opening refrigerator makes me jump.

"Beer?" Buzz Cut chuckles.

"Only one?" I joke.

Our clinking bottles cut through the tension in the room, and Buzz Cut sighs strongly enough to blow open the curtains of his brave facade. His face blanches with each step back to the couch. Looks like he's seen a ghost, but I can't fault him too much. It feels like we've all seen one.

The one with jet-black hair breaks the deafening silence. "Are we ready?"

"Do it." Buzz Cut nods, and somehow we've gone from strangers to a team in under thirty seconds.

He reaches for the three books on the table and opens the first, extending it out to me. I guess I'm Dean.

"Hudson."

"Matt."

"Dean," we sound off.

Hudson glances between Matt and me, running his hands over the top of his close-cut buzz. I'm not exactly a small guy, but he's a personal home defense system, and his deep blue eyes are an unsteady ocean of trouble. Polar opposite of Matt, whose blue eyes are much lighter, like the clear waters of a fresh spring that reflects the color of the sky. Really piercing, yet somehow comforting. It would be hard to hide anything behind them. His shaggy black hair would be a shield if it were slightly longer.

That leaves me . . . hair too long to be short, but too short to be long. Build too lean to be ripped, but thick enough to be intimidating.

Dean.

How long does it take for someone to recognize their own name?

By the third read-through of my book's short-written explanation, our circumstances begin to make sense. It's New Year's Day and we've been given *The Gift of Forgetting*, courtesy of our generous government. We live in this apartment together, and none of what happens this year will matter in the next.

Lifting his beer bottle, Hudson clears his throat.

"Cheers to a fresh start, gentlemen!"

My gut twists at the uneasy tone hidden beneath his excitement. Call me a coward, but I don't think I'm ready for whatever's to come.

- 2 -

January 2096

The History of Psychology 2335

"Good morning, class," the elderly professor greets us with a calm, commanding voice. Immediately, a wave of silence cascades throughout the seats.

"We're here to learn about the History of Psychology. If you're not here for the History of Psychology 2335, sections 4–9, then now is the appropriate time for your walk of shame." He gestures toward the double doors, hopeful that at least one student will realize their mistake and make a break for it.

A long pause is filled with shuffling papers of students double- and triple-checking their schedules. No one dares to take the walk, but I highly doubt that not a single student is in the wrong place. I've made it my entire personality to get to know all of the psychology majors, and there are about four faces in here that don't belong.

"Excellent, then we shall begin. My name is Mr. Holiday." Pausing, he waits for a few of the chuckles to cease. "Yes, you heard me correctly, and if I hear a single one of you referring to me as Mr. Christmas, there will be hell to pay in the form of a twenty-page paper. There are plenty of other noteworthy holidays."

In the front row, a girl shoots her hand in the air. She must be a freshman, all eager and way too excited to be noticed. Despite her excitement, Mr. Holiday stares back blankly.

"What is your favorite holiday, Mr. Holiday?" she asks.

The shoulders of my classmates tense as we wait curiously for his reply. It was bold of her to assume his apathy was an invitation to ask the most insignificant question on the planet, but after pausing for a few seconds of contemplation, he finally answers.

"Groundhog Day." He smiles, and our eyebrows collectively furrow in judgment. Seriously? The audacity of this man to choose arguably the most forgotten holiday!

"It's a day that reminds me to look at the light."

That's all he offers before diving into the lecture over chapters 1–3 in our textbook, *The Historical Accounts of Psychology and the Human Heart.*

Like most of the other students in this room, I binge-read all three chapters at midnight, desperately holding on to the last seconds of summer. Whoever altered the universe to allow professors to assign homework *before* the first day of class deserves a life sentence in prison. The jury finds the defendant guilty of stealing away our freedom and forcing us to think about the inevitable responsibility of growing up. To that, I have to say, eat glass.

The chapters were underwhelming at best, but aren't most textbooks? It was all introductory, briefly explaining how the semester will be spent—studying The Experiment. Or, as they called it back then, The Gift. My information retention would probably fail a pop quiz, considering the notes I took are a mix of average doodles and frustrated illegible scribbles, but who can blame me? The entire textbook feels like a marketing ploy. The author promises real and honest experiences from people who lived during The Experiment, but nothing was real back then.

How could it have been?

Time was merely a construct created by the government, controlled and orchestrated through a microchip. Once The Gift won the majority vote, there was not much to be done. Civilians were lined up like animals in a shelter, waiting to be chipped. It was carefully inserted into the back of their neck until, with one push of a button on New Year's Eve, bodies with souls were turned into hollow shells of who they had been. The loss was controlled, leaving behind basic skills and functionality but removing any personal intricacies. What a cruel form of "freedom." They turned an entire population of humans into machines and forced a master reset on history's hard drive. Life, liberty, and the pursuit of happiness really ran them down the wrong road.

Psychology is incredibly captivating to me. That's why I declared it as my major. My performance in history, however, is average at best. Don't look at me like that. I know it's important; it's just hard to grasp the concept of time when you didn't exist during most of it. If it were up to me, I'd have avoided this class altogether, but it's a prerequisite for the research lab next semester.

The research lab? Can't wait.

History? I'd like to leave it in the past.

The remainder of class stays fairly surface level. Mr. Holiday breezes through this semester's schedule in under twenty minutes before politely kicking us out for the day.

"I know that the majority of you are here because you are forced to be, whether by a parent, guardian, or the university. I am here because I choose to be. By the end of the semester, I hope you will look back and realize that somewhere along the way, you started to choose to be here too. For what is life without choices?" His rhetorical question echoes through his long pause. "This is a lot of information to remember, so if you have any questions, just ask. I value vulnerability."

Overall, his relaxed vibe makes me feel relaxed too, and that's not an easy task to accomplish. It feels like an hour passes in the silence before one student decides it's been long enough and starts the avalanche of students cascading to their next lecture. Crowds are not exactly my comfort zone, so I hold off until the initial rush of traffic slows down by casually gathering my things. That's my first mistake of the semester. Within seconds, the click of approaching footsteps drops my stomach like a rollercoaster ride.

Meeting the professor on the first day is never my intention; however, it does happen occasionally when I time my exit poorly. Bracing for the common questions about my name, major, and hometown, I spin to face him, but rather than greet me, he reaches down to retrieve a piece of paper.

Shit.

The first impression of my note-taking skills won't be an impressive one. I remember writing "boring" in all capital letters down the side of—yep. The page he's holding now. As his eyes land on the writing, his expression shows no change.

"Interesting critique coming from a sophomore. I'll keep this in mind and make it my goal to be worthy of being remembered," he declares with his commanding calm.

Before I can explain, or even apologize, he limps out the door. Risking the crowd would've been better than that.

Much, much better.

- 3 -

Hallee

Maybe if Marlowe and I don't move, then we won't be hit with the uppercut of everything we've forgotten and an ache for a place that feels like home. If we don't move, then we won't have to face whatever is to come.

I break our staring contest first and meander back through the perfectly placed living room. The centerpiece, a light gray sectional, is covered in furry white throw pillows and, finally, a pop of color! Three fuzzy blankets—yellow, cream, and pink.

My heart stretches toward the yellow one, but before I get my hopes too high that the happiest color might be mine, my eyes turn to a TV mounted cleanly on the wall. For a moment, I contemplate turning it on and distracting myself from reality with whatever show pops up first. Instead, not one, not two, but three books sitting on the round coffee table steal my attention from the remote next to them. Those must be the books mentioned in the sticky notes. But if there are three books, then where is our third roommate?

One turn down an empty hallway, my feet freeze before a closed door. Nerves are unnecessary. It's not a warzone waiting for me on the other side, but this is a little nerve-wracking—right? Another catfight could be awaiting me, and I don't think I'd fare well. Inhaling some grit, I clench my fists and get ready to rumble.

Knock, knock, knock.

Three times because three is good luck.

"Where am I?" a terrified voice reaches out. How do I comfort someone I don't know?

Marlowe is the "fighter," poised to strike and drag this girl out by her hair next, I'm the "flighter" that ran directly into a vanity, which leaves—the "freezer." We're the perfect trifecta.

"May I open the door?" I ask gently.

"Yes," she whimpers.

The approval was faint, but existent, so I proceed with caution, careful not to enter unless explicitly invited.

"Hi," I sigh, slowly cracking open the door.

Best guess? This girl's the youngest of us. Textbook beautiful, with a short blonde bob framing her delicate face. She'd be prettier without last night's makeup streaming down it. Probably didn't need the makeup in the first place, but most of it has been cried off anyway. The comforter she's using to hide her trembling body is soaked in tears. Runny mascara has stained it like spots on Dalmatian puppies, and a wave of nausea passes through me. Is there a way to get those stains out?

Marlowe struts directly into the room, reaching out her hand to the timid stranger. It's a gentler approach than she used with me, but still causes the girl to flinch, and her wide green eyes lock onto the outstretched hand. As Marlowe's shoulders fall, she finally accepts and willingly follows us to the living room.

Book is a generous term for the stack of papers on the coffee table. Surely I've amounted to more than just these few pages?

"Hallee," "Marlowe," and our third roommate, "Avery."

"Hi, Avery," I gently answer her silent question. "My name is Hallee, and this is Marlowe."

Passing around a few comforting glances, Avery is the first to reach for her story. I guess a "freezer" can still choose to move.

"Where. Am. I?" she asks again, braver than before.

"We're wondering the same thing," Marlowe replies. "I'm sure you heard the events unfolding out here and I'm happy to report, I would've won the catfight."

The joke was a good attempt but missed its mark in the fog of fear still surrounding us. Avery couldn't look less impressed, but entertains Marlowe in a conversation that dims to a steady hum as my fingers fan the few pages resting in my hands.

Most days, we don't know when our whole world is about to change . . . when a dramatic event will alter the axis we live on. We're blissfully naive to when information that could shatter us, rebuild us, and shatter us again will be dropped on our doorstep, or when a stranger will become a friend who introduces us to our new favorite thing. We simply exist in the ever-evolving world, doing our best to not fall face first in a big pile of failure. However, at this very moment, I'm keenly aware that everything and nothing is about to change, simultaneously.

Am I really ready for that?

- 4 -

January 2045

Dean

The first week of the year is always spent re-familiarizing yourself with the neighborhood, my book had explained. So, here I am. Exploring the city that is apparently my own, with no destination in mind and a cherry-red nose numb from the air's freezing chill. Anonymous faces pass me on their own adventures to unknown locations.

In a few minutes, my fingers will be useless. My jacket isn't suitable for this killer cold, but it's hard to dress appropriately when you don't know where you live. Ann Arbor, Michigan, is listed in our address. Apparently, Michigan winter has a bite that my wardrobe isn't ready to deflect.

Our books weren't exactly thorough. There are a lot of loose ends and, even though my room looks like a library, I don't care to search for answers I'll only forget. How long ago was it that reading was my escape? Two years or two days?

My mind's lingering questions accompany me and the wind as we pick up our pace—because freezing to death isn't on this year's bucket list.

In one area of interest, our books were crystal clear: government officials are the only ones who don't have their minds erased. They're the givers of The Gift and ensure the safety of civilians by watching us carefully. I should be thankful, but it's hard to appreciate their generosity when none of us can recall why we needed it.

Forcing my attention back to the sea of strangers, I can't help but wonder if any of them are government officials who remember me. The majority have focused their eyes on the city, familiarizing themselves with the forgotten town as it comes back to life, but to anyone who glances up, I give a soft smile—just in case.

Tracing my turns onto a mental map to home, I walk until my chattering teeth risk chipping and settle outside of a quaint corner shop. A trail of dormant ivy has grown up the navy matte siding, pointing each passerby toward an antique arched door. The warm light shining through its old stained-glass window beckons me to enter and find reprieve from the cold.

As I walk inside, a rainbow of colors shines across my feet, and the warm air shoots pins and needles through my hands.

Oh, this entryway is picture-perfect for an awkward side step with a stranger. Tight hallway, short ceilings—claustrophobic as can be. What a choice for my first stop post-"event." That's what my book called it: *The Big Event.* The lack of creativity is disappointing, but not surprising. It is the government, after all.

A part of me had hoped I'd stumbled upon a bar. A drink to take the edge off would've been nice, but after a slight left, the room expands into a cozy coffee shop warmly lit by the new morning light. The floor-to-ceiling windows on the farthest wall are excellent for brightening up the place, but a particular form of cruelty to the birds that might fly into them. Hanging plants cascade down from the ceiling, soaking in the rays of the sun. They have the perfect life, really.

Inhaling the peace of this place, I glance toward the line. A smiling barista is silently waiting for me to approach the counter. Is this level of patience always offered, or is this a first-week practice to bring ease to the nervous city?

Either way, I'm thankful.

"Good Morning! Welcome to The Marmotte. What can I get for you today?" she asks cheerfully, but my heart begins to race as I stare blankly at the letterboard menu behind her. It looks like it's written in a different language.

"Make me something as sweet as your smile," I say with a smirk. In a world where you'll be forgotten, there's room for some pretty big risks. Small ones too, like hitting on your barista.

"Yes, sir." She salutes, blushing and barely meeting my eyes.

Hopefully I didn't make her uncomfortable in the attempt to save my pride. Asking her to explain the menu would've been a little embarrassing, no?

Before I can make any more choices I'll regret, I turn to find a seat. Bench seating lines the wall to my left, spanning five fully occupied tables. To the right, past the bar, there's a living room setup where three women are sitting, one in each of the minimalistic leather chairs and another on the loveseat. The smallest of them laughs so hard she snorts, and hot coffee pours all over her hand. The other two join in laughing, and I swear the room brightens because of the sun-kissed, sandy blonde. That woman is a living, breathing sunshine. Even as coffee stains her rainbow striped sweater, she's radiant. Electric, really. Can't take my eyes off her, so I stumble to a seat in the middle of the room. This might sound crazy, but I wasn't ready to pick a side yet.

With every glance at the women, a pang of jealousy punches me in the gut. They look like they've known each other for a lifetime. Guys are slower to warm than girls, but not *that* much slower. These ladies have skipped a few steps. Or a hundred. Maybe they work for the government.

"Here is one smiley-sweet coffee," the barista says, laughing as she carefully sets a full cup in front of me. "Next time, call it a white-chocolate mocha."

Before I can thank her, she's off to greet the next customer. Considering it's the first week of the year, this place is already packed. I can't imagine how busy it will be once people stake their claims as regulars at their favorite places.

Warming my hands on the mug, I slowly raise it to my lips. Despite my steady touch, coffee pours all over my hands, pants, and table. The woman with the auburn hair chuckles, but I'm too preoccupied to connect if she is laughing at my faux pas. I hope the blonde didn't notice it.

Even more carefully, I lift the mug again, and hot coffee laced with white chocolate meets my lips. It's sweet, like she said. Feels sentimental to me somehow, but nostalgia is a topic for a therapist to dissect.

Thoughts pass with the hours as I sit peacefully. This is the first place that's actually felt like home, and I'm not ready to leave it.

Hallee

Avery and Marlowe are fun friends to have. Can I call them that already? Feels like I can, and I have, but maybe that's wrong to feel so soon.

We tried a new coffee shop this morning before going our separate ways for work. Avery is a florist down the block, and Marlowe works at the craft store across town. I wonder if we got to choose our jobs—those seem fitting for them. Will mine be fitting for me, too?

I've been standing in this parking lot like a lost child for twenty minutes, and I'm still going to be late. The coffee's caffeine is exacerbating my already anxious stomach, and twenty minutes hasn't been enough time to build up the courage to go inside. Actually, maybe it's been too much, and ripping the Band-Aid off would've been easier.

Is there a *right* way to have a first day of work? That's all I want—for this to go right, but reading about where I work and seeing where I work are two very different things. There's less to lose in a mere idea.

If I stare any longer, the vintage "Happy Bookday" sign above the door might send me into cardiac arrest. Apparently, I'm a sales lady here. Maybe I'll get to take some books home at a discounted rate? The apartment could use some love.

Well, *my* apartment.

I've got to get used to calling that place mine.

Inhaling bravery, I force my foot to take one step. I can do this. One step after the other—that is how I'll face my fears.

Meeting new people is an unfortunate thing to be anxious about, considering it happens all the time. There's a lot to be lost in a poor first impression, and label me insecure, but I just don't want to let anyone down. It'd be helpful to list off the reasons why I feel I'm not disappointing, but how can I reassure myself when I don't know who I am?

The store bell dings loudly, startling me as I enter. A thin, quirky man with thin-framed glasses hops across the aisles, and I can't help but smile at the sight of his boldly colored outfit. He is walking proof that someone can dress colorfully and professionally all at once.

"Who let the sunshine in?" he exclaims, reaching out to me. His perfectly gelled salt-and-pepper hair jiggles with our firm handshake.

"Good morning! I'm Hallee. I'm so sorry I'm late. Nerves got the best of me."

Although, they've been immediately curbed by the comfort of a thousand stories staring back at me. I'm at home here.

As he looks me up and down, there's a suspicion in his pause. He's probably assuming this'll be a regular occurrence.

It won't. I don't know how to explain that I'm sure of it, but I am. Sure of it.

"Hi, Hallee. No need to be nervous. You fit right in here, remember? I already know you."

"Oh, of course you do!" I shout like a *totally* relaxed, and not at all anxious, person.

"Business owners fall under the umbrella of government officials."

"Right, my book did teach me that." How could I forget? But, honestly, how could I remember? "I didn't catch your name."

"Miles is the name, bookselling is my game." His shoulders teeter back and forth, shrugging in time with his rhyme. "Follow me to the back of the store. I'll train you today from back to front, and in the wink of an eye you'll know the store from front to back. See what I did there?"

He clearly gets a lot of joy from his work—from talking to other people. Will being timid hurt me as a saleswoman?

"Bookselling isn't an easy business these days. Readers' shelves are stocked with books they get to enjoy for the first time again, every year." A small frown lowers his joyful facade, just enough to catch a glimpse of sorrow.

"But fear not!" he exclaims as his cheerful smile returns. "We have some steady regulars who can't seem to get enough of escaping into another world."

That's how I'll sell these stories. They're real-life magic—capable of transporting us to a hundred different realities. Hate it? Jump to the next and leave the others behind. Love it? Find comfort in its friendship, because when the pages of our life flip to a new year, the books will remain. They'll hold on to our memories.

"This is the children's section," Miles explains, stopping at the back of the store. "It's small, but mighty."

"It sure is." I smile, taking in the dreamy space.

It's the perfect place to foster imagination—to stop time as we know it. Twinkly lights frame a sparkling stage, puppets hang on hooks by the steps, and fluffy cloud-shaped poufs await in a semicircle, ready for an audience to enjoy a show.

"There's not much to know about this section, except that all are welcome. Age does not get to steal away youth—unless we let it."

"Let's not let it," I reply.

"I knew I liked you." He smiles, pausing briefly before continuing. "Any questions?"

"No, sir."

"Oh, please. Call me Miles!"

Miles who smiles—a lot.

"The store grows increasingly more professional as we walk toward the front," he explains while we pass through the aisles. "We increase the personality of the store as customers walk through in order to draw them in. The further into the store they get, the more likely they are to walk out with not only what they came for, but another item as well."

"Makes sense," I say with a nod, doing my best to keep up. In only fifteen minutes, he points out the bestsellers, up-and-coming authors, and the entire layout of the store.

"Okay, Hallee, let's test your memory." The joke snaps me like a rubberband. "Lead me through the store from front-to-back."

"Okay, Miles, the—"

Consider me saved, and startled, by the bell's announcement of the next employee-in-training's arrival.

"Well, excellent work, Hallee. You can go for the rest of the day. No sense in information overload. I'll see you tomorrow—same time, same place."

Without leaving room for a reply, he skips to the wide-eyed girl. My sheepish wave does nothing to bring color back into her face, but I can't blame her. It wouldn't have made a difference for me either.

Does he really want me to leave? Maybe this is a test to see how I respond to authority figures, or maybe he understands how challenging the start of the new year can be.

Taking his word at face value, I pack up my things and head out into the cold winter wind of Michigan.

- 5 -

January 2096

The History of Psychology 2335

The attention of the class follows Mr. Holiday as he rises from behind his podium, walks to the board, and writes *The Experiment* in bold chalk letters. Crazy that he still uses chalk, but he insists it's important to preserve history. Really, the clicking noise it makes on the board matches the pitch of his shoes when they click across the floor, and I think he likes that. Perhaps it's like the Pavlov dog, and the sound is his conditioned reward.

Ashamed of my first note-taking impression, I was much more thorough going through the assigned readings last night. Was I anticipating a pop quiz? Possibly. Did the anticipation drive my attention to detail? Absolutely. As dry as the content was, it seemed like the building blocks for the rest of the semester.

"Who can tell me about The Experiment?" Mr. Holiday asks, looking at us like a cat waiting to pounce.

This is about to get confrontational—it always does when politics are involved. Like clockwork, the hand of the eager freshman shoots into the air.

"Anyone except our overachiever?" He waits for any other student to take the bait, but again, she takes his apathy as approval to speak. Psychology is going to hand her own ass to her on a platter if she can't learn to pick up on social cues.

"The Experiment was a study performed by our government to test the validity of the idea of permanence. In a world where all is forgotten, are we permanently marked by the experiences of our lives? By the traumas we have endured . . . the interests we have grown . . . the people we have loved? In the midst of memory loss, is there an invisible string connecting us all? It was a true test to see if the human heart is stronger than the human brain."

Her cocky attitude overshadows her brilliance, so it's an effort to not roll my eyes at her impressive answer. Life needs to hand her a hearty helping of humility.

Mr. Holiday paces back and forth.

"Excellent," he praises.

Here comes the jealousy bomb, dropped just above my head. It shouldn't bother me to see another woman succeeding, but it does.

Time to go to therapy, my inner critic taunts. It's probably right.

"How did they gain consent to conduct this Experiment?"

Before I can place a bet with my neighbor that *little miss overachiever* will be the only one to participate today, Mr. Holiday raises his gaze to me.

"Ah yes, our sophomore critic. Maybe you would like to join us in today's discussion?"

It's more of a challenge than a question. If I'm involved, maybe "BORING" won't be written all over my notes. He's probably right, but being forced into the spotlight doesn't sit well with me.

"I'm sorry, Professor. I can't seem to remember. Maybe I was a part of it."

Tension floods the room as a flicker of rage ignites across Mr. Holiday's face, and a few near-silent chuckles fan the flame. A student in row two swoops in before my guilt for having such a curt response does.

"Seeing the low morale of the citizens, the plummeting mental health statistics, and the quality of life disintegrating, the government presented the idea to the public as a gift. *The Gift of Forgetting*."

Lack of hope can drive a nation to do desperate things for an ounce of it . . . for the *promise* of it. They promised an increased quality of life, the resuscitation of mental well-being, and a more unified nation.

Our textbook claims it had the potential to be the world's greatest gift, to erase the history of a devastatingly broken world. If I were as hopeless as them, I would've fallen for it too, grasping at every straw offered to keep from hitting rock bottom. But the great lie of rock bottom is that it's definite, rather than subjective. The potential was there, but did people actually enjoy the "free" and "unapologetic" promise of living from ground zero—every single year?

"Yes, very good. Now, before you cast your judgment on those who voted in favor of this gift, I want you to embrace and understand how freeing it could feel to live without the consequences of your actions. Without fear of regret. After all, these citizens thought they were being given a gift. They were not consenting to being the pawns of an understudied experimental trial."

I hadn't thought of it that way—as a villainous deception of the general public. The people trusted their government to protect and serve, not to deceive them.

Civilians are not at fault for the information withheld from them. They thought it was a means to restore the well-being of the world, not a corrupt preservation of control. Yes, the government wanted to gain knowledge, but in the midst of their quest, power was an added bonus.

"Your homework over the weekend is to write a paper. You can decide how long it is. The length makes no difference to me."

The fraternity boys in row three snicker.

"I do want you to be thorough. Be honest and be vulnerable, with yourself and me." Mr. Holiday turns, writing the essay prompt inches below his earlier writing.

What would you do if you could live a life without fear of failure? Without anxieties and burdens?

"What would matter to you, students? *Who* would matter to you?"

The question hangs in the air, accompanied by devilish smirks from the third-row frat pack, and Mr. Holiday holds their gaze with a steady, vicious wisdom that makes me second-guess my first judgment of him. Maybe there's more to him than being a grumpy old professor after all.

- 6 -

Dean

Dispatch sirens sound throughout the station. In under three minutes we're halting traffic in our midst, speeding toward the first fire since completing our new-year training. Our fire chief, Chief Boswell, has the luxury of remembering his crew, being a government official and all.

"You are fully capable and equipped," he swears, but they need to redefine "equipped" if only a few days of training is the current accepted standard.

Despite the circumstances, it's nice to be driven beyond the invisible borders I created during my first few outings. Before this moment, I've stayed within those borders and settled into the daily routine of returning to The Marmotte. Seeing familiar faces is comforting somehow. Being a regular feels like the beginning of rebuilding a life—*my* life.

Racing through town, we fly by a couple grocery stores, too many Starbucks to count, a few fast food chains, and the strip of bars Hudson begs me to go to every other night.

"Come on, man. No memory, no breakups. There's never been a better time to shoot your shot," he's insisted, always pretending to sink a three-point shot.

After the fourth time, I decided he's trying to convince himself rather than me. Settling in looks different for everyone; let the man live a little. The job we do is heavy, and Boswell continuously reminds us to celebrate life outside of our taxing work. That's all Hudson is doing—coping by celebrating.

Our training transforms into reality as the truck races around the corner. Releasing our held breath, the crew shares a sigh of relief at the still-standing strip mall. Seeing the streams of smoke pouring out of the shattered windows makes me clench and unclench my sweaty hands. I'm not ready to lose someone.

Never will be.

Boswell's the first to make it to the building. Not surprising, considering he *is* the most experienced. His yell overpowers the ringing in my ears as he breaks in the door with one swift kick. "Stick to your assignment, stick to the plan!" Like dogs on a scent, we follow him closely inside.

It's either the best news or the worst news that there's no sign of civilians, just tables and chairs thrown every which way. Without hesitating, the crew begins to extinguish the flames swallowing the booth seating, and I head out to search for any wounded escapees. For a moment, a steady calm overpowers the chaos, but with one sharp inhale, I double over and empty my stomach.

"Adrenaline gets the best of you every year," Boswell admits, sighing as he rubs my back.

How much of this has happened before?

"Don't they need you?" I ask, gesturing to the team inside.

"They've got it. My first priority is my crew. *Your* first priority is the fire, and this was an excellent first one to get called to. I'm never thankful for being needed, but I'm always thankful when we can fill the need at hand."

For a moment, his hard features soften.

"Thank you," I whisper, regardless of how weak it sounds.

"You're a good kid." Turning his face back to stone, he takes off to help the others, running like a man with the weight of the world on his shoulders.

It must be a long, hard life to remember all of the loss and destruction. This fire is minor compared to what we've been trained for, and I still can't stomach it.

Thank God I'll forget—it's the best gift I've ever been given.

Hallee

"Happy one-week Bookday-versary!" Miles shouts as I walk through the doors, right on time. Still can't believe I was late once—even that is one time too many. He insists I'm too hard on myself, but something inside me isn't as forgiving as it should be.

"Thanks, book bestie!" I call back, grinning from ear to ear until a small flame rises above the romance shelf. "Oh my gosh!" I gasp. "Miles! Fire!"

"Surprise!" Marlowe and Avery yell, popping up from behind the checkout counter.

"Happy Bookday to you," they sing. "Happy Bookday to you! Happy Bookday dear Hallee . . ."

"Happy Bookday to you!" Miles joins in, concluding them like a well practiced choir.

The potential for disaster widens my eyes. "Move the flames away from the shelves! Jesus Christ, we work in a bookstore!"

"My name is Miles, not Jesus Christ, and if you want the fire gone so badly, make a wish on your Bookday cake and blow out the candles!"

What do you wish for when you don't know what you've had?

"Bookday cake. Clever," I say with a chuckle.

Eyes closed and empty-handed, I blow them out. Maybe by my birthday I'll think of something worthy of a wish.

"Yay!" Marlowe cheers, rushing in for a hug.

"Happy Bookday, Hallee." Avery smiles, gently patting my back. She still hasn't hugged me. Doesn't seem to be the physical touch type, but that's okay. We all have our own ways of showing love.

"You guys! Don't you have to be at work or something?"

"Yes, *Miss Picture-Perfect Punctuality*," Marlowe answers, rolling her eyes.

"Being late doesn't matter when the attendance record is erased." Avery blushes.

She doesn't like disappointing people. I know, because I recognize the look on her face when she thinks she has. Will anything actually happen if we do?

"This was such a special surprise!" I say. "Thank you, thank you, thank you. I'm so thankful for our little family."

Immediately, my stomach jumps to take back the f-word, and Avery's shoulders flinch as her eyes fall to the floor. There was no mention of family in any of our books. The government only included our concrete personal information. Apparently efficiency doesn't include the intricacies of families. Details like last names, marriages, or gaining and losing family members are too fluid and have been discarded as "expendable." If you had a great family, then you suffered a great loss, but if you had an awful one, you gained an awful lot of freedom.

To live without boundaries—that's the gift. Mostly, I'm thankful to not have anyone to disappoint. Pretty sure Avery feels the same.

"Let's cut this cake!" Miles cheers, raising the knife high before plunging it into the middle. Strawberry, with real fruit and buttercream icing—the girls must've told him about New Year's Day.

After using up all our tears, I had turned on the TV and immediately clicked on the picture of a cake, because what could be better for three emotionally unstable strangers? Everyone's a dessert person, and if they say they aren't, then I'm not a *them* person.

Thus, our first roommate binge-watch began with the baking competition. One of the bakers, Peter, insisted you can *hear* when cakes are done. We shared a good laugh watching him lean in and listen, and promptly ate our words when the judges crowned him star baker. Listening to cakes went from crazy to cute in about two seconds.

"Did you attempt the Peter method here, Miles? I'm not sure you have the same ear he does." Marlowe holds back tears in silent laughter.

The cake is beautiful, but atrocious. The strawberries have outed Miles as a rookie baker by all sinking to the bottom, and the middle is . . . stodgy, as one of the judges would say.

"Okay, *Magnificent-at-Everything Marlowe,* next time *you* get to try and find out how good you are at listening," Miles counters, and Happy Bookday fills with the wonderful sounds of memories being made and life being lived to the fullest.

My friends took the risk of looking silly to make an ordinary day a great one, all for little old me. This kind of living—it's contagious. It'll catch on like wildfire, calling to others to dare to live *more.* More intentionally, more wholeheartedly, and more courageously. *This* is exactly the gift the government intended. It's a relief, really, and I'm happier than ever to accept it with open arms.

- 7 -

January 2045

Dean

Time flies when you're having fun—isn't that what they say? Well, fun isn't exactly how I'd describe getting reacquainted with your entire life, but the last month has been . . . *something*.

The Marmotte's barista officially recognizes me as someone who prefers the sweetest coffee available. A week-long adventure of spontaneous orders taught us that for me, we must erase the bitter bite with however much sugar is necessary. My visits are less about the actual coffee, anyway. Much more about being known.

A hot white chocolate mocha has yet to be dethroned from its top-tier position, but the peppermint mocha has made quite the effort. It's seasonal, so I have to order it more before it's just another thing lost to time.

A few other regulars are on the same schedule as me, and when our eyes meet every morning we dip our chins in a kind, silent hello. It lessens my anxiety about going to the fire station but never completely medicates it. This storm cloud is persistently swelling as the days tick toward losing our first victim. It has to happen eventually.

It's an adjustment period, Chief has reassured me.

Apparently, this year is the best I've handled it.

Maybe I should actually apply his advice to enjoy life outside of work and go out with Hudson and Matt tonight. They've offered enough, and my declining chuckle has started to sound a lot like *it's never gonna happen*.

Taking a step forward, I glance up to order. The barista is patiently smiling at me again. "Oh, I'm sorry!" I mumble to the long line of eager customers behind me. Her patience may have extended beyond the first week of the year, but theirs has not.

"Good morning. What can I get you?"

"I'll take my usual."

Usual—really?

"Sure," she answers, chuckling cautiously. "Coming right up."

Rushing to escape the awkward moment of silence, I turn to my usual table in the middle of the room, but mid-step, my feet freeze. Why is that woman sitting in my chair?

She's one of the other regulars, here almost every day with her two friends. Sits on the loveseat. It's strange that I know that, but it's hard not to when she walks around looking like the sun.

Her warm, wide smile breaks my stare and mind. Startling me is rare, but damn—she's done it. Shrugging my shoulders to shake it off, I loudly thank the barista, grab my coffee, and run out the door. The fresh air will piece me back together.

Even in the cold, I walk everywhere. It's independent and less intimidating than the bus. Chief insists public transport is just another learning curve, but there's no need to learn that one. The fire station is only a few blocks away anyway.

The coffee cup warms my hands as I take my first sip. Convulsing at the bitter flavor, I mumble, "What the fu—"

"Excuse me!" a faint voice yells from behind.

The impressions I make are few and far between. No one needs my attention. Closer this time, the woman yells again, "Excuse me!"

"Hey!" she exclaims as her delicate fingers grip my arm and pull it backward.

Spinning to regain my balance, my entire cup of coffee becomes her newest fashion statement. Honey-colored coffee drips from her face as she lights me on fire with her eyes. My training didn't prepare me for this one.

It has to hurt, that hot of a drink in this cold of weather. Probably feels like a million needles prickling her skin. What do I—

Holy—Sunshine.

Time is lost as I hold her rage-filled stare, careful not to let my eyes wander. Even pissed, she's radiant. Instantly burned away my anxious storm cloud, just by being close to me. Reaching up, I gently wipe away her coffee tears like tissues absorbing sadness. It's the least I can do after being the one to cause the rain.

For a second, it feels like she leans into my touch. Must be magic, because her brows unfurrow and eyes widen a bit. My heart seems to widen, too. It feels more now than it's felt all year.

She's the main reason The Marmotte became my favorite place. There are plenty of coffee shops in the city, but there's only one that has her light. That smile of hers stops time, and I wish more than anything it'd make its grand appearance for me right now.

Hallee

It hasn't taken long for The Marmotte to become my favorite place. The coffee is great, but the experience is unmatched. The barista is always smiling, and the sun shines through the floor-to-ceiling windows in this romantic way that makes me feel warm and cozy. There's no better start to the day. After panic-ordering a vanilla latte during my first visit, I haven't strayed. Life is adventurous enough already.

Avery opened at work today, so I walked with her. She's the smallest of us, barely five feet tall, and we're extra protective of her. Maybe it's her height, or the fact she wouldn't defend herself in a crisis. Either way, I arrived ten minutes earlier than usual to The Marmotte, so someone else was sitting in my seat. Well, it's not *my* seat but it is, okay? It's the *right* one, and the shift in schedule must've cracked my mind because rather than waiting for it to open up, I somehow ended up in the wrong one. The *middle of the room* one. Clearly, I wasn't thinking, because never in a million years will this be considered right. I blacked out on the way here, actually. Came to by tapping my fingers on the table and counting the seconds until my coffee hits the bar. The longer I sit here, the more my shoulders tense.

Is someone watching me?

Check left. Check right. Stay calm, Hal.

Surprise, I talk to myself these days. I'm really all I have and—I knew it!

That man standing by the bar. Why is he staring at me like that? Like I'm an ex-girlfriend breaking his heart all over again.

Gently swiping my hand across my cheek, I brush my hair over my shoulder and shoot him the widest smile I have.

Nothing. Not even a wave back.

Annoyance builds with every second this stalemate continues. My roaring, anxious thoughts had finally turned to embers, only to be viciously reignited by *Mr. Stand and Stare.*

After grabbing the first coffee to hit the bar, he bolts out the door and honestly—how dare he? Did he really not realize I ordered before him? Now he's left me with his . . . peppermint mocha. Of course. Peppermint toothpaste is barely acceptable, but peppermint coffee? Unbearable. Certifiably insane.

My gut curdles as I catch a whiff of it. Ugh, Mr. Stand and Stare is a sneaky coffee criminal. I paid good money for that vanilla latte and it's privileged to care this much about something so minor, but it's the principle of it! Logic runs me out the door as I transform into a feisty lawyer, thirsty for justice.

"Excuse me!" I yell.

The audacity of this man to keep walking as if he hasn't heard me, the only person yelling on the street.

"Excuse me!" I yell louder, significantly more annoyed.

"Hey!"

Grabbing his arm, I pull him around, and—oh my god, he's hot! I mean, that's hot. Really painful, actually, feels like my skin is melting, but it's fine. Totally fine. Wowee, drinking coffee is so much better than wearing it.

Tears mix with what is, unmistakably, *my* vanilla latte, and fall off of my eyelashes like raindrops from the sky. His mortified expression does nothing to stop my glare, even as my vision blurs.

I deserve an apology. Instead, he reaches up slowly and wipes away my tears. Magic, that touch. Soft, deliberate, and gone before I realize how much I needed it.

His eyes are dangerous—hazel, with a honey halo circling his pupil. Swindler's eyes, powerful enough to steal your heart in the night, or convince you to offer it up for a feast. They're a one-way ticket to a world where fairy tales exist, and soulmates do too. I don't believe in that kind of love, but maybe I do? I could never say no to those eyes. They feel like home, but home's just a figment of imagination when you don't have the time to build one. Don't have the time to connect safety to another person. Damn him for his coffee crimes, and damn his eyes for giving me something worth remembering.

"I'm so sorry," I spit out, breaking the long silence.

Him tipping his head back laughing is my final straw. This is precisely why I don't stray from routine. Now, my favorite crewneck is ruined and an irresistible, socially unaware man is practically laughing in my face.

"I don't need this," I mutter, turning to leave.

Grabbing my arm, he yells, "Wait!"

There should be a universal wardrobe for those who startle easily. Some sort of warning label that screams *tread with caution around this one,* because his loud voice makes me instinctively drop his peppermint mocha all over my shoes.

"Great," I sigh. "Just great. It's not funny! Why are you still laughing?"

Honestly, this can be the end. The world can go ahead and take me now.

"You apologized to me." He bends over, nearly breathless from laughing. "*You* . . . apologized to *me* . . . because *I* . . . dumped coffee on *you!*"

Marlowe says I apologize too much, as if I'm apologizing for my existence, but it's a hard habit to break.

"Right," I draw out. "Well, go ahead, sir."

"Go ahead with what, ma'am?"

"You've got to be kidding me!"

Ironically, I have not had enough coffee to be giving etiquette lessons this early in the morning. Does he even realize he hasn't apologized? Well, he *is* a man. The world doesn't expect their every move to be followed with an apology, even when one is warranted, and I don't deserve much, but I do deserve one now.

"Go ahead with your sincere apology for being a coffee criminal and then discarding the evidence all over my favorite, perfectly pristine, crewneck."

"Now, wait a minute. That is an extremely serious charge. We need to bring in a jury before officially convicting me of any coffee crimes." His voice is sarcastic, but his face is stone-cold serious.

"Okay, Mr. Stand and Stare," I scoff, "it's been a pleasure."

Hurt and embarrassment flood his galaxy eyes, and my stomach sinks. Clearly, he's insecure about the whole *staring* thing, but I'm not apologizing again for something that's not my fault. Women are not responsible for healing the insecurities of men.

"I'm not sorry for appreciating a beautiful thing when I see one, and your smile is absolutely captivating. However, for ruining your beloved crewneck, I do apologize."

Captivating? What is this guy on?

"Please, have this." Taking off his *Firefighters of Ann Arbor* sweatshirt, he holds it out to me. "It's freezing out here, and you're drenched. I insist."

Pausing for a moment, I silently welcome his muscles to the gun show. Firefighter is right, but if love were a fire, would he fight it or let it burn?

"Are you sure?" I ask.

Yes, his eyes blink as he dips his chin.

"Thank you very much."

"You are very welcome."

Pulling his sweatshirt over my head, I hesitate slightly to hide my burning cheeks. It smells like fresh snow, salt, and a touch of sandalwood. Somehow exactly what I expected.

The sun is a paid actor, illuminating him from behind and forming a perfect halo around his ruffled chestnut hair. Unfair, how much it emphasizes our height difference. I'm 5'5" on a good day, and his chin starts where my head stops.

A vision of him hugging me flashes through my mind, and I can almost feel him touching me like his sweatshirt is. Makes me nervous, so I glance at my phone.

Oh my gosh, is that the time?

My jaw unintentionally clenches, and the tension between us returns. Being late really *really* bothers me. The rigidity of my schedule doesn't leave much grace for myself. If other people are late it's acceptable, but if *I* am late then I will not sleep for days. Flexibility is something I want to work on this year, but it's hard to find the drive to self-improve when I won't remember how far I've come.

His standing and staring interrupts my thought spiral before his voice does. "Well, I won't keep you from bringing light to the rest of the world. Do you want an escort to work?" he asks, discreetly hopeful.

"The sweatshirt will keep me company. Thank you, though."

Take *that* eyes. That was a runaround answer for a no.

His disappointment flickers and fades.

"Then have a great day, *Sunshine*." Confidently chuckling, he walks away with a single wave.

Regret hits me like a brick with each step he takes. Why didn't I get his name?

- 8 -

January 2045

Hallee

My roommates are undoubtedly the ones blasting "You Belong With Me" loudly enough for the entire third floor to hear. One step out of the elevator, and I'm imagining Avery dancing in her homemade junior jewels T-shirt while Marlowe slides a frozen pizza into the oven. By default, we eat frozen pizza every three days. It's all Marlowe ever tries to cook, but I can't blame her. Rediscovering our world and interests has been overwhelming enough. Of all the things we've tried, Taylor Swift is where we bond the best. Her timeless music has become the soundtrack to our first roommate tradition—dinner dance parties.

Turning my key in the door, I run in just in time to scream shamelessly about cheer captains and bleachers—female empowerment at its finest. Too bad I couldn't have gambled on my predictions; I'd be one rich woman. Avery's dancing on the island in her T-shirt and plaid pajama pants, and Marlowe's sliding a frozen pizza into the oven.

The first dance party was Marlowe's idea. Avery and I had both been timid to join, but now Avery is the wildest of us. Although elevated surface dancing is usually reserved for after the third glass of wine, there's no way the glass of chardonnay in her hand is her third. With a pour that heavy, she'd be under the table if it was.

I rush to grab my favorite glass off the counter before she can accidentally kick it off. They're slowly wearing down my stubbornly rigid walls, so I hold my tongue about how careless it was to leave it there. It'll be good for me—to change. By the end of the year, I'll be a certified professional in the art of living unapologetically.

Marlowe wastes no time pouring my drink. It's way too full when her eyes catch a glimpse of the sweatshirt. As irritating as it had been to accept, I haven't taken it off all day. Somehow, the lingering cologne is comforting.

"Wait a minute, HALLEE!" she screams, smirking mischievously.

Avery gasps, jumping off the island, and I brace for the impact of ten thousand questions as the music pauses.

"Tea time, Hal. Spill it," Marlowe insists.

"It's *nothing*," I tease, drawing out the last few syllables of the word. It was absolutely *not* nothing. It was definitely something. A confusing something, but something nonetheless.

"Who's the mystery man that gave you that?" Avery presses, batting her eyelashes to charm the answer out of me.

"I didn't get his name, but it's the least he could do after ruining my favorite crewneck. He almost made me late."

Marlowe cackles as Avery asks, "Wait, the cream one?"

I nod and her eyes fall. She loved it too.

Most of her clothes are neutrals; it honestly fit in her closet better than mine. They both have an appetite for the details but don't want to place an order, so they patiently wait for me to deliver. Like clockwork, silence and a long sip of wine propel me to overshare.

"I made it to The Marmotte earlier today after walking with you to work." Avery nods and mumbles an appreciative *thank you.* "There were people in our usual seats, so I sat at the table in the middle of the room."

Marlowe's hand flies up and smacks her forehead. "The one time you go to the center of a room and we weren't there to hype you up?!"

They don't share my affinity for the quiet, invisible places. Probably because neither of them want to remain invisible, like me.

"Okay, spit it out!" she pushes.

"So I was panicking, per usual and—"

"Were you counting?" Avery asks.

"Yes, but still panicking because there was a man staring at me!"

"No there was not." Marlowe laughs. "You were being paranoid, Hal."

"No, really! Like actually staring. A perfectly still statue by the pickup bar."

"Okay, so . . . ?" she asks.

"I smiled to cut the tension, but I think I made him nervous? He grabbed a coffee without checking it and sprinted out the door."

Unified *ahs* salute my storytelling.

"Since I had some extra time in my schedule—" a scoff from Marlowe cuts me off, and I side-eye her before continuing, "—I chased him down."

"You did not!" Avery gasps.

"I did."

"Bullshit," Marlowe impersonates Matthew McConaughey from the romantic comedy we watched last night.

"Read it and weep, Lowe. I've got the sweatshirt to prove it."

Their jaws fall to the floor.

"When I grabbed his arm to get his attention, he whirled around and dumped *my* vanilla latte all over me."

Simultaneously sipping their wine, they attempt to hide their building laughter.

"He offered me his sweatshirt, and to walk me to work, but I declined. He was gone before I could get his name."

My rambling has become a solo conversation. The other participants have exited the chat.

"What?! Why are you looking at me like that?"

Marlowe smirks. "Based on the size of that sweatshirt . . . that was one tall man . . ."

"Yes, how tall was he, Hal? Definitely taller than six feet," Avery teases.

A territorial needle pricks my side at the film-reel flashback playing through my mind.

"Mr. Stand and Stare's name is a mystery to me, so his appearance will remain a mystery to you!"

With a wink and another drink from my glass, I spin to my room to change.

"Boo, you're grounded. We don't gatekeep in this house, Hallee!" Marlowe yells, but I'm too lost in the memory of his galaxy eyes to reply.

I've got a strict after-work routine. First my hair is thrown into a top knot, then my bra sinks a three-pointer into the hamper. I pair biker shorts with a sweatshirt three sizes too big for me, and then the evening can continue.

Mr. Stand and Stare's sweatshirt fits the bill. Might as well leave it on to rub in that I'm the first one to bring home a trophy. It's definitely not that I'm not ready to let go of its comfort. Nope, not that at all.

Taylor's voice summons me to the dance party on the other side of my door. "Blank Space" blares—certainly a calculated choice by Marlowe. Yet again, she proves to be the sassiest of us.

As I slide across the hardwood and into the kitchen, Avery cheers, "Yes, girl! Show it off!"

"I don't know what you're talking about," I lie, turning to open the fridge. Snacks are required before I drink any more, but the magnetic whiteboard stops me in my tracks.

Blank Space: <u>Mr. Stand and Stare</u> is written in Marlowe's handwriting.

It's clever, really, and proves she understands what I'm too afraid to admit out loud. Somehow, someday, I hope that I meet him again. Only next time under better circumstances.

Mid-song, the music stops, and I turn in time to see Avery grab the phone from Marlowe. Both of their eyes shift intentionally to mine as twin Cheshire-cat grins form on their cocky faces. Chill bumps cover my arms as lyrics of first looks, dark rooms, and time moving way too fast fill the apartment. A gasp of half laughter and half shock heaves out of my chest.

What the heck is happening? Why am I so emotional?

Blinking away tears, I glance at the ceiling. My friends don't need to see me like this. They don't need to view me as a mess to clean up.

A net would be handy right about now, to catch all of the butterflies unleashing in my stomach and to contain this insistent need. That's what this pressure in my chest is—a desperate need to see Mr. Stand and Stare again.

Dean

Chief Boswell threw my ass onto the street after one attempt to hold a conversation with me, but how was I supposed to carry on normally? Her sunshine gave me the mind of a man on vacation—no new information in, no new information out, and I've been walking around mindlessly all afternoon.

I don't actually seem to mind walking, even in the freezing cold. The sting of the wind reminds me I'm human, and we have the promise of changing seasons—in nature and in life. Usually it clears my head, but today it's only emphasizing how cold I feel without her warmth next to me. Why didn't I ask her name?

I'm still carrying her crewneck around like a puppy clinging to its favorite shredded toy. Saw her drop it on the ground when I was doing everything I could to not watch her put my sweatshirt on. Surreal, how much it looked like it belonged on her. It cracked her outer shell of indifference, and flustered insecurity started to peek through. It was then that I knew—our encounter struck her as silly as it did me.

My apartment door is already open when I exit the elevator. Must be a trap set by Hudson or Matt, maybe both. We've gotten into a little prank war—The Pyramid Pranks. Similar to a pyramid scheme, it started as a very small thing and quickly took over our entire lives. Hudson pranked Matt first by putting cling wrap over the toilet seat and, well, it ended with lots of yelling and a lifetime's worth of ammunition for teasing. Matt struck back, sprinkling glitter on the top of Hudson's fan. When he turned it on, as he does every night, a glimmering rainfall from hell poured down. It'll be years before the glitter finally goes away, but it took about ten seconds for his one night stand to.

They've gone easy on me, so I've made it through mostly unscathed. My soap has been replaced with water, and my turkey sandwich replaced with tuna, but apparently my time has come. This open door must be my end.

To test for any motion sensor, I throw my keys through first. *Hmm,* nothing. Slowly peeking around the doorway, I survey the area. There, in the living room, Thing One and Thing Two are dressed in matching tuxedos. Joy lights up their faces as they see me. Suspicious, coming from Matt. Less suspicious, coming from Hudson. Tip-toeing in, I pick up my initial sacrifice and throw it on the counter.

"Gentlemen, am I officiating your wedding this evening?" I ask, carefully walking over to them, but their faces don't change.

Surely no one we know died? We don't know anyone.

Hudson gestures for me to take a seat on the couch while Matt turns on the TV. A PowerPoint presentation loads onto the screen.

Matt and Hudson's Last Effort to Convince Dean to Party with Them.

With the day I've had, letting loose is just what the doctor prescribed; however, I wouldn't dare waste their hysterical dedication to the bit by admitting defeat before the show begins.

After a thorough twenty-minute speech, they finally conclude in unison, "That is why it would be of great benefit to us all if you graced us with your peaceful presence this evening."

Matt and Hudson eye the crewneck as my fingers tighten around it. Jesus, how long am I going to carry this around? Thankfully, they don't ask as I carefully place it on the couch.

"It's your lucky night, boys. I'm in."

"Excellent! That's the outcome we hoped for."

Hudson scoffs at Matt's formal presentation voice before saying, "Your tux is in your closet."

"Oh, you don't think I'm actua—"

"If you're finally joining us for a roommate debut on the town, then we're dressing to make an impression," Matt informs.

"Whatever you say," I mumble, hiding my excitement about being included behind a stoic face.

"Remember, it's not about the tux. It's about the confidence you have in the tux," Hudson yells as I saunter to my room.

"Give me twenty minutes" is my only reply before slamming my door like a disgruntled teenager. I always forget how light it is.

Damn, an impression is right. What that impression will be is to be determined. Matt and Hudson are also firefighters, although we're rarely scheduled together. Something about the government wanting us to feel a sense of camaraderie at home, but not enough at work to be distracting. Working with friends is not acceptable, but one week of training is? I still can't let that one go. Anyway, we're not a bad-looking group of guys. Put us in tuxedos and it'll be game over for any women we set our sights on, which is good. Perhaps a new warm body will be the cure to this sunshine hangover. Only way to find out is to go out.

As I walk out of my room, Matt laughs and claps his hands together like a proud dad gearing up to pep-talk his kids. A smug grin forms on his lips as he glances at me and asks, "Who's ready to party?"

"Ah shit, we're a stone-cold pack of foxes," Hudson slurs, already drunk from pregaming. Dragging him out the door, we stumble our way to the car waiting downstairs.

"Where to?" the driver asks, glancing at me.

When I hesitate, Matt answers, "Main Street, please."

"Do you ever listen to Sean Kingston?" Hudson half-yells at the driver.

"Not usually," the driver responds, which prompts Hudson to begin a very loud, *very* unsolicited karaoke session.

Maybe I'm high on life, or on her light, because no amount of alcohol could make me proud of my choice to join him, yet here I am. Belting as loudly as possible to try and distract me from thinking about her. At this rate, I'll never stop.

Hudson gets even louder when he hears me, smiling all excited like a little kid who just made their first friend. Matt's even smiling, bigger than he ever has. I need to surprise them more often. It might be my favorite thing I've done so far in this new life of mine.

After only a few minutes, the driver pulls over and parks it.

"The drinks are cheap, the music is loud, and the girls never miss," Matt explains, swaying slightly into me as we get out of the car. "Welcome to paradise, my friend." Clapping me on the shoulder, he points to the glowing neon sign.

Friend.

He said it so casually, I almost missed it.

Is this how it happens? One minute we're all acquaintances, and then something snaps and we're tied with the "friend" tether?

I had one rule—don't get attached to anyone or anything that will be gone so soon. But there's always an exception, right? They won't really be gone; only my memories of them will be. The here and now, that's what I live for. I can do that with friends, I guess.

Hudson sways to the muffled music as we approach the bouncer outside of the door. With a half-hearted glance at my ID, he waves us through, making no effort to check Hudson's or Matt's. Must be their perk of being regulars here.

As we make our way to the bar, neon strobe lights shine a colorful pattern across the sea of strangers grinding on each other.

"The usual," Hudson yells to the bartender.

With the pulsing music, I can't quite make out what she says as she turns to take my order.

"I've never ordered at a bar before . . . at least not this year," I admit, too quietly for her to hear.

"First time?" she asks.

I may be too prideful to ask for help, but I'm excellent at panic ordering. "Whiskey sour, make it a double." Heard someone say that in a movie. Look at that, Hudson's romantic comedies have actually paid off.

Our drinks hit the bar as we observe the crowd, plotting our next move like a well-trained group of offensive linemen. A pretty blonde makes a play, locking eyes with mine and waving me over to dance. With her or on her, I'm not sure. I'd do both, I guess. Liquid courage, don't fail me now.

Whiskey burns my throat as I swallow it down with the last of my nerves and head to join her.

"Hey, sexy," she says with a smirk as I grip her waist and tug her close to me.

Lowering my head, I lean in to whisper in her ear. "Hey sunshi—"

Wait, what the fuck?!

"What?" she asks, face as confused as mine.

"Nothing. It's nothing."

Her shoulders fall with her eyes, but we dance anyway. When she spins around, I sneak a glance at my roommates. Thing One and Thing Two are frozen—absolutely dumbfounded that I was the first to manage a catch this evening.

Mouthing *CONFIDENCE* as dramatically as I can, I send a wink their way and try to refocus my attention on the beautiful blonde grinding all over me. Some of my attention, at least. She's never had all of it.

Her hands climb up my body, until they're tangled in my hair and pulling me in for a kiss. She's hot, this dance is hot, but somehow this is so wrong. Feels like I'm cheating or something, so I swerve left at the last second. She plays it off well and as the song transitions to the next, our dance follows along with it again . . . and again . . . and again.

When our touches start to walk the line of publicly inappropriate, I break away for a second whiskey sour. Bar, dance floor, bar, dance floor, bar, dance floor—my steady routine matches the music's endless rhythm.

These tuxedos have done the trick. Hudson's smile screams this is the most fun they've had all year, and Matt just followed a girl out.

It is fun . . . really. Don't know why I'm trying to convince you. Maybe to convince me, too, because even dressed in their best, every girl that summons me to dance pales in comparison to this morning's sunshine.

I'm not attached—I don't get attached—but an all-consuming, desperate desire to see her again has been stapled on top of everything I do. Another dance, another girl, and another whiskey sour does nothing to wash the wanting away.

- 9 -

February 2096

The History of Psychology 2335

"Today's lecture will be a continued discussion over the papers you turned in last month regarding your choices if you could live a worry-free life."

Mr. Holiday is captivating without an ounce of effort. He knows it, and continues to demand respect during every lecture with his perfectly poised posture.

"I was incredibly impressed with the vulnerability shown by most of you. I'm here to facilitate a healthy and productive discussion; however, today I hand the baton over to you. Class is in your hands."

Limping over to his chair behind the podium, he takes a seat and folds his hands on his lap. His encouraging smile grows wider and wider as he waits patiently for our participation. The silent treatment works every time, so before I can stop my hand from betraying me, it catapults high into the air. The relieved glances of my classmates sweep my shaky ship out to sea.

"I can start . . . if that would be okay?"

No one nods in encouragement. They're waiting to see if my ship clears Mr. Holiday's reef of criticism, but his unchanged expression offers no guidance for my journey. Is this when I'm supposed to take his apathy as a yes, and start talking? Even the overachiever is expectantly staring, shock written all over her face at my prompt participation.

"Thank you, Rayne. Your powerful essay—or, poem—is an excellent place to start with this discussion."

My classmates' faces soften at his approval. I can't believe he got my name right—pronunciation and all. Usually, people assume it's "Rain," when really it's pronounced "Rain-ey." My mother insists that rainy days are her favorite, and so am I.

You will not be for everyone, just as rainy days are not, she always says. Apparently it's something her mom told her anxious friend once. It helped, so she never stopped saying it.

There's no reason to try to be everything to everyone. Those who need you will find you, and you will feel their love.

I steady myself with her words. Those who need me will find me. Those who get this will get this.

Come on, voice. Sound sure.

Sound strong.

"Then class, welcome to discussion. I'm Rayne, and I think you'll be pretty surprised by how thorough you can be in a one-page paper."

My nervous chuckle is the last thing I hear before beginning.

The gift of a world forgotten
is an intriguing gift to receive,
It's promise of freedom and hope,
an easy thing to believe.

When anxiety and worry knock on my door,
declaring what could have been,
I welcome the offered defense against
thoughts claiming they're a friend.

What could have been glory,
what could have been riches,
what could have been love everlasting,
Erased by the gift that sets our souls free,
erased by The Gift of Forgetting.

The year begins and the fun soaks in,
the most lavish parties I've seen,
Living invincible,
a feeling restored from when I was only sixteen.

But then we arrive at the first glitch in time,
and I see my found family,
A year spent building a life worth remembering,
victim to the system's depravity.

The grim reaper arrives and stares in my eyes,
my gaze a plea for him to wait,

As yet again the clock strikes midnight,
challenging the course of fate.

My soul grows weary of longing for more,
for a purpose beyond the fun,
Did I even live, or learn, or love
if forgotten by everyone?

This wandering life is not enough,
to live without leaving a mark,
To know the pain of loving a man,
but not recognizing his heart.

Stuck in the labyrinth of eternity alone,
an impossibly forlorn destiny,
The protector of the general public
has become our own worst enemy.

To have to let go of the life I've built
every time the year concludes,
The purpose of living fully,
what a dangerous thing to lose.

Impossible to erase the volcanic eruption,
our past left covered by obsidian,
Our souls set free only to be lost
in the damning grip of oblivion.

To answer your question of how it would feel
to live then, Mr. Holiday,
To live in a world where all is forgotten . . .

I think I would wither away.

My voice cracked during my final sentence, spooking my fragile strength back into the cave of my chest. Looking around for any form of comfort, I'm met with the stare of a hundred wide-eyed dolls. Someone needs to pick the overachiever's jaw off of the floor and hand the three best friends in row four a box of tissues.

Even Mr. Holiday is speechless, his eyes filled with glimmering tears. As the freshman begins to clap, he clears his throat. That's right, she's clapping. Oh god, everyone is. My goal was never to become a public spectacle, only to silence the aching guilt in my chest when no one was participating in discussion.

Too afraid I'll cry if I speak, I nod a silent *thank you* and sit down to hide my burning face. A voice from the third-row frat pack cuts through the clapping, ending my standing ovation.

"It's an interesting idea, but if you couldn't remember anyway, then you wouldn't feel sad. And if you did, it would be the New Year and The Gift would nullify the sadness."

Here's the conflict I'd initially anticipated, but I've done my part. My opinion is my opinion, so now I get to sit back and watch the train wreck.

"Not necessarily. If we knew that to be true, then the government wouldn't have had a reason to experiment at all," counters a girl from across the room.

Solidarity, sister.

"The entire Experiment was to test the strength of the human heart. If the heart really can remember even when the brain can't, then eventually the memories would catch up with you emotionally," replies another girl.

Over the next thirty minutes, the room divides into two groups—those who side with the frat pack, and those who side with me. Ironically, the support for each side is almost evenly split by gender, with a few stragglers sprinkled in. Most of the men support the idea that it would be a gift, and most of the women agree that they would desire more in life; forgetting would be too empty.

It makes sense, with women's affinity for a good fairytale, but I don't actually believe that either side is wrong or right. Everyone should be able to choose to live how they feel the safest and most authentic.

That's the point—they should get to choose.

Mr. Holiday has remained still and silent most of the discussion, so when he stands, the room immediately grows quiet.

"We are out of time for today, but I congratulate you on a well-managed discussion. You all should be getting paid a professor's salary," he jokes.

"Well, who was right?" the freshman blurts. How typically freshman to assume he'll answer.

"This exercise wasn't about being right, but about proving that decisions, however obvious they may seem in hindsight, can be quite intricate when you're living in them."

"But—"

"It's not so easy being the group to agree and decide on the course of history . . . is it?"

Sorrowful silence is the only reply. Without another word, he gathers his things and limps out of the lecture hall.

- 10 -

February 2045

Dean

Spending the entire morning hunched over the toilet is a rough start to the new month. At one point, I even fell asleep with my face on the seat, which of course prompted me to empty my stomach yet again when I woke up.

"Hangover meals!" Matt yells, opening the apartment door.

The smell of greasy food fills the air, and my stomach turns over again. Clearly, I hadn't built up the alcohol tolerance I had assumed. Maybe last night was an exception to a long life of staying in. The books on my shelves taunt me through the crack of the bathroom door. Makes me smirk, even with the overwhelming urge to puke. If reading was my favorite hobby in a past life, wouldn't the idea of it fill me with some sort of peace, or joy? Then again, I felt a lot of joy last night while searching for some peace, and look where it's gotten me. Empty-handed and empty-stomached.

I thought I could drink myself into it, a place for my soul to settle, but the more I drank the more I ached. It's becoming harder and harder to claim I'm not attached.

A crush—that's all it is. A minor infatuation.

"Rise and shine, it's hangover food time!" Hudson bursts through my door, holding four bags of McDonald's, and the smell triggers another dry heave.

"Yikes, did you have a little too much *confidence* last night, Dean?" he mocks.

"Do I even want to remember?" I groan, wiping a hand down my face and smearing the stream of vomit left on my chin.

"That's for you to decide, but the blonde was a true ten. You also wouldn't shut up about the girl with a cream crewneck, whoever she is." He winks before proudly yelling, "Let's eat!"

Peeling my arms from the toilet, I slowly push myself off the ground. The spinning room steadies as I place a hand on the wall and take one last glance at the books. What would life be like if I read them?

"Don't you have to be at work soon?" Matt calls from the kitchen.

"I've got twenty-six minutes," I grumble, hobbling to meet them.

Boswell will probably send me home again the second he gets a whiff of me. Regardless, I scarf down a breakfast burrito and sprint to the shower.

In ten minutes, I'm out the door, speed-walking and sweating off the leftover alcohol. With each step away from The Marmotte, my shoulders visibly flinch and my head pounds louder, protesting missing my morning coffee. Or, maybe it's begging to return to the sun, but *hungover and barely functioning* is hardly a better impression than standing and staring. It's good I'm skipping this morning. Gives her a chance to miss me—if she's thought about me. Surely she's thought about me? I've thought about her enough for the both of us, but . . . another day, then. I'll see her another day.

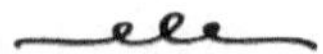

With how the morning went, I wasn't so sure today could be good. Funny how the universe surprises you. It must have been offering me a shred of grace because there weren't any fires to fight. Always a great day when no one's life is falling apart. Around 4:30, the next crew trickles in, Matt and Hudson with them.

"Well, Chief, you owe us twenty bucks." Hudson grins, holding his palm out in front of Boswell. "A deal is a deal. Pay up!"

"I didn't think you'd ever get this hermit out of his shell," Boswell replies, chuckling as he pulls two crisp twenties out of his pocket. "Good work, boys."

"Thank you," Matt says, plucking one from his hand.

Their faces are a perfect display of cocky arrogance as Hudson winks and mumbles, "Pleasure doing business with you."

Like a proud father, Boswell pats their shoulders and heads back to his office. No wonder they made such an effort to get me to join. Stings a little, but I'd rather not get tangled up in the details.

"Since when do you two work together?" I ask, gesturing between Thing One and Two.

"Substitute shift," Matt answers. Always a man of few words.

"Three of the night shift guys are out sick. We're still one short, though, if you want to join?" Hudson hangs the question in the air like candy in front of a baby. "You don't have to. We all know you've had quite the day, with all that *confidence* you displayed last night."

Watching them laugh together, pride stomps down exhaustion.

"I'll stay," I say through clenched teeth.

"Yeah?" Matt's voice lifts with Hudson's eyebrows.

"Of course."

"Well, shit. First time working together." Hudson chuckles.

"The three musketeers." I smile, intending it to be fake, but realizing it's real. I can't seem to shake the feeling that this'll be a night I'll want to remember.

The alarm goes off in the middle of dinner, urging us to gear up, and within five minutes the truck is speeding into the city. As we fly by The Marmotte, I let out a thankful sigh—my favorite place is still intact.

The truck finally stops outside of a four-story apartment building nearly identical to our own. First assessment, there's no visible flames or smoke. Regardless, the street is lined with residents nervously glancing between their home and us with crushing, reliant hope.

Find and evacuate—that's my mission, and Hudson and Matt trail me closely as I barrel through the door.

First and second floor are clear, but chaos has struck the third. Heaps of smoke are pouring out of the open door at the end of the hall.

"Keep low!" Hudson shouts, in case any residents are still escaping.

A screaming voice cuts through the air, followed by a howl of laughter. What kind of person laughs during a fire?

Entering the apartment, Matt calls out "Fire department!" and uncontrollable belly laughter explodes from two women clutching their stomachs on the floor. Another one is tip-toed on the kitchen island, frantically waving a towel to push smoke away from the blaring alarm.

Despite it being our first call together, the Three Musketeers fall perfectly into our places. Matt helps the two women up off of the floor, quickly escorting them out the door, and laughter resounds through the hallway as they make their great escape. Hudson gets to work extinguishing the fire contained in the oven. Little fire, lots of smoke.

As I turn to help the third woman, a note on the fridge catches my attention.

Blank Space: <u>Mr. Stand and Stare</u>

My eyes snap to the woman on the island, and panic punches my chest. Adrenaline surges through my fingertips, numbing them as I clench and unclench my fingers.

That navy sweatshirt . . .

The glow of her smile cuts loose a primal need to protect.

"I have it secured!" Hudson yells as I rush to her, but my pool of logic evaporates in the heat.

Small fires surge all the time, and her bare legs would burn in a millisecond. She will not be a part of an accident. Not on my watch, and not ever.

Tightly grabbing her hips, I pull her down to safety. I mean . . . to me. I could be her safety, though. This is good practice for it.

"It's okay, Dean!" Hudson assures as I toss her over my shoulder, but it's no use.

In record time I'm through the hallway, down the stairs, and on the street. The cheering crowd snaps me from my protective daze, just in time to hear her protest, "Put me down!" as her friends fall to the ground, again, in unapologetic laughter. I can't believe I didn't recognize them when I first ran in.

The fresh air dims the roaring in my head enough to slowly lower her off my shoulder, and my hands fly to her waist, steadying her as she sways. She clings to my arm like a girlfriend, but lets go so fast I question if it happened at all.

It's *her.*

I'd never forget that face. Couldn't—I've tried.

With one look in my eyes, light breaks through her fury, and my heart skips because it's written all over her face.

She remembers me too.

Together, we giggle over the odds of this, and her laugh feels like coming home. Like being recognized, or admired, or connected to something other than time. She's a deep breath in a shallow world.

"Really?" she asks. "Over the shoulder?"

Really, I think.

Not attached, that's the rule. But holding her honey-golden stare, I've never been more thankful to be called to a scene.

Looks like I didn't miss my daily dose of sunshine after all.

Hallee

Marlowe and Avery can't get off the floor. They're doubled over, wheezing because the fire alarm is going off . . . again. My nights cooking dinner rarely end well, but it's never been this bad. Usually, I try my best, cuss like a sailor, and we grab cereal instead of whatever meal I tried to cook. Tonight, there's actually flames.

"Shut up and help me!" I scream, laughing out my nerves.

It was all going well, until it wasn't.

I was tossing the salad while the chicken tenders and sweet potato fries baked in the oven. Basically, a five-star meal at the rate we've been going. One minute it was going perfectly, and then the next?

Bang.

Marlowe and Avery startled off the couch, and we opened the oven to a graveyard of chicken tenders and shattered glass. The pan—exploded?

It didn't take long for the fallen tenders to catch fire, filling the entire apartment, hallway, and third floor with smoke. Our personal fire alarm led to the entire building evacuating and the fire department being called. Major inconveniences all around, caused by yours truly. Very classic of me—selfish too.

Wait until the firemen get here and realize their dinner was interrupted by a woman who simply can't cook. Well, in my defense, the cooking was going well until the pan decided to disintegrate.

Pan, you had one job.

Hold. The. Dinner.

The universe is sending me a sign. For what? I'm not sure. But it feels like something. A tug on a tether connected to something else.

"You are no help!" I yell at Marlowe and Avery, jumping on the island to wave our dish towel at the blaring alarm. They're still on the floor laughing when the firemen announce their arrival. They got here incredibly fast, considering the station's across town. One glance, and Marlowe shoots an impressed look in my direction.

"You should start a fire more often, Hal," she mumbles, quietly enough it's barely audible.

Upon entry, one of the firemen immediately rushes to them.

"There's no immediate danger." Avery snorts.

"Just a glass pan coming for our lives." Marlowe wheezes, and their laughter echoes down the hallway.

The remaining firemen assess the oven. I wasn't scared before they got here, so why is my heartbeat faster now? They're used to entire buildings engulfed in flames. This campfire is elementary at best.

Inexplicably, one of them rushes to me and grips my waist. Okay, wow, strong hands but wait, why is he—?

"Over the shoulder? Really?" I yell, but it's drowned out by the siren.

"Really?" I try again, louder.

As he runs me out the door, an utterly embarrassing gasp slips out of my mouth, and suddenly I'm thankful for the alarm I was cursing two seconds ago. Who can blame me? His speed and strength are . . . impressive.

He's dedicated to his work.

The second he carries me outside, Marlowe and Avery hit the sidewalk, laughing uncontrollably. This is ridiculous; the only real threat here is the one to my pride, and it's not the only thing hanging out in the open with my butt in the air like this. Changing into more appropriate pants wasn't on the top of my to-do list in the chaos.

"Put me down!" I playfully hit his board of a back, and that seems to do the trick.

Here he goes with those hands again, wrapping them around my waist and lowering me slowly. When I sway slightly, his grip tightens and I cling to his strong arms. Didn't need to, but might as well milk it. Sculpting my face into rage, I raise my chin to cut him with a sharp stare, but all the air leaves my lungs.

Those eyes—*his* eyes.

My cheeks burn as he joins in with my nervous giggle.

"Really?" I ask. "Over the shoulder?"

What in the world?

Mr. Stand and Stare is here, doing what he does best. The silence starts my mind's marathon, running it back through the last few minutes. His urgency upstairs was directly after he glanced at our fridge where Marlo—

"Oh my god!" I gasp.

"Hello, Sunshine." His low, raspy voice cushions my fall into the pit of social humiliation.

With kind eyes, he reaches up, gently tucking a loose strand of hair behind my ear.

Punch me.

In the.

Face.

Please, knock me out.

A suspicious cough snaps the tension, tearing apart our glances. Marlowe and Avery are waiting, watching behind a calm and collected guise.

"Hot damn, Hal!" Marlowe's eyebrows raise to her hairline. "Please introduce us to your knight in shining armor."

Avoiding eye contact, he responds before I can properly ask his name.

"Mr. Stand and Stare, at your service."

Shock widens their eyes, mine fall to the floor in fifty shades of mortification, and Marlowe's lips curve upward as the other two firemen approach.

"Everyone still feeling alright?" the largest asks, undressing Avery with his eyes.

"Better now," she says with a wink, and Marlowe and I freeze, dumbfounded because she's usually the shy one.

"Hudson." He reaches out his hand.

Marlowe locks eyes with the mysterious one. "And you are?"

"Matt."

"I'm Marlowe, and that's Avery."

All eyes shift to me as I nervously tug at the sweatshirt. Hudson and Matt give a devilish grin seeing me in the logo and glance at their friend.

"She's cream crewneck," he explains.

"*Ohhh*," they sound off, and there's something oddly comforting about the three of them. Friendly, almost.

"Hallee," I blurt, reaching out to my nameless rescuer, "but my friends call me Hal. So either one works, I guess."

Time felt strange as I said that, blurring in the sea of his galaxy eyes, and I could swear his face shifted, a little confused.

Did I just friend-zone him? I didn't mean to. Don't want him to think I did.

"Dean," he finally unveils, and his name crushes the spider web of insecure thoughts spooling in my brain. It's an answered call to my soul, and an explanation for the exploding glass pan.

Order has been restored.

We are together again.

Dean—the owner of the world's most captivating eyes. Makes me blush when they travel up my body like they're doing now.

"Hi, Dean," I say, and conveniently, our friends all have somewhere else to be.

Holding back my smile is more challenging than it should be as he closes the space between us. Leaning in, his warm breath caresses the top of my ear.

"My sweatshirt looks good on you, Hal," he whispers, pulling away before I can melt. With a single wink, he turns and heads back to the truck.

"Dean," I breathe, quietly begging him to stay. Begging for him to look at me, smile at me, touch me just one more time.

My left hand reaches out and I smack it down with my other. What the hell am I doing?

Evidently, his soul speaks a different language than mine because he doesn't glance back, and the ache in my chest grows as he's driven away by the very truck that brought him back to me.

- 11 -

February 2096

The History of Psychology 2335

Passion has driven our differing opinions apart since our last discussion, and the room has divided into two groups equally convinced that their stance is correct. I don't actually think it's that simple. Life is way less black and white than I was raised to believe. It's a thousand and one shades of gray that appear lighter or darker based on your priorities. Based on what you value.

Last night's reading briefly reviewed defense mechanisms and self-actualization, topics we studied in great detail in *Introduction to Psychology*, but it's been a few years since I've thought about the concepts, or Maslow's Hierarchy, because it always unsettles my stomach.

How do we know when we've reached our full potential? Would we know if we achieved it in the moment, or only if we were to lose it and be forced to look back longingly, yearning for that version of ourselves to return?

Is it long-lasting?

To me, it's always felt like a trap to keep us on the hamster wheel of achievement, change, and obsessing over perfection. It implies there's a "correct" way for a person to live, but if that's true, then who is the guidebook's keeper?

This is what happens when I think too deeply. My thoughts push me down and capture me in the quicksand of facing the fact that I might be ordinary.

I might be average.

Hence why self-actualization scares me—what if I never achieve it?

Mr. Holiday's entrance silences the class. "Let's get started. Please open your textbooks to chapter thirteen."

One by one, the shuffling of backpacks and clunks of textbooks ring out across the room.

"Someone please explain why we're studying defense mechanisms at this specific point in time."

The air is split by at least fifteen eager hands slicing through it. Mine is not one of them. I haven't spoken much since sharing my poem.

I think I would wither away.

My opinion has remained the same.

Without being called on, the freshman answers. "It's important to know how individuals defend themselves against vulnerabilities and unhealthy behaviors."

Annoying, as usual. My eyes roll at her dance around the real reason Mr. Holiday asked that question, which was: why now?

The truth is, no one knows.

"Yes, but the important part of that question was, *why now?*" Told you.

An entire minute of silence passes before he shakes his head in disappointment.

"If any of you had been honest, we would've gotten somewhere by now. If you let down your pride and admitted you don't know, then time wouldn't have been lost to the silence of solitude. We would've laughed as a group and further discussed the reasoning." His tone shifts into slight indignation as he continues. "Instead, you chose fear. Unfiltered, brave vulnerability will change the world, and you all are lacking it. I suggest you find it before our next lecture. *Timing* is crucial."

Our sea of embarrassed faces, some blushed and some blanched, all look down, ashamed. Mr. Holiday has never used embarrassment in his lessons before. This has to serve a purpose, but it's hard not to be angry at him for making an example of us. We are students, after all; we don't have all of the answers. Even if you aren't a student, you don't have them all. We're forever destined to be a student in the class of life.

My stomach flips as my steady voice echoes through the room. "There are many ways to be brave, Mr. Holiday. Bravery will appear differently in everyone."

The entire class holds their breath as he nods, gesturing for me to continue, but that statement didn't have a destination. It was merely an idea. Despite his burning stare, I can't find the words. It's the first time he has made me feel afraid that maybe I'm a coward.

Maybe I won't change the world.

"Silence i—" I stutter, begging my mind to work, and the eyes of my classmates urge me to continue. Are they rooting for me to succeed, or for good entertainment?

"Silence is our defense mechanism against the embarrassment of admitting we don't know—admitting we let you down."

A few heads nod and glance back to Mr. Holiday, pressuring him to let me down gently. Luckily, his voice has returned to his commanding calm when he answers.

"You wouldn't have let me down with honesty, but you let yourself down with fear. It has held you back from powerful knowledge, and I'll enjoy watching you figure out what you missed over the rest of this course."

Will I ever feel like I understand it all?

The Experiment . . . this class . . . life . . . ?

"The homework for this weekend is in the syllabus, but unless anyone has anything to add, I have somewhere to be. My time is precious, as is yours. My TA will teach the rest of class."

Deep down, something whispers that this lecture is one I should remember.

- 12 -

February 2045

Hallee

I've officially altered my morning routine and now arrive thirty minutes earlier to The Marmotte in avoidance of Dean. Whatever game my body has started with the butterflies and pounding pulse, I'm not here to play. It's not logical to love only to lose. I'm doing us a favor by preventatively snuffing out any spark that could light up our world.

Sometimes I cut it too close and run to the bathroom when I see him turn the corner. The other day, I hid in there for fifteen minutes before working up the nerve to come out. He was gone, like I had hoped, but somehow his absence still stung, which triggered a thought spiral. Some thought spirals are good, but most are all-consuming anxiety about the idea of him and me.

Of him *knowing* me.

It's paralyzing, the overwhelming feeling that we could be something great. Irreplaceable, even. Because we could. At least,

I think we could—does he? Surely this isn't one-sided. Two encounters in and I've known him for a lifetime. Not actually, because that's impossible, but maybe?

I must be losing my mind.

When I step up to order, the barista recognizes my face but not my name. Never anyone's name; that's too much effort in the long run. Handing over my daily charge of $5.07, I pay to feel life pumping through my veins. I can almost hear the medical commercial . . .

Do you suffer from paralyzing anxiety? Then I have the cure for you! Band-Aid over it with a daily dose of chihuahua shakes in a cup. Best served with a side of cynicism and a splash of disassociation.

Am I addicted? Depends on who you ask.

Am I going to Coffeeholics Anonymous to change my behavior? Absolutely not.

Amused with myself, I make my way over to the pickup bar. Grab and go, that's the new routine. No sitting, no lingering, because that would heighten the chance of running into Dean, who I'm obviously trying to avoid. I definitely don't want to see those eyes again, at all.

Not even for a second.

Being in public already makes me so uncomfortable. It's sad to think of losing this place too. *This* is precisely why relationships are embarrassingly messy. They drop in unexpectedly and suddenly you're running away from your favorite place.

After I admire the process of the barista making my latte, she hand delivers it to me with a smile. Within a second of it touching the counter, she's off to provide the next cup of life to Jack. I learned his name last week when he dropped his pocket watch. It's engraved with the letter "L," but he can't remember why. Perhaps he used to belong to someone and carries it lovingly for a partner who knew him the best. Now, the "L" stands for "lost and waiting to be found." Maybe that's why I've never seen him leave this place—he's hoping someone will find him.

Is anyone out there to find me?

Before ruminating on the idea, I rush out the door. Walking to work makes me feel less isolated. Strangers pass me by like pages flip in a book. What are their stories? Is life being kind to the woman walking alone? Does the man across the street stare up at the moon and ponder eternity, like I do? Do they need a smile today?

Everyone does, I suppose, so I give the best one I can to each hurried commuter. My extreme aversion to being noticed doesn't seem to nullify my dream to change the world for the better. A mere bookseller, the ripple that will start it all. My inner critic scoffs at the delusion, but in the book series Miles recommended, the world was changed by an illiterate teenager. She's proof—even the most unassuming can be impactful.

Every second of reading the series has felt like a small tug toward healing. Healing what parts of me? Don't know. I can't even remember the parts that needed it, but it's helping me. I'm, mostly, sure of it. Can't be too sure. It's hard to trust your gut when you don't know who you are.

As the store bell startles me again, Miles leans out from behind a bookshelf. "Well?!" he draws out, widening his eyes in anticipation.

These morning meetings have become one of my favorite parts of the day.

"I finished the entire thing."

"You did not!" He gasps.

"Oh, it was so good. I can't believe Cas—"

The bell cuts me off before I can divulge my juicy theories. It's time to sell these amazing stories to other people.

The day slows down after lunch, so I start the newest book added to the banned book list. Selling the banned books feels like some rebellious adrenaline rush, and that's about as strong as rebellion runs in me. Two things should be set in stone—rules and routine.

A mystical shadow casts across the most likely haunted historical fiction section. Despite the stagnant window pattern, the shadows ebb and flow in different patterns every day. Thinking about it too long gives me the creeps, so I think of other things. Happier things, like the group of friends laughing in the romance section.

What happened to my old friends? Did we laugh together too?

An elderly woman with a yellow balloon tied to her walker is in the young adult section, lingering over our new bestseller. She sparks a seed of hope in me that aging doesn't have to imprison my spirit. Taking notice of my observing stare, she smiles kindly. As her eyes start to glisten, her voice cracks, "My body may be old, dear, but my soul is still twenty-two."

How old is my soul?

"Cheers to staying young, adult." I wink, and pull the book off the shelf. "This one's on me."

This is the first rule I've broken since being here. I get one free book a week because of the reward program, but it's employee exclusive. Technically, it has to be for myself; however, this woman has a magnetic energy that calls courage out of me.

"Thank you, dear," her aged voice answers. "I'd like to enjoy the store for a bit longer. Would you stay with me?"

Anything to feel less alone.

For the rest of my shift I follow her yellow balloon, listening to her imagination spiral into ideas far beyond anything I could think up. If I didn't know better, I'd say she remembers a lifetime of experiences with a great love. If I didn't know better, I'd say she would be an extremely hard person to forget. But I know better. None of us are immune to the changing tides of the year.

What happens when I'm her age? Will I have anything to hold onto? Nausea shocks my system. I won't remember what I had, but at least I'll be clueless to what I've lost. Somehow the thought doesn't medicate my growing discomfort.

- 13 -

Dean

Two weeks is a long time for Hallee's warmth to be missing from The Marmotte. I've still gone every morning because the coffee is good, but the hope of seeing her is better. Regret swells in my chest the longer she's not around.

I thought I'd see her again. Should've been more clear about how badly I wanted to. Mysterious and sexy was the target, but when I rolled the dice and played it "cool," maybe it came across as arrogant. Hopefully I didn't embarrass her as much as myself.

My "down in the dumps" playlist has teamed up with the overcast sky to keep me kicked down on my morning commute, yet I can't turn it off. It feels cathartic, worshiping sadness.

The apartment will be empty this weekend. Well, except for me. Today is my Friday; then I'm off for the next four days. Hudson and Matt are scheduled for the long shifts, so they'll stay at the station.

It's strange, I only have two people to call and they don't even really know me.

I don't even know me.

Being alone is a great excuse to fix that. Explore the city, maybe try out basketball like Hudson or gaming like Matt. Spending time with myself will be good for me. I'll enjoy it.

And with that, I've been promoted to CEO of lying to myself. Not attached . . . I'll enjoy it . . . what's next?

Flurries fall down from the sky, twisting and twirling in the wind. They land on my coat and melt away in under a second. I wish they'd stay.

The daily dash for caffeine is shorter this morning due to my quickened pace. I had thought I was trying to outrun my racing thoughts, but now I see. Not even The Marmotte's frost-covered window could dim her light. The universe was realigning the stars.

There she is, standing and waiting by the bar.

Here I am, standing and staring . . . again.

How did I not come up with a plan for what to say after weeks of wishing for this?

Walking inside, I'm struck silly, so distracted by her in my sweatshirt that I can barely order, but how is anyone supposed to focus when she's out here looking like that?

Her hair is perfectly curled, and rosy cheeks are highlighting her freckles in this really cute way that makes my heart race. My eyes trail down her body and connect with hers as they climb back up.

Oh my god, she's looking at me. Okay. Everybody stay calm.

The nod that breaks out of me absolutely demolishes my chance at a redeeming impression. My gut twists in embarrassment as I pay for my coffee and approach the pickup bar.

"When do I get my check for modeling the fire department's merchandise?" she jokes.

"Before we offer payment, I need to observe what kind of reputation you're giving us."

A great one, that's what. I hope she's worn it every day since I gave it to her.

Grabbing her latte from the barista, she hesitates before walking away. A sip of coffee fills her eyes with a sneaky shimmer, and her smile glows bright enough to warm me up.

"Well then, Dean, go ahead and observe. Unless you have somewhere else to be, you're walking me to work!"

Like clockwork, my drink hits the bar and Hallee struts to the door without a glance back. She knows I'll follow her. Who wouldn't? Without missing a beat, I grab my coffee and chase her into the flurries.

Hallee

It was too late to run once I saw him, and my backup plan was thrown out the window by an adult taking a toddler into the bathroom. Did I really think I could avoid him forever? He comes in every morning, so gorgeous it's almost gross. It's rude to be that beautifully distracting. Even on my very first visit, I'd noticed him—and worried *he'd* noticed *me* spill my drink.

This morning he's a force of nature, ready to blow away any heart in his path. My heart tried to run. It even picked up its pace, sweating through my hands as I hid them in the sleeves of his sweatshirt. I can't believe I'm still wearing it, but the lingering smell of cologne defeated panic, blowing out fear like a birthday candle and crowning humor as the victorious coping skill of the day. Humor that led me to strut and spin down the sidewalk like a New York runway model.

Horrified is how I should feel.

Instead, I feel free.

My laughter is the soundtrack to Dean's pretend photoshoot. Winking and lowering his voice, he teases, "Come on, show me the sunshine."

Flurries have turned the sidewalks into a slippery ice rink, so I spin and blow him a kiss.

"That's the shot!" He cheers, laughing through each syllable, and I swear it feels like a dream. Who knew life could feel so light?

"Okay, okay, your check will be in the mail next week. The Ann Arbor Fire Department is thoroughly impressed with the reputation being modeled by the most beautiful member of our marketing team."

"That's interesting," I mutter.

"What? That we still write a check, or that we still use the snail mail delivery system?"

"That you think I'm beautiful."

Rose blush blooms on his cheeks before his smirk is replaced with a calm, cool facade.

"Why can't we appreciate beautiful things? Life's too short to withhold an appreciation for beauty."

"I didn't say we couldn't appreciate them. I said it was interesting that you consider me that." Self-deprecation arrives to teach me a lesson, my shield of confident humor rusting in the snow.

"I think of you as a lot of things, Hallee. Beautiful is only the start of a very long list."

I open my mouth to reply but quickly slam it shut. I'm so happy, walking with him. Really, really happy. The scary kind of happy, where it's almost too good to be true. Where the first walk feels like the tenth, but this comfortability is a lie because he's the perfect wave. The water will recede eventually, sending me diving into the reef.

It's exhilarating though, this happiness. It's the start of something that'll change my life. Not sure how I'm sure of that, but I am, okay? It makes all the sense and very little sense all at once, and butterflies have swarmed my voice box, so I do the only thing I can.

I smile.

A full smile that talks through my eyes and says, *I want to learn every little thing on that list.*

About halfway to work, he reaches out for me. My head shakes no but my hand overwrites the objection as if it's magnetically drawn to his. Walking with his hand in mine makes sense in every possible way, like when you find the piece to a puzzle that changes the perspective on everything, and suddenly the remainder of the pieces fit just right. Holding his hand is like that—just right.

He tried to hide his smirk as our fingers intertwined, but I caught it. I caught it, and now I'm all warm inside because his eyes sparkle a little extra when he smiles. His expressions are a language I speak.

How different would I feel after a year of walking with his hand in mine?

Would I feel any different if I didn't remember it?

The thought shatters the glass I'd been walking on. We could never be anything but fun for a year. We could never be lasting. What a gut punch.

A hopeless romantic, Miles will call me when I come inside flustered and unraveling. It'll be a constant effort to remind myself to keep it fun. A continued reality check that the love stories I dream of don't exist anymore.

Dean's hand tightens around mine as he studies my face like it's his favorite subject. It's cute, and it's confusing.

"What are you thinking about?" he asks.

Why does he care so much? I can't say no to those eyes, but could I lie to them?

"I'm thinking about the odds of our paths crossing again, despite my efforts to avoid you."

Please walk through the door I just opened, my eyes beg. *Show me I'm not the only one wishing for more than just fun.*

"Ah, thank you for concluding my investigation. I'll be sure to inform the FBI that you *were* purposefully avoiding me." I drop his hand dramatically, and he pulls his phone out of his pocket. "Please close the case regarding Hallee."

The commitment to the joke is hot, and his confidence is too. Makes me want to be confident in myself.

"They're always listening, you know." His face falls with my stomach and I nervously giggle, buying time to conjure up the right response to such a serious twist.

"Well, Hal . . ."

"Well, what?"

"Explain yourself. Why were you avoiding me?"

"You carried me out of my apartment, in my underwear, in front of the entire building!" Technically I was in biker shorts, but they're practically the same thing and I want him to feel as flustered as I do. "A little embarrassing, no?"

Mission accomplished and confirmed by him clearing his throat before leaning down.

"No. But something tells me, Hal," he whispers in my ear, letting out a breathy laugh as my body sways closer to him, "this was our first test against fate. It appears that fate has won."

A chill snakes down my spine. "I like this game," I say, rising up on my tiptoes to kiss his cheek. "Looks like we'll play again tomorrow."

Channeling his overflowing confidence, I spin one last time and flip my hair over my shoulder. I throw him the most flirtatious wave I can muster, but my smile is crushed as I walk through the doors and smack directly into Miles.

"What was that?" he asks, pointing outside.

I shrug innocently. "Best to keep 'em guessing."

Dean

The sound of my keys hitting the counter echoes through the empty apartment. It's both intriguing and depressing. On one hand, I finally have some time to myself. On the other hand, the quiet might feed me to the wolves of wondering when I'll see her again.

Somehow, after our absolutely perfect morning, I still managed to fumble and forget to ask her on a proper date. Fate has pulled us into a game without a guidebook, and I'm placing a whole lot of pressure on it. I don't know if it can withstand the weight of hope rising in me. Don't know if I can withstand it either, honestly. Hope hurts a little.

After she made it inside, my head grew cloudy. The cold wiped away the lingering warmth of her lips on my cheek, and I ran like a mad man, chasing the wind and the feeling of her holding my hand again. The bookstore was way further from the station than I thought, and the sidewalks were slippery. It nearly doubled my commute time, but things were going so well—I wasn't about to bail halfway through. Plus, she was holding my hand and I'd be dead before letting go first. I told her I'd walk with her, so I did. End of story.

I'm a man of my word.

At least, I think I am.

I want to be.

"Hello!" I yell down the hallway. My echoing voice is the only answer. Two minutes into this extra special alone time and I'm already talking to myself. Excellent.

We grocery shopped earlier this week, so the pantry is full. That's a love language to me—a full pantry. All this potential locked and loaded on the shelves, waiting for me to experiment, is intriguing. Trying new combinations challenges me in a way that keeps my mind sharp. Makes me feel clever. Most nights, it's a stress reliever. I put on some music and get lost in the process of making something great. I'm, undoubtedly, the best chef of us all; however, the process occasionally ends with me calling in takeout and enduring some grade A taunting from Hudson and Matt. As a joke, Hudson got me an apron that says *this daddy can cook.* Regardless of the intention, I've actually been putting it to good use. Never underestimate the value of a pocket and a man who's secure in himself.

It's nice to hear myself think in the silence, but I do miss their yelling. The apartment feels lonely without them. It's the people that make up a home, not the walls.

Searching for a silence-filler, I click on the TV. One of Hudson's romantic comedies keeps me company. The dude has a soft spot for love and I do too, I guess, because they're pretty good. All cute and lighthearted, as long as I don't think about them too much. If I do, my chest feels hollow, as if it's missing everyone it ever loved. I still haven't gotten a read on if Matt likes them. He's quiet most of the time.

The oven interrupts the dramatic reunion of the characters, and I rush to make it back before missing the grand gesture. The delivery is always so predictable, but it never fails to leave behind a box of warm fuzzy feelings. Taking a swig of my beer, I glance at the couch. Its emptiness is emphasizing my fizzing loneliness. Damn, it's pretty pathetic how reliant I've become on distraction to avoid the lack of control over my own thoughts.

The credits roll while I clean up the kitchen, and then silence greets me again. Feels like an uncomfortable run-in with someone I didn't want to see. Glancing at the clock, I tap my fingertips on the counter. Together, we count the passing seconds. I've resorted to making friends with a clock.

Yikes.

After deep cleaning the entire apartment, putting away all of my laundry, organizing the pantry, rearranging my closet, and performing an intense karaoke concert, I glance back at it. Only one measly hour has passed.

My dark keys contrast against the white counter, and my eyes fly back and forth between them and the clock. Before I make a choice I'll regret, I rush to hang them on their hook, but nearly tripping over a shoe on the way is my final straw.

Honestly, how bad could it be? I've got nothing to lose. Might as well go out tonight.

- 14 -

February 2045

Hallee

"I need your red lipstick!" Avery's voice slides down the hall as she runs to Marlowe's room. Her high heels click three times as they pass by my doorway, and it's another eight until the sound finally fades.

Our girls' nights are usually filled with laughter from the comfort of our couch, paired with our favorite pajamas, wine, Chinese takeout, and a classic romantic comedy, but tonight they are in the mood to be wild.

Correction—*we* are in the mood to be wild.

I'm definitely included in that. *Totally* ready to party.

It took an hour to perfect the "I didn't try too hard" aesthetic. Surprisingly, it takes a whole lot of effort to appear natural. Who gave society the credentials to define "beautiful"? Chasing it sure makes me feel like I'm not already it.

My full face of makeup taunts the inadequate parts of me. The foundation to cover my uneven skin buried my freckles in their graves and depleted any sign of life from my face. Powdering blush atop the mask awakened my look, but the highlighter was the cherry on top. It's my favorite because it makes me sparkle in the light. The eyeshadow, however—what a choice. Sexy and mysterious might not have been the move, but the inspiration pictures didn't seem as dark as it actually looks on me now.

Should I wipe it off? I don't have time to redo it.

The sun's golden spotlight shines on the three dresses laid out on my bed. Two of them I borrowed from Marlowe's closet. The other matches the rest of my clothes, walking the line of colonial style with a loose fit and high neckline. It tells me enough about who I've chosen to be in my past lives—someone who allows clothes to hide her as if she doesn't deserve to be noticed.

Tonight is opposite night. It's about embracing change and feeling beautiful because of longing stares from strangers. It's about being new, and I can't be *me* if I'm also being new, can I?

Well, I guess all of me is new. I just met me not that long ago. Met them not that long ago, too.

The dress on the left is the right one to wear. It matches my eyeshadow and is the furthest thing from typical Hallee; although, it *is* actually my favorite. I knew it the second I saw it because it made my heart race toward the idea of being someone else. The other two are placeholders in case I chicken out, which I won't. But, I might?

Marlowe and Avery are laughing in the kitchen, waiting for me to pick my poison. Probably curious to see if I'm still a coward. I was at the beginning of the year, glancing away from my reflection, and I still feel like her.

I don't want to feel like her.

Closing my eyes, I take a deep breath and inhale a new personality. One where I can wear a tight dress and high heels, where I can wear red lipstick and show some skin, where I'm confident in my body and the personality inside it. No matter what happens, if it's heaven or hell, it will be forgotten.

Just live, Hal.

Live. Live. Live.

Opening my door turns Marlowe's attention to me. "You've been holding back on us!" she yells, raising her hands and gasping all dramatically.

An impressive whistle sounds from Avery.

"Give us a spin, honey," she catcalls, lowering her voice a few octaves to impersonate a man checking me out.

"Call the fire department, we've got a smokeshow!" Marlowe jokes, overexaggerating a wink.

It feels good, showing off a little. Maybe I'll do it more often. Spinning away my leftover insecurity, I reach my hand out.

"Lipstick, Lowe."

She glances at Avery before making a kissy face and handing it over. With one last glance in the mirror, I paint my lips red. The confident new me is complete, and we're out the door before I can change my mind.

Luckily there's no wind to drop the night's freezing temperatures even lower. None of us were about to allow a jacket to ruin our outfits. They slay, and the driver's heated gaze proves it. Doing a double take, his eyes lock onto Marlowe's low-cut dress. *Chest out, best out,* she had joked when I'd first seen it, mumbling something about putting her best foot forward. What part of me is my best?

The driver's lingering stare threatens to shatter my fragile filter of confidence. Regret bubbles in me because wearing so many things out of my comfort zone suddenly seems like a recipe for disaster. Marlowe rolls the windows down, cranking the heat and music up. The freezing air rushes in to calm my anxiety. Not quite sure why it helps, but it does. Is that something I used to know?

My hand reaches out the window, soaring below the stars. This is the epitome of youth and invincibility. Capturing the magic of this moment, my eyelids morph into camera shutters and snap an image to store away in the archive of my mind. The writing on the back says: *It's exciting to grow—to try new things.*

The club is dark except for the neon spotlights shining across the dance floor. *That* is a lot of bodies. The room doesn't feel so big anymore.

"Vodka sour, please," I beg the bartender while winning a staring contest with one of the four guys standing on the edge of the crowd, huddled and ready to pounce.

"Tequila shot," Marlowe orders, followed by Avery: "White wine, please."

She always keeps it classy, but this is a hurricane brewing. Wine always makes us cry; that's why we drink it at home.

The drinks hit the bar and Marlowe throws hers back, straight-faced. Badass. She orders another before the bartender can even walk away. Together we scan the room and search for our first victims of the night. Catch and release is the game. Rules? Dance with a few strangers and maybe hit second base. Nothing more, and no feelings. Sometimes a girl just needs to be kissed.

One scan of the sea of bodies, and my eyes lock onto *him*. Even with a blonde hanging on him like drapes, he's gorgeous. She is too, actually, and that hurts more than it should. His hands are on her waist, attention locked in the moment and the swing of her hips. I feel a little sick, squeezing my hands tight and remembering how his held mine this morning.

Is he thinking of me? Would he touch me like that if he could?

My blood heats on the spot, rising to a boil in record time, and some deep, territorial string stretches, shoving jealousy through my paper thin walls.

Avery and Marlowe take notice of my suddenly empty drink and stop talking. Their eyes follow the line of my heated stare, and they know exactly who they're looking at . . . how could they not?

Marlowe begins a pep talk, but tears have already lined my eyes as if I've just caught a boyfriend cheating, which is crazy because we haven't even gone on a date. He's not *mine*. He knows nothing about me, save for where I work . . . and where I live . . . and my coffee order . . . shit. Maybe *I* just don't know much about *him*, but I want to. Seeing him there, with someone else, I want to know him.

Leaving us up to fate was reckless. What if fate is that he ends up with someone, but not necessarily me? It has to be me. It didn't have to be, but now, it has to be. His hands on her are all wrong, and his hand in mine was all right. The universe sings when we're together. My heart is lighter when we're together.

Nausea kicks my stomach to the floor. Blinking away my tears, I bite my lip and hand Avery my empty glass.

"Do your worst, babes," she encourages, winking like what I'm about to do isn't the opposite of who I am.

One second of fear is all I allow before nodding. Emphasizing the sway of my hips, I give my best spin and slide onto the dance floor. Two can play in the game of jealousy, and I am *definitely* going to win.

Dean

Her spin is unmistakable. Saw it enough times this morning to recognize it immediately. This time she's modeling a little black dress, skintight and doing very little to hide her flawless figure. She's glowing brighter than the spotlight that's illuminating her sun-kissed legs. Breathtaking, those legs.

Treasure on earth.

Spinning again, her long hair fans out behind her and casts a spell on everyone close by. The girls want to be her, and the guys want to be with her.

On her.

All over her.

She eyes the crowd, raising her arms and tracing the outline of her body as she drags her hands down her frame. The rest of the room blurs, and it takes about two seconds for the first lion to pounce.

I hadn't even realized I stopped dancing until the blonde grinding on me shoved my chest. Her killing scowl was a formal goodbye, but it won't be long until another guy is pining after her. She's at least an eight. Pales in comparison to my Sunshine, though.

There I go again, calling her mine.

She sure doesn't look like it while a sleaze with a man bun gropes her and I watch from the sidelines. *Mr. Stand and Stare strikes again*, I can hear her tease. Truly, I can't help it, and neither can the rest of the club. The men are charged—lightning bolts waiting to strike, one after the other.

There'll be nothing left of my molars if I keep grinding them like she's grinding on him, but it's something to focus on other than my pounding pulse. She must've been a dancer in a past life. The more I watch the more I want, and *Man Bun* feels the same. His hands get a little too handsy and her face shifts uncomfortably before she drops low, forcing him to let go of her. As she slowly rises back up, her eyes meet mine and I could kill everyone in this room for looking at her like they own her.

I am too, I suppose, but I don't want to use her. I want to know her—more than just her coffee order or where she works. I want to know her favorite things, the different tones of her laugh, what keeps her up at night. I want to see her in my sweatshirt, in her favorite shirt, and in nothing at all.

She's putting on a show for me and every guy at this bar. We all want her, but I want to be wanted by her. I want to be needed by her.

My throat's desert dry as she spins, placing the creep behind her. His wandering hands tightly grip her inner thigh. For a second her eyes shift to sadness, and my heart shatters on the floor. I hate it more than I've ever hated anything. He doesn't deserve to touch her—no one does.

Her gaze is an emergency alarm, declaring checkmate on the fastest game of chess to ever exist. Am I going to punch someone tonight? Not much of a fighter, but I could be. My fists clench, ready to throw down as his hands move higher and higher up her body. I break through the circling crowd and pause before I do something I'll regret. Swear she's not even breathing as she spins and shoves him off of her. Without missing a beat, she backs into me and laces her fingers through my hair. Nearly kissing her collarbone, I freeze. It's not mine to kiss.

Not yet, anyway.

"A kiss on the cheek isn't enough, Dean? Already wanting more?"

My body comes alive when she says my name, the evidence confirmed as she leans back into me, and I cement my hands on her waist. If I hold them still, maybe she won't notice how much they're shaking. If I hold them still, I can't touch her in a way that will make her eyes sad.

Regardless of how she dresses, or dances, she deserves respect. Every woman does, and I refuse to cross a line she might not be asking for. Wasting a first touch, or a first kiss, in a room so loud I can't hear her consent? Not happening. She's too precious to me, and it all feels very delicate.

"You haven't noticed, then?" I chuckle.

"Oh, I've noticed." She laughs, pressing back against me.

"No, not *that*. You haven't noticed how the entire club is looking at you."

Her stomach tenses as she spins to face me, immediately laying her hands on my chest.

"You don't get it, do you, Hal?" She really, really doesn't, and her eyes turn glassy, pooling with fear, as I continue, "They're waiting for the encore."

The spotlight of attention shatters her confident guise, leaving behind a woman ten seconds from falling apart. She opens her mouth, but nothing comes out. I'm not even sure she's breathing. For a second I question if she's even heard me, but then she takes one step in.

One step and I know—she needs to get out of here.

I don't know how I know, but I do. There's no mistaking her body language. As she swallows, her bobbing throat waves me down and tells me she needs this. She needs me. Her eyes blink three times. *Get me out*, they beg. They don't have to ask me twice.

Jealous stares burn into our backs as I grab her hand and lead her off the dance floor. Her high heels sound off a pitter-patter of thank-yous all the way out the door.

- 15 -

Hallee

Throwing up in a plant was not on my bingo card for the evening, especially not in front of Dean. I'm sure he assumes it's because of alcohol, but it's not. Not even close.

I really did enjoy escaping into a different life, surrendering to a new personality and sealing it with red lips. It was all fun. Well, could've been fun. Should've been fun? It was, until it wasn't—until it ended with this.

Dean's holding my hair back, which is sweet, but it's kind of making it worse because he's behind me and I'm in a dress that looks like *this.* He keeps looking up, away from me, as if the sky is super interesting. It's literally dark, and the stars are washed out by city lights. There's nothing up there, but it's better than me, I guess. Most things probably are.

How am I? Embarrassed barely scratches the surface, and Dean's near-silent chuckle confirms that this isn't the night he expected. Well, it's not the night I planned for now, is it?

A strong arm reaches out to hand me a cup of water, and I glance up to see the bouncer smiling down empathetically.

"Thank you," I mutter, taking the drink and sipping it slowly.

Expletives set sail in my head, but never out loud. My sailor's mouth is my dirty little secret—something a parent would probably be ashamed of. *Not very ladylike*, I can hear a mother scold. Not my mother, because I can't remember her.

I think I miss her.

The thought spirals another wave of nausea through me.

Dean's hands brush my arms as he wraps his jacket around my shoulders. It's another trophy I'll have to show for our spontaneous encounters. How many clothing items can you acquire from the same guy before you're considered an item? Surely I'm teetering the line.

The fabric of this is different. Heavier. Fancier. It's—

Oh my gosh, a tuxedo jacket!? Forget teetering the line. This is the final shove to the other side. What is he doing wearing a tuxedo to a club?

"I called a car," he says, still rubbing my back. "It'll take you home, and when I see you've made it up safely, I'll leave. I just want to make sure you make it home."

"How did you know where I live?"

His blank stare reminds me.

"*Right* . . . do you think we're doomed to an eternity of unfortunate events every time we see each other?"

"Seeing you could never be unfortunate, Hal."

My heart pounds faster, and each thump emphasizes the stare of his eyes.

Ask me, they insist.

You ask, mine blink back.

My mind runs wild in the open field of silence, now and always. Nine times out of ten, it ends with melodramatic tears and realizing I have no one to call. I just want to belong to someone, for one night. Or at least feel like I do.

Just one night.

"Dean," I whisper, blinking away my tears and pride. "Can I come over?"

To his credit, his shoulders didn't flinch as my voice broke in desperation. I wonder if his heart did.

"Hal, I'm not sure that's the best idea . . ." he trails off, glancing at the plant.

"I'm not drunk."

He lowers his chin and glances up at me, smirking. It's unfair, how weak it makes my knees. This fickle thread holding me together will snap with a denial. Can he tell by my shallow breath?

Willing my voice to sound stable, I continue. "I'm not drunk, Dean, I'm withdrawing from the dangerous border of an incredibly embarrassing and near socially fatal panic attack."

His eyes widen, and there it is. The pity.

It's slight—a minor shadow—but it's there. This is why I haven't told anyone about the attacks. I already know I'm broken; I don't need them to know it too.

Surely, somewhere along the way, someone taught me coping mechanisms, but time took them away. If only they could be ingrained into me like my anxiety seems to be. Maybe then I'd have a shot in this fight, or at least a shield for when my mind is triggered into autopilot.

Being looked at is the biggest trigger.

Disappointing people is another.

It's a gift, they told us . . . *a gift to forget.*

Ain't that the truth?

Although . . . it'd be nice to be able to find the shattered pieces of me and puzzle them back together. Maybe then I wouldn't be here, and Dean's demeanor wouldn't look like he's about to approach a stray dog. Shoulders dropped, eyes soft, watching me shiver in his jacket. He thinks I'm cold, but it's really the suspense of wondering if I'm wanted. Which one makes it more likely he'll take me home?

He opens his mouth, but changes his mind mid-thought. As he takes my hand, smiling gently, my lungs start working again.

"I hope you like to read," is all he says before helping me into the car.

The passing lights twinkle in the dark like a galaxy of stars weaving itself into our city. It's one of my favorite things, seeing the city at night. Chill bumps raise on my arms as we pass The Marmotte. Fate's the ultimate wing woman, bringing us back together like this. Clearly she's on our side.

Placing his hand on my leg, Dean gently strokes my knee. It's rare, this familiarity with a stranger. Almost feels like we've done this before. I can see it—us doing this again, but the details fade to black before I get stranded in the daydream.

It's reckless, hoping for a future like that. Like driving in the dark with no headlights. But maybe if I want it badly enough, I can will it into existence.

The thought dissolves as we pull up to Dean's apartment. He runs around the back of the car, rushing to open my door for me, and I'm hit with a vision of us doing this again, and again, and again. Hurts a little, being teased by my mind, but his hand reaching for mine sedates the sting. Like a perfect gentleman, he helps me out of the car, steadying me with a hand on my lower back. It makes him feel good that I accepted the help. His smile says so.

"Thank you," he says to the driver before sweeping me off my feet and carrying me into the building.

"Dean!" I laugh, trying on the idea of us by playfully hitting his arm like a girlfriend would. The first-class ride lasts in the elevator and down the hall, until we reach his apartment door.

"Welcome to my castle, Sunshine." He winks, pushing it open and setting me down carefully. "Hudson and Matt are on duty this weekend, so we've got the place to ourselves."

I really need a filtration system for these fleeting moments of confidence. I didn't think enough before coming here. Astonishing, truly, because have you met me? I always think enough. Too much, probably.

"My room is this way." He laughs, eyeing my twiddling thumbs. "Nervous, Hal?"

Yes, very.

"No, why?"

"Call it a hunch."

"Well your hunch is wro—" my voice stops with my steps. Dean just got about ten thousand times more interesting.

His room is a library. There are all types of genres here, but there's no rhyme or reason to his organizing system. The books of a series aren't even placed together—the blasphemy! My eyes linger on a few of the dark romances, and my face heats at the images of us flashing through my mind.

"Hey, you okay?" he asks, gently touching my arm.

"Yeah, sorry. Just distracted by the books. You've visited a lot of different worlds."

His head tips, confused. Mine tips back. Did I speak a different language? He shrugs a little, as if shaking off a thought, and curiosity reconnects his gaze with mine.

"I must've been a reader in a past life, but I can't get myself to pick any up this year. I hope if it was important to me, I'll find my way back to that passion somehow."

Ah, Dean just got about ten thousand times less interesting. Call it a wash, I guess.

I turn to hide my growing disappointment, but the series Miles suggested calls to me. It feels like a weird violation of privacy to pick it up, considering Dean hasn't even done it. I blink, and my heart projects a vision of me placing a book onto these shelves. Maybe one day they'll belong to me too.

"The bathroom is through here." He walks by, and the familiar smell of his cologne stops delusion from driving me off the cliff. It's officially faded from his sweatshirt. Smell doesn't withstand the test of time. Feels like a brutal reminder that we wouldn't, either.

"Nothing like a shower after the club," he says, laying a clean towel on the counter.

Hard to read, this one. Can't quite tell if he's excited to be alone with me or bothered that he's not actually alone.

"Wait just a second." Holding up a finger, he jogs out the door. "Now, these might not fit," he says with a chuckle, before turning the corner with a T-shirt and sweatpants, "but you are free to try."

"Thanks," I whisper, and time stalls as my hand grazes his.

"Anytime." He smiles, eyes glancing down to my lips. "I'll be out here if you need me."

Stay, my eyes blink, but he's out the door.

Is this round two of the cat and mouse game? Of course I don't want to shower with him. But maybe I would, if I could? I mean, look at him.

He *did* leave the door open . . .

Before making another decision while disguised in confidence, I rush to close it. Feels like I can breathe again as I strip off Marlowe's dress. It was claustrophobic, despite how little it actually covered.

Releasing a long exhale, I step into the shower. The water drops wash away every part of the personality I tried on tonight, leaving behind nothing but the version of me I want to like best.

Dean

She is in my shower. *She* is in *my* shower, and I have forgotten how to exist. She almost left the door open. Would've done me in if she did.

The sound of popcorn pops me back to reality and I race against the clock to turn this night into a seamless romantic surprise. This isn't exactly what I had in mind for our first date, but when opportunity comes knocking, you answer the door. Especially when opportunity looks like her.

I grab every blanket I can find and the candles from Hudson's bathroom. He swears a candlelit bath isn't girlie, and I've given him shit for it—until now. I'll have to thank him later and replenish his stash.

As quietly as possible, I slide the coffee table under the mounted TV. The shower turns off as I'm grabbing the pillows from my room.

Tick tock, Dean.

Throwing the softest blanket aside, I lay the rest out on the floor, prop the pillows against the couch, decorate the coffee table with the candles, and light them before running to the kitchen.

She said she wasn't drunk. Does she want to be? I'm not the most qualified in coping with a panic attack—maybe she wants to drink away the aftermath.

If I can't give her the world, I sure as hell can give her whatever drink she might want. Wine—red and white—water, Sprite, and two mugs stuffed with hot chocolate packets from the pantry. Her footsteps approach as I set it all down. Lingering timidly in the doorway, she reaches up and twists her wet hair.

Oh, I am in so much trouble. Suspected it when I saw her in her dress, but seeing her in my favorite T-shirt confirms it. It's more modest than her dress was, but somehow more intimate in this exciting way that makes me unsure of where to look. If I look at her,

I might never stop. But if I look away, I can't hear anything except my heart roaring to look at her again.

"There you go again, standing and staring," she teases.

How do you tell someone you barely know that you could spend forever staring at them without sounding like a total stalker? It's true. I could spend an entire life like this. Can see it, too. Us dancing in the kitchen like a couple without a worry in the world.

So much for not getting attached—I never stood a chance.

"Feeling better?" I ask, patting the empty space beside me. As she hesitates, I hold my breath.

Dressed up or dressed down, she's a knockout, although I prefer her this way, with her makeup washed off and her hair drying naturally. There's something extra beautiful in the exclusivity of seeing the rawest part of someone. Bold of me to assume this is exclusive, but that's the grand mystery of Hallee. She has me believing we're something we're not. She has me believing in something we could never be.

"I wasn't sure what you'd want to drink, so I got some of everything."

The look she flashes is a curious one. Not seductive, but thankful. A look you'd offer a friend, but that's not the goal now, is it? There's no way the friend zone is the end zone here.

"Wine's great, thanks."

Her eyes look a little sad again as she sits down beside me, and queasiness accompanies the memory of Man Bun's hands traveling over her body without consent. Me causing her eyes to look like that might be my biggest fear, so I sit patiently still. She's the captain of this evening. Whatever she says goes, no questions asked, but staring at her in the silence, I know exactly what she needs.

The opening credits to one of Hudson's rom-coms roll as I crack open the white wine. I pour her a perfectly portioned glass before topping mine off with a little extra to curb my shaky hands and mind.

"Cheers to new beginnings and a night we'll never forget," I toast.

She scoffs, clinking her glass against mine, and downs half of it before cutting me a sassy glare.

"What? What did I say?"

"We'll always forget, but cheers to the sentiment."

Oh, that one hurt. Knocked the wind right out of my lungs. She's right, I guess, but it's kind of ironic she had to remind me.

"Then cheers to the time that we have."

However much it is, there will never be enough of it.

"Cheers, Dean."

Hallee

A night we will never forget—really? That's what he chose to go with? It was all going very well before that annoying reminder.

The shower felt so good that I lingered a little longer than I normally would. The longer the water hit me, the more vulnerable I felt, yet what should have felt like a foreign vacation felt like returning home after a long voyage. A miracle, considering how easily I startle. A promising sign—for what exactly, is to be determined.

Gently shoving his shoulder, I push him against the couch. He drapes a blanket over us like I drape his arm around me, and my body finally relaxes. Can't say the same for my mind.

Is this all I've amounted to? Relying on a man's comfort to save me from the battlefield of being alone?

Shame isn't a very good friend, but this is the soul I have to live with. All I have is me. Please, let me be enough.

We haven't discussed expectations for tonight, but I don't feel pressured. If anything, I'm a little worried he's disinterested. Jam-packed silence and lack of eye contact aren't exactly crystal clear signals of interest. Maybe lover boy has some nerves to shake off too.

Passion is romanticized, but his innocent gentleness is endearing. It's incredibly irreplaceable to feel safe with someone. Weird though, isn't it? Feeling this safe with a stranger. He would put me above himself—would hurt *for* me but never hurt me—if he cared for me. Which he does.

Doesn't he?

With one blink, I envision us laughing on the couch. We're watching a different movie, but drinking the same wine. My hair is shorter, and his hair is longer, emphasizing the passage of time. How many times could we do this in one year?

As quickly as it came, the vision goes. What would fate charge to ensure that my wildest dreams would come true? What would the currency be?

"You good?" His question pulls me out of my head.

Oh shit, he's looking at me. Can he tell that I'm crazy?

"What? Yeah! So good," I reply, inching closer to his comfort with each breath. His kindness is almost as captivating as his eyes.

My head falls onto his shoulder as if it belongs there. I'm pretty sure it does, because my body knows exactly where to lie for the best fit into his. As he leans his head over mine, my soul ignites, glowing in the dark. I'd spend forever resting in his security because nothing could be more right, but *forever* is just an increasingly depressing trick of my imagination.

Dean's eyes follow me as I reach for the wine again. He's trying to hide his worry, but it's written on him like a billboard. It's the only tangible proof he might care about me as much as I already care about him.

"I thought it'd be fun to try something new. You know, no lasting impressions and no consequences if I crashed and burned." His head nods, but his silence coaxes me to continue. "Isn't that the grand design—to live freely and unburdened?"

Gazing to the floor, he shifts slightly. He's misunderstanding my heart.

"I'm so lost. I'm exhausted from trying to choose who to be. I thought if I tried on a different personality that I'd enjoy it. Maybe I'd feel like I'd saved a past version of me. Instead, people stared, and courage crumbled, and all that's left is little old cowardly Hallee."

He flinches as if I struck him.

"Hallee, you don't ha—"

"I keep thinking it'll get easier, dealing with the panic. Clearly, I am mistaken."

Dean's hand stills before he pulls it from my leg. Shame passes through me like a salty tidal wave, burning my eyes and discarding me violently on the shore. My vulnerability is embarrassing, so I down the rest of my wine.

"Hallee," he starts, but I cut him off, eager to clean up the mess of myself. Tears show up just in time to wash away the stains.

"I'm sorry, this is a lot. This was your alone time and I begged you to bring me here like some damsel in distress. I can go home, really. I'm okay. Totally fine."

Right, because *totally fine* people force what they want rather than focusing on what's real.

"Hal." His voice is soft, holding gauze to my clotting wounds. "Thank you for trusting me."

A wavering breath exhales from my lungs, and I press my hands to my eyes like a kid playing hide and seek. Before I can count to ten, his gentle hands nudge away my shield.

"Irrational jealousy." His eyes steal my inhibitions as his voice breaks. "That's what I felt seeing him touch you tonight. Your dress? Stunning. Your body? Breathtaking, Hallee. But now?"

I brace for it. You're crazy . . . you're too much . . . you're—

"Underneath the mask of whatever you were pretending to be, you are even more radiant. It's astounding."

I'm sorry . . . what?

"I hear you, and I see you for all that you are—a messy, complicated, intriguing, and devastatingly beautiful ray of light."

My melancholy eyes rain down tears. He understands, and is already piercing my protective distractions, shredding through the parts of me waging war against myself.

Delicately cupping my cheek, his thumb brushes away my flowing stream of insecurities.

My heart pushes me to kiss him—honestly, to do a lot more with him, but gaining a relationship also means losing it.

For him, I'd love and lose. Would he? I'd never ask him to, but would he want to? I want him to. Happy me needs love too, almost more than messy me.

Pulling me close, his strong arms are my weighted blanket until the lingering tears evaporate and my self-loathing fades away.

- 16 -

February 2045

Hallee

Avery's text to meet at the apartment woke me up this morning. Well, almost afternoon. Apparently we all had nights that led to sleeping in.

"Spill the tea, Hallee. We saw you leave with him." Marlowe nudges my leg, and I take a sip of my coffee to hide my growing smirk.

"There's nothing to tell!"

Oh, there's plenty to tell . . . it's just not the story they want. Dean was everything I needed without having to ask. In my weaknesses, he comforted me. In my strength, he watched me like I was a shooting star—like he was making a wish on me and couldn't bear to let it burn out. We weren't overcome with passion, crossing all boundaries like jumping off a bridge, but it was absolutely perfect. Slow, respectful, and laced with self-control. Connection through tears, laughter, and vulnerability in conversation, going no further than a forehead kiss. He thought I'd already fallen asleep, but I hadn't. I hadn't and I felt it, and now I can't unfeel it because I know that he meant it.

He held me all night, careful of where his hands fell. Requested nothing, expected nothing, and accepted me wholly as I was. It was a form of protection, his lack of expectation, relieving me from the guilt of being the one to say no. He not only saw the invisible boundary, but held it and defended it. I was safe and cared for, and isn't that what love really comes down to?

Not that I love him. No way. Not yet, but *belong* to him—I might. Could swear I have for a lifetime, but they don't need to know that. It's safer to hold a few secrets sacred in the hope of whatever's to come.

Marlowe's glare cuts into my widening eyes. Holding her stare, and my ground, I repeat, "There's nothing to tell! Really. Avery, why don't you share the details of your night?"

Their eyes roll, but deep down Avery's excited. Her foot is bouncing, and that's her tell.

After the beginning of her story, my mind trails off, adrift in a Dean daydream. He's holding me, he's walking me home, he's lending me the heaviest sweatshirt he has. It's another item to tip the boat toward a label for whatever we are, which is the nerve-wracking in-between of something to imagine and nothing to hold.

"...and then he called a car..."

I'm not a very good friend. A good friend would pay more attention, but here comes the vision again, sweeping me away into the bliss of his hand holding mine, of us grabbing coffee, of him taking my heels off and carrying me so my toes don't freeze from the cold sidewalk.

I recall the shock of Avery and Marlowe as he kissed my forehead when I hugged him goodbye this morning. I lingered a little too long, desperate for the comfort of him to not fade like his smell would the second the door closed. Their giddy cheers followed him down the hallway and out the door to the street.

"Whatcha thinkin' about, Hal?" Marlowe nudges my leg, interrupting my escape from reality.

"All of the details that you don't have to share?" Avery teases, winking and theatrically fist-bumping her.

"I'm sorry! Ugh . . ." My hand flies to my forehead. "I can't stop thinking about him! Backtrack to the car ride, Avery. I'll listen this time, I promise."

Their silent stares burn into me.

"Come on! Tell me about your fun nights!" I insist. "That's what this was, right? Our night of *fun*!"

My voice cracked, and they flinched, and now it's weird. They're waiting for me to unravel, which I won't. Except, maybe I might. My mouth goes dry, and there's a lump in my throat that wasn't there before, and the fluffs on this blanket aren't distracting enough because I'm still feeling. The truth is, I failed at fun. Who the hell fails at fun?

They play a game of hot potato with their eyes, bouncing them from me to one another before yelling, "Intervention!"

Marlowe runs to the kitchen, grabbing three wine glasses and the bottle of red. Red over white? They mean business. Avery runs to her room, returning with three more blankets, nail polish, and a face mask for each of us. Within a minute, we're settled back in the living room, and they're staring at me a little too patiently, as if they could break me. Silly girls—you can't break what's already broken.

"Let's say, theoretically, you didn't have the same definition of fun as us. That doesn't mean we don't want to hear about it," Avery encourages, gently touching my knee.

Marlowe reaches for the red nail polish and shakes the bottle before handing it to me. "It matches the fire on his sweatshirt," she says.

"Why am I this smitten over a man who will only forget me?"

Avery's jaw hits the floor, and Marlowe's eyes flare. Told you, I'm broken. Devastation kicks open our door, sucking out the oxygen in the room.

"I sound crazy, but I can see it already. Going on dates, watching movies, dancing in the club. Riding bikes in the park, painting and laughing together. Coffee runs and calling in sick for work because we can't bear to part. What is wrong with me?"

Avery grabs my hand as a tear falls from my face, crashing onto her skin like the first raindrop in a rainstorm. Her eyes line with pools of empathy.

"There are no rules to this life and how you want to live it. Don't judge yourself too harshly. There's nothing wrong with you. You just don't know what you want."

Her words press the gas before the clutch, stalling my mind in place.

"What if I do know what I want, and it's just not what we're supposed to want?"

"Then you make your choice and we rally behind you," Marlowe answers.

Apparently, you can belong to friends too.

"If *he* is how you want to spend your year, then we will cheer for you every step of the way," she continues.

Together, we take a deep breath and they absorb the rest of my insecurities.

"Here's to living out our own version of fun," Avery says, smiling as she raises her glass.

"To many more days of girl talk." Marlowe laughs, joining in.

My voice comes out barely above a whisper. ". . . And to *maybe* falling in love."

- 17 -

March 2096

The History of Psychology 2335

Mr. Holiday greets us from behind an unfamiliar, rickety card table as we walk into class. "Please grab a pen and paper and place your phone in the basket. Leave your backpack at the front of the room."

My teeth grind together at the alteration to my routine.

"Did I miss an email?" I whisper to the overexcited TA.

"Go sit, Rayne. You'll be okay."

I'd like to punch the giddy smile off his face. Instead, I timidly obey and shuffle to my seat. The uneasy stares of my classmates are oddly comforting. Even the freshman is sitting wide-eyed and twiddling her thumbs.

There should be a quiz today over the last four chapters we've read. Can't say I felt super confident about it, so maybe this schedule switch-up is a gift. Typically, I've got a strong pulse for when something will be on a quiz, as if the noteworthy section is bolded in our textbook. In this instance, I didn't feel the pressure once.

Picking at my cuticles makes them bleed on the blank paper we were instructed to grab. A quiz full of questions I don't know the answers to would've been better. I'd kick myself for not being more prepared, but at least I'd still have a sense of security over the circumstances.

Eleven, twelve, thirteen.

Row thirteen, seat three. Something I can control.

The final students roll in, late as usual, and I rush to sit before Mr. Holiday begins. Out of all of my professors, he is by far the most respected. His energy demands it, and, in my opinion, he actually deserves it. Maybe that's why it's so easy to give it to him.

The attention of the room shifts as he claps three times. "Thank you all for cooperating with our change of plans. I know you were expecting a quiz today. However, I didn't promise it would be a traditional one."

The shoulders of the freshman tense as he slips his hands into his pockets. A near-silent laugh snickers out of me before I realize, mine did too.

"You grabbed a blank piece of paper and a pen on your way in, and as you all now see, you have a phone on your desk. These are given to us by the psychology department to conduct our immersive experiences. Welcome to round one."

The echo of his clicking shoes bounces off the walls as some students immediately pick up the phone. Others, like myself, wait for further instruction or courage—whichever comes first.

"Okay, students, let's begin. Please write your name on the paper."

Hands shoot up all around the room.

"I won't be answering any questions until later. Do your best. Trust your gut."

Write your name . . . on the top?

Across the entire page?

"Make your decisions promptly. We're moving on in ten seconds. I trust you all remember your names," he jokes.

Ten . . . nine . . . eight . . .

There has to be some sort of rubric, or how would he grade this?

Five . . . four . . . three . . .

I scribble *Rayne* in the top right corner, the same place I normally would.

"That's time. Put your pens down and hold your paper in the air, please."

Papers fly up throughout the room. It's a pretty even mix of people who decided to take up the whole paper and who repeated tradition.

"Excellent, next question. Who is the first contact on your phone?"

Again, the vague question crawls over me like a spider. Does he mean my personal phone, or the one sitting in front of me? My phone is organized alphabetically by last name, so it's—

It *is* organized by last name, isn't it?

Other students are scrolling through the phone on their desk. They're probably right, if the phone isn't here for this reason, then why do we have it?

Searching the contact book, there are only two listed—Amy and Jenn.

"Ten seconds and we will move on."

Ten … nine …

My heart palpitates. I don't know. I need more time. More instruction.

Six … five …

I'm excellent at following directions, but the lack of structure is going to make me fail this quiz.

Three … two …

I'm a lot of things, but a failure isn't—

One.

"That's time."

My hand scribbles, *Amy.* Surely that's what he was looking for.

"Finally, you have one minute to write down as much important information about yourself as you can."

My grade just went down the shitter, flushed by the open-ended directions.

"Go."

Isn't importance fairly relative?

A few students set their pens down. Either they don't think anything about themselves is important, or they are just as stumped as me.

A deep breath forces my thoughts through my pen.

Birthday, address, phone number.

Family, best friends, hobbies.

"Time. Put your pens down."

Analyzing myself on paper in the aftermath of the rush, I don't seem so interesting after all. I seem painfully ordinary.

There are plenty of interesting things about myself. I can lick my elbow, juggle almost anything, and eat eight hot dogs in under two minutes. Why didn't I include any of that? Why didn't I include what makes me unique?

"Excellent. Please bring your paper to the front of the room."

Gently rubbing my face, I try to physically wipe away the mental stress I feel about my decisions.

"This information will be used in a lecture in the future. For now, let's move onto discussion about the homework from last week."

Just like that, class continues as if Mr. Holiday hadn't rattled any of us who require guidelines and rules to hold us together.

- 18 -

March 2045

Hallee

My alarm expects me to get up and participate in society, which is a little rude, honestly. I could snooze it for the eighth time, but the angle of the sun shining through the curtains is higher than it should be. For how important keeping a schedule is to me, starting the day on time should be more of a priority.

Should be, but isn't.

Sleep—the ultimate defying factor to any and all schedules for today, tomorrow, and always.

Releasing a sigh to whatever spirit is listening, I kick off the comforter. The bitter bite of the cold floor pisses me off every morning, so I shuffle to the bathroom quickly to speed through the steps of making myself presentable. Regardless of the late start, I'll stop by The Marmotte on the way to work. Morning coffee is a requirement now, and I'm not too proud of that, but it is what it is. There are plenty of worse things I could indulge in.

Within fifteen minutes, I'm grabbing my keys and muttering goodbye to Marlowe and Avery. Their keys are missing from the hooks so they aren't here to hear it, but leaving a room without acknowledging it dooms me to fulfill a bad outcome of fate.

A character I read about didn't tell her boyfriend she loved him before he left. He never came back, and it's haunted me since the moment I read it. Now, I'm destined to a lifetime of sharing a whispered farewell to the places and people that have carried me this far everytime I leave a room. He had a mantra about not being afraid, and it's stuck with me. Every morning, I look at my reflection and declare the words over myself. My anxiety has shuddered at the strength growing inside me, trained and sharpened by a book. *That* is a gift.

Goodbye, I mutter as I step out of the elevator, and again as I open the first-floor door. The fresh air is still cool, but the breeze is less biting these days. We're in the calm before the great awakening of nature. That's how the nature documentary Avery and I watched had described it—a great awakening. Why does it feel like my soul is a part of it?

Experiencing things for the first time all over again is one reason I'm thankful for my circumstances. Life would be so dull if I became desensitized to the little moments. How long would it take before that happened? Before I didn't notice the light glistening on the snow, a smile from a stranger, the smell of a new book. Blooming flowers, the grass turning green, the birds chirping a little louder than before. Little love notes from the universe to us. Thinking of them brings a smile to my face, and I share it with every stranger I pass on the way to The Marmotte.

I've run into Dean a few times since staying at his place a few weeks ago. It hasn't felt uncomfortable, but he hasn't taken the initiative to see me again, and the lack of effort has stung—more than I'd like to admit. He smiles, hugs me long enough to make me question everything, and then runs out the door. Walks to work like I do, which is probably a sign we're soulmates. Those don't exist anymore, but maybe they could? He could be mine for a year or mine for a hundred, but having him for one rather than a hundred doesn't make it matter less . . . right?

Call it self-preservation or acting old fashioned, but I'll follow his lead, even if it's only stale breadcrumbs from weeks prior. It's not like time is completely fleeting and the overarching deadline of our memories is approaching or anything—that would be totally crazy. Even crazier than loving a stranger, which I don't. He's simply a force of gravity, constantly and unknowingly drawing me to him.

The Marmotte's line is long, filled with the unfamiliar faces of later morning regulars staring at me because they know I don't belong. At this rate I'll be twenty minutes late to work, proudly displaying the explanation of my tardiness. Surely Miles will understand—I've only been late once. Still think about it, too. Am still ashamed of it.

My feet step forward, following the line. An older couple is snuggled up on the same side of the booth. What would their story be if they had the collection of their lives to tell? How many loves have they had, jobs have they worked, lessons have they learned?

The line moves again. A woman not much older than me is waiting by the bar in a chic pinstripe pantsuit. Her hair is pulled into an elegant ponytail that hangs down her back in large curls, and her stilettos click when she walks. She looks like the epitome of success, but does she feel as alone as me?

A gentle touch on my arm pauses me mid-step, and comfort overwhelms my senses. There's only one person who does this to me—his touch is ingrained in my heart.

"Did you know . . ." Dean asks, "that sunflowers turn their face toward the sun during the day?"

A sarcastic chuckle escapes me, as I glance up. Did I hope to see him? Yes, but I didn't plan for it. I'm already running late, and those eyes could be the final thing to derail my emotions for the rest of the day. It's confusing how even a good thing can set me off.

"Well, I wanted to test that theory. Upon further review, I can confirm." He smirks, raising a flower and turning it to me. "They do, in fact, face the sunshine."

An uncontrollable smile lifts my cheeks, squinting my eyes so much I can barely see. Sunshine is a nickname I'd like to get used to.

"One hot vanilla latte for Hallee," the barista calls out.

My name and my drink? But I haven't even ordered . . .

Dean smiles at me, eyes flaring slightly as he says, "Better go get it, Hal."

This wouldn't be the first time my mind's played a trick on me, but I swear he winked as I walked away.

As I reach for my drink, the barista spins the cup. There, written on it, is a note. One simple question, proving that he feels it too.

Can I walk you to work?

Dean

The timing of that plan couldn't have been executed more perfectly. I did wait for over an hour and order five different vanilla lattes under her name to try and get it right, but when it really counted, it was as flawless as her. The barista, Lea, rolled her eyes the third time she wrote the question on a cup, but her smile was hopeful that my plan would work, and the surprise on Hallee's face when Lea called her name? I'd buy endless amounts of lattes to see it again.

My gut is pushy these days, insisting she's not an ordinary hookup. This delicate beginning might grow to redefine my idea of love. Nothing and no one will stop me from pursuing her like a prince would.

"Well, Hal?"

She taps her cup three times before mumbling, "I'm running really late, but if you walk fast, then yes."

Message received.

Meeting her step for step, I push open the door and follow her onto the sidewalk. Her hurried steps call out, begging me to break the silence. She's on edge, like one wrong move could push her over the cliff. Won't make eye contact and is biting her lip as if she's trying to keep it from trembling.

What the hell did I do?

It's been a bit since she stayed the night, but it's not that I didn't want to have her back over. I didn't even want to drop her off! I wanted her to stay all day, tangled up in the blankets and bliss, but she seems to startle easily. I didn't want to suffocate her with too much attention too fast. That night was the flint to spark a flame that requires a steady and consistent effort to burn.

Steady and consistent—that's what I'll be for her.

"You look really beautiful today, Hal."

"Are you bullshitting me?" she asks, glancing at the flower in my hand.

"What?! No, you're gorg—"

"Do they *really* face the sun?"

"Oh! They do. Hudson and I watched a whole nature documentary on it."

"Intriguing," she mumbles, squinting suspiciously to hide her growing grin.

"Although, I think they should rename it," I bait her with a mischievous smile.

"Is that so?"

"The Hallee Detector is much more accurate. After all, they follow the sunshine."

She scoffs, but her shoulders relax a little.

"I got it for you, but maybe I should keep it so it'll lead me back to you."

Playfully shoving my arm, she giggles, and I swear that sound turns the gray sky blue, the cold air warm, and a boy into a man. I'd give my whole life to hear it again.

"Sunflowers face the sun . . ." She pauses, nodding as if the gesture will lock the memory into place before her shoulders tighten up again, uncomfortable from the moment of silence.

"Talk to me. What's going on in that pretty little mind?" I ask.

Her weighted sigh is crushing, and she does that adorable thing where she twists the ends of her hair. You know, the way she did while standing in the doorway of my bedroom. Man, she looked like she belonged there.

"I don't like being late."

That was, at best, an incomplete statement. She'll continue if I stay quiet. Did I mention how much she hates silence?

"Do you not have work today?" she asks, shifting her demeanor to hold her head a little higher than before.

The change of topic is a clear protection against something bordering on too personal. She must not realize I don't startle as easily as her.

"Not today."

Honking horns fill the pause in conversation and I'm not going to lie, her icy exterior is flustering. Not startling, just . . . nerves aren't something I'm used to. If I wait any longer, the butterflies in my stomach will carry away the rest of my thoughts.

"Hallee . . ." I grab her arm, conscious to keep my grip a soft request rather than a forced decision.

Her usual glow is absent—hidden by clouds on her face—and her eyes are ready to rain, still refusing to meet mine.

"Would you like to go on a date with me this weekend?" I ask, and tap my feet to distract from how long it takes her to answer.

The clouds on her face darken, lightning strikes, and then nothing. Her eyes are a ruined city, exhausted from weathering the storm, and I can't get myself to look away.

How do I rebuild it?

"Well," she pauses, finally raising her glassy eyes to mine. "What took you so long?"

Oh.

She isn't preparing for battle, she's recovering from feeling discarded. Makes me feel sick, so I clench my jaw tightly to keep it from gaping open.

"There—" I try to explain, but every thought sounds like an endless list of excuses rather than an actual reason for waiting so long. Nothing was good enough in my strive for perfection, but now I could lose her to the wasted time. Maybe love is less about perfection and more about the intention.

"There was a brief lapse in my judgment about what amount of excitement would be flattering, but not scare you off." I swallow down my nerves. "Let me make it up to you, Hallee. Let me take you out. I promise it will never happen again."

Fighting a smirk, she side-eyes me and asks, "You'll never take me out again, or you'll never make me question your intentions again?"

"Hallee," I sigh. Her tone may be playful, but the words still feel like a punch to the face. Stops me in my tracks, actually.

"Dean." She freezes, batting her eyelashes as a grin breaks free.

"There will never be another question about my intentions here."

"Are you sure about that? Because I ask *a lot* of questions. Queen of the questions," she jokes, tapping her forehead three times.

"Queen of the questions!" I exclaim, grinning from ear to ear. "Thou shall never again be put in a position to feel anything less than irreplaceable!"

As I pretend to bow, the star finally shows up to the show. Her full smile is worthy of a record-breaking standing ovation. Before she can notice, I snap a picture with the Polaroid camera hanging off of my shoulder.

"Hey!" she shouts, laughing through the end of the word. "Have you had that the whole time?"

"*Someone* was too distracted by her change in routine to notice," I tease.

"Ugh, Dean!"

My name on her lips is like seeing a familiar face in a crowd of strangers. Her laugh? Has me flying. She's feisty for her size, quick on her feet, but not quick enough to get this picture from me.

"No fair, you're tall!" Pouting, she crosses her arms over her chest.

"Oh, and that's a bad thing?"

"Yes!"

Tipping my head to the side, I shoot her a knowing smirk. "Really? Wow, ladies and gentlemen, mark it down in the books! A man being tall is a *no go.*"

"Are you done?"

"Are you?"

Letting out a frustrated grunt, she circles me like a shark on a hunt. She disappears, and I'd think she's given up . . . if that were something she's capable of.

Her full weight slams into me as she conducts her sneak attack. Bold move, to jump on my back without warning. Already trusts me enough to know I'd never drop her.

"Clever girl." I laugh as she pulls at my raised arm.

"Move your arm down!"

"Your wish is my command." As she hops off my back, I obey, but slip the picture into my front shirt pocket.

"Happy?" I chuckle through the word, letting her spin me around to meet her wild glare.

"Picture," she demands, holding out her hand like she's commanding a dog to drop its toy.

Flirtatious irritation looks good on her. Has her cheeks all pink and lips all pouty.

"I think that this," I tease, plucking the Polaroid from my pocket, "is what you're looking for."

Her eyes flare as I brush her hair over her shoulder. The touch holds her attention while I slide the Polaroid into my back pocket.

"You can have the picture, Sunshine. You just have to get it." Her breathing stops as I continue, holding her stare. "It's in the back left."

She swallows as I turn my pockets to her. Hesitating for a second, amusement raises her eyebrows.

"Now I'm really going to be late to work."

Rolling her eyes, she resumes her speed walk.

"So—is that a yes?" My heart skips at her nod, but she's extra cute when I tease her, so I continue, "Need to hear ya say it, Hal."

"How could I say no to those eyes?"

"Ah, it's the eyes you like, then?"

Hers widen, and suddenly cracks in the sidewalk become more interesting than me.

"I'll pick you up on Saturday, 9 a.m. sharp. That is, unless you have another date we should work around?"

It's a joke, mostly. Also my way of finding out if she's seeing other people.

"That works! Don't be late."

Not exactly a jackpot of answers to my question, but it's enough for me. She always will be.

Her fingers interlace in mine as if we've done this every day of our lives, and it feels like we have. The walk to Happy Bookday doesn't feel long enough this time, and as we turn the corner, her pace slows.

"You better take the sunflower with you," I insist, smiling as she turns to face me. "It belongs in the sun."

Pink paints her cheeks as her hand grazes mine.

"One more thing," I say, doing my best to not come apart at the way her touch lingers for a mere few seconds. "Will you take a picture of me?"

"Why?"

"Trust me."

Tipping my head barely to the right, I tuck my hands into my pockets and give the biggest smile I can while keeping my eyes locked on her.

Click.

I grab it before she does, but immediately hand it over.

"A picture to permanently wash away any doubt of how I feel about you. Look at your effect on me."

She smiles and I wink, and I want to stay here forever.

"Remember me happy, Hal."

It hurts my heart to walk away without another word, so I sneak a glance over my shoulder after a few steps. When I do, she's already inside, but through the window her eyes find mine, and the smile she gives me makes it true—my life will never be the same.

Hallee

It's official. My life will never be the same, all because I love a man.

Miles throws me a taunting grin as I cradle the Polaroid in my hand, extra careful not to bend the corners. He doesn't say a word, but his eyes tolerate my late arrival for the day. They tolerate it, even if I don't. I'll be thinking about this until the day I forget.

Choosing to run late rather than rush here this morning contradicts my goal of being the world's most reliable employee. Not that it's extremely pressing; there are no customers yet, but the sentiment still matters to me. It was my turn to help open, and I wasn't here for him. The guilt string of my heart stretches so thin it hurts. What age did I start to believe that every single moment has such high stakes?

What age will I be when I start to believe that my existence isn't an inconvenience?

It's all-consuming, the swell of my degrading voice repeating all of my shortcomings. Being late, burning dinner, being too distracted to remember to smile at a stranger who looked sad. Has my brain always been this mean? Forgetting really is a gift if the alternative is a lifetime of being my own worst enemy.

The corner of the Polaroid pokes my finger. I forgot it was in my hand, but my pocket isn't safe enough for something so irreplaceable. I flip it over, finally looking at the developed picture. Dean's joyful smile reaches into the darkest corners of my mind, illuminating them until every degrading thought scatters. There is nothing but hope in the presence of the light.

This morning he proved he has enough hope to carry us both. Regardless of the terrain, I'm ready to walk the path with him. If we end the year holding hands, the journey was worth it. If I end up alone, at least I was brave enough to risk it—to risk my heart in the fall for the man that brightens up the darkest parts of me.

My feet rarely carry me to the romance aisle, but here I am. Seems like a sign, but before I can choose a book, the bell dings and the familiar click of a walker announces my favorite customer's entrance. A pink balloon floats slowly through the doorway as if it's rolling out the red carpet for her. She's only a few feet inside when I skip to greet her.

"Good morning, ma'am. I see you chose a pink balloon this morning. It complements your lipstick well."

It's almost identical, actually, as if it were color-matched and created for this moment entirely.

"Thank you, dear." The raspy texture of her voice is proof of the many lives she's lived so far.

Content to be alone, she disappears between the aisles. It must be nice to be happy spending time in the company of yourself.

Her balloon renders it impossible to lose her location in her quest for the next adventure, and I follow along from afar as it pauses in the romance aisle. Love must be in the air today. Signs all around.

After about thirty minutes of shuffling back and forth, she turns the corner. Miles rushes to her side, immediately offering to carry her three books.

"I like your balloon! French Rose pink suits you well," he compliments loudly, biting back at the passing judgmental stares of the other customers.

"Oh my stars, you know your colors!" she cheerfully replies, approaching the counter.

"Did you find everything you were looking for?" I ask as clearly as I can without sounding like I'm talking to a child.

"I sure hope so, dear. I always allow the characters to choose me."

That's a crazy idea, but I'm a reader, so to me it makes perfect sense. What doesn't make sense is that she didn't apologize for saying something that could be labeled as odd. Time has made her bold. Could it make me bold, too?

"Would you mind sharing your story about the balloon?"

Her face lights up, negating my assumption that she is asked about it often. Perhaps fewer people are brave enough to connect with strangers than I thought.

"There's not much story to tell, dear. I like balloons. Life is too short to not spend it in the space of things you love."

"Like books?" I giggle, gesturing to the hundreds of companions on the shelves.

"And balloons!" she exclaims, and our laughter intertwines.

"Between you and me, I have always thought that names are forgettable. It's our hearts, and their unique characteristics, that are worthy of being remembered. At the end of the year, my name will be lost in the wind along with every other civilian's. Yet deep down, something calls to me, promising that somehow, someday, *someone* will remember the old woman hobbling along with her balloon."

Her unsaid words linger in the air between us.

"It's an act of defiance," I breathe, quietly enough that her aged hearing fails her, and quickly mask my widening eyes behind the same face I give to every customer as they check out. One that says, *We are thankful for your business.*

"The top one is for you, dear," she says, and her shaky hands slide the book off of the other two, plopping it onto the counter.

"No, take it with you! I get a free one each week for working here."

A stubborn edge sparks in her voice as she replies, "These characters didn't choose me. They chose you."

"Thank you," I whisper as tears well in my eyes, and we pause for a moment, holding hands and slowing down the day.

Together, we take in a breath so powerful my bones rejoice. Connection—how I've missed it. Pockets of it have started to weave their way back into my life, and it only makes me want more of it. With a wink, she pulls her hand away and walks to the exit. Her pink balloon marks her path the entire way out the door.

The book she left is face down on the counter, so I skim the summary on the back. It's a forbidden love story about two people with the entire world against them, and—

A gasp of shock flies out of me as I flip the book over, and chill bumps cover me from head to toe. Lingering tears overflow in streams down my face at the title.

The Symbolism of a Sunflower.

The entire world stills as I glance behind me to the sunflower Dean gave me, hidden underneath the checkout counter. My pulse pounds, guiding me toward the question I didn't dare ask her.

An act of defiance implies that there's something to be defied. Could what she believes really be possible? Somehow, somewhere, someday, will I be brave enough to defy authority?

I ponder the question for hours, but hope is the only answer I land on.

I hope that I will.

- 19 -

March 2096

The History of Psychology 2335

Backpacks line the front of the room, and the basket of phones is sitting on the end of the rickety table. As we file in, the TA hands us each a thin binder personalized with our names. My heart rate takes flight at the all-too-familiar lack of control.

"Please leave your binders unopened until I give permission," Mr. Holiday reminds us as I climb the thirteen rows to my usual seat.

The anticipation is always the hardest part, but counting ceiling tiles fights against my nerves. I make it to forty-three before a loud pop explodes from the front of the room and streamers rain from the ceiling. The TA puts on a gold sparkly *Happy New Year* headband as another confetti popper shoots and, despite being more prepared, our shoulders still flinch. The back row bandits cascade down the stairs, laughing as they toss glitter over the rest of us. Glitter, of all things. Months from now, I'll still be finding leftover sparkles.

"Okay, okay, back row bandits, thank you for your assistance. You may make your way back to your seats," Mr. Holiday says, wheezing through laughter. "Welcome to our second immersive experience," he continues. "Happy New Year!"

Crickets and dropped jaws answer him.

"Before we officially begin, let's take a walk down memory lane and remember our special quiz from a few weeks ago." He pauses expectantly. "Well, who remembers the quiz?"

Hands fly up across the room.

"Good, I was worried The Experiment already got to you."

A few students snicker as he continues.

"You wrote your name, the first contact in your phone, and then as much important information as you could about yourself in one minute. I must say, it was entertaining sifting through the items you deemed to be important."

I lower my head to hide my insecurity.

"Would anyone like to explain how you decided which items to include?"

As hands urgently raise, mine sink further into my lap. A girl from row eight answers first, "I wrote the first things that came to mind."

"I wrote information that would identify me in an emergency," the freshman cuts in. I laugh under my breath until it hits me—we are more alike than I'd like to admit.

"Yes, you are all *very* important people. You have a lot to be proud of! I'm lucky to have such an involved group of students this semester." Mr. Holiday grins suspiciously. "Of course, we can't actually simulate The Experiment, but we've worked hard to create an interesting lecture that, with enough imagination, can transport you to the emotions of back then."

Wait, are these binders—

"Happy New Year, class. From now until further notice, you have no memory of life before this."

My stomach plummets as the thought of being studied sinks in.

"Please take the next few minutes to familiarize yourself with your identity, your role in society, and any interests listed in your paperwork. The phone on your desk has been doctored to your specific needs. Be sure to also go through it."

I curse at my shaky hands as they open the binder. There's only one page of personal information, and the ghost of quiz past haunts me.

Name: Rayne
Birthdate: 11/04/2077
Roommates: Amy and Jenn
Address: 19476 W. Holiday Avenue
Family: None known
Interests: None available
Occupation: Barista at the downtown coffee shop

Frantically flipping pages fails to give me more information. The next only briefly explains The Gift and the general well-being of society. *You're safe,* they claim. Physically, maybe, but this is a sick joke. There has to be more to my story than this. Did the civilians know this was all they'd be left with?

Peering over my neighbor's shoulder, I glance at her open binder. Hers is the same as mine, except *I* am listed as one of her roommates. Is she Amy, or is she Jenn?

My eyes' search is interrupted when Mr. Holiday's voice splits the air. "Something wrong?" he asks the scoffing student in row two. "I'm sorry, I can't seem to remember your name. What is it?"

"There's nothing to go off of. You want us to familiarize ourselves with our identity? What identity? There are no interests, no family—nothing. I wrote down so much information you could've used—"

Another student cuts him off. "I wrote down everything I was proud of, and none of it is here!"

Mr. Holiday nods with the audacity of an entitled teenager, knowing full well the game he's put into motion. None of us had the choice in playing. Did the civilians really know what they were voting for?

"Oh, when did you write those things down?" he asks, raising his eyebrows and tipping his head to the right.

"During the quiz—"

"What quiz? We've just rung in the New Year! Look around, there is even glitter from the celebration."

The crime sinks in, convicting the government of first-degree larceny.

We knew the civilians were given very little information, but not this little. I'd assumed they were kept in the dark of the happenings behind the closed doors of government meetings, not held hostage from their identities.

In the snap of some fingers, my entire life has been erased, leaving behind an empty shell of who I used to be. They even took my last name.

Looking to my right, I make eye contact with either Amy or Jenn. I still couldn't tell you which name her blanching face belongs to, but she looks as nauseous as I feel. In some ways, this is all too real.

Anticipating more information, I finally unlock the phone on my desk. It's completely blank, except for one unknown application. Clicking on the icon opens me to an address book with—right. Amy and Jenn.

Surely I missed an explanation in my binder?

Electronics are erased alongside the memories of their owners in order to maintain the integrity of The Gift.

Shit.

What a crucial piece of information to leave out of our textbook. Who wrote it? And who decided what to teach through multiple generations? If that job fell into deceptive hands, it would be so easy to alter the perception of the past. What other information has been omitted from our studies?

In the silence, fear ricochets around the room.

"It's not so easy to let go of things that matter to you, is it?" Mr. Holiday's gaze burns a hole through the boy that was appalled his precious achievements were not included.

"It's not easy to move forward with very little information about who you are, what built you, and what matters to you."

Today clarifies any lingering confusion about his opinion on The Experiment. There's no hiding his disdain, and the point has been driven home. None of us are unique. Not anymore. My poem echoes in my mind as I re-count the ceiling tiles.

I think I would wither away.

Not that it matters now, but I'd change it.

I *know* I would wither away.

- 20 -
March 2045

Dean

Four in the morning, I wake with the amount of energy I'd get from three cups of coffee. Hudson and Matt have been on duty for the last two days, so there's a decent chance they're still awake. It's hard to sleep at the station. If they wanted to come home immediately after their shift I wouldn't blame them, but it would alter my plans for our date.

Rise and shine, it's almost date time! I text our roommate group.

My phone vibrates as a text from Matt comes through.

Mission "help Dean land a girl way out of his league" is on.

Hudson enters the chat before I can reply.

I don't know Dean, I might be changing my mind. It's only fair I take her out first. Test the waters for you.

Sarcasm is in every letter, but the thought has me clenching my phone like a letter on a windy day.

If you fumble her, don't worry. We'll be here to recover the play, Matt replies.

Double tapping the message, I react with a *haha*, close my eyes, and hope that sleep will find me again. Instead, the Polaroid picture of her projects onto my closed eyelids. It starts with one, and then more images pass by like an old-time film reel. I sweep her off her feet in the snow, spinning to the tune of her laughter. We're dancing in the rain, kicking off our shoes to splash in the puddles. She's asleep on my chest while I tickle her back.

Laying still for a few more minutes, I stare at the shadows on my ceiling that spell out the word reckless. Building a mental life with her is, but my world has already become a kingdom for her to rule. There's no hiding it. Don't really want to, either. If I don't leash my hope, maybe it'll lead me into the shoes of a man who deserves to rule alongside her. There will be no other end than us being together, because life makes infinitely more sense together.

Four thirty, I finally roll out of bed, drag a hand through my hair, and throw on some gray sweatpants. My body might as well accompany my mind on its run. At the very least, exercise should shed off the shaky energy in my hands. All of the planning I've done for today will matter.

It has to.

The run lasted about forty-five minutes before I started pacing around the city while it still slept. It's different without its people—a display of sadness rather than a painting of welcoming nostalgia—but it's coming back to life as people rise and start their days alongside the sun. Even the city changes with the times.

From the inside of my apartment, sunrise has always served as a brutal wake-up call. But from the outside, the windows sparkle with the warm orange reflection of its light. Reminds me of my favorite person, and suddenly the wake-up call doesn't seem so brutal. I get to spend time with her today, which means it'll be a good one. Smiling at the symbolism, I jog inside to get ready.

The timing matters and is a detail I refuse to let slip, but my overthinking almost has me running late. It's a good thing I headed back to the apartment when I did, because getting dressed is impossible. Every outfit falls flat, missing the mark on the impression I hope to make. At this rate, I'd be better off wearing the tuxedo. At least then my confidence wouldn't be at risk of wavering.

Someone who is put together but not a tryhard. Confident but not arrogant. Attractive but approachable. Real and worthwhile. What would that someone wear?

Staring in the mirror, I start by fixing my hair. A hat would be too casual, and maybe send the message I overslept, which is the exact opposite of what I did. Next, I clean up my face by shaving my five-o'clock shadow. It's how I looked at the club, so Hallee already knows this version of me—already trusts this version of me, and that counts for something in my mind.

Pairing my light-wash jeans with the nicest T-shirt I have, I take one last glance in the mirror. My white tennis shoes squeak on the floor as I hop away from the last of my nerves and into excitement. The anticipation of her sunshine is already highlighting my best qualities. She's the sun and I'm the window, proudly reflecting her light on me.

Hallee

Avery and Marlowe are giggling on the couch as we wait for Dean to arrive. Everyone loves a good love story, but in this apartment we *really* love a good love story. Love the story almost as much as the love. Maybe more.

The connection between Dean and me could be in my head, and it feels so good it might be; I can't seem to tell what's real once I look into those hazel eyes. But, if it was all in my head, he wouldn't be knocking on the door and my feet wouldn't be running to him like he's my home.

"Girl!" Marlowe whistles, smiling wide as my eyes snap to her. "Go get your man."

My man, my heart skips.

I sure hope so.

Excitement swarms my stomach as I reach for the door handle, touching it three times. I need all the luck on my side today. With one deep breath, I twist the knob and pull the door open. As my eyes adjust to the change in lighting, Dean's pale blue T-shirt fades to a pure white.

"You match!" Avery squeals, and Dean laughs through his color-stained cheeks.

We do, even down to the wash of our jeans. Somehow, this is exactly what I expected and nothing I expected, simultaneously.

We are, too.

"Hi ladies," Dean says, grinning as he waves, and I steal an up-down glance before he looks back at me.

"Good morning, Hallee."

Oh, so he's going formal instead of funny. Alright, I'll follow that narrative. We are multifaceted—capable of many different realities.

"Good morning, Dean."

"Yet again, you prove my theory to be true." Raising a sunflower to me, he winks.

The callback is cute, but now I can't breathe. We have memories together I never thought we'd have.

Weaving his fingers into mine, he tugs me out the door, leans around me, and waves to Marlowe and Avery. "Goodbye ladies!" he calls, tone sing-songy like he knows how excited they are. Then he smiles, completely unaware that acknowledging my friends might be the most attractive thing he'll ever do.

Without a doubt, it mattered to them too. Avery will gush about it at dinner tonight, confirming that he won them over with that simple gesture. It's another thing added to the list of reasons why he feels like home to me. Deep down, I hope this first date feels as monumental to him as it does to me.

"Goodbye, lovebirds!" Marlowe shouts over Avery's giggling.

As he closes the door, our eyes lock. I've been in the guy's shower, yet this is somehow more nerve-wracking. Now there's actually something to be lost.

"Ready, Hal?" he asks, tipping his head like he did when I took his picture.

"Ready," is all I can muster.

With his hand over mine, he leads me outside. The sun bathes our backs in warmth and elongates our shadows in front of us. I can't tell where his stops and mine starts, and it feels a lot like our souls. Our silhouette makes sense which means we make sense, and a swirling shadow of leaves dances around us, cheering us on. We could keep doing this. Again and again. As many times as possible before the end of the year.

"Does my date want to be surprised, or know the plans for the day?" Dean asks, looking down at me.

"Hmm . . ."

Knowing would actually calm my stomach. Letting him plan the date was enough loss of control.

"I want to know."

"Somehow, I knew that's what you'd say."

"Predictable is she. Hope you don't get bored of me."

"With rhymes like that? Never."

"First, we're grabbing coffee. The Marmotte will not suffer the loss of your sunshine today."

"Good start!" I encourage.

Excellent start, really. The one I'd have picked.

"Second, we'll walk a few blocks to pick up some bagels. I placed the order this morning, so they'll be ready for us to grab and go to our next destination."

My eyebrows shoot to my hairline.

He ordered for me? Gutsy. If he got it right, it was a confident decision, but if he got it wrong, it was a cocky assumption that he knew me well enough to already know what I like. Although it kind of feels like he does. Know me . . .

"Interesting. Go on."

"We're going to the park for a picnic, where you will proceed to stare into my dreamy galaxy eyes and fall madly in love with me."

Mid-step, my feet freeze. The man really can read my mind.

Those eyes of his—they cause a head rush, heart rush, all the rush. Every kind of rush. Except the kind that speeds up time, because we already don't have enough of it.

"Alright, you don't have to fall madly in love." He glances at me confidently, tugging my hand gently to resume our walk. "You can fall a socially acceptable amount in love. Although, that is much less exciting."

"You . . ." I laugh, hitting him playfully on the arm with the sunflower.

"Me?" He pretends to gasp, but before I can return the flirting, I'm distracted by a man standing outside of The Marmotte.

He's leaning against the wall, harmless enough, but this street is usually just a passing stop on a commute to or from somewhere. Can I switch sides with Dean, or would that be too obvious? I don't want the man to think I'm afraid. That might hurt his feelings. Sidestepping closer to Dean, I lean into the comfort of his height and strength. Luckily, I don't even think he notices.

As we approach, the man pushes off the wall and steps in front of us, hiding his arm behind his back. Adrenaline shoots through my fingertips, tightening my grip on Dean's hand.

Please protect me, my eyes blink as he glances down.

"It's okay, Hal. It's Matt."

Dean's smile is sweet, gentle, reassuring but—should I know a Matt?

"For the lovely lady," Matt says, bowing slightly and pulling a sunflower from behind his back.

My mouth gapes open as I glance at Dean. This is how the women must feel in the movies I watch. No wonder people try to capture this feeling.

"Did you—?"

"Did I what, Hal? *Plan*?"

"Now is the time to accept," Matt whispers, moving the sunflower closer to me.

"Oh my gosh, thank you!"

"You didn't think I'd show my entire hand when you asked for the plan, did you?" Dean asks, the corner of his lips raising into a teasing grin.

"Yes, actually, I did."

"A man never tells all his secrets," Matt jokes.

"Thank you for your service, Matt. We will see you later," Dean replies, giving him a single nod before leading me through the door of The Marmotte.

The smell of coffee welcomes us home as a couple of regulars who belong here, together. *This place* just became *our place*.

Dean

My phone vibrates twice with messages from Matt telling me he's in place at the park. Hudson was waiting outside of the bagel shop, exactly as he said he'd be. The plan has been executed perfectly, although I never considered how it might feel to be a woman and have an unfamiliar man approach you—until Hallee stepped toward me. That little moment was unexpected, but not unnoticed. Thankfully when it was Hudson's turn, she merely blushed through profuse gratitude, absolutely clueless as to how serious I was when I promised she'd never question my intentions again. The most serious I've ever been, I think.

Nature is slowly coming back to life. The ducks in the park are dunking their heads in the water without a worry in the world. She makes me feel like that—all carefree and light.

As we make our way to the blanket by the pond, Matt and Hudson step out from behind a large tree with sunflower bouquets in each of their arms.

"Oh!" Hallee gasps, hopping in this really cute way that makes me proud of myself.

As if they are here to take them instead of giving her more, she pulls her collection close to her heart. With how happy she looks, God so help me, I will find every single sunflower in this city and give it to her by the end of the year. Every sunflower will be returned to their sun.

When we planned the route, we'd settled on Matt holding all four bouquets of flowers. Hudson would've had to haul ass from the bagel shop to get here, especially without running into us along the way. Makes me happier than it should, how hard he tried.

Surprising Hal is intimidating because of how easily she startles, but that doesn't mean I shouldn't do it. Her face right now is proof of that. The absolute highlight of my year.

"You really shouldn't have—" she starts, but I cut her off.

"I should have, and I did. Now I think they'd really appreciate seeing your strut, you know, for application purposes to continue to model for the fire department."

Rather than slowing down after the momentum of my initial push, she spins melodramatically and rules the catwalk. Hudson whistles as she twirls again, right before them, and Matt's jaw hits the grass. I didn't expect her to actually do it, and didn't think through that if she did, I wouldn't be the only one wanting to take her home.

Probably wasn't anyway. I mean—look at her.

"That's my girl," I whisper, heading to join them before drool runs down their faces.

"Nice to see you again, gentlemen. For me?" she asks, doe-eyed and batting her eyelashes.

Damn—I'm proud to show her off, but do they have to look at her like that? Like they might love her too. Everyone might. It's impossible not to.

Wait, love? No, not yet.

Right?

Matt clears his throat, shaking me from my daze. "Our final flower delivery for the day, ma'am."

The sunflowers fill her arms, blocking her vision as they bow to her. Barely lifting their gaze to mine, their devilish smirks are the flashing reminder—I fumble, they recover.

"This is where we leave you, milady," Hudson says, his subpar British accent making her giggle.

They straighten to wave goodbye, and I'm too distracted to hear anything more than a gracious *thank you* from Hallee. With one drop of the attention she actually deserves, she's glowing. My girl's the brightest thing on this planet.

Her giggle reminds me in a gentle way to help her with the flowers, but as I carefully take them from her arms, her bag tumbles off of her shoulder.

"No!" she shouts, reaching out as if she can stop the fall mid-air.

A relieved sigh comes out of her as she bends down and pulls out a book, looking it over like it's her most prized possession.

"It's a paperback. I was worried the fall bent the corners."

Her face flushes in this endearing, bashful way as she rubs at her arm. Bent corners would be very serious business, I'm not patronizing that. My heart's just happy because she's so cute, and my face wants to be happy too.

"I'm glad it's okay," I say, and I am, but she stares me down contemplatively. "Did you think you'd have a lot of reading time during our date?"

Sue me for grinning, I dare you. She's just too damn adorable not to.

"No, I always keep one with me." She gently places the book back into her bag. "I swear, Dean, I didn't know what to expect for today, but I carry one with me wherever I go."

There go her hands, nervously twisting the ends of her hair. She doesn't want to hurt what she's the keeper of. Doesn't want to hurt my feelings.

I stand still for a few seconds, and she shifts uncomfortably under the pressure of my lingering stare. Somehow this woman doesn't understand that she deserves love. That'll change after one year with me.

"What?" she snaps, sitting down quickly on our picnic blanket.

"I just like looking at you."

I join her, close enough to extend my arm out behind her as I lean back onto my hands, holding her gaze while I do it to see how much she trusts me.

"Alright, smooth talker, we've had plenty of laughs. Tell me something that matters."

"Something that matters?"

"You heard me." She tilts her head back, watching the sky like I'm watching her.

"There are many ways to matter," I tentatively reply.

"Are there?"

The appropriate amount of time for me to think about a response approaches at full speed. I planned for a lot, but you can't plan for how the tide of a conversation will go. I couldn't plan for her to surprise me too.

"This matters," I answer, holding up a single sunflower.

Chickened out from what I wanted to say—what I know she needs to hear. She waits for an explanation, so I double down.

"You matter."

Sinks my stomach, her doubt-filled eyes.

"You'll come to learn, Hal, that I'm not the best with words. There are never enough of them to amount to what I feel, and if there are, then their importance isn't good enough. Actions are the easier way for me," I mutter, my voice dripping in disappointment, but it's not about being perfect. It's about trying, and this is me trying.

"You've told me a million little things about yourself today, from what you planned, how you've treated me, and how you treated your friends."

She reaches over, tilting my chin up so my eyes meet hers. Hers flick down to my mouth and back up, so quickly I almost missed it. Couldn't miss anything she does, though.

"You are confident but not arrogant. Punctual but not inflexible. Attractive but not cocky." Leaning in, she freezes with her lips a hair's breadth away from mine. "You care about people, friends or strangers, and you are very *very* bad at hiding just how much you like me already."

Holy—Sunshine. My woman is a mind reader.

"How'd you know that's what I was going for?" I ask.

"Probably the white shoes." She smirks, and my laughter becomes her laughter.

"Well, what else would you like to know?"

"Everything," she whispers, pulling away casually as if she didn't just have me in a chokehold in the middle of the park. Laying the back of her hand across her forehead, she jokes, "Oh, Dean, whatever will we do?"

"What do you mean?"

Her silliness turns to seriousness in one second.

"You and I both know we are one step away from falling off the cliff. One step from the point of no return for whatever this will be."

The tremor in her voice hurts. She's forgotten that one step is all it's ever taken for me to understand her.

"If you're not ready to break my fall when we reach the bottom, then I need you to let go before you take me over the edge with you.

It's irrational, and crazy, and fast, but there's no halfway here for me, so please, Dean. This is the only time I'll ask. Let go. If you don't feel the same, then let me go."

The desperate ache to comfort her is filled with the words I'd been missing. Taking her trembling hands in mine, I gently stroke my thumb over her palm.

"Look at me," I insist, and her eyes immediately obey while a single, fear-filled tear falls from her face.

"I've got you, Hal. Let's fall."

- 21 -

March 2045

Hallee

Marlowe and Avery started blowing up my phone around two o'clock. We all assumed I'd be back before noon, at the very latest, ready to debrief the date sleepover-style. Snacks, face masks, nail painting—the whole deal. Avery even made cupcakes.

"They'll sweeten the sting of the date being over, or comfort you if it's dumpy," she'd insisted.

But here we are.

One turned to two, which turned to three, to now four forty-five and I don't want to go back. We've taken as many detours as possible on the way back to my apartment. There was a crack in the sidewalk on Main Street that caused quite the scene because Dean, apparently, is very superstitious. He said it was bad luck to step over it and made us turn around. My laughter drew the attention of everyone on the street, and I didn't even care, because him killing time means that he feels this too. I already miss him and he's not even gone. Will I miss him next year when he is?

Call in a pizza and I'll pay you back. Be home soon!!! I text Marlowe and Avery.

Send three question marks if we need to call the police, Marlowe replies.

No, don't do that! Avery jumps in. *Marlowe, you know she sends three of everything, always. SEND TWO!*

Laughing under my breath, I inhale a rush of bravery.

"The girls think you've taken me hostage. Let's send them a picture!"

Butterflies swell in my stomach as I raise onto my tiptoes, leaning back against him for balance. Wow, he's strong. Knew it, but now I can feel it. Has he always been this tall?

Before I can talk myself out of it, I lay a kiss on his cheek, and the camera captures his entire reaction. It's minimal, but the change in his eyes is there—surprise mixed with desire. My feet flatten out as I sink down to my normal height.

"Wait, take one more," he insists, leaning down beside me. My eyes roll, but any excuse to be closer to him is good enough for me.

He kisses my forehead, lingering for a second like he doesn't want to move. Is this love? Green flags are all I see.

No police, but maybe a doctor??? I text back.

Wait, why a doctor? Avery quickly replies.

Because I've taken a hard fall!!!

Imaginative cheers echo through my mind as they "love" the picture.

You better not hold out on us! SEE YOU SOON! Marlowe replies.

"I have a question," Dean says, grinning as I slide my phone into my back pocket, and nerves run to me like an old familiar friend.

"I may or may not have an answer!"

The more I think I know, it always turns out to be the opposite.

"Why do you smile at everyone you pass?"

Fear, loss, kindness, all come to mind. Mostly fear. Fear *of* loss.

"Everyone has a story."

"And?" he asks.

"Who of these strangers has been interwoven into my life? Someone out there is the reason why I'm happy when I hear Taylor, flinch when I hear about baseball, laugh when I see a moose, feel sad eating tacos, and scared in the club. Someone is the reason I run instead of stay, apologize for my existence, startle easily, think breakfast for dinner is superior, and believe in mermaids."

"You believe in—?"

"Fairytales. Someone out there is why I believe in fairytales. Am I the reason anyone believes in anything? Loves, or hates? Who do these strangers have in their lives that cares for them? Do they feel valued? Has anyone smiled at them today?"

"Wow, that's—"

"Crazy, I know."

"Amazing. Your mind is—"

My cough of shock cuts him off, and I look everywhere except at him as he continues.

"Extraordinary. Your mind is extraordinary."

"Anyway," I say, completely ignoring his wildly inaccurate compliment, "obviously, they're answers I'll never get, and the people will continue on completely unaware of the girl who cared enough to wonder about them. But what if I'm their last hope for kindness, and I don't give it? What if they need it to want to live?"

"That's a pressure you can't put on yourself."

"Well, even on my worst day, I will give them my best smile, because my worst day is someone else's worst day too. I'll never know when someone has met their breaking point, but you better believe I'll do everything I can to let them know they are not alone."

Dean blinks, squeezing my hand tighter while his chest freezes as if I just knocked the wind out of him.

"Do you disagree with me?" he asks, stopping in the middle of the sidewalk.

"With what?"

"That your mind is extraordinary . . . that *you* are."

I try to change the subject from the least favorite part of me, but the words get caught in my throat.

"You think I'm perfect, and if I tell you, then I won't be perfect anymore."

"I don't want perfect, Hallee. I want to know *you*."

"Right. Extraordinary . . ." I close my eyes, blowing out as many of the scary feelings as I can. "My body, maybe. My mind? Damaged—broken beyond repair. I'm a mess, really."

"How do you feel, admitting it?"

"Free."

"That's my girl." His eyes are a galaxy of pride, shining just for me.

"Come on, Mr. Stand and Stare," I tease, reaching out my hand. He hesitates but eventually gives in, and his hand comes home to mine again.

"You know, I loathed that nickname at first, but it's starting to grow on me."

"Oh yeah?"

"People stand and stare at art all of the time. They even make a hobby of it, and you, Hallee, are the greatest masterpiece of them all."

Art is valued; does he value me? If it's all art, then maybe we're continuously being sculpted into our final design. Each day is one step closer to becoming our own personal masterpiece of experiences that make us unique. There is still hope, then—that my happiest days are to come.

Reaching into my bag, I grab my annotating pen. The cap clicks as I pull it off and flip my forearm over.

This is art, I write in chicken scratch handwriting.

He believes it, and his smile confirms it. This unfamiliar flicker in my heart gives me permission to hope that one day soon, I might believe it too.

A popping wine cork greets me as I walk into the apartment. I barely set the flowers and Polaroid on the counter before Marlowe and Avery nearly tackle me to the ground. Grabbing my hands, they drag me over to the window.

"What are we doing?" I yell over their ear-splitting squeals.

"There!" Marlowe points as Dean comes out of the first-floor door.

"Look at that *walk*!" Avery screeches.

"It really is a good walk," I mumble.

He runs a hand through his hair and the crowd goes wild.

"He glances back within ten or I cook dinner all week," Marlowe bets.

"Twelve," Avery counters, shaking her hand.

"Three, and we get ice cream," I say, laughing through my burning cheeks.

Three.

Two.

That's my man, giving the people what they want.

"Oh my god!" Marlowe gasps as we duck under the windowsill.

Avery's eyes widen as she whispers, "Oh, girl. What did you do to him? He's whipped!"

Marlowe's laughing so hard it's quiet—more of a wheeze, really. She grabs her stomach as I shove her over. Tears roll down her bright red cheeks, and Avery snorts next to me. This kind of joy feels never-ending. Right when we think the wildfire is under control, one of us lights a match and ignites a new burst.

A knock from the pizza man only adds to the situation. Poor guy is just doing his job, but Marlowe can't stop laughing in his face.

"Sorry about her," Avery apologizes, giggling while I sneak up behind them and mouth, *She's crazy.*

With one nervous smile, he leaves, and we fill our plates and file into the living room like a well-oiled machine.

We have a dining table, but the coffee table is our favorite place to eat. Every night feels like a special girls' night when we eat here, criss-cross applesauce like teenagers without any rules.

"Okay, well—" I begin, but Marlowe cuts me off with a gasp.

"Girl," she draws out.

Avery looks at her and then back to me before asking, "After one date?"

"What are you talking about?" I question, nervously sipping my wine.

"You've got that look," Avery mutters, eyes flicking from Marlowe to me about ten times before finally landing on Lowe.

"What look?" I ask.

"You wear love well," Marlowe replies, winking and clinking her glass against Avery's.

"Love? I am *not* in love. It was simply a really good date. A great start."

Marlowe strikes my rebuttal from the record. "Call it whatever you want, Hallee, but you can't hide the sparkle in your eye."

"Dangit," Avery mumbles, reaching into her pocket. She pulls out a crisp twenty and hands it to Marlowe, shaking her head at me.

My finger shifts, pointing at each of them. "What is this? What are you doing?"

"We may or may not have bet on how head over heels you'd be when you returned," Marlowe confesses, proudly pocketing the twenty.

"We've got to quit it with the betting—"

"My money bet you'd be sparkling, utterly enchanted and unable to contain your love," she admits.

"My money bet that it'd be a slow burn. At least three dates before you committed," Avery says, smiling directly at me.

"We aren't formally committed—"

"BUT YOU'RE IN LOVE?!" they scream.

Marlowe hits her hands on the table, and Avery simultaneously drops her pizza and her jaw.

My hands fly to cover my face, and the reality of their words set in. "Oh my gosh, am I crazy?"

I didn't say the "L" word, they did. But—I couldn't deny it. Denying it the first time felt wrong, like putting your favorite dress back on the rack. Denying it again? Book me for lying on the stand.

The room's energy shifts into the danger zone as I peek through my fingers and meet their knowing stares.

"I am—aren't I?"

The sympathetic shrug of their shoulders is answer enough.

"He coordinated his roommates to hand me a sunflower outside of every place we went."

"He did *what*!?" Avery springs to a stand, pacing frantically. "He got his friends involved?"

"You. Are. Kidding," Marlowe says, absolutely dumbfounded.

"I'm not."

Their eyes shift to the sunflowers on the kitchen island.

"Shut up!" Avery squeals, feigning passing out before crawling her way back to the table.

"Did you kiss him?" Marlowe asks.

"No—well? Only when I kissed his cheek for the pictures I sent you. I almost did plenty of times but it never felt right." I lower my eyes shyly and finish off my wine.

His hug goodbye didn't bother me. It felt like the natural progression for us, but now insecurity sweeps in to shove me down the rabbit hole of overthinking.

"Do you think it's bad that *he* didn't kiss *me*?"

"I don't think so," Avery instantly replies. "Everyone moves at their own pace. If it felt right to you, then it was."

It's what I wanted to hear. Not as comforting as I'd hoped, though.

"Oh my gosh, do you think I should've made the move and kissed him? He planned this extravagant date and I didn't even—"

"You don't owe him anything, Hallee. Not today, not tomorrow, not ever." Marlowe slams the door in self-doubt's face and lays her hand on my knee. "Don't let worry win this one. You had a great date."

"I had a great date," I repeat.

"When are you seeing him again?" Avery asks.

"We're getting coffee tomorrow."

"Attagirl." Marlowe winks, pouring my second glass of wine.

Avery raises hers for our girls' night toast tradition. "To Hallee."

"To Dean," Marlowe calls.

"To love," I toast, smirking as the sound of our clinking glasses fills the air.

- 22 -
April 2045

Hallee

Darkness surrounds me, pulling the breath from my lungs. Screams of neighbors ring out in the distance. Avery . . . Marlowe . . . my chest tightens. I need to help, to help, to help, but my weary muscles won't hold up my body.

A disappointing whimper escapes through my parched throat.

No one can hear me.

No one is coming for me.

No one knows I'm here.

My frantic eyes search for something, anything at all to hint at where *here* is, but all I see is blackness. Oblivion—it has come to take me.

Please, anyone . . . come save me from the abyss.

I can't breathe.

I'm suffocating.

I—

—jolt awake in bed as if the sheets have burned me. My room is spinning uncontrollably as my chest rises and falls to the beat of my pounding heart.

It was only a nightmare.

I've never actually needed the water on my side table, but there's not a single night that I've gone to bed without it. Avery and I call it my emotional support water—there just in case.

Tonight, I'm thankful for it as the cool sweat on the glass drenches my fingers, and I dab the drops carefully on my neck to curb the nausea tossing my stomach like a laundry machine. The first sip of water stops the tumble, but leaves the queasiness.

I haven't thought a whole lot about why I always sleep on the left side and not the middle of my bed, but now the empty half is mocking me, laughing at my longing for comfort. Laughing at my longing for Dean.

The short-term leases on this life have started to chip away at me. Shouldn't "freedom" bring peace? If so, why do I only feel it in the presence of him?

Tonight is the first night since getting his sweatshirt that I haven't worn it to bed, and that coincidence is almost funny. Propping my extra pillows up, I arrange them to imitate his presence. My shaky hands clench together and I inhale deeply, counting to six, before exhaling too quickly to be helpful.

Jesus, why haven't I figured out how to handle this yet?

Too much. I'm too much. How can I expect someone to understand me when I don't even understand myself?

A pool of shame gathers in my eyes. With another deep breath, I sink further and further into the pillows. What if I suffocated in the darkness? The moon would be the only witness. Trying hard to focus on its light, my imagination transforms it into a balloon floating in the sky. The conversation with the old woman replays in my mind like an audiobook.

Somehow. Someday.

She wasn't hopeless. She was certain someone would remember. Hearing her desire to leave a mark made me realize how deeply I desire the same thing.

What is my purpose here? A near-silent, consistent tug on my heart has made me wonder about it. If we could maybe—no. We could never.

This world is an empty one.

This love is a fleeting one.

I need to accept that before it eats me alive but—what is life without love? What is love without memories? What are memories without time?

Was *this* really the grand design?

My cascading tears are the waves that hold me under, drowning me alive in the growing grocery list of doubt. When I finally come up for air, it feels different somehow.

Sharp. Enraging. Powerful.

I'm a handful, but I don't deserve to be alone. No one does.

It's been a few weeks since our first date, and Dean has brightened up every part of my days. The little moments have become my favorite ones. Getting coffee in the mornings, holding his hand on the walk to work, knowing who is behind the knock on our door, his familiar touch on my lower back, the way his grip tightens when he kisses my forehead.

Now that I have something worth losing, fear is lighting the path to our inevitable end. Each day is a steady and constant train ride through time, propelling us along a perpetual cycle of countdowns that turn the past into the present, the present into the future, and the future into the past. Well, the future that doesn't exist, because does anything exist if we can't remember?

Some *gift*.

Losing the low also means losing the high, and the only thing worse than feeling the pain of loss is to feel nothing at all. If only it was my choice. I think I'd choose to remember.

Thoughts circle like a lion waiting to pounce.

I have no purpose.

I will make no difference.

I'm the sum of a life forgotten.

The weight crumbles me as I roll over and lay my hand on the side where I wish Dean was. Tears soak my pillow as I close my eyes tightly. Sleep, please take me anywhere but here.

- 23 -

April 2045

Dean

"Are you nervous?" Matt yells through the open door.

He and Hudson have been sitting on my bed for the last forty minutes "helping" me get ready for my date.

"Why would I be nervous?"

"Our offer still stands to take her off your hands," Hudson jokes, but it's starting to sour, so I walk back into my room. Want to look them in the eyes for this one.

"She's mine, and only mine."

Their tensing shoulders receive the message.

"You love her?" Hudson questions, his playful tone on vacation.

"Already?" Matt asks.

"Are we talking about this right now?"

Raising his eyebrows, Hudson asks, "Do you want to?"

Yes. No. Yes.

"She had me before she even looked at me. She's . . ." My voice trails off.

Breathtaking, captivating, exquisite—none of those are enough. I'll have to create a new word just to describe her. One that means *a culmination of all of the good things to ever exist,* because she's all of it and then some. Hurts a bit, how much I love her.

"You guys have seen her. Her body is drop-dead flawless in every single way. But her mind? I can't imagine a world without it. She sees everything so vibrantly, it's contagious. It challenges me to live fully—freely."

I both hate and love that they nod like they agree. For the first time, Hudson doesn't have a sarcastic reply, and Matt's face softens. They know it's reckless to get attached.

"Spare me the warning. I know what I stand to lose and I'll stand anyway, because *yes.* I'm in love with her, and I'll spend the rest of the year making sure that when it all goes to shit on New Year's Eve, it was worth it."

They wear a look of pride, like military cadets accepting their next order, as they each give a single nod.

"Then we will stand with you," Matt gently replies.

"Wear the tan pants today. They look better than the jeans," is all Hudson says as he walks out my bedroom door.

Matt and I share a glance of acceptance for the end of whatever's to come before I return to my bathroom and finish getting ready.

He sits on my bed the entire time, doing what he does best—being there for me without saying anything at all.

Muffled music welcomes me to the third floor as the elevator doors open. It's coming from the girls' apartment. There's no way they'll hear my knock, so I hesitate for a few seconds. Hal would be embarrassed if she knew I was listening to their three voices scream-singing "Love Story," but for all I know this is her pre-date routine, and I wouldn't dare interrupt that. Makes me smile that she has such thoughtful friends to enjoy life with.

Once the song tapers off, I knock loudly.

"*Ooo*, Hallee!" one of them squeaks.

"Shhhh!" she protests. "Coming, Dean!"

She's definitely pretending to be annoyed, side-eyeing her roommates while prancing to the door. Wish I could see it 'cause I know it's cute.

The lock clicks and my heart skips.

"Hi!" she half yells as the door swings open.

A perfume cloud of sweet vanilla crashes into me before she does, and her arms wrap around my neck. While I hug her tightly, my eyes close and our bodies sway. In my head, we're dancing. I'm about to lead her into a spin, but she pulls away before I can fully imagine it. As if it's second nature, I lean in. Her shoulders tense as her eyes open as wide as the world—what the hell am I doing?

Shrugging my shoulders a little, I play it off as me waving goodbye to her roommates. Her knowing glance heats my cheeks, but she shouldn't be surprised. Not when she looks like that.

The light blue sundress makes her legs look extra long. As it shifts, I envision her up against a wall with me, kissing her like I can't get enough. Her back closing the door and my hands holding her legs around my waist. Might be the death of me, those legs, or at least the death of my innocence. That is, if I ever had it.

"Are you ready?" she asks, self-consciously tugging down on her dress.

I take a beat, purposefully letting her watch my eyes drag down and back up her body. Down—strip off her insecurity. Up—flood her with confidence.

"Spin for me, Sunshine."

Flashing a flirty smile, she flips her hair over her shoulder and spins into me. My arms cradle her in a mid-air dip, and her head tips back in unabashed laughter. This is what it feels like to hold the sun without getting burned.

Suspended in time and nearly suffocated by desire, we breathe in time with each other.

"We better get going," she whispers, glancing at my lips.

"Right, can't be late," I reply, smiling as I glance at hers.

I wonder what her lip gloss tastes like. Sugar and strawberries seems right. Time glitches as her grip tightens on my shirt.

"There's a car downstairs. We don't want to miss the sunset," she says, pulling away and skipping down the hallway.

"A car?" My face falters.

Surprising choice, with how much we both love walking.

Glancing back at me, she winks as she says, "It'll be quick, I promise."

Placing a hand on her lower back and guiding her into the elevator, I whisper, "Oh, Hallee, I can assure you, it will not be."

Curiosity lines her widened eyes as she imagines it—all of the ways it could be not so quick with us. Makes my heart skip about four thousand beats, until we slide into the car and my hand rests on her knee. Bizarre, how someone can be both a shock to your system and a sedative to the shock.

The golden-hour light is stunning, and I could look out the window, enjoying it, the entire ride. Instead, I watch my Sunshine stare at the sun, and that's even better. She is my grand, magnetic center star, and is completely unaware of how lucky I am to exist in orbit around her.

Hallee

My love for the city lights has started to turn to hate. They aren't very calming to my increasingly restless soul, so as the driver pulls out of the city, I release a much-needed exhale. There's no fluff or frills to the date I have planned. It's only us and the setting sun, and I hope that's enough.

The temperature has dropped with the sun, and chill bumps cover my legs the second Dean opens my door. I'm not sure him helping me out of the car will ever get old. It's nice to feel cared for, even in the littlest ways.

He closes the door behind me and we wave goodbye to the driver watching us in the rearview. Do you think he can tell we belong together?

"Come on. It's not too much farther," I say, linking Dean's hand in mine.

After five minutes of walking, we wander into a meadow of wildflowers. Nerves build in me with every step. Now that there's a chance someone else will think this is silly, it feels a little less inspiring than I remember.

"Well, Dean, you said you wanted to know me."

He stares, blankly.

"Welcome to my favorite top-secret hiding spot." I giggle, gesturing to the open field before throwing my hands behind my back and twisting like I usually twist my hair. I tap my toes three times because I can't control his reaction, but I can try to summon some luck.

Finally he looks at me, eyes sparkling as he asks, "How did you find this?"

"I had a hard day and wanted to escape the city, so I walked to the edge and kept going. Stumbled upon this little oasis. It's too far off the road for everyone to know it's here, and far enough outside of the city to not hear honking horns. It's a calm pocket of peace when it doesn't feel like I'll ever hold hands with peace again."

His index finger traces a star on the back of my hand as I lean into the dream of doing this forever. He bites his lip, and my stomach jumps, and underneath the spotlight of his stare, I do what I do best.

Bolting away, I sprint wild and free through the flowers like a little kid running with their best friend. So light, so carefree, before they know the weight of growing up. He chases me closely, pretending to struggle catching up. This is the whole reason I wore tennis shoes with this dress—so I could run away with him, if only for a minute. Each breath in and out propels us into a new round of uncontained laughter.

The edge of the flowers is the finish line, and I spin through the soft, green grass on my victory lap, throwing my arms out wide. Dean catches me within a few steps, wrapping his arms around my waist and lifting me off the ground.

This is what it feels like to fly.

This is what it feels like to fall.

He throws himself under me as we land on the ground. Eye to eye and breathing as one, we are ambushed by a second wave of laughter. His happiness is my favorite song. It awakens my soul from sleeping. It makes me want to live.

"I could stay here all night," he admits.

Like a camera flash, I see us intertwined with one another. Tightening my grip on his shirt, I roll over and pull him on top of me.

"I picture us more like this at night," I whisper inches from his lips.

Even now in the heat of his hungry stare, he makes no move forward. Never fails to lead with respect and self-control. I wish he'd let go a little, if only for me. If he won't for me, he wouldn't for anyone, right?

Holding his gaze, I ignite my eyes. My city's on fire, Dean. This is your smoke signal. A muscle in his jaw tenses and his breathing hitches.

He wants to, doesn't he? If he wanted to, would he?

Instead of being my remedy, he climbs off and rests his head in the grass. My cheeks burn the city down at his silent denial. Why won't he kiss me?

Why won't I kiss him?

The sunset does nothing to ice the impact of the punch to my pride.

"I hope I get to paint a sunset someday," I blurt, desperate to distract myself.

Rising up halfway, he props his head up on his hand.

"What do you mean?"

"I've recently had this idea that maybe we can be whatever we want when we pass on. Maybe whoever controls the skies will let us paint a sunset to light up the sky for those we left behind."

He's looking at me like I hung the moon, encouraging me to continue.

"This one was painted by someone who left too soon. Someone trying to remind all of us that there is a lot of life to enjoy in the small moments. It's chaotic, but beautiful, like a painting at the hands of a child. Look." I point to an area of colors mixed so aggressively that it's impossible to decipher what the original one was. "They used every color they could to remind us to live a bright life—to live boldly. What a legacy to leave."

His eyes break and lower as sadness peers through the cracks. The brief pause stitches me together, preventatively providing reinforcement so I don't fall apart right here.

"Do you think about it often—leaving a legacy?" he timidly asks.

"Do you?"

"I have to admit that it's crossed my mind more recently." His eyes flicker to me. "Life could be really beautiful if we could remember, but that doesn't mean it can't be beautiful this way too. There isn't much use in wishing life were different when the outcome is already chosen."

"My mind doesn't work that way. We only get one life—why would we willingly accept anything short of everything we hope for?"

"I'm just trying to do the best I can with what I've been given."

"But what if—?"

What if what, he blinks.

"There was an old lady at work the other day. She carries around a balloon with her everywhere she goes." I guide the conversation toward the idea that has haunted me over the last few weeks. Maybe The Gift isn't so permanent.

"When I asked her why, she gave me a suspicious look and lowered her voice. She thinks that somehow, someday, someone will remember her, and she doesn't just hope, Dean. She *believes* that someone will. What if she's right?"

It takes less than one second for hope to be ignited in the heart of someone who's desperately searching for it. He too will now cling to it like a life raft. Hope—the ultimate lifeline of our love.

"Do you really think it's possible? To remember each other?" he asks.

"I don't know, but I officially have something worth remembering, so I won't go down without a fight."

His hand cradles mine as he gently kisses my hairline.

"Naive of me to think that I could be the exception to the rule. It's a little bit embarrassing, isn't it?"

The security blanket of his arms wraps around me, pulling me closer into his chest.

"It's not embarrassing to have hope, Hallee. It's essential, and you've given me a great deal of it."

We share a charged glance, like two people walking into a battle they don't expect to walk away from, and his head rests onto mine. My shame cowers at his touch.

"Let's be whatever we want to be right now, Hal. There's no time to waste."

Surrounded by the wildflowers, we watch as the sun sets and the stars appear one by one like freckles in the sky.

- 24 -

April 2096

The History of Psychology 2335

"Have you enjoyed reading the accounts of the survivors from The Experiment?" Mr. Holiday greets us, and our heads collectively nod.

Our textbook is a devastating timeline of civilians' lives. We're flying high above the scene, able to see the immediate approaching danger, but unable to stop it from happening because it's in the past. There was no justifying the government's actions once we realized firsthand how many things were lost in their heist. It's astonishing, the speed at which we went from thinking it was a gift to realizing it was a tragedy—the ultimate crime against humanity.

The most recent chapters have explored the heart of The Experiment, diving deeper into the debate that our emotional and physical reactions to certain triggers are connected. Are we permanently changed by trauma? By core memories?

"Can someone begin discussion by telling me how long The Experiment lasted?" he asks.

"Six years," the freshman answers without raising her hand.

"Yes, six years. That's not a very long time, now, is it?"

Depends on who you ask.

A boy from the frat pack joins in. "Does the duration really matter? The first year is the one that damned them all, erasing all of history."

His buddy backs him up, as if they have a monumental point to prove. "Yeah, what was lost couldn't be recovered."

"And what exactly was—lost?" Mr. Holiday tips his head to the right, inhaling a deep breath.

"Tradition, culture, family lines," a girl in row ten calls out.

Mr. Holiday nods, encouraging her soft voice. "Correct, those were just the beginning of the casualties. So how did we get to where we are now?"

"Those brave enough to weather the beginning years. Those who rebuilt life from the ground up," the freshman answers, and as her voice wavers, I almost wish I could hug her.

The discussion fades to a hum in the background while I consider my grandma and grandpa. It must've been so lonely to be the first ones, but they had amazing friends who were their safehouses through The Experiment and onto the other side. When it came crashing down, they were left standing on the clean foundation of a new beginning, together. They don't talk about them much, but the glow in Grandpa's eye when they do is all I need to understand their importance.

It's easy to understand how they fell for it back then, and it's equally terrifying to realize how easily we could all be tricked again. At first, our assigned readings were in support of The Experiment, convincing us that our initial stance was accurate. However, over the course of the semester, they've uncovered boundless amounts of missing pieces falling ominously into place. The closer we get to finishing the puzzle, the more revolted I feel.

For a few chapters, I'd felt like I'd become friends with the civilians, deeply wanting so much more for them than what they were left with. I can't help but wonder if we will get answers to their stories, or if it will end like the closing of a year—open-ended and abruptly.

With my hand raised, I wait patiently for Mr. Holiday to call on me. He probably won't answer my question, but you never know what can happen if you don't ask. Passivity doesn't get anyone very far.

"Rayne! Nice of you to join in." He smiles, a little too excitedly to be normal.

"What changed so that we're learning about The Experiment as the past, rather than living in it? And if knowledge is power, then why is it so taboo to talk about?"

No one talks about The Experiment, and in most majors it's not even mentioned. The information is deemed irrelevant to their studies, but if so many of *us* thought that reinstating it could have been beneficial, and we're the ones studying it? We'd be screwed. All of the psychology majors in the world wouldn't stand a chance against the majority vote.

Fifty-two percent.

Only fifty-two percent of the population voted in favor of The Gift, yet it happened because it won the majority. It's the ultimate proof that *the greater good* means something different to every single voter. Must be why it's so hard to get shit done.

"That's a great question, Rayne. One that I can't answer right now, as it will be answered at a later time. But I applaud your curiosity," he says, softening the sting of denial with his most encouraging smile.

"Could you at least tell us if there was a conclusion? Or did they cease The Experiment because it was deemed invalid? Inappropriate? Cruel?" the freshman pushes, clearly not satisfied with having to wait. We have more in common than I care to admit.

"I'm merely the vessel educating the next generation, doing my best to ensure a tragedy like this does not reoccur. It's no secret where I fall in support or opposition to this. As much as I try to keep my personal opinion out of my lectures, it can be hard when you're so passionate about something."

Unsatisfied hands shoot up all around the room. It's Mr. Holiday's job to emulate the emotions felt during that time. He wants us to feel the rising anxiety, to ache for answers we may not get, and to know the fear that can overtake you when you've lost all control of your life.

"Can you at least tell us if they get to stay in love?" I beg, defeated.

His eyes widen slightly at the question, and mumbled requests blend together in an uproar. It only takes two steps of his clicking shoes to silence us.

"This uneasy feeling, let it fuel you to ask yourselves some of the hard questions. Sit with the uncertainty of what's to come, like the subjects of The Experiment had to. Sharpen your skills of emotional self-control as you would teach a client to do. Compartmentalize fear from what is real. Fear can be a debilitating disease when uncontrolled, but hope is the healing cure. Have hope, students. Have hope."

- 25 -

June 2045

Hallee

Summer in Michigan is my favorite so far. The sun feels closer now and my days are brighter. I can finally breathe.

Birds are always the first to greet me, and the spring rain has pushed the flowers into bloom. They line the sidewalks, waving in the wind on my daily commute. Feels like I'm being waved at by a friend.

Dean continues to sweep me off my feet, I have amazing friends who I trust with my life, and I'm happy with my job. Panic has become a stranger, replaced with the friendship of thankfulness. It's a much better friend to have.

This life is a beautiful one, and it feels true to myself. Never thought I'd know me, but I'm starting to. I think I like her.

With how supportive our friends have been of Dean and me, it's probably time to officially cross the borders of our social circles. After all, they're the only permanence we have each year, and that counts for something. But it's intimidating, introducing the people you love to each other. No one else can love them like I do, but could they love each other like I do?

Marlowe and Avery's support was secured by the many times Dean acknowledged them like a gentleman. His support for them was secured by the way I feel so much better about myself around them. I'm kinder to myself around them.

He's the perfect gentleman. They are the perfect friends, and hope keeps airdropping perfect pictures of our future together—of what we'd build in a year, and what we'd build in a lifetime. It's turned my mind into a scrapbook of images reminding me of everything I'll lose. It stings, but I can't stop. Painful, to be a dreamer.

With each step toward The Marmotte, a new dream flashes in my head. We're dancing together, and he's leading me, spinning me, dipping me, and kissing me, as if he has a hundred times before.

A few steps further, and I'm opening the door as he picks me up for a date. His shirt is pale blue, but could almost be mistaken for white in different lighting. I jump into his arms, and he spins me around. His hands know just how to hold me, and I feel at home with him.

"Excuse you!" a frustrated man yells as his shoulder bumps into mine.

"Sorry!" I say, smiling at his frown, and my pace quickens to a near skip, the closest feeling to flying I can have unless Dean is lifting me.

Our coffee dates have turned me from a night owl into a morning person. Nights have always been when my deepest thinking takes place, but there's something special about a fresh, clean slate to be whoever and whatever I want to be, every morning.

With my newfound appreciation for a fresh start, I should be more thankful for The Gift. Instead, paralyzing fits of insomnia leave me awake and craving to be held by Dean—in that moment and forever.

Forever, what a wish.

Should've wished on my Happy Bookday cake candles, but how could I have anticipated longing for "forever"?

Will my soul be longing—forever?

A text from Dean flashes on my home screen as I approach The Marmotte.

Running late! No, I'm not mad or hurt or second guessing or any of the other things you are wondering. Hudson caught his towel on fire (and is perfectly okay.) See you soon!

Why am I not surprised? Sometimes, even my favorite routine has its hiccups.

See you soon, xoxo, I reply, hopping up the front steps.

Soon is roughly three minutes and thirty-three seconds.

His clear communication is intentional, and is one of my needs I haven't yet thanked him for noticing. My man knows me the best. Teaches me how to love me, too.

Stepping up to the counter, I order for us both. The barista takes my payment, smiling as always.

"Thanks, Hallee. I'll have it right out."

Shame floats in on a buoy. I smile at this woman every day, but I've never treated her like a friend. After all this time, I've never learned her name. When I turn to ask, she's already greeting Jack. Later, then. I'll ask later. There's not an expiration date on kindness.

Subconsciously, I walk to our table. Weird to be alone and choosing the middle of the room, but this is what growing feels like. Being alone isn't going to kill me. Being in love might.

I assumed the initial butterflies would fly away one day, but just when I think they've been ceremoniously released, they return. Maybe seeing him will never feel ordinary. I hope it never does. For all the time I get to spend with him, I hope it always feels this electric.

"Hallee, I have your drinks at the bar," the nameless barista calls out.

Blinking farewell to the warmth of the sun on my face, I walk to the counter. My hands grip both cups as my phone vibrates again.

Walking in now! Dean texted.

Excellent, just in time to walk me to work. The barista doesn't notice as I raise the coffee in my left hand in an awkward goodbye, so I choose to say nothing. Shouting something generic like "ma'am" or "miss" would only emphasize the absence of her name. I'll get it next time. There's always another day.

Dean's text warned me he was coming in, but I still jump when I see him.

"Oh, hi! I ordered for us bo—" My breath cuts off my words mid-sentence and my hands drop the drinks, pouring coffee all over myself and the floor. Normally, I'd panic and move quickly to minimize the damage, but shock has chained me in place. The *flighter* has frozen.

"I—" I stumble to apologize, but no words come.

Sound is replaced with ringing and feeling is replaced with numbness as time glitches. Dean's face flares with worry, and his gentle touch pushes play on reality. His voice is an airplane soaring through my clouded head.

"Hallee?"

"Dean?"

"Hi," he says gently, as his hands grip my forearms.

"Hi! I'm so sorry . . . I don't know what came over me!"

My strained voice is iced by his comforting embrace, but my eyes won't close. They can't. They're transfixed—on his pale blue shirt. A blue so light, it could be mistaken as white in different lighting.

Surely the light is tricking me again, like it did on our first date, but shaking my head doesn't change its hue. Backing away, I nervously pull my hair into a ponytail.

"Are you okay? Do you feel sick?" he asks, reaching for napkins to clean up the mess I've made.

"I'm okay. I—I like your shirt."

He's never worn it with me, and what I think is happening can't be happening, so I just need to hear him tell me.

Tell me it's new.

"Thanks, I thought you might like the blue."

See? Totally new. Except, it's not.

It's not. It's not. It's not.

My heart accelerates as I frantically grab napkins, fighting through my increasingly shaky hands.

There he is in *first date trick of the light* blue. In *daydream from this morning* blue . . .

"*Ha, ha,* even with your warning I still got startled," I joke, laughing at myself to cover up my oddly delayed reaction to his entrance.

There's no reason to tell him until I'm sure this isn't a mistake but—it's not.

It's not, it's not, it's not.

His hands reach to steady my shaky ones, and my face shamelessly displays a garden of emotions. Fear, confusion, excitement, hope, the gang's all here, because deep down something is whispering the truth.

My desires haven't been a vision of the future at all.

They are memories.

I remember him.

Dean

Miles approved her day off, reassuring me that he'd cover Hallee's work for the day. Now, I need to convince Hallee that it's a strength to allow others to help you when you need it. She tries so hard to be strong for everyone else and fatigues herself in the process, but when my woman makes up her mind, she doesn't change it without a fight. Especially when she believes someone else will be inconvenienced because of her.

It's cute when she's frazzled, her raw emotions all out on display. But she wasn't just spooked when she dropped the coffees. She looked stunned.

Confused.

Afraid.

Her deflection was clever, but I know her. She's my girl, and it's absolutely ridiculous that she's claiming to be fine when she can barely form a sentence. I've never seen her like this, and I've seen her a lot of ways. Something is very wrong, but if she isn't ready to talk, then I'll hold her in silence until I flood her with every ounce of peace I have.

"Here you go, guys. I'm so sorry about that!" The barista, Lea, slides two fresh coffees across the counter. Leave it to a woman to apologize for something that was in no way her fault.

"Oh, let us pay! That was totally my bad," Hallee insists.

"No way, you're here every day. It's on me."

"Thank you, Lea," I say, cutting off the polite female back-and-forth. "That's extremely generous."

Makes me flinch a little, the way Hallee's head snaps to me.

"You know her name. It's Lea?" she whispers.

"Yeah! You didn't—?" I stop as her face falls. It's odd that she didn't know that, right?

"Hallee, please prepare the runway for round two of landing!" Pretending her coffee is an airplane, I fly it directly into her open hand. "Got it?" I ask, raising my eyebrows as I smirk.

"Yes."

Oh. That crash landing was brutal but probably should've been foreseen. Lacing her fingers in mine, I nod and lead her out the door.

"Alright, let's get you home," I insist.

"No, Dean, I have to go to work. Really, I'm okay."

"If I didn't know better, Hal, I'd say you are trying to avoid me." I wink, but her eyes don't find mine.

Wait, shit. Why won't she look at me? Is she actually trying to avoid me?

"Miles insisted."

Oh, I'm in for it now. Her eyes pierce me with arrows of fiery rage.

"You called my boss?!"

"Who did you think I was on the phone with in there? Do you know another Miles?"

With the chaos of the spilled drinks, she didn't even realize she left her phone on the counter. Unlocking it was easy—her passcode is set to our first date, and she's talked about Miles enough to know who to call.

"It's already handled. Come home with me, Hal. Let me hold you through it."

Her hands search frantically for her phone as I dangle it in front of her. One look at my cocky smirk, and she taps out in the fight, the quick surrender confirming that she's definitely not *okay.*

"Let's put Mr. Stand and Stare to work." Spinning me around, she hops onto my back. "Carry me home, Dean."

"Home," I say, turning and ignoring that her definition of home is different from mine.

"My apartment is the other direction!" She laughs, and I'd do anything to hear it again.

"You will come to know that I'm not very good at following orders, Hal."

Her breathing hitches, and the strong thump of her heartbeat pounds against my back.

She liked that, then.

One point for Dean.

"That could be an issue because I can be *very* demanding."

Her breath touches my neck, tensing every muscle in my body, and I force the vision of her below me out of my head.

Ten points for Hallee.

The game clock is swiftly decreasing, counting down the time that our flirtatious teasing is no longer just that. There are only so many places I can look to distract myself from her body, and only so many ways I can hide my trembling hands.

I want to take my time with her, leaving no room for her complex mind to question the order of my priorities. Her body matters, but her heart matters more, and I'd never forgive myself if she ever believed that all she is to me is a successful day of catch and release.

The closer we get to the apartment, the more she demands that I set her back down. Regardless, I don't want her to get any ideas and make a break for work, so I only obey when we reach the foot of my bed.

Immediately, she crawls to the left side. Seeing her on that side makes sense; she belongs there. Funny, I always sleep on the right. Never wondered why I don't sleep in the middle, until now.

She's most comfortable in my shirts. Makes her feel safe, I think. Makes me feel valued, so I grab the largest T-shirt in my closet and toss it in front of her.

I'll never grow tired of watching those eyes fill with different emotions. A twinkle of trouble is the last thing I notice before she tugs her dress over her head and tosses it on the floor in front of me.

White matching lace hugs her curves, and her chest dips into my line of view as she reaches for the shirt. The respectful thing would be to look away, but I can't. Don't think I ever will again. Hesitating, she shoots me her familiar inviting look.

"Put it on, Hallee."

Woah, that was more tense than I'd intended, but dammit, look at her—I'm doing my best here. My feet back me into the bookshelves, parking my body until she puts the shirt on.

"Now look who is the demanding one," she jokes, and her nose scrunches up in the cute way I love when she giggles.

I'm barely hanging on here, and she's giggling? This *woman*.

With a wink, she pats my side of the bed. My feet don't wander, but my eyes do, following the outline of her body.

"You are astonishing," I whisper. Can't say it too loud. It would be my final undoing.

She pats the bed again, but I hold my ground, emphasizing every word as I insist, "Put. It. On."

To my surprise, she listens.

"Happy?"

No.

Yes, but no.

Her cheeks blush as she twirls her ponytail. Somehow, I thought seeing her in my shirt would make it easier to maintain my self-control. Clearly I didn't realize how much trouble I'm actually in. Have to clench my hands to not rip it right back off of her.

"Ecstatic," I reply and slide in bed next to her. "Talk to me, Sunshine." I reach up, brushing her ponytail over her shoulder.

"You know I love it when you do that," she groans.

"What happened, Hal?"

"I was startled. It happens all the time!"

"You were—startled." My voice lowers at the last half of the sentence. She wants to go head to head? Fine. We'll go head to head. I'm not settling for a lie.

"Yes," she snaps.

"Did you see my text that I was coming in?"

"Yes."

"So, you were expecting me."

"Yes."

Her stubbornness is sexy, but her silence is deafening, and my skin crawls with anticipation of getting kicked to the curb. Can you get dumped if you've never even labeled it?

"Hallee?"

Tears burn in my eyes as I reach up slowly, tilting her chin so she's in the perfect position for a kiss. I lean in and stop just before her lips, ready to shut her up if she tries to end it. If I'm going to lose her, I want to kiss her goodbye.

"Come on, Hal, don't let the clouds win. Shine for me."

Her exhale is warm on my lips.

"I don't want to talk about it. I *can't* talk about it."

"You always want to talk."

"I can't," she whispers, and the crack in her voice feels like stepping on a LEGO brick.

Unshakeable worry explodes out of me. "Then talk about something else. Anything else, Hallee. Please, talk to me. I can't handle you slipping away."

"Slipping away?"

She shoots up and I follow, sliding backward and leaning against the wall. This is it—we're driving full speed on a crumbling bridge.

"Yes, slipping away. Looking afraid. Dropping our coffee. Avoiding me. Are you ending this?"

Sympathy shines in her eyes as she replays the morning from my perspective.

"Ohhh," she draws out. "I don't know what to tell ya, babe. There's not a world where ending us is an option. I'm your girl."

Those words on her lips—that is my undoing.

My last chain of self-restraint snaps as my hands cup her face, pulling her mouth onto mine. Tastes like sugar and strawberries.

In a split second we're back in the position from the flower field, me on top of her. This time, her legs wrap around me and nothing else exists. Our kiss deepens as she slides her hands into my hair. The sparks leave a smoke trail, pointing to where we're headed—us tangled up in these sheets, riding the high of surrendering to loving each other deeply.

I need to hit the brakes. Slow us down. Take it in. My heartbeat protests, pounding against my chest as I pull back. Her face is flushed, and man it feels good to be wanted, but if I don't stop now I never will.

"You're my girl," I whisper, kissing her forehead. My lips already miss hers. "Now, unwrap your legs."

Hesitantly, she obeys.

"Good girl."

Ten thousand points for Hallee.

Hallee

How did he think I was breaking it off? We're not even official yet! *He* led *me* down this reckless path on our first date, so whatever we are, I'm his until memory fails us—if mine does. This new development has thrown a wrench in the security of knowing what comes next for me.

Laying in his bed is so natural, as if I've been here enough to have established this side as my own. As if my weary bones have been wandering around homesick, and he is the precious cure.

How much of this has happened before? Tossing me his shirt, demanding I put it on, crawling into bed next to me all flash through my mind, and every time he's wearing something different.

This must be a psychotic break.

It's impossible—emotions are making me irrational. Except maybe they aren't. Do I really think they are, or was I taught to think they are?

Every part of me came to life during that kiss, responding to his soul's call for its long-lost partner. Everything and nothing made sense all at once, but hasn't it always been that way with us?

His peaceful embrace smothers anxiety's uncontrolled burn into a mere ember, glowing in the dark without the pain of panic. Our breathing unites in a steady rhythm as we lay together, my nose nuzzled in the nape of his neck. The silence is comfortable, but internally I've been conducting a heated debate over telling or not telling him about the vision turned memory, future turned past.

He wouldn't judge me. In fact, he'd be the first to believe me capable of nonconformity, but it wouldn't change anything—would it?

What would I even say? I think maybe . . . I might have . . . possibly . . . had a memory of us?

We'd still be on the same path, riding straight toward a dead end at full speed. He'd be crushed under guilt because he's entirely incapable of walking me through this unless he remembers too, but my heart isn't prepared for the likely denial. I'm not ready to hear that he has permanently marked me, but I haven't done the same to him.

I need to tell him, now.

I can't tell him, yet.

"Sunshine," he says, hammering down the gavel in my mental debate.

I'll tell him—later. Dangling the hope in front of him would be cruel.

"Mr. Stand and Stare." I hug him a little tighter, suddenly aware of how much I have to lose.

"I've been thinking . . ." his voice trails off.

Is he as lost as me?

"I would hope so," I joke, trying to cover the complicated tone with a laugh, but he caught it. Skipped a breath because of it. When will we stop feeling like such a fragile, breakable thing?

"Would you like to label us? Would you *formally* be my girl?"

His question rings through my head, again . . . and again . . . and again, transporting me to a multitude of places. We're here tangled up in the sheets, we're in the park eating a meal we haven't had this year, and we're in the wildflowers staring at a solid pink sunset.

Three visions, clear as day, all linked to those words—*will you formally be my girl?*

I grasp for more memories to reassure me of reality, but nothing comes. Crazy, is what I am. I've officially gone crazy. Yet, a montage of answers to his echoing question rings through my head.

Of course, in the sheets.

Of course, in the park.

Of course, in the wildflowers.

"Of course!" here, lying in his arms.

The same response I gave then, and then, and then, I've given now, and it's the only one I'd ever give.

"Yeah?" He laughs, pulling me on top of him and squeezing tight.

"I can't breathe," I say, dramatically gasping for air.

Have I breathed at all today?

He spins me back over and lays me down gently. Brushes the side of my face as he leans in. Our lips meet softly and the trigger is unleashed, shooting memories through my mind of today and years past.

Our first, our third, our thirteenth kiss.

What number kiss is this?

A shock runs through my system, troubleshooting years of caged passion. I could stay here with him forever, and it would be enough for me. It *has* been enough for me. Our hearts have been fighting a secret battle, continuously coming out victorious by repeatedly reuniting us.

Love is unstoppable. At least—ours is.

It's not such a gift, to be forced to forget. Losing the hardest days doesn't outweigh losing the best ones. Maybe the real gift is living a life built of experiences that make us wonderfully human. Sickness, pain, heartache, loss, laughter, growth, passion, love—it's all a gift. We'd never appreciate happiness without sadness.

The hope of a lifetime with Dean radiates off of me. With all that I have, I'll fight for us.

Somehow. Somewhere. Someday, the old woman's determined belief rings through my head.

The Polaroid camera on Dean's bedside table catches my eye. Please, don't let falling asleep reset the progress I've made. Please, let him stay. I'll help—I'll do whatever I can, just please—don't take him away.

- 26 -

June 2045

Dean

Wine-drunk and swaying in the kitchen, arms hooked around Hallee is exactly where I belong.

It's group dinner night. *Combine the friend group* dinner night, and we've been a shaken bottle of soda waiting for it. Hallee's being a little rule breaker, drinking on an empty stomach because her appetite is finicky when she's nervous. The intention of tonight wouldn't be a secret if it had the world's best security, and the pressure couldn't be hidden by the world's best disguise, but the nerves are good. They mean we care. After all, our roommates are the only "family" we have.

Three of us and three of them.

This could be really, really fun.

Hallee proposed dinner at their place, casually and seamlessly mentioning that I should invite the guys. Hudson and Matt were shockingly excited when I pitched the idea. Didn't even take a PowerPoint to convince them.

Based on our first impression of the girls' cooking skills, we *did* flip a coin to decide if we'd invite them here instead, but tails told us to just accept the invitation. We're putting a lot of trust in tails.

The three of them welcomed us at the door, passing glances and silently engaging in conversation the way only women can. After a mysteriously confusing few seconds, Marlowe hugged Matt. Avery didn't look too happy about joining in, but I watched her notice how happy it made Hallee. Feels special to see someone love your person well, and these girls do that. I'd give my life for them because of it.

As we made ourselves at home, Hudson popped open the white wine. Marlowe, the spitfire she is, ran up to Hallee, startled her as usual, and mouthed, *Oh my hot.* Caught me by surprise, her eyes falling on Matt.

It took us less than thirty minutes to drain three bottles of wine. Everyone finished their first glass in under five minutes. Normally, I'd brush it off. Tonight, I'm in my head about it. They feel the pressure too.

There's lots to lose.

There's lots we will.

I try not to think about it, but it's getting harder and harder not to.

A loud smack across the kitchen makes my shoulders tense.

"Ow, Matt!" Marlowe squeals, laughing as she grabs the back of her leg.

The dumbass snapped her with the kitchen towel. Weird way to flirt, but . . . works, I guess? She seems to be intrigued, and he's looking at her like she's the only one in the room. Feels like an out-of-body experience, watching your friend catch the love bug. That must be how I look when I'm looking at Hallee.

Hudson's barely left Avery's side by the stove. He's playing dumb, asking her how to stir pasta sauce, and she's laughing like she never wants it to end. Ten out of ten technique—way better than snapping her with a towel—but the way he glances at her as her hand falls over his drops my stomach. Curiosity mixed with desire, the perfect cocktail for the start of something new. Although there's an added shot of something I can't quite decipher. He's not usually timid, could be voted life of the party, actually, and it's not quite gentleness. Maybe caution? Like he'd be careful with her. I never thought he'd settle down, but his focus is locked in. Her touch has tamed the stallion.

"Hudson!" she shouts, giggling as he fishes out two noodles.

"Throw them with me," he insists, handing one over to her.

"What?"

"You can tell they're done if they stick to the wall!"

With that, he got the girl.

There's no hiding the intrigued blush on her cheeks as they toss the noodles. She laughs so hard she snorts, and uses it as an excuse to grip his arms. I'll be damned—she'll be careful with him, too.

"We're pretty good matchmakers," Hallee whispers, raising on her tiptoes to kiss my cheek.

"Wouldn't that get messy?"

"Hope, Dean. You never know what could happen."

Exactly. You never know what could happen, and she would never forgive herself if someone got hurt.

Right now, it's like watching a comfort show before the plot gets too messy, but it always does. That's why we watch. It makes us feel better for being messy too.

Spinning out of my embrace, she snaps a Polaroid and turns up the music. Skips to join Marlowe, dancing like there's no one else in the room.

Hal seems lighter these days, like whatever storm clouds rolled in in the spring were blown away by the warm summer wind. She's living fearlessly, wild and untamed. She's kinder to herself, too. Must've finally realized taking risks is fun when there are no lasting consequences. So far none of her risks have ended poorly, but to be fair, they never will. Wearing pink instead of gray or kissing me in front of people won't make life fall apart. Her innocence is cute, though, and it gives me a purpose—I want to protect it for her.

I love her.

Still haven't told her, at least not while she would remember, even though I say it in my mind all the time. It's slipped out a few times holding her while she's asleep, but watching her now, I can't believe I've waited.

This time is precious.

This time is little.

Matt steals Marlowe away, pulling her into a spin, and Hallee whips her head to me. Time stalls as she reaches out her hand.

Wait, have I been here before?

The question rolls off of me the second I grab her hand.

"You okay?" she asks.

A gift and a curse, her ability to pick up on silent social cues. Sometimes I swear she knows me better than I know myself.

"Yeah, I—"

What do I even call it?

"You what?" she asks, all doe-eyed and expectant.

"I'm better than okay," I answer, pulling her into a soft kiss.

Loud cheers fill the room and Hallee pulls away, burying her blushing face into my chest.

"They're happy for us, Hal. This is exactly what we wanted," I mutter, kissing the top of her head as it tilts up.

Those wide eyes turn glassy as she says, "This, right here, is exactly what I want forever."

Forever—what a heartbreaking impossibility.

"Who wants more wine?" I instigate to ease the sting.

Looking around the room, I etch the evening into my memory. If only this would become the future too. This life is a pretty good one.

Hallee

I love him more than the end we will get. I love them all more than the end we will get.

We didn't miss a beat when they arrived, easily skipping over small talk and introductions. No one else seems to be questioning why, as if there's this innate understanding that we already care for one another. Seeing us together is like watching an old home video. The trigger guard on my mind has been flipped, releasing years of memories from captivity.

Hudson walked in, holding a bottle of white wine. Last year, it was red. He started raving about romantic comedies, and I time traveled back to my first memory of us together.

Three first-friend dinners have played in the theater of my mind as events from previous years repeat. Matt and Marlowe dance together, looking scared enough to want to dash and involved enough to want to smash. They looked like that last year too, except Matt was in black instead of gray. Funny, Marlowe was in the same thing as today.

Avery wasn't as shy as I thought she'd be. Settled into cooking with Hudson, and within seconds they were looking at each other like they'd never look away again. He wanted to scoop her up and take her to the couch to cuddle. I know, because last year he did.

Dean was surprised by the pairings, and it's taking everything in me to pretend I am too. It's some kind of cruel dream come true, reliving years of history in real time. The worst of it is that I still can't remember how this ends. There's no way to prevent the bad from repeating if it all went up in flames.

The guys looked at us funny when we gathered around the coffee table rather than the kitchen table to eat dinner, but it'd feel wrong not to be ourselves. We've finally found an *ourselves* to be. Avery keeps slowly and ever so slightly scooting closer to Hudson. Matt has cast a spell on Marlowe, and Dean? I'm enthralled by him. Really, I can't stop looking.

There was a moment earlier when his vibe shifted from relaxed to riddled with anxiety. There was no explanation for the abnormal change, but I can't help but wonder if there was.

Did he have a memory?

If he did, would he be bold enough to recognize it, or would it flutter away faster than a paper airplane in the wind?

Knowing I'm lost in thought, he gives my hand a reassuring squeeze. He seems to know everything about me these days, except the biggest things. There'd be more glass to shatter if he were to drop those. More of me to break.

Forever.

I told him that this is what I want, forever.

It's the first arrow shot at the system, planting the idea that permanence could be an option for us. We will burn brightly, and nothing will dim our light. End of discussion. The balloon of hope has convinced me—I have the power to choose, and maybe it's irrational, but having something to strive for has given me a purpose that's lightened my soul.

Even if it can't be undone, there has to be a way to prevent the continuous cycle of being forced to forget. Small acts of defiance—speaking in terms of forever, asking indirect questions, choosing my words carefully. Things so subtle they won't even realize it's become the steady drip eroding the strength of The Gift.

I'll continue what the old woman started, spreading hope across the city, and I'll begin in the quiet places—at the table with my found family. Even standing alone, I'll fight, because we are worth far more than letting go. We've been ripped apart for years, but not anymore. Never again.

"Gentlemen, you've come into our home, so you are subject to our traditions." Avery's voice comes out bold rather than bashful. Hudson's effect on her is already resurfacing. Her eyes flick from Marlowe to me, leading us in silent conversation.

Nearly pushing Matt over with a teasing glare, Marlowe jumps in. "Since it's your first time, you can observe. Next time, you'll be expected to give it your heart and soul."

First time. This isn't their first time.

Next time. There will be a next time.

"A toast!" I cheer.

Avery raises her glass to start us off. "To great food, great company, and whatever is to come."

My eyebrows lift at her absence of the word friends. Maybe I'm not the only one playing mastermind.

"Cheers!" the men yell out, and we erupt with laughter.

"To more nights like these, and the couple of the evening that brought us all together!" Marlowe raises her glass.

Raising mine, I declare proudly, "To forever."

There's an uncomfortable silence, the first one of the evening, and Dean's stare shifts from love to pain.

"To forever," he echoes timidly, and our glasses clink together as his words close the toast.

His first punch in the fight for us, thrown without even knowing it.

- 27 -

June 2045

Dean

Hallee's nails digging into my chest wake me up. Tears are pooling underneath the pained expression on her face.

"Hallee," I whisper, gently rubbing her back.

"Hal!" My voice is louder this time, more demanding, but she still doesn't stir.

As I kiss her forehead, she finally startles awake. Immediately pushes off my chest, and the distance slaps me in the face.

"It was a dream! It was a dream, you're safe. I've got you."

"I'm so sorry." Her hands reach up, wiping away the flowing river on her face.

"Why? You have nothing to be sorry for."

"I woke you up! Did I wake them up too?"

She points to the living room, where Hudson and Matt crashed on the couch. We were all too shit-faced after dinner to even think about calling a car. Hallee insisted we stay, grabbed my hand, and led me through her bedroom door as if she'd done it ten times before. Was a little too confident, actually. How many men has she led in here?

"No, you weren't loud—you were crying."

"Oh," she breathes.

"Are you okay?"

Her hesitation cracks my heart.

"It hasn't happened in a while. I thought I was over it."

"Over what?"

"My nightmares. They used to happen often but have slowed down."

"Wait, this is normal for you?"

"I'm okay. Really. I don't know why it came back tonight."

The uncertainty in her voice argues against her claim.

"What was it about?"

I don't want to know, but I want to know. Think I already do.

"The best I can come up with is fear. Fear of being forgotten. It's always me, alone and surrounded by darkness. No matter how much I scream, no one comes because no one remembers and I'm oblivion's next victim. It drags its claws as it creeps to collect me."

"But—that's our life."

"Yeah," she sighs, eyes all glassy.

Her deepest fears have sucked the breath from my lungs. If I inhale too quickly, I might throw up.

"Dean?"

"Yeah?"

"What do you think the purpose of it all is?"

Her vulnerability hangs in the air, begging for Superman, but the answer I have is simple. It won't be enough to ease the screaming complexities of her mind, but it's the only one to give because I really do believe it.

"To enjoy it."

"But—" Closing her eyes, she takes a deep breath and I know. The voice in her head just got a hell of a lot louder.

"But everyone is unique. What if enjoying life means something different for every single person? How can an umbrella decision be best for all of us?"

My woman's angry. Her tone is laced with disgust.

"I don't—"

"My thoughts, Dean. They never stop. It's a constant stream of overwhelming questions, but when I dive further into them, I'm left circling back to square one with empty hands and an anxious mind. It's vicious, exhausting, and overwhelmingly unsettling."

"You have to let them go, Hal."

"I've been trying all year! No matter what I do, they won't shut off. They demand to exist."

"No, I don't mean turn them off. That would change *you*, and there's nothing about you that needs to be changed. Acknowledge them, and release them with the next breath. Don't hold them under a magnifying glass, and don't allow them to dim your light."

"I don't understand how I'm supposed to not think about the thoughts that literally exist to be thought about. There has to be a reason . . . or some sort of way I can use them."

Holding her is the only defense I can offer, and as her eyes find mine, she shatters into a million pieces.

Shards slice into my arms as she sobs. "I want to be defined by a great, lasting love."

"Hallee—"

"I want to be great, Dean. Someone who changed the world for the better. Who made darkness feel less scary and sadness feel less lonely. The kindest, the selfless, the extraordinary, empathetic, authentic, brave. *That* is how I want to be remembered but—"

Her voice breaks as tears send stripes down her face.

"They took away my potential, and now I'm anxiety's favorite meal, plated and served every time I'm alone, or every time I look in a mirror, or close my fucking eyes. I just want my mind to stop. Please, how do I make it stop?"

"I don't think you do, Hal."

Her nails dig into her skin, and there's no air in this room to breathe.

"What are you doing? Hallee, stop!"

"I don't know, I just—I need it to stop. I feel dirty. Like it's written all over my skin that I'm crazy and I—"

"You're not crazy."

She's going to rip herself apart.

"I'm so afraid—of the here and now, of the then and later. Deep in my bones I wish that we could be marked by a lifetime of our great love, but time races on, and while I dream about forever, it slips through my fingertips like a handful of sand, falling to be carried away by the tide. Everything I dream of is impossible. I'm insignificant. I have no reason—"

"I'll be your reason."

Her hand flies up to cradle the pain on my face.

"I will be your reason. Me, Avery, Marlowe, hell, even Matt and Hudson now. They love you already."

"I know," she bites. Odd, considering the great night we just had.

"Smiling at strangers on the street. Surprising Lea by knowing her name. Reading. Selling stories you believe in with Miles. Experiencing changing seasons. Beautiful sunflowers. Carefully painted sunsets."

"What are you—?"

"Laughing with your roommates. Setting off the smoke alarms. Drinking too much wine. Drinking too much coffee. Dancing to Taylor Swift. Singing in the shower. Looking at the light. Me."

She sniffles. Thank God, she's breathing. At least one of us is.

"All excellent reasons, and next year, you'll find a million other ones. Selfishly, I hope none are as great as me. I hope I'll always be your favorite because someday, something will happen that will make my heart remember you. You will always be mine."

"Please don't leave me," she begs. Knows it was an unfair ask, and her eyes apologize for it.

"Never." I hope.

"Will you hold me?"

"Always and forever."

- 28 -

July 2045

Hallee

Dean and I have been playing house since he found out about my nightmares, but he won't admit it's less about sleeping over and more about not wanting to leave me alone. It's almost like he knows my mind has convinced me he's dead if I'm not touching him, but he couldn't know that—right? That would be wrong. That would mean his presence is out of pity, and pity is great at masquerading as love, but can it be both at the same time? Am I a bad person for not caring which it is?

Loving him is like driving through an underground tunnel with no headlights. Can't see much except a small beam at the end surrounding him, and I'd always drive to it.

I will next year too.

The work days feel longer now that I have something to be excited about in the evenings. I've been hinting to the guys that having a few visitors at work would be nice, so my stomach jumps as three tall figures appear in the store's frosted window. Miles's head snaps to me as I skip-hop over to Dean and jump into his embrace. Wrapping my arms around him, I accidentally whack the back of his head with the book I'm holding.

"Sorry," I chuckle onto his lips, refusing to break our kiss.

Only the sound of Miles's tapping foot and clearing throat could pull me from Dean's gravity.

"What can I say, sir? Look at her. I can't help myself," Dean says sheepishly, shrugging his shoulders, all nervous that I'll be in trouble.

It feels respectful rather than rude that Miles doesn't actually look at me as he extends his hand to Dean.

"You must be the man Hallee rattles on about," he jokes, pausing in a weird man-to-man handshake moment.

"Yes, sir. I'm Dean."

Knowing that I talk about him turns him on. As his eyes steal a glimpse at me, they shift from bashful to tempted, and he lets out a skittish giggle before clearing his throat.

"These are my friends, Hudson and Matt."

"It's good to finally meet the men who saved Hallee's apartment from utter peril. I'm Miles."

As they laugh, I slide Miles a silent thank you for cutting the tension. His approval matters more than I'd like to admit, but I guess it's easy to find family in strangers when strangers are all that we have.

"What brings you in, boys?"

"Just here to browse, sir. I'm not much of a reader, but Hallee's putting up a noteworthy effort to change that. Thought it might be time to let her show me a reason."

Confusion fills the pause as everyone waits for the punch line to our inside joke.

The book in my hands, *The Human Brain and Psychological Trauma: A Comprehensive Study*, grows heavier under Dean's attention. Hudson would ask too many questions if he noticed the title, so as nonchalantly as possible, I spin around.

"Miles, I was restocking the shelves when the guys came in. Do you mind taking over for me while I show them around?"

"You were . . . restocking?" Miles's glare beams into me as his eyes squint.

"Yes," I reply, widening my gaze and leaning into Dean's touch.

After a suspiciously long pause, he agrees, but his eyes pass me a note that says, *we'll talk about this later.*

"Alright boys, you're going to read! Where would you like to start?"

Matt fakes a cough, punching Dean's arm. "Maybe with the ones in his room."

"With romance." Dean laughs, knocking Matt into the romance section, and he jumps away as if it's on fire.

"Not a romance fan, Matty?" I ask, doing my best to hide my growing chuckle.

"Books don't have cooties, bro." Hudson rolls his eyes. "Your commitment issues are screaming."

"Yeah, Matty, you could probably pick up some tips. You know, to use on a certain someo—"

"I don't need any tips, and I don't have a certain someone."

After a few seconds of eye-contact Hot Potato, Hudson starts the laughing train.

"Whatever you say," Dean teases, grabbing my hand and pulling me down the aisle.

Hudson follows close behind, actually picking up a book. There's a happy couple on the cover, standing and holding hands on the beach. "I'm sold. Check me out, Hallee. And I do mean *me.*"

Dean's hand squeezes mine harder as I fulfill the request.

What? It's my job . . .

"Hal, don—"

"Oh, come on. Aren't you the one that said it's important to look at beautiful things?" I taunt.

Matt plays into the bit, slowly dragging his gaze up and down my body as he mutters, "So important."

Letting it get to my head, I strut down the aisle runway. Hudson and Matt drop to their knees, and within three seconds, Dean pulls them off the floor by the back of their shirts.

"Okay, *ha, ha.* Joke's over."

"Oh, but—" I fake a pouty face, "you're so fun to tease."

Hudson breaks our stubborn impasse. "But really, I'll buy the book."

"Really?"

"Yeah! Might as well."

Smirking, I put my nose where it doesn't belong. "Looking to spice it up with Avery?"

"Sis, you know I never kiss and tell. My bedroom, my secrets."

He winks, and I've never been happier that he is the guy who holds my friend's heart. Well, I think he does. Whatever they are is a little confusing.

"Dean, you want to add to your collection?" I ask, discreetly hopeful.

"I'll read at least one of the books on my shelf eventually," he swears.

It'd be life-changing if he did. Can almost guarantee he'd love it as much as he loves me.

"As long as you promise."

"Anything for you, Sunshine." Pulling me close, he kisses my forehead.

"Alright, I've got to get back to work, but I'll see you later. Thanks for actually coming in."

"Anything for you, sis," Hudson teases, patting my head like you'd pet a loyal dog.

Blowing them a farewell kiss, I turn back to work and smash directly into Miles. His tapping foot is angry, as if it's disciplining me for having an afternoon that wouldn't win me a star employee award.

"Girl, you're in so much trouble."

"Miles, I'm sorry! I thought you'd be cool with it. I won't let it happen again, I promise."

"Oh, trouble with me? Absolutely not."

"Okay, then wha—"

"I'd never get in the way of young love, but you, honey, are on a one-way plane to paradise, and there's no runway to land on. That boy is head over heels for you."

"I know. Good thing I feel the same, or this would be awkward," I admit, shrugging away the fear climbing up my back.

"Enjoy it," he replies with the most genuine smile. "Enjoy every second. You make a great couple."

"Wait, do you—?"

"Do I what?"

"Nothing." He stares at me as I shake off the thought. "Good talk, Miles."

"Hang on. Tell me—why were you reading up on psychology and trauma?"

My shoulders tense, and I grind my teeth together to keep from wincing. It crossed my mind that he might catch me with the book, so it's not hard to skirt around the question. I carefully crafted this answer.

"I just miss learning sometimes."

Our staring contest lasts far too long before he yields. "In-ter-est-ing."

Every drawn-out syllable is filled with the unsaid words.

He knows I'm up to something.

- 29 -

May 2096

The History of Psychology 2335

Never underestimate the power of a symbol is written on the board behind Andrew, our eager teaching assistant. His greeting smile is bordering on *I'll hold you hostage* territory, so as usual, I climb the stairs as fast as possible.

Seeing a new face at the end of my row so close to finals week breaks my confident stride. For the most part, maintaining student attendance isn't an issue for Mr. Holiday. His lectures are entertaining, and the lack of control isn't my favorite but it *is* intriguing.

My interest in the content probably points me toward the path of pursuing psychology rather than psychiatry, but every time I finally make a decision, doubt creeps in and confuses the logic I worked so hard to find. My guidance counselor insists that deep down I know what I want, but I'm only nineteen. Choosing your life path feels like quite the tall order.

It's not for lack of trying. I've lain awake imagining my life a thousand different ways, and nine hundred and ninety-nine of them make me happy. The one scenario that didn't ended with me homeless and freezing in the heart of winter.

"What gives you a sense of purpose?" my advisor repeatedly asks.

My high school advisors asked me too, and every time, my answer was the same. Still is.

I don't know.

What I do know is that all I want is to make people happy, but sharing joy doesn't exactly put a roof over your head and food on the table. The more I focus on that vaguely cloudy goal, the more confused I become, because there are countless ways to make people happy, yet one career will not make everyone happy, so none of them are good enough for me.

The medical field, how prestigious! But remember, there's a chance I wouldn't get into medical school. The arts, how important! But only the greats make it far. Do I really think I'm one of them? Nonprofit, how generous! But how will I pay my bills?

There's always an angel saying *go for it* and a devil saying *you'll fail miserably,* and apparently after college your life goes down the shitter anyway, so I better enjoy it. It isn't exactly encouraging to be reminded by every adult who's made it out alive that these are the best days of my life. The days that feel like my very worst might actually be the best I'll ever have? What a bleak thing to tell someone without knowing how deeply they're struggling. Package that together with my lack of direction, and I'm a gumball spiraling down the chute, destined to be chewed up and spit out by adulthood.

Attempting to command the room as easily as Mr. Holiday, Andrew clears his throat and the stranger a few seats down opens a writing pad stamped with the University's crest. No wonder he looks like he'll come unhinged with one more sip of coffee—he's getting graded on this.

"Hello, class. You're stuck with me today, as Mr. Holiday has taken . . . well, dare I say . . ."

No way, he's not about t—

". . . an extended holiday."

Yup, there it is.

The freshman offers an overly forced laugh as I grind my teeth together, refraining from dropping my jaw. Andrew's cheeks blush at the crash and burn of what he'd probably assumed was his most interesting talking point.

"So," he continues, "you're stuck with me. Let's begin by discussing the elderly woman with the balloon. Please open your textbooks to chapter thirteen."

"Geriatric Psychology is a senior-level class," one of the smug frat boys calls out. "If you'll excuse us, we can call this lecture complete."

What age will he learn that purposefully trying to embarrass someone actually makes you an asshole? Surprisingly, there's a fierceness to Andrew's tone as he replies, "I'm well aware of your class requirements, and I suggest you sit down. We'll be discussing the most useful, or perhaps dangerous, tool of them all."

The class shuffles at his intriguing word choice, and even the observer sits up a little straighter.

"And what would that be? A balloon?" The frat pack scoffs, but is silenced immediately with one word.

"Hope."

"Hope?" the freshman questions.

"Yes, hope. You may think you have all of the answers to the perfect plan for your life."

Actually, no. Literally seconds ago I was thinking the opposite of that exact statement. However, I do believe some people are ignorant enough to think they have control of the reins.

"But you never know what life will throw at you." Andrew's shoes click like Mr. Holiday's when he walks over to the chalkboard.

"Never underestimate the power of a symbol, and never misjudge the power of hope when all seems hopeless."

His deep sigh rebounds off the walls, only to be soaked up by blank stares.

"Can anyone give me an example of how hope could be a dangerous thing?"

Crickets.

"No one?"

Here we go again. I feel bad for the guy, and we all know what happens when I feel sorry for someone.

My hand is the only one in the air, but I still respect him enough to wait for his acknowledgment. "Rayne! What is your example?"

"The pain of lost hope could be worse than never having it at all. If you set an expectation and are let down, you'll be sad, but if you never had the expectation at all, you'd probably be satisfied with your circumstances. People do unprecedented things in the pit of despair, but should they find their way out someday, the very things that helped them cope might come back to haunt them, pushing them back into a vicious cycle."

Andrew throws me a nod of gratitude as hands shoot up all around the room.

"Similarly," a back row bandit calls, "hope could be used as a tool to maintain control. Plenty of people can endure excruciating circumstances as long as there's a light at the end of the tunnel, but if it goes out, then there's no reason to push for improvement."

"In this instance, yes. Hope can be stifling. Does anyone have anything to add before we continue?" He waits approximately ten seconds before continuing on. "Then what are some examples of how it could be powerful?"

"It's powerful either way," I mutter.

Unfortunately I wasn't quiet enough, and the observer took notice of my classmate's annoyed glares. "A student back here has something to say," she sternly declares, and Andrew blanches.

"Rayne, I'm sorry. Did you have something to add?"

"No, it's just—hope is powerful either way. Sometimes the most dangerous things are the most powerful. Asking for examples of how hope could be a wonderful thing might be a more effective question."

His eyes flare with pride. "Well, you heard her. Does anyone have any examples?"

A sharp gasp comes from the second row, from a student we've started to assume is mute. She's never spoken before, and her words now are barely above a whisper.

"It can change the world, like the woman with the balloon."

The class's eyes collectively fall on the chapter we'd forgotten was open in front of us. Chills travel over my entire body as I recall the personal accounts in the textbook regarding the impact that one woman had—all because of the hope of one helium balloon.

$$- 30 -$$

August 2045

Hallee

Miles isn't usually picky about the entry table, but this is our third reorganization this week. He's avoiding eye contact, flipping two books back and forth as if he hasn't done it twenty times already.

"The woman with the balloon hasn't been here in a while," I say, trying to distract him from whatever mental battle he's fighting.

He's always been kind to her, attentive to her needs and generous in listening to her stories. I can't believe it took her absence for me to realize how connected they've always been, laughing over their shared love of stories. Isn't that how it works, though? Absence gives you time to think about someone—to miss someone.

His silent fidgeting is deafening.

"She's pretty hard to miss, but I haven't seen her recently. Have you?"

My blood becomes liquid worry, pumping through my body. Why won't he even look at me?

"I didn't know how to tell you. After a couple weeks of her absence, I reached out to the elderly transportation service that brings her here. They informed me that she unexpectedly passed last week after a brief illness."

"She what?" My voice breaks as the news slaps me in the face. My frown is the lasting handprint.

His tone was almost robotic—devoid of all emotion—but there in his eyes is a glimmer of devastation deeper than my own.

Reaching over, he rests his hand on mine. "I'm sorry, Hallee. I know you really enjoyed your time with her."

"Unexpected illness, so she was—" A sob travels up my throat, releasing silently through cascading tears. "Alone. She was alone."

As he nods, fear freezes my lungs. We're all damned to the same fate. Regardless of how much I fight against it, oblivion will collect me too.

"She was so much braver than me," I whisper over the ache in my chest.

Business owners belong to the government. How much of what he remembers is he willing to disclose? Grief and fear move me to press on the subject, and my dissatisfaction with The Gift radiates off of my every word.

"Did she come here every year, Miles?"

His weary eyes find mine, flaring before he admits, "She did."

Miles, the man of many words, has settled for two? What kind of training has he endured to warrant such a bland response?

"Were you close with her?" I push.

"Hallee," he sighs.

"Miles, were you close with her?"

"It's very hard to be close to anyone when they forget you."

The answer implies he wasn't, but his watering eyes beg to differ. A slideshow shuffles in my mind, projecting memories of Dean and I. My heart cracks more and more as each one passes by.

Come on, Hal, his voice is the soundtrack, lifting me up to channel the bravery of the old woman, and my tears shamelessly flow as my eyes close.

"What is it like, Miles? To remember when no one else does?"

I need to hear his oblivious warning for my upcoming fate.

My disrespect of questioning the government is a stun gun, locking his empty stare onto me. Clearly no one has ever dared ask. The public has chosen acceptance over curiosity.

"She believed someone would remember her because of the balloon. Do you think it's possible for the civilians to remember, Miles?"

Silence overrides my hope that the humanity of hearing his name would drive him to talk to me, and anger bubbles in my voice as I try again. "Come on, Miles. You're a *person,* not their pawn."

"It's an incredibly lonely prison," he whispers as a single tear falls from his face, crashing onto the book in his hands. The raw vulnerability of his fear-filled stare cracks the door for me to continue.

"Are you happy, Miles? This *gift* they have given us—do you really think it's that?"

Holding my stare, he breathes out a strained, "No."

No he isn't happy, no he doesn't think it's a gift, or both?

I'd never have known the pain that the happiest person I know has carried alone, but the implication of my tone if I ask for clarification might startle him back into his armor, so I don't.

"Someone should change that, don't you think?"

Desperation seeps from the well in my eyes. Staring straight into their reflective pools, he offers me a single nod of bravery—of hope.

Maybe we're all not as different as I'd assumed, civilians and government employees. We share the similarity of being forced into solitude by either forgetting or being forgotten. Taking three steps closer to him, and I replace the book he's holding with my own hands.

Hope did not die with the old woman, and I'm not the only one she ignited it in. Allowing the unspoken words to settle, I gently squeeze his hands. The pressure is the final crack in the dam, and his shoulders shake as bone-deep sorrow breaks through.

"You're okay, Miles. I'm with you," I cry, pulling him into a hug.

"She—" A sob swallows his voice. "She was my mother."

His exhale of grief circles us like a ring of smoke, filling and suffocating my lungs. Waterfall tears fall to the floor as I pull away and look into his eyes. He needs to see the determined strength behind my words.

"I'm so sorry for your loss. She was an irreplaceably beautiful flower in a world filled with dirt."

"She was," he responds, nodding once as his grip tightens.

"My friend." I swallow down fear and breathe in her bravery. "I will remember her and her balloon. I promise."

"Promise is a big word, Hallee," he whispers, but I stomp down his doubt.

"I promise."

As we hold each other until our tears subside, my heart pounds the promise into my bones.

His mother's legacy will live on through me.

Miles

The first year was the hardest.

The adults had it better than the infants and children, who were separated from their parents and placed into group homes to be raised by government educators. They were only allowed one personal item. I was allowed whatever I could fit in their standard moving box. I'm not sure what happened to the rest of my belongings after they moved me into assigned housing. They were probably erased like the rest of me was.

I was the only member in my family whose job qualified them as a government official and was immediately trained on the "appropriate" way to conduct myself if I ran into people I have known—have loved.

It all amounted to one conclusion: *act as if you don't remember.*

Under no circumstances is it acceptable to break character or insinuate that we've known someone in a past life. Should we fail to uphold our duty, the government will gladly . . . handle us. They didn't have to explain what that meant—it'd be incredibly easy to make a problem disappear when there's no one to notice the absence of their loved ones.

At first it was freeing that no one held onto an opinion about me from when I was still young. When growing pains hurt, ignorance made me rude, or mistakes made me bitter. There are hundreds of apologies I owe to others because, at the time, I didn't know any better. I carried the shame of learning wisdom at the expense of others, hurting friends in the name of growing, until The Gift was given to us. The load had been lightened, and for a week I began to think that underneath all of my grief there could be a free life, filled with happiness.

I thought that until I saw her.

The bell to the store rang, followed by the click of her walker, and the familiar sound transported me back to the day she'd been given it. Dad tied a bundle of French Rose pink balloons to it, attempting to break the news as softly as possible. He thought introducing it as a present rather than a reminder of her declining health would help her cope with the change. After a lifetime together, he should've known that she was the one most in favor of such a thing.

To his surprise, she was ecstatic for the extra stability and expressed nothing but gratitude. It was one of the reasons I admired her—her uncanny ability to remind others that aging is a gift and should be celebrated as one.

As she hobbled along toward me, I had hope that memory was what led her to my store. The store she listened to me dream of for over twenty years. The store we spent a year trying to name.

Surely, I thought. Surely she remembers.

Then, her eyes met mine.

A yellow balloon was tied to her walker, floating along her path as she passed the entryway table. A friendly smile lifted her cheeks as she saw me, yet there was an emptiness behind her eyes. My mother looked at me without an ounce of recognition. I wish I had the luxury of forgetting her unmistakably soul-crushing blank stare, but it's forever burned in my mind like her words from the opening day of Happy Bookday.

Be intentional with your customers. They will always buy books, but will choose to return here based on how you make them feel.

She would want nothing less than for me to continue on—to live a good life. So, regardless of the hollow hole in my chest, I promised myself that day that for her, I would not be swallowed by grief. For her, I would continue on and cherish whatever fleeting moment I could have with her as a customer in my store.

She always found her way back to me. For five years, I got to spend time with her as her favorite book salesman. In the end, it was never enough. I still wanted more—for her and for me. The feelings of unrest continued to grow, and do so even now.

"Are you happy?" Hallee asked.

No.

The answer resounded in my mind five times before my whisper slipped out. Five times for five years of faking it, but honesty won as the knowledge of my mother's death urged me to courageously disobey my training.

I have nothing and no one to lose anymore.

Let them take me away.

"She was my mother."

For everything she had been to me, it was the last thing I could give her. Acknowledging and sharing who she was by recognizing her favorite title—*Mom.*

As Hallee looked into my eyes and called me a friend, my heart shed away the shell of darkness that encapsulated it.

No one has called me that in five whole years.

"I will remember her and her balloon," she promised.

"Promise is a big word, Hallee," I reminded.

There was an eerily pointed edge to her words, paired with a ferocity in her eyes that caused the doubt in my mind to shudder as she repeated, "I promise."

For the first time since that very first year, I had hope.

I believed her—and hold on tightly to that belief as the store bell's *ding* pulls me back to reality. A little girl is skipping in, holding a yellow balloon. My mother must've sent her my way.

As a warm ghost of wind passes me, I almost swear I hear her whisper, *I remember you now, my Son. You are not alone.*

- 31 -

September 2045

Dean

"He looks guilty," Hallee whispers, overly paranoid that her voice will carry.

"No, he looks nervous. There's a difference."

"Did you see the way he lowered his head before walking in? That man doesn't want to be seen!"

She's got me there. I tried to give him the benefit of the doubt, but he did duck down. Nothing goes unnoticed by Ann Arbor's star detective, Hallee Sunshine.

"He was looking at the door handle."

He wasn't, but when I argue with her she defends herself in this adorable way where her eyes look sure. It's one of the only times she looks like that.

Some people need to be liked; Hallee just needs to be understood. She cares too much—putting all of her empathy into the universe for others to freely take. We may never know the full extent of her impact in our lifetime, but she's essential. Makes this world better just by existing.

I got a lesson about how differently we view things, laying here on the picnic blanket with her for hours. A circus of clouds floated across the sky, and Hallee swore she saw an elephant when I saw an obese man smoking a pipe. Laughed so hard that my side still hurts, but the disagreement smoothed over quite nicely once I agreed that most of her ideas were superior to mine.

Most.

I don't lie, not even about the little things, and there were a few where she swore she saw a puppy when it was clearly a stack of donut holes. Yes, this was all going very well until I found the hill this woman would die on—interpreting clouds.

She grew tired of watching them, rolling to her stomach to watch the cars instead, and that's when she saw him. Once she did, there was no going back. The FBI investigation immediately began . . . and will absolutely not close until this poor man walking into the jewelry store alone either pays or leaves.

His first offense? Being alone. How dare he.

His second offense? Wearing a baseball hat.

According to Hallee, it does a suspiciously excellent job of hiding his identity. Never fear, I did ask for clarification and we concluded that if he were with someone else, the hat would be acceptable. Being alone and wearing one? Criminal offense—unless it's backwards, in which case he can do no wrong.

"That man is buying an apology diamond. What do you think he did?" she asks, gasping and leaning closer to me. This is an extremely delicate case, and she won't risk being heard. Even if he's across the street and inside.

"Dean, do you think he cheated?"

"Definitely."

"Oh my gosh, then who is he buying it for? The girlfriend, or the other woman?!"

I inhale a deep breath, failing to fight off my growing smirk.

"Probably the other woman."

"I knew it."

Her eyes roll as she finally glances at my cocky grin.

"Don't patronize me! If you have a better explanation, do share. It's not like he's buying a ring!"

"He could be!"

"You know he's not, that's not even funny."

"Fair."

The market for engagement rings dissolved into thin air alongside the hope of happily ever afters.

"Let's name him John," I say. "Johnny boy is madly in love and planning to shower his partner with a gift he knows they'll enjoy."

Come on, John. Don't fail me now.

"No way. Too easy. Men don't walk around buying shiny things for their partner without an explanation."

"Maybe it's an anniversary?" I counter.

She scoffs. "In a world where we start over every year? Try again."

"Birthday?"

"Possible, but unlikely."

"Why are you so sure he isn't simply surprising someone he loves? There doesn't always have to be an ulterior motive."

"Oh, yes there does! Have you?"

"Have I what?"

"Surprised the one you love? Because last I checked, I'm diamondless. So unless you love someone else—" Her suspicious eyes tease me.

"Oh no. Nope. Why do girls do this? Let's not displace the facts. This isn't about me, we're talking about John."

"That wasn't an answer."

"*That's* not what you want, Hal. Flowers, quality time, back scratches, takeout coffee—all make you happier than a diamond ever could."

"That is fair. But—" She casts the line, staring blankly until I bite.

"But what?" I ask, sighing because she's the best fisher out there.

"No woman would ever turn down a shiny new thing, especially if it's accompanied by a grand gesture."

"Interesting." So she might like it more than I'd originally thought, but I have to capitalize on her slipup. "Then you agree that maybe he *is* plotting a grand gesture."

We'll have to agree to disagree, because my woman never bows out of an argument. She did huff a little as her face fell, and that's the closest I'll get to her admitting defeat. This man's fake profile is not going to say *I'm a cheating asshole* on my watch.

We were planning on grabbing some lunch, but Hallee can't leave things unfinished. She has to know how this story ends or she won't sleep for days, and John is quickly getting added to my shit list. I'm starving, and the man has been in there for over two hours.

Literally, why?

It's very suspicious. The security guard thinks so too, because he steps closer to him every five minutes. Give it thirty more, and he'll cuff him for loitering.

We've started taking shifts, keeping watch for checkout. It takes two shifts each before he finally pulls his wallet out of his back pocket.

"Hallee!"

Resting her eyes turned into a sunny afternoon nap. She wouldn't be able to sleep at night without knowing what happens, but can sleep perfectly fine in the middle of trying to find out what happens. Complex, my Hal. Endearing, though, that she's able to relax around me even in the middle of the park.

"Hallee, he's checking out!"

Jolting awake, she springs up like a jack-in-the-box.

"Did I miss anything good?"

Detective Sunshine strikes again, forming binoculars around her eyes with her hands. A satisfied smirk raises on her face and oh—

"Do you see what I see?"

Shit. Come on, John. I was really rooting for you.

"Two! Items! Wrapped and bagged identically, but separately." Rage bubbles in her voice, and her eyes widen as she whispers, "One for his partner, and one for the secret lover!"

"Now we don't know that! It could be—"

"If they were for the same woman, they'd be wrapped together or wrapped in different colors so each one would still feel special."

It's cute, her little temper tantrum for the two women being done dirty by John. Honestly, whatever case I'd built was closed by the double bag. Someone update his bio.

"Alright, Hal, you're right. The grand mystery of John has been solved. Let's go get some food."

We hit the sidewalk at the same time cheating John exits the store. Spinning around, Hallee snaps a Polaroid selfie of us. Sure enough, it develops the perfect picture of us smiling with John suspiciously escaping in the background. He's even looking down, shielding his face behind his ball cap, and I've never been more impressed—Hallee's judgment and timing are impeccable.

- 32 -

October 2045

Hallee

The air has shifted back to cold winds, bringing along frost-filled mornings. The leaves are saying goodbye to us—changing colors in a loving farewell. We've all enjoyed the fall festivities, but playing tag in this corn maze is my personal hell. Matt insisted it'd be fun, but fun is continuously getting more and more subjective.

Twenty minutes have passed and I still haven't found my way out, loud shrieks keep startling me, and if one more person runs in front of me too quickly, I'll throw a punch. *Flighter* turned *fighter*, real quick. Even the smiley scarecrow is starting to give me the creeps. Paranoia made its eyes move on my third pass by.

Are the sloshing footsteps approaching my aisle friendly? Are they hunting me? Realistically, it's one of us, but reality is blurring with the horror movie Avery made me watch last night, so I sink into the corn and camouflage myself like a child.

"Hallee?" My shoulders relax as Dean slides around the corner. "I know you're here. I followed your footprints."

Wearing white tennis shoes to the pumpkin patch was one of the greater lapses in my judgment, and my stomach falls as I gaze at my mud-covered feet. Messes are the worst. They make me feel like there are a hundred little ants crawling on my body. Sometimes I lean into the feeling. Sometimes I run from it like a squirrel crossing the street. It's rarely a linear journey—healing.

Today we've passed the point of no return, so as Dean tiptoes past my hidden body, I put all of my strength behind a lunge and tackle him to the ground.

The smack of our bodies hitting the mud flips our laughter switch, and we slide a good five feet before settling and sinking into the mud. Dean blocked the majority of the damage so my shirt is still pretty clean . . . until he does the meanest thing he has ever done. Reaching out, he plasters his handprint across the front of my chest. Now it looks like we were fooling around in the freaking corn maze. Thank God my arms catch my fall before the back of me is painted completely brown.

"Oh! Ah!" Avery squeals, catching us unaware. Couldn't hear her and Hudson's footsteps because of Dean's overly exaggerated laughter.

"Sorry, Mom and Dad!" Hudson yells, snapping a picture and then dragging Avery away before we can explain.

He fought us for the camera this morning. Like, he literally took us to a fake court in our living room where Matt was the judge, Marlowe and Avery were the jury, and we were the witnesses. We carefully weighed the odds of him breaking it versus providing the funniest pictures ever taken, and Matt gave the verdict that it was a gamble worth taking.

"That's going to be one interesting picture," Dean says, grinning and staring at me like he's making a wish on me again. His happiness is a drug I never want to quit.

"I'm going to have to sneak that one away before he tries to use it as blackmail."

He tips his head back, and his laugh is a choir singing the melody of our memories. With each verse, another laugh joins in and replays years and years of this angelic sound.

My senses have clocked overtime hours, working tirelessly to piece back together our puzzle, leaving me high on the history of us, starving and raiding my mental pantry for more. As I suspected, I can only remember things we're repeating, mixed with a slight glimmer of memories connected to his laughter . . . his smile . . . his eyes.

Reaching up, he draws eyeblack onto my cheeks, and I see us covered in blue paint, recreating a scene from my favorite book. I draw a mud heart on his arm and remember the time I drew it in pen, desperate to tattoo him so he'd never forget how to love me. We'd just learned that it is, in fact, possible to forget how to ride a bike, and it made me realize that it's possible to forget love, too.

The sun shining on his hair blurs the lines between laughing now, and laughing then. *Then,* we were sitting in The Marmotte, we were skipping on the street, we were walking to work. *Now,* we're covered in mud, beaming with joy, and saying *fuck you* to time. She's a greedy little bitch, turning my life into a constant coin flip of the good days of *then* versus the crushing fears of *now.* Although, on the nights I can't sleep I've been held by the memories filed away in my mental archive of comforting things.

"Why don't you lead us out, Sunshine?" Dean asks.

As he helps me up, my grip tightens subconsciously, and he smirks at the secret that reflex revealed.

"Unless . . . you can't?" he taunts.

"You're really gonna make me admit it?"

"Absolutely."

"Ugh. Dear knight in shining armor, I'm trapped! Please, come rescue me," I call like a damsel in distress. Makes me realize how rarely I feel like one these days.

"The smartest woman I've ever met couldn't find her way out of a silly corn maze?"

"Okay, was that totally necessary? Felt a little personal."

"I was hoping you had, because I couldn't either."

Smart man, admitting it before I was too hurt.

"Well then, shall we?" I ask.

Sifting through the mud hand in hand, we retrace old steps and pass the smiley scarecrow. There's no rush to our stroll and no panic in my pulse. Seems silly that there ever was, but being stranded alone is so much different than being stranded together. Everything's better with him by my side—I am better with his hand in mine. Always will be.

- 33 -

October 2045

Dean

"The Sexy Six, together again!" Hudson cheers as Marlowe and Avery walk through the door.

They don't bother knocking anymore. This place is as much theirs as it is ours. Like a lost puppy, he runs to Avery, slinging his arm over her shoulders. With one wrong move he'd crush her.

"Dean, what are you *wearing*?" Marlowe screams, bending over in her signature contagious laughter.

Did they pregame? Alcohol makes her as loud as an air horn, and that was pretty loud.

"Oh, this little old thing?" I tug at the apron. "The pockets are life-changing."

"You look very nice, Dean," Avery whispers.

"How much have you all had to drink?"

She always whispers when she's drunk, as if she could get in trouble somehow.

"What do you mean?" Marlowe asks, blinking rapidly and feigning innocence.

"I don't know what you're talking about," Avery whisper-yells as my sunshine finally lights up the room, skipping over and kissing me on the cheek.

"I'm *so* sorry. I left the wine in the car, but the driver waved me down before I made it inside."

Her hands rest on my chest, and I'm a goner before the night has even started. She never shows this much skin without a liquid-courage kickstart.

"Wine before carving pumpkins? Bold move, Hal."

"Questioning my decisions? Dangerous move, Dean."

My eyes tap out of the stubborn stare-off as she bites her lower lip. That mouth gives her an unfair advantage. It's impossible to hold focus around it.

Leaning in, I steal a kiss.

"Wine, sugar, and—"

"Strawberries," she cuts me off. "Your favorite."

"That's where you're wrong, Hal. *You* are my favorite."

Her eyes glisten, blinking three times. *I believe you,* they say. *It's about time,* mine blink back.

She spins and dances away, lost in giggle city with her friends, but she'll come back to me. Can't stand being too far away, although it's brave of her to twirl around the island while drunk. She's the least coordinated of us by far.

Right on cue, her foot slips out from under her. She knocks a pumpkin over and the domino effect begins. One by one, they fall and crack open on the floor. Only the smallest one survives, and a moment of silence fills the room for the fallen fruits. Grief is different for everyone, so no one's sure how to react.

Avery breaks the silence, bursting out in laughter. From a mile away I'd be able to tell that Hal's embarrassed. The tip of her nose is bright red and her hands are twisting her hair again as Avery hops around the pumpkin graveyard.

Lifting the lone pumpkin like a champion trophy, she cheers, "Small but mighty!"

Our cascading laughter starts slowly but builds until we each forget why we started laughing in the first place.

"Someone should vote for me as least coordinated," Hallee jokes.

As we all pass confusion like a frisbee, I try to get a grip on her tone. There was something unrecognizable, but I could swear her eyes blinked, *Please understand me.*

I love you, I blink back, empty handed. Still haven't told her, but my eyes do every day.

"Least coordinated. Interesting," I chuckle, frantically pulling at mental straws to explain her expectant expression.

She's worked so hard to speak kindly to herself. I'd hate for this to be the final drop that makes the tears fall. Our friends feel it too, so in their silence I shoot around a look of gratitude. Hallee's too busy getting paper towels to notice.

"Wait!" I yell.

She pauses like a TV screen as I run to the living room and grab the camera. It never fails to come in handy during our dinners.

"Everyone get in!"

While they're distracted, I check on Hallee. Grab the sides of her arms and sink down on her level.

"You good?"

She nods as tears form in her eyes.

"Everything matters, remember?" I remind her. "Messes too."

"Messes too." She kisses my nose, slipping away to join the others, and smiles proudly in front of the chaos as I snap a picture. *Click.*

"Because you were such a good sport, you can keep it."

She'll probably trash it, but it was worth the sentiment.

Thank you, she mouths, relieved to accept the only piece of proof that this mishap occurred. The oven beeps and time blurs as I picture us kissing, but the second beep interrupts before I can make the vision a reality.

As I check the food, Hudson swoops Avery off her feet, spinning around and tossing her onto the couch. Matt and Marlowe are staring at each other like they want to get a room, and Hallee seems to have snuck off. She hides sometimes when she's sad, so after five minutes I head to our bedroom.

Catching her carefully placing a book onto the shelf, I ask, "New read?"

"Not new to me, but it could be to you!"

"You practically read a book a day. I could never keep up."

"How many books is too many books, Dean?"

"Depends on who you ask."

"It's fun to escape! You must've thought so too at some point. Look at your room."

"*You* are my escape. You are my love story. You are all I want."

My arms open as she runs to me.

"You'll get it someday." She giggles as I spin her around.

"Will I?"

Hudson's voice interrupts, yelling from the living room, "It's romantic comedy or bust."

"For once can we please just watch a show?" Matt begs.

"Time to sway the vote," I say with a laugh, pulling her out to join them.

"Four against two!" Hallee cheers.

"Every. Single. Time," Matt complains, his hand flying to his forehead before we pair off into couples like a group of middle school friends.

Hallee falls asleep about thirty minutes in instead of her usual forty-three. Watching her breathe makes me more aware that I'm living in *the good ol' days*. I won't let them fly by without being thankful, especially for my little night light. Somehow, she even shines in her sleep.

- 34 -

October 2045

Hallee

All it took was one look at my grade A insecure face for Avery to attempt to calm me down. "Come on, Hallee. It's for *fun*!" she insisted.

Fun—I'm starting to hate the word.

We were pretty indecisive about what to be for Halloween until girls' night a few weeks ago, when we watched a romantic movie with the world's hottest cowboy. It took approximately five minutes for us to agree that it'd be fun to save a horse and—well, with one look at our sexy cowgirl inspiration—the boys jumped overboard on their Three Musketeers idea.

I was excited . . . until I wasn't. Isn't that how this always goes? The longer the outfit lays on my bed, the more I question all of my life's decisions.

Bless her heart, it taunts.

I swear it said it with the sweet Southern drawl of a country woman. Wearing a literal bedsheet wouldn't deter Dean from being excited to see me, but this nervous pit in my stomach is pulsing with desperation to not be disappointing to him, or to myself. There's no actual standard that constitutes failure in my head, just an overarching idea that I want to *feel* a certain way. It's wrong if it's not just right.

"Do you want tough love, or do you need to be coddled?" Avery asks. I hadn't realized she was still standing there.

"Tough love."

"Brace yourself."

Obeying, I tap my fingers together three times. Although, what she thinks is rude is usually rock bottom of one of the nicest things you could say to someone.

"Ready?"

No, but I nod yes.

"For the love of God, stop being such a little bitch."

"Ope."

"You've got it, babes! Flaunt it. If not for yourself, then for your man. You want to be someone he'll proudly show off? Stop thinking about wearing that bedsheet to the club." She points at the wrinkled sheet on my floor.

"I didn't. I—"

"Finish your hair, paint your lips red, and put on the fucking cowgirl boots or so help me, Hallee, I will take a bottle of vodka and shove it down your throat."

"Yes, ma'am!" I cheer, playfully tipping an invisible hat to her as she continues.

"You will not be for everyone, just as rainy days are not, so stop trying to be. It's annoying and unhelpful. Shine where you can."

A pin drop would be audible in this silence. She's right, I won't be for everyone. Rainy days are really nice, though. They serve their purpose.

Avery's face grows a deeper shade of red every second we stand frozen. I'd never heard her cuss before. Didn't know she had it in her, but we've all changed since the beginning of the year. Tonight will be the proof of that.

"I'm sorry, Hal. You wanted tough—"

"Stunned," I whisper, exhaling and holding up a hand as I brace myself on the edge of my bed. "The woman is too stunned to speak."

Laughter spills before I can continue to scare her.

"I hope someone spills a drink on you tonight!" Rolling her eyes, she frowns and stomps off.

"The guys are meeting us there, right?" Marlowe calls from her room.

"Yes, why?"

"Because . . ." She pauses, sliding into my doorway. "I don't think we'd make it to the club if they came here."

Matt is one lucky guy. At least, I think he is. I still haven't asked.

"I can do this." The words leave my lips before embarrassment shuts me up.

"You can do this, babes. No time like the present." With a wink goodbye, she closes my door, leaving me to drown in thoughtful silence.

If I'm doing this, I'm going all in.

These jean shorts are a surefire way to gain some attention, but if they don't catch it, then this sheer white crop top will. It ties together at the front and does nothing to hide my firetruck red bralette. I wanted to go with black, but Marlowe insisted. The boobs match the lipstick, the lipstick matches the boots, and the black glitter cowgirl hat matches her soul.

As I head to the kitchen to join them, the sound of my clicking boots practically snaps their necks. Marlowe's mouth hangs open as Avery shouts, "Yeehaw, cowgirl!"

"Yee-hawty!" Marlowe screeches before whistling.

"Is yeehaw our new catch phrase?" I ask.

"Yes," they say, nodding in unison.

"It's scientifically impossible to say it without smiling," Avery smugly answers.

"Well, how do you feel?" Marlowe asks.

"As sexy as I look!"

"Attagirl!" she cheers.

Glancing in the mirror, we do some final touch-ups. Best guess? We're running eleven minutes late. Telling time without looking at the clock is what happens when your largest personality trait is remaining on schedule. Glancing at it anyway, I chuckle under my breath. Only ten minutes late. How *dare* I be one minute off. Still my gut twists a little. Maybe the cold wind will freeze my nerves and remind me—things that scare me can be fun, too.

Dean

The music should be able to beat away my nerves about Hallee running late, but I know my girl. She doesn't *just run late.*

Whiskey warms my cheeks as I down the rest of my glass. How much time can pass before I freak out? Because I'm kind of freaking out. Hudson and Matt are unphased by their late arrival. It's not uncommon for Avery or Marlowe to run late. Hallee, though. Well, you know.

Voyaging to the bathroom, I scan the sea of bodies in search of my treasured sunshine. The search continues as I pass the long line of women waiting for the restroom. Yet again, I'm thankful to be a man, but if there's any part of womanhood that seems fun, it's the drunk bathroom conversations. If the entire world were as supportive as a women's restroom, world peace might actually be attainable.

Closing the men's restroom door cuts off a loud compliment about a girl's red lipstick. Apparently it matches her bra. The cold sink water fails to wash away the anxiety written all over my lovesick reflection. There's no harm in checking in, right? Might as well send a text.

Howdy, baby. Where's my pretty lady?

An ironically timed *ding* resounds as I exit the restroom, but it's just a random guy uncomfortably standing alongside the women's bathroom line. Maybe he's waiting for his date? Don't know, and don't have time to find out. I've got my own girl to worry about.

Fear, the bull, bucks me off, kicking my gut as I spot two sexy cowgirls flanking Matt and Hudson. As nonchalantly as possible, I push through the crowd and tip my hat to the ladies. I may be injured from the rodeo, but I'm not a jackass.

"Evening, ladies. You look mighty fine tonight, but you seem to be missing one. Where'd my angel get off to?"

Avery opens her mouth but, out of thin air, a lasso appears and tugs me backward. My balance wavers as small, familiar hands spin me 'round.

"Howdy, stud. Lookin' for me?"

Does that confident voice really belong to my girl? Takes me three takes to believe it. There she is—hook, line, and sinker.

Here I am, mouth agape like a fish out of water. If I'm not the luckiest man on this earth then I'd love to meet whoever is. One look at her on my arm and I'd prove him wrong.

She's so fit. In apple-pie order, really. I'd always run up the barrel of a gun for her, but with that red lace on her chest? Might run a smidge faster. Love it so much, I could almost swear I recognize it. Wait a second—do I recognize it?

"What's the problem, darlin'? Barn cat got your tongue?"

She makes fishing look easy, but all the words I try to reel in break the line as the lasso slides down my body, pooling at my feet.

Normally I pride myself on self-control, but tonight I'm a bull seeing red. I've seen a lacy bra before. On her, even, when one thing led to another, and I couldn't care less about the red lips or boots.

Why is my attention so fixated?

"Dean?" Her hand shakes my arm. "Is it okay?"

Insecure innocence has replaced the confidence in her wide eyes. She's bracing for an insult, tugging at her shorts as if she can stretch them longer. Feels like a shot in the foot. Reaching up and twisting her hair is the shot in my other foot.

"Sorry, Sunshine. Your getup has me speechless." The country accent butters her up, relaxing her shoulders and restoring her confidence. Still, the situation has me rattled more than a tail on a rattlesnake.

"Dance with me!" she yells.

"Drink some water and I will!"

Her eyes roll, bowling over every expression except mischief.

"If you won't, I'll find someone who will." Glaring at me, she takes a swig of her drink.

As she whispers something in Avery's ear, I hold my ground, but my stomach sinks as Avery nods. Shit, she wasn't bluffing, and now she's pulling Hudson to the dance floor.

"Hallee," I call, but it's no use.

My woman's on a mission, and Hudson's gladly cashing in the one free pass to dance with her. There's a chance he would've turned her down if he were sober, but even then it's slim. Avery and I sip our drinks as we watch her man touch my girl in places only I should.

"Crazy, isn't it?" she asks, chuckling half-heartedly.

"I'm sorry," I say, and I'm not sure why.

"If I cared about that, I wouldn't have told her to do it. It's crazy how much I trust him already."

"More than I do," I admit.

"You're her everything, Dean. Only someone secure in their relationship could tease their man with his best friend. After all, she's watching *you*."

Avery might be the wisest of us. She's definitely the most comforting.

"You gonna step in?" Matt asks, handing me another drink.

"I called her bluff but she delivered. I'm going to see how this show plays out. My bet is she folds first."

Avery nearly spits out her drink, shaking her head as she says, "Absolutely not."

"No chance," Matt scoffs, stepping forward.

Before his foot can hit the ground, I grab him by the shirt collar.

"Take one more step and I'll kill you."

He lets out one loud "ha" before muttering out of the side of his mouth, "Down, boy."

"It's all a game until it's not," Avery taunts, and anger bubbles in my blood as Hudson's fingers climb up Hallee's thigh. Watching them slip under the edge of her shorts makes the tips of my ears hot and my steps heavy.

"Enough," I yell, shoving him off of her. Harder than I meant to, if I'm honest.

"It's about tim—" she tries, but I shut her up with a kiss. Her lips open for mine as our bodies close every inch of space between us, and the room spins as kissing turns into missing her lips on mine.

"Jealousy looks good on you, Dean," she admits, giggling as she sways into me, yet I can't help but remember how sad her eyes got the first time I saw her in the club.

"And you look good on me," I reply, sliding my hand into her right back pocket as I give her another quick kiss, just to remind everyone in this place that she's mine.

"Well, stud," she says, laying her hands on my chest. "How 'bout you and I skip the rodeo and head out into wide open spaces?"

"Lady, that's a mighty fine idea."

Don't even know if I used that correctly, but her cheeks turn pink as a pig. Same color they turned when she was talking about a cowboy who said it in a movie.

"Leaving so soon?" the bouncer asks, adding a mumbled, "Have fun, buddy," when Hallee's too distracted to hear.

Matt and Hudson said the same thing, probably assuming we're headed off to take advantage of the empty apartment. More than anything, I want to talk to my best friend, and I think Hallee feels the same. It's uncanny how we can be on the same page without saying anything at all.

Hallee made Marlowe take a Polaroid of us before we left. She's been keeping all of them recently, and as much as I want this one to be mine, in the end I'll fold in the fight. Placing it in between two fingers, I hold it out to her.

"Back left," she insists, winking as she turns her back pockets to me. Sliding it in, my fingers swipe over one that's already there.

"What is—"

Oh.

It's her in the red lace—and only the red lace.

"Consider it an early Christmas present."

So that's why they went with red. Call 911, her mischievous smile has set me on fire.

Wait—*I'm 911.*

Barely holding on to composure, I smile widely and admit, "You just keep surprising me, Hal."

Loves to see me flustered, my girl, so she skips in celebration of a mission accomplished as she changes the subject. "It's a beautiful night out here."

Talking about the weather usually means she doesn't know what to say, which in her case is rare. It's my turn to lead, but there's no good way to say, *I'm shaken up by the color of your bra, but not for reasons you might think. Actually, I'm frazzled because it feels familiar?*

That practically screams, *I think I got blackout wasted and cheated on you,* which isn't what I think. Is it? I'd never allow that to happen, right?

There's so much about me that I don't know. I can't remember what type of guy I am. I only know who I've been because of her, and he wouldn't cheat—ever.

She's all I want.

Forever, her voice rings out in my head. Makes me nervous again, like it's our first date.

"Do you know how to say your alphabet backwards?" I blurt.

Really, Dean? What the hell was that?

Her high-pitched giggle draws a smile out of me like an artist draws on paper. If this is all I ever get to do, live a slow life walking around in circles with her hand in mine, then it's enough for me.

- 35 -

November 2045

Dean

A sea of smoke engulfs me as clanging debris rains down, clashing with distant cries of devastation. The pounding in my chest intensifies as my shuffling feet drag me around to every corner of this home. Lives depend on me and my mental clarity. Now is not the time to fall victim to my quivering bones.

Get the civilians, Dean. Save the civilians.

"Hello?" I call.

There's not a single sound of life.

"Hello?!"

The cracking wood replies, threatening to fall in on me.

"Hello?!" I scream as my eyes attempt to adjust to the darkness.

There's no life raft here for me in this all-consuming sea, but I'm supposed to be one for others.

I'm going to die in here.

My training has taught me how to escape, but all of it is failing me. I can't carry myself out.

I am trying.

I am trying.

Am I trying?

Will anyone even realize I'm gone? It might not be so bad, to be set free. There's nothing for me out there anyway.

Let them take me away.

My last few moments will not be spent trembling, so as I exhale my fear, I sink to the ground. It's eerily peaceful laying here as the world around me falls apart. It won't be much longer now.

Where is the rest of the crew? Why am I alone?

"Dean!" A familiar scream pierces my ears. It's a glass shattering on the floor, crashing and exploding shards into the darkness.

"Dean!" she begs, relentless in her search for me.

Pain and despair fill the air with her every breath, but no footsteps follow her call. Wherever she is, she's trapped and only I can help her.

"Hallee?" A question and request for her to come to me.

"Dean?!" Her unwavering scream saws through my hopeless heart.

Agonized adrenaline pushes me to get her, but my boots have melted to the floor and my feet have melted to my boots. She is desperate, I am desperate, we all are fucking desperate.

She needs me.

She needs me.

She needs me.

"Hallee, run! Get out of here!"

My pleading tears write a letter, but it burns in the fire before delivery.

"Run for me, baby!" My voice comes out hoarse, broken from begging. Taste blood in my mouth from screaming.

Please, God, hold up this house. Please, I'll do anything. Take me instead. Give her more time. Give her that lasting love, and let her love him more than she loves me.

"Find me, Dean."

Please, tell her I'm trying. Let her know how hard I tried.

"Find me, Dean."

We are destined to lose to this great divide.

"Find me, Dean."

"Hallee, RUN."

A loud crack in the ceiling resounds with her final plea, and hands shake me awake before the rubble engulfs us both.

"Dean."

Clear air fills my lungs as my eyes open to darkness. Through my curtains, the moon is shining onto my bookshelves. Gentle hands wrap around my waist. The familiar smell of sweet vanilla slows my racing heart.

"You're okay," she whispers.

Relief cools the burn as my head catches up to my heart in realizing she's safe. We both are, and we're together.

Laying back, I pull her into me. Feel her chest rise and fall. Feel the warmth of her living body.

"What was it about?" she asks.

Shaking my head a little, I summarize it the best I can.

"Losing you."

"You'll never lose me," she exhales, wiping away my tears.

In a month and a half, I will—when we are reduced to nothing but the rubble of a burned house.

She's been doing this recently. Talking as if we have a different fate than what's coming for us. I only nod in response. She thinks I'm agreeing with her. Don't have the heart to tell her I'm not. Really, I'm saying *yes I will*, and there is nothing I can do to stop it. My boots are burned to time, and it will drag me along no matter how hard I try, so I'll hold her.

I'll hold her until the roof caves in.

- 36 -

May 2096

The History of Psychology 2335

"At what point in the year do you think you'd flip the self-preservation switch?" a jock in the fifth row whispers to the blonde bombshell sitting next to him.

He's been hitting on her relentlessly, and either he has no pulse for social signals or he has the audacity to ignore the glaringly obvious ones she's been shooting his way. The poor girl has tried, but can't seem to escape the ever present ego of this overly confident man. He's followed her all four times that she's moved seats this semester. The shiny diamond on her left hand should be reason enough for him to back off, but nope. Even a ring won't deter the determined. I can count on one hand the amount of times I've told a man no and it has been respected the first time. This is a perfect example of that.

If he'd been paying attention a few classes ago, he would know her answer. A month is how long she suspected she'd last before shutting out any new relationships. She fiddled with her engagement ring, eyes heavy, probably thinking about losing the love of her life to time's cruel grip. The ache in her gaze remained as we all filled out our questionnaire.

It categorically placed us into different personality types, honing in specifically on a person's flexibility. Last night's homework was to review our results and write four predictions about the trajectory of our lives if we'd lived during The Experiment. My results were shockingly accurate, concluding that I'm a direct, patient, and loyal introvert. My weaknesses? Inflexibility and anxiety in unconventional situations. Science has confirmed that—to live in a world where all is forgotten—I would be royally screwed.

Class has begun to guide us in growing a distaste for The Experiment, but this exercise was excellent at highlighting how it could've ever been discussed in the first place. The world had developed into one big mistake, and no one wants to be remembered for the culmination of their worst moments. Forgiveness was rare, compassion nonexistent, and depression held a steady reign.

It's ironic, no? Depression prides itself on isolating people, on making them feel alone, yet it was the only thing that nearly everyone had. When you're already used to isolation, a lifetime of it wouldn't seem so bad to just be able to breathe again. It's easy to understand how the civilians jumped on the first option of reprieve.

Despite our collective agreement that The Gift was horribly inhumane, there are individuals who admit they'd have the potential to thrive in that circumstance. Where introverts might seclude themselves, meeting people too slowly to form meaningful connections, extroverts would quickly and easily form relationships.

The government did try to combat natural seclusion by forcing roommates upon civilians, but it's not hard to hide behind a bedroom door.

Those with an affinity for spontaneity would blossom in the lack of structure, and those with traumatic or challenging family dynamics might be thankful for the release.

"Were anyone's results similar to mine?" Mr. Holiday asks, unveiling his assessment.

Surprisingly, about half of the room's hands raise.

"The flexible, please keep your hands in the air."

A few hands drop as he continues.

"The flexible and spontaneous, please keep your hands in the air."

There go a few others. What is he doing?

"The flexible, spontaneous, even-tempered extroverts, who enjoy taking risks—please keep your hands in the air."

About half of the remaining hands to drop.

"Those who are logical in decision-making and nonconfrontational in relationships, as well as the already listed characteristics, please keep your hands in the air."

Down to eight.

"Excellent. You eight are seemingly the perfect fit for The Gift, as am I. Textbook shining stars—what an honor," he scoffs, pacing back and forth. "And what is your stance? Do you think you would thrive as a subject?"

"It seemed intriguing at first," a girl from row two answers.

"But then?"

"I think even the wildest of us need a place to call home. Traditions that build it, people who feel like it, and laughter to fill it. Everyone needs to matter to someone. Everyone needs somewhere they belong."

Unified nods come from the class.

"We are a perfect example of how people connect over shared circumstances," she continues. "What started as strangers has turned into companions on a quest for knowledge."

She's not wrong. As much as I hate to admit it, I've even grown to care for the frat pack. They can be charming . . . when they aren't being total meatheads. Isn't life just a continual acceptance and celebration of our unique complexities? The world would be so boring if we were all the same—all hollow.

Together, we could raise a community that's strong in every way. Where I lack humor, they would step up. Where the freshman lacks social awareness, the sophomore from row three would direct her with patience and grace. Where Mr. Holiday lacks energy, the annoying jock, who's still staring at that poor girl's chest, would carry him on his back.

Everyone has a special and essential role in this experience. We've grown to cherish even the smallest moments of this little life. In any and every existence, I am positive my bones would feel the deep devastation of forgetting them.

- 37 -

November 2045

Hallee

The Polaroid camera has risen above my comfort book to take the throne as my number one accessory. Dean forgot it on our last date and after we'd spent forty-five minutes backtracking to his apartment, I finally convinced him to let me keep it. There has to be tangible evidence of us. We deserve that.

Tipping the camera down, I snap a picture of our intertwined hands. Now I have proof that he usually walks on my left side. Sometimes he switches sides, claiming that if a car ever ventured off the road he would block it for me. The sentiment is cute so I play along, but the man is crazy if he thinks he'd actually stop a moving car. Regardless, I'd never hurt his pride by refusing to let him love me in this way.

Purposefully repeating a gesture from this time last year, I tap each of my fingers on the back of his hand. I've been doing that a lot lately—repeating past lives, convinced that something will trigger a memory for him.

There've been a few times where his eyes squint in this way that makes me wonder if he's started to question *the future*. If chaos can jolt him into my version of reality, dropping the craziest conversation I can remember from last year should do it.

"What if we got married?" I ask, ignoring the fact that marriages aren't acknowledged anymore. Why would they be?

His eyebrows raise like a hot air balloon in the sky, and I snap a picture of the expression. When the Polaroid develops, I'll have a permanent image of him wrestling against the memory loss. A permanent image of the entire reason I continue to hope. He's oblivious to his effort, but I'm not. He shakes off the shock, but it served its purpose.

It made him think.

"Just say when, Sunshine," he replies in his sexy raspy voice that he only uses when teasing me.

Last year he said something similar, more of a *name the time and place* situation, but this year he used my nickname.

"Would you actually want to? You know, if we could?"

He's staring at me with squinty eyes again and my stomach crunches like a coke can, as if his answer holds the power to change our circumstances anyway.

"Without a doubt."

Thank God he's sure. Would've killed me if he wasn't.

"There would be no greater honor than making you my wife," he whispers, pulling me into his chest.

"Well, honey, you dodged a bullet. You've been spared from a lifetime of being forced to eat scorched dinners, read cheesy romances, and witness countless mental breakdowns, followed by many tears and unnecessary fights."

"That's all I want."

His heart cracked with his voice. It was nearly silent, but I caught it—he's coming undone, too.

"What? Huh? You want to fight with me?" Staying light on my feet and light in my mind, I lift my fists. "Be careful what you wish for, Dean."

My first punch meets his arm with half of the force I intended. Who am I kidding? I can't even throw a punch! His lack of engagement in this joke of a fight doesn't discourage me. Throwing a left hook with a little more strength, I laugh off the embarrassment of how weak it is, despite switching hands.

"Oh, honey, this is a sweet massage. You're going to have to hit a whole lot harder to get my attention."

My eyes RSVP *yes* to his invitation. There are plenty of ways I can steal his attention. Grabbing his shirt, I tug him close, plant my lips onto his, and kiss him passionately before pulling away too quickly to be anything except a tease.

"Come on, baby. Fight for me," I whisper onto his lips.

My eyes desperately plead for him to understand the weight of that request, but his are just desperate for me.

Faking a frown, I saunter back to his side, but on step three I jump onto his back. Even when he's least expecting an attack, he'd never drop me.

Joining me in laughter, he finally taps out in our fight. The surprise attack gets him every time.

"Okay," he sorely sighs.

"Okay?"

"Okay."

"Dean!" His name comes out in a half laugh, half warning as he starts to spin. *My* world is spinning on *the* world—that's dizzying.

Letting me down slowly, he holds me upright until our hands naturally fall into each other's grip. My left in his right, his covering mine with an unwavering confidence. Our feet fall in stride together as if we're one, even as we hop over the crack in the sidewalk on Main. Finally stopped walking around it last month.

"Hallee . . ."

"Dean?"

"Did I tell you that you're absolutely radiant today?"

Somehow being complimented all the time still hasn't taught me how to accept, so I silently nod.

"Call me a sunflower because I can't take my eyes off of you, Sunshine."

"Speaking of," I hesitate. Keep 'em guessing, remember? "My room has been sad and sunflower-less lately. It's almost like the man got his woman and stopped surprising her."

The side eye I throw him is wholeheartedly playful. He's done nothing but treat me like royalty. A queen deserves sunflowers on her side table, though.

Clutching his chest tightly, he feigns a gunshot wound and yanks out the invisible bullet.

"You devastate me, my queen. Shall I compare thee to a—"

Shoving him into the empty oncoming traffic lane takes his breath away before he can finish taunting me.

"How kind of you to push me onto the runway. Finally, my turn!"

Laughter bubbles out of me, growing louder and louder as he struts. Confidence is the world's sexiest accessory and he's dripping in it, dragging his hands up his torso as he gives me a swoon-worthy spin.

When he reaches up and turns his hat backwards, I'm ready to jump into traffic with him. He knows it too, but luckily before I make a fool of myself, a car honks. Startles him, which is rare. Startles me, which is less rare.

"Sorry," he says, waving politely before returning where he belongs.

"I love you," I admit.

Woah, hello? Hallee, what the hell? We had a plan.

We were going to orchestrate a grand reveal, but—his face, and those eyes, and that laugh, and his hand—this feels just as special. Simply being together is grand enough.

"I love you too," he answers, grinning as wide as the sky.

Every step we take, I'm transported back to a memory of us doing this over and over again.

I love you, then.

I love you, there.

I love you, last year.

I love you now, I blink.

Now and a lifetime of tomorrows.

- 38 -

November 2045

Dean

After a full day of cooking, I was nearly asleep when a very excited, very awake Hallee pitched this idea to me. Turkey-coma must've clouded my judgment, because there's no way a fully conscious Dean would've agreed to this.

I have an idea, she said.

It'll be fun, she said.

Fun doesn't include scaling an old rusty ladder, but here we are. I went first, of course. There's no world in existence where I'd let her be the adventure test subject.

I can hear her down there, second-guessing how great of an idea this really is and calculating the distance of the fall I'd take if this ladder snapped.

"You're halfway!" she yells, coated in worry.

She'd hear it in my voice too, so I take a hand off the ladder to give a thumbs-up.

"Put your hand back on the ladder!"

To be a smartass, I throw a more dramatic thumbs-up. The momentum makes the ladder sway and Hallee, you guessed it—startles. Her startle startles me more than the ladder did.

What a mess.

Picking up my pace, I reach the rooftop quickly.

"I'm coming up!" she calls before I can even look over the edge.

Sure enough, here she comes. Stress climbs up my spine with every rung she fearlessly relies on. If she falls, I'm not there to catch her. I promised I always would . . . but didn't expect for it to be taken so literally.

"Steady hands, speed racer," I joke as she reaches the top.

Calm down now, heart. She's safe.

Are any of us, though?

Woah, hell no. Now is not the time for rogue questions.

"Everything you hoped and dreamed?" I ask, pulling her into a tight embrace.

"Crazy how a perspective change can make the city go from daunting to dazzling," she whispers. "Come this way." Tugging my hand, she leads me across the moonlit rooftop.

"But the city is that way."

"It's even crazier how beauty amplifies without all the noise."

"You don't like the lights?" I ask, surprised because she used to love them.

"They drown out the stars."

Without waiting for me, she sits on the edge of the roof. What a rush, dangling our legs off the edge like this. Reckless, to act as invincible as we feel. My heart skips a beat as she leans her head on my shoulder.

"I love you," I whisper into her hair.

Time dissolves as we sit in silence. There's no doubt she's silently counting the stars. Her fingers are fidgeting, which means her mind is a windmill, creating loads of energy. Nervous energy, sad energy, all the energy, because this woman never stops. Never thought of it as a privilege until now—the ability to quiet your own mind.

"I love you," I repeat, just to make sure she knows.

I'll never say it enough.

Lately there've been days where she's the happiest I've ever seen her, but those days have also highlighted the amount of times her shoulders have sagged under the weight of a silent burden. There's a heaviness to her that she refuses to acknowledge, and repeatedly avoiding it has peeled back the scab before it can heal. Her face is raw, bleeding, and begging me to understand the ache of her heart, but I love my woman patiently. She'll share when she's ready.

Three.

Two.

"Do you think there is anything out there?"

There it is.

Can't help but chuckle before I reply, "Do you actually think I've contemplated extraterrestrial life?"

The differences in the depths we think were learned long ago, but that's what makes us work so well. She talks and I listen, which is all she wants now. She wants me to listen.

"So contemplate it now, with me. What is out there?"

"I don't know, Hal. It wouldn't change anything to know."

"But maybe we aren't alone."

"Alone is not such a terrible thing to be."

She shifts back and forth like a seesaw as her face deflates.

"Alone is the most terrible thing to be." Tears pool in her eyes as she continues, "I like to think that in a different world, there's another version of us, and they get the ending we deserve."

Pretending to touch the sky, she drags her hand across the constellations. "Right now, they're sitting on their rooftop, telling all of their favorite memories to the stars for safekeeping."

A lump forms in my throat. "A constellation of memories at their fingertips."

"The stars—our ultimate friend." She sighs.

"I'm scared, Hal."

"Me too."

"We deserve better," I finally admit.

"We really, really, really, do."

Choking down my fear, I point to a particularly bright star. "That one will hold onto the first time I saw you at The Marmotte. And that one," I move my hand across the sky, "will hold the stubborn stare that glared up at me through coffee raindrops."

Her face is love, shining in the dark. Always has been, and I hope it always will be, even if it's not for me.

"That one," her voice cracks as she points to a faint little dot in the distance, "will hold your shock when I kissed your cheek outside of Happy Bookday."

She got me there; that had to have been a sight to see. It was that moment that I realized I'd never grow tired of being surprised by her.

Pointing to another, I whisper, "When I saw you in the smoke-filled apartment."

Her mischievous eyes glance at me. "The time you kissed my forehead while you thought I was asleep."

"You've been holding onto that all this time and you never told me?"

"Maybe."

"Wow, Hal. I didn't know we were in the business of keeping secrets from one another."

As if my words have struck her, she flinches before her eyes fall.

"I was just holding it until I could let it go. It's the star's now," she mutters.

"That one," I point left, forcing her to look in my direction, "will hold all of my love for you."

The warm honey in her eyes sweetens the shade of heartbreak in them.

"That one," she whispers and points straight ahead to make me look away from her, but I'm fixated on the earthside star sitting next to me, "will hold onto us."

"Us," I sigh, wrapping my arm around her as a kaleidoscope of moments collect between us.

Together, we hand them over to the constellations. All night, we reminisce and designate our favorite memories to their own star, wishing on every falling one that we could have a lifetime of nights just like this one.

- 39 -

December 2045

Hallee

Decorating for Christmas is our way of bandaging over the approaching change. The twinkling lights are doing their best to restore the serotonin that time has stolen, but even they feel dim.

"Do you guys ever think about what could have been if life wasn't like this?" I ask, tossing the Christmas lights around the tree to Avery.

She's been paying extra close attention lately. Makes me wonder if she's catching on when she asks, "What do you mean?"

"Like if we didn't forget every year."

"I haven't really thought about it," Marlowe answers, pursing her lips as her eyes widen. "Shit, I'd have a lot to apologize for!"

"I've thought about it," Avery says, eyeing me suspiciously before continuing, "but try not to focus on things I can't change."

"You're so much like Dean, it's scary."

"I take that as a compliment," she replies, smiling as she shrugs her shoulders.

"Would you change it—if you could?"

"I'm always down for a surprise," Marlowe answers, waving a hand as if it would be no big thing.

Avery gasps. "Coming from you, that's a royal endorsement for change!"

"Really, Lowe? I assumed you of all people would say no," I press.

She hesitates for a second, and I could almost swear there's a sadness behind her fire as she says, "What can I say? I keep it spicy."

"What about you, Avery?"

"I think I'd change it!"

No one elaborates, and I don't push further. That was enough of an answer for me to sleep soundly. It's ridiculous to worry this much . . . my plan might not even work, but on the off chance it does, at least I won't be ruining their lives.

We couldn't have spaced the lights more perfectly. They run out right when they reach the bottom of the tree, and I run to the light switch.

"Three."

"Two."

"One!" we sound off, and I flip off the big light.

A wave of nostalgia washes over me as I see Dean and I cuddling next to a tree identical to this one. We'd almost invited the guys over, too. There's not enough time to spend together before the year ends, but we needed our girl time. There's an inexplicable sweetness to female friendships—a role reserved uniquely for them.

"You guys—it's time," Avery whispers with a grin brighter than the lights.

"Time for what?" Marlowe asks.

Without a word, Avery sprints down the hallway, returning quickly with three identical bags. One for each of us.

"Santa came early!"

"Avery, you didn't ha—"

"Don't thank me yet, girl. This is mostly for me." The wink she shoots my way is all I need to know. These are—

"Matching jammies!" Marlowe squeals, pulling out an adult-sized reindeer onesie.

Through my giggling, I manage to muster, "Of course you would take this opportunity by the antlers, Avery." She's always trying to match with us, and other than Halloween, we've mostly turned her down.

Separating into our bedrooms, we change and prepare for the grand entrance of Santa's cutest reindeer. Avery's excitement is unmatched.

"Are you ready?" she calls.

"On Dasher!" Marlowe yells, jumping out of her doorway.

"On Vixen!" I yell, and prance out of mine.

"Wait, wait, wait," Marlowe interrupts. "I didn't realize we weren't going in order. This is *so* not fair. Why does Hallee get to be the sexy one?"

Avery drops to the floor, wheezing out a near silent, "What?"

"Oh, don't you *even* lie about it! You both know that Vixen is the ten of the group. Top-tier name, top-tier reindeer."

"I need an inhaler." Avery's hysterical, her face so red it could light the way for Santa's sleigh.

"Which one should I be then, Lowe?" I ask.

"I don't know, probably Donder!"

"WHAT?!" Gut-splitting laughter drops me to the floor with Avery. "Screw that, I'm not Donder! People don't even know his real name!"

Marlowe does her best to cover her tracks. "He's the sophisticated one, and you're always reading."

Our laughs turn into sobs, like there's so much joy that our bodies don't know what to do with it. After about five minutes, we finally compose ourselves.

"I will not settle for being the Donder of the group. Let me be Cupid!"

"Fine, but only because you're lovestruck and have been playing matchmaker all year. Don't even try to deny it. We're onto you, *Cupid*."

"I bought them. I get to choose," Avery declares, as if she's the oldest child. We let her without arguing, as if she's the youngest.

"Hallee is Cupid, Marlowe is Vixen, and *I* am Prancer."

"Prancer?!" Marlowe questions as her eyebrows lift.

"Yeah, Prancer?" I ask. "Avery, you're the freezer."

"Unless Hudson sees a side of her we don't get to." Marlowe winks.

Avery's finger flies between the two of us. "Jail, both of you."

"Cool, I'm into handcuffs," Marlowe mumbles.

"Marlowe!" I scream, cackling through the end of her name.

"Play nice! We've got a tree to decorate!" Avery insists.

As we spend hours perfectly placing every ornament, I can't help but notice how much this apartment has grown with us. Life has brought color to every room. Even if Avery and Marlowe won't remember that the fuzziest blankets are from Matt, the best Tupperware is from Dean, and the candles are from Hudson, I'm thankful that when the year changes, I'll still have them.

Dean

"I don't know, guys, she's been acting differently."

"Well, Dean. Do the math. Your expiration date is approaching like a home-run hit," Matt says.

He's much better at giving advice than setting the pace for our evening run. The women called a girls' night, so we decided to have a guys' night. Rather than drinking away our feelings, we settled on a short jog. Well, the run hasn't been short—or a jog.

"I wish I knew how to help. I worry about her." The admission slides through my gasping breaths.

"As you should. Those girls are crazy, but we love them." Hudson says.

"Love?" I push.

"You know what I mean, man," he pushes back. This could get ugly . . . fast. Hudson doesn't talk about emotions very often, just uses humor to Band-Aid over them.

"Actually, I don't. What *are* you and Avery?"

"Nothing."

"Nothing?" Matt chimes in. "What do you mean, nothing?"

"We can't be anything when there's nothing to be. We are what we are, until we aren't what we were. Okay?"

Sounds like he's about to cry, so I let that statement push me over as Matt presses his lips together.

"Matty, what about you?" I ask. "What are you and Marlowe?"

"Everything."

"Oh, fuck off, man." Hudson nearly shoves him over, laughing as he stumbles.

Nothing, everything—a mess is what we all are, and our footsteps slow as our hearts turn sad. It's a weird thing we're forced to deal with. The reality of it all set in the other night on the rooftop when there weren't enough falling stars to wish for everything I want to come true.

"I don't say it much, but I'm going to really miss them," Matt admits.

Hudson reaches over and pats his shoulder. "Me too."

"That makes three of us," I say. "We're the perfect pack."

Matt pauses for a moment, smirking before he declares, "The Sexy Six."

The light on Hudson's face snuffs out. "The apartment will feel empty without them."

"You okay?" I ask, tugging the end of his shirt sleeve.

"Are any of us?" he replies.

Matt blows out the pain from that knife to the chest.

"The apartment isn't our home anymore, Dean." Devastation pools in Hudson's wild ocean eyes as he admits, "They are."

He's not wrong. Will life feel empty when they're gone?

- 40 -

December 2045

Hallee

The year has come and gone too quickly. Does it feel like this every year? Like dying a slow death. Like days are being held hostage by time, and time is a greedy spirit taunting you with the inevitable expiration date.

Next week is Christmas already, and the anticipation has wreaked havoc on the peace Dean has brought me. He's held my hand every time I take one step forward and two steps back, healing parts of me I didn't even know were hurting. Our unbreakable friendships have built a home for our family, and our memories are worth more than a fleeting blink in time.

We're worth more than being lost.

Our love is worth more than being erased.

The slowly creeping deadline crushes my chest in with each passing minute, rendering it impossible to take a deep breath and leaving me longing for the summer days when I could finally breathe. Being underwater again over the last month has taught me that I'm better at suffocating than I used to be. But is that really such a victory?

The others haven't shown any anxiety regarding our inevitable end, only hints of sadness here and there. Marlowe's still celebrating life without consequences. Hasn't brought anyone new home, though. Haven't seen her bring Matt home, either. Avery's living in the moment of each day. Her and Hudson are . . . whatever they are, and Dean's still the steady calm in my silent stormy chaos.

He's the only one who's picked up on my energy shift—his grip is a little tighter these days—but he still hasn't addressed it. Doesn't want to rock the boat in our final days together, but he doesn't realize I'm already overboard. Time is dragging me along the jagged ocean floor while sharks circle above me.

The Christmas lights we hung in my room are supposed to be comforting, but each bulb has turned into a mocking symbol warning me of what's to come. Even the snow globe Dean surprised me with is staring me down, brutally reminding me that we're stuck. Nowhere to go except to be shaken or shattered.

I think that I'll shatter. Think I already have, actually.

The boys are coming here for Christmas, insisting it's easier for them to pack overnight bags. Reality is, our apartment has a better aesthetic than theirs, because no one needs an overnight bag anymore. Our apartments have merged into extensions of each other. Most nights we sleep in the same one, and we live and laugh in both.

We belong to both.

Will their apartment feel empty without us, as if it's built for more than it's achieving? Will Dean's room miss me like I'll miss it?

In a few days we'll have to pack up our things and bring them back to our original homes, like returning the belongings of an ex-lover. I can't bring myself to get a box, but the thought of losing the few items I've acquired over the last year feels like giving away hope that somehow something will jog my memory at the start of next year. I'm not ready to be another lost soul floating in existence, tethered to no one and nothing. This newfound gift of mine cannot go away. I will remember.

I have to.

Marlowe and Avery will still be mine, but I'm losing my home. I have to open my hands, release this love to the universe, and will it to come back to me.

My phone dings, flashing a text from Dean across the screen. He knows that I used to wake up overwhelmed by an invisible pressure to achieve. The weight of it all made my bones feel heavier, so Dean's grand mission has been to lighten the load with a good morning text. He claims that I'm his sunshine, but I only shine because he breaks apart the clouds for me.

I should probably tell him that . . . before it's too late. He'd deny it, still too humble to believe the true impact he's had on me, but in a world where I've felt overwhelmingly lost, he has given me a purpose. He's anchored me in the rocky seas. He's given me a reason.

My stomach sinks as I read the message, *Good morning, Sunshine. I can't wait to see you today!*

Can't wait, see you soon, I type, wiping away my tears, but my fingers won't press send.

With one glance at me, he'll know the weight on my shoulders and try to help, but he can't. Scrambling to take away my pain, or empathizing in sadness with me, is not the ending of the year I want for him. He shouldn't have to love me today. Shouldn't ever have to love the darkest parts of me.

Erasing the old, I replace it with the new:

Good morning, babe. Marlowe needs us today. I'll just see you tomorrow if that's okay?

As it sends, I drink in the guilt of lying to him. It's a good thing his eyes aren't here to wrangle the truth out of me.

Lol. Keep me posted on all of the drama. You know I live for it. I'll see you tomorrow.

A second text comes through seconds after the first one.

I love you.

The words are the final cut to unleash my shattered heart.

To be loved in such a deep way, in such a short time—that is a gift. I have so much more love to give than what time allows. A lifetime's worth, really.

"Liking" his message, I flip my phone back over and finally allow myself to unravel. The pillow on the right smells like him, and as I sink into its comfort, I can only hope that it will for a long while after the year concludes.

Dean

The walk to The Marmotte is surprisingly enjoyable. Cold weather is less bothersome around Christmas time. It belongs together, like Hallee and me. Any other way would feel wrong.

My shoulders fell as her text came through. It's not the first time Marlowe's called an emergency girls' day, and it'll be prime entertainment when Hallee fills me in later. Never fails to be, but the timing is rather odd.

"The most wonderful time of the year" has turned into a looming storm cloud. Time is about to pull the rug, and as much as I wish it wouldn't happen, I'm better at coping with reality than Hallee is. "Liking" my response is fairly alarming, considering her affinity for having the last word, but her friends have got her. Will next year, too, and if this year could be so amazing after losing whatever had come before, next year could be amazing, too.

Being recognized hasn't gotten old, it still brings a smile to my face when Lea waves as I walk in. "Hi Dean! One smiley sweet coffee?" she asks.

"You know me so well! What will I do next year?"

"Something tells me you'll be back."

"I hope so," I admit, offering her a somber grin.

"I'll get it right out!" She spins off to create my cup of comfort, and I spin to sit at my table of comfort.

The old couple is back on the same side of the booth, the businesswoman is on a high-stakes phone call, and the girls are in their usual spot.

Wait—the girls?

Well, Marlowe and Avery . . .

There was a weird twist in my gut when Hal texted me. The timing and the tone were off. It was a careful lie, crafted in a way she knew I'd believe, and with every pulse, my heart is insisting that something is wrong.

Panic holds my hand as I reflect on carrying her through some of her most vulnerable times. Why did she want to be alone today?

She never wants to be alone.

Last week, she brought up purpose again.

What is the purpose of it all anyway? she'd asked.

The purpose of what? I'd replied, chopping vegetables and not paying the closest attention.

. . . of living.

Her broken whisper snapped my bones. Hit an artery, and I was bleeding out when she changed the subject. I think she could tell how much it had scared me. Time went on, but the implication of the question, the hurt in her eyes when she'd asked it . . .

Dashing over to Marlowe and Avery, I almost hold it together, but don't. My calm facade is burned away by the fearful flame in my eyes.

"Where is Hallee?"

Shifting nervously at my terror, they glance to one another.

"Don't do that, don't cover for her. Where is she?"

"She said she wasn't feeling well—" Avery's voice is defeated, ashamed, and I don't let her finish before running out the door.

Come on Hal, answer the phone.

Hi! You've reached the ph—

Hang up. Try again.

Hi! You've re—

Again.

Feels like I'm running through water, and reality is blurring as panic chokes me alive. Is this how she felt that night in the club?

Hi! Y—

What is the purpose of it all? she'd asked.

I can't believe I didn't say it. Can't believe I let her brush it off. My veins pulse, screaming the unsaid words.

Love, Hal.

Love is the purpose of it all.

The words accelerate the treadmill in my mind, forcing my feet to run faster. Every inhale is painful, and every exhale is a plea of desperation that the weight of the world has not crushed her.

Please, let her be alive.

Her apartment door is locked, and I thank God for my emergency training as I kick it in, no problem. For one second, my hand lingers above her bedroom door handle. Just one second to brace for the impact of my worst nightmare coming true.

One.

The bedroom door opens easily—wasn't locked, and that's a good sign. A little fucked up that I know that, but I do. It looks like she's sleeping, motionless on her bed, but is she sleeping?

Come on Hal, please be sleeping.

I'm not ready to know.

Not ready to settle for her voicemail when I need to hear her voice. Not ready to be cold all year without her light. Not ready to forget what it feels like to belong to someone.

I'm not ready to let go.

Moving forward feels like ripping off a Band-Aid, but she jolts awake before I can touch her. Always aware, my girl. Even in her sleep.

Her hands fly to my chest, instinctively shoving me away, and tears slide down my face like my back slides down the wall. Never thought I'd be so relieved to see her startled. My voice box is locked and my hands held the key, but they've dropped it in the stream of my falling flood. I'm frantically broken and silently shaking under the microscope of her stare. The thought of losing her shattered me. Will *actually* losing her shatter me too?

She's breathing, her chest is rising and falling.

She's wearing my shirt. The one from the first night she stayed over, before we knew how scary it would really be to love and to know we'll lose it. Before life was hard, and dreams were unreachable, and love maybe wasn't enough.

She's wearing my shirt and it's holding her like I should, and I can, so I will. I always will, until I won't. Because soon, can will be can't, and will will be won't, and forever will dissolve in our tears.

"Dean, what—"

My hand flies up, cutting her off. I need one silent minute to realize all I thought I'd lost is still here.

My Sunshine is still here—until she's not.

Climbing out of bed, she sits down in front of me, criss-cross like how she sits at her coffee table. Rests her hands on her knees, palms up for me to hold, and my muscles relax as mine cling to her warm touch.

"I saw Marlowe and Avery at The Marmotte, but you weren't there. You weren't answering my calls. I couldn't get here fast enough. I couldn't get to you. I—"

She gently brushes my tears away, her face now covered in her own.

"How are we supposed to do this?" she asks, voice as broken as her eyes. "How are we supposed to live knowing we'll lose it all?"

Her shoulders shake as she combusts into a full-body sob. I feel it too—the pain that's ripping her apart. It's nearly too much to bear.

"I don't want it, Dean. It's not a gift to forget. I want the highs and lows, the light and the dark, the clean and messy, the joy and the pain. I want ten thousand bad days for one good day with you. I want to laugh with you, cry with you, and grow old with you."

"I know, Hal. Come here."

Snuggling in close, she cries into my chest. "They've stolen the purpose of life. They've stolen it, and sold us all a lie that a life without regret would set us free."

As I scratch her back, she continues, "They trained us, rewired us, and handed us our priorities on a silver platter so beautiful we never questioned their promises. Their pretty gift bow has trapped us all." Screaming through her sobs, rage coats every single word.

The cold floor is a chilling reminder of how cold life's about to be, so I cradle and carry her to the bed.

"I didn't want to let them steal more than they already have—to allow the fear of losing you to overtake our last few days. It's paralyzing, Dean, the burden of feeling deeply."

A year of loving her through panic has taught me that it's worse when her neck gets too warm. Pulling her hair back, I try to meet her gaze. "You're not alone, Hal."

Eyes locked on the floor, she sighs.

"Hallee."

Lights are on, no one's home.

"Look at me," I whisper. Breaks my heart watching that lip tremble. Delicately lifting her chin, I lead her gaze to mine. "There's no part of you that's a burden to me. I love you—even the parts you hate. You believe this world has broken you, but even our brokenness will be used, Hal."

"How could they do this to us? What are we going to do?"

"You will be you."

"I don't even know who I am. I'm just broken pieces of who I wanted to be."

"You are radiant, every piece of you. They may take my mind, but my heart will remember and follow your scattered pieces of sun. Time and time again, my soul will carry me home. You're mine. Not theirs."

My lips seal the wish with a kiss on her forehead, and her breathing finally calms.

I believe it. I really do, every word of it. There's no world in existence where I wouldn't find her again.

As she holds up her pinky, I interlace it with mine.

"It's a pinky promise now," she whispers, nodding three times, "and you know how seriously I take my pinky promises."

- 41 -

December 2045

Hallee

Focusing on my five senses seems to calm my pounding heart. Sight: Dean. Gray sweatpants and morning hair all tousled from waking up early. Smell: homemade cinnamon rolls. Sound: a TV fireplace, crackling in the background of our friends' laughter. Smart of the landlords to not include actual fireplaces in the apartments. I nearly burned the building down without one; imagine the damage that could be done with one. Touch: the cold countertops. Taste: Irish coffee topped with whipped cream and peppermint chips.

The taste was my way of proving that I *can* be helpful in the kitchen, and Marlowe and Avery seem thoroughly helped. Cuddled under a blanket by the tree, they're two princesses waiting patiently for their breakfast.

Beaming with satisfaction, Dean plates the food. He looks happier this year than last. What a strange thing—to be able to compare where we started to where we are.

What an important thing.

Makes my love for them stronger.

As we gather around the coffee table, Matt turns on Christmas music. It feels like a knife to the chest and sounds like a funeral procession. As our forks hit the plates, we laugh over the montage of memories made this year. Tiptoeing around the elephant in the room is our strongest talent.

"I'd give anything to see Dean's face again when he realized it was Hallee standing on the counter," Hudson quips. Nods of agreement are passed around as everyone finishes their bites.

"I'd like to revisit the look on Marlowe's face while Matt walked them out. What did you whisper to me, Marlowe? I can't seem to remember," I tease.

It's all in good fun, but what even *are* they? They still haven't come clean, and my need for control is making me pushy. The blush on her cheeks signals for a subject change, and Dean jumps in to save the day.

"Who's ready for presents?"

As the guys clean up, I take a long drink of my coffee and lean toward Marlowe.

"I'm sorry, I didn't mean to—"

"We aren't together, okay? It's complicated. Please, drop it."

Everything is complicated these days, but the embarrassment on her face hints that it isn't Marlowe who chose their label. Were they ever anything? All those times I've teased her—could I have been rehashing a wound?

Dean is listening intently to Matt, who looks like he might throw up, and that's enough to make me retire. *Cupid* is done shooting the arrow. What will be will be. They would've been great together, though.

I don't dare let my eyes linger as Avery and Hudson break off on their own to exchange gifts. Matt and Marlowe do the same, exchanging *together but not together* gifts, and Dean and I settle onto the couch.

"Buying a gift for you was hard, okay? I did my best." I sigh. "Nothing was good enough . . . for me, anyway. Anything would be good enough for you."

His eyebrows raise, flagging me down.

"Wait, that sounds wrong! You'd love anything I'd give you. That's right."

"I'm going to love it, Hal."

The silence as his hands carefully unwrap the present is loud as hell.

"It was so important to get it right that I could barely pick anything at all, but after countless sleepless nights, I recruited the help of an artist in town."

It's priceless, the vibrance that art adds to the world.

"A mug," he cheers, chuckling as he glances up at me.

"Your very own handcrafted mug, and look!" He spins the mug as I point.

Reading the hand-stamped clay, he smiles. "Meet me at The Marmotte."

"She painted the front of the shop. Absolutely crushed it, right?"

"Right. You did too."

"Even if you won't know who you're looking for—"

"I'll know where to find you."

Tears fill those galaxy eyes, and I can't help but think about the first time I saw them, but if they overflow, my eyes will too.

"Look inside," I squeak, ignoring the obvious tension in the room. "The artist painted a marmot! We thought if there was a cute little mascot it'd ease the sting of finishing your coffee."

There's been a lot of sting to ease lately. Carefully setting it down, he cups the sides of my face.

"I love it."

"Yeah?"

"Yes. It's perfect."

As he kisses my forehead, I rub the side of the mug three times. Lots of threes happening lately, but we need a lot of luck. Maybe somehow it'll release a genie to grant us three wishes. I'd probably wish that the genie would bottle us up, put us on a shelf, and save this moment forever. How many years would it take for that to feel like a trap too?

"Your turn, Hal," Dean says, sliding the present into my lap.

"Why are you looking at me?"

"We've been over this. Life's too short to not appreciate beautiful things, like watching the love of your life open their Christmas present."

"Can you not?" I ask, laughing and tearing it up quickly to get out of the spotlight.

Oh.

My.

"Cream crewneck!"

"I knew it!" Matt gasps from across the room.

"Oh my gosh, it's pristine. Softer than I ever remembered. How did you fix it?"

"Fix it? Nah, that thing was long gone from the moment we said hello. This is a new one."

Well, that's the sweetest thing he's ever done. I knew I'd picked the right guy to love.

"Dean, I looked for a replacement for months! Searched high and low, scavenging the internet from dead end to dead end! I couldn't remember what store it came from!"

"What can I say? I'm an excellent detective."

Oh my gosh, no wonder I could never find it. Holding it up now, I remember—it was always a present from him.

"Did you get this at the same place as last time?"

Subtle, Hal. Very subtle.

Puzzled expressions fly around the room, and Dean's head tilts like it always does right before he smiles.

"What?" He asks, smiling.

I knew it.

Giggles flow out of me like champagne bubbles. There's no taking it back once the nervous energy flows. Time for damage control.

"Where did you find this?"

"A magician never reveals their tricks," he whispers, leaning in and kissing my cheek.

"Psssst, Hallee," Avery mutters, pointing to Hudson.

"Did you keep a secret, Hudson?"

"He's been looking for that since the day he walked through our door with your ruined one. He clung to that thing like a lost puppy, it was actually a little embarrassing."

Dean's bashful stare confirms it. Shoving aside the wrinkled wrapping paper, I climb to snuggle on his lap.

"Thank you," I breathe, laying my head on his shoulder.

"You're welcome."

While he holds me, we take mental pictures of the family we've built. The next holiday is the one I dread the most, and these are the memories that will break my fall when we plummet down with the landslide.

- 42 -

December 31, 2045

Dean (3.5 hours until Midnight)

"We have to make one stop. It'll be fast, I promise." The words come out carefully, treading lightly around the tension growing in Hallee because of the change. She's clueless, but I've already calculated this stop into the schedule. I told her I'd pick her up for the New Year's party an hour earlier than I actually needed to.

Like clockwork, she exhales. Sounds pretty annoyed, but I let it slide because I know who I love. "Dean, we're going to be late to meet everyone."

No we won't, I want to scream, but I settle for, "Trust me, Sunshine."

She must be extremely frazzled to have not caught on yet; we've taken this walk almost every day this year. When I picked her up, I thought my clean-shaven face blew my cover. A wide grin squinted her eyes into a sliver of suspicion at me ending the year looking how she likes me the best. Although she wanted to ask, she let it rest.

It's one of the few times she hasn't gone digging for details, and I'm proud of her for that.

Flurries fall down, shining in the glow of the street light, and her clicking heels settle my nervous stomach.

Click, we're in the park.

Click, we're dancing in the kitchen.

Click, we're anywhere but here.

Nerves come back with a vengeance at the sight of The Marmotte's sign. It's, literally, now or never, and every step closer to our home away from home makes my hands sweat.

Click, we're sprinting through the wildflowers.

Click, we're dancing in the club.

Click, she's drawing a heart on my arm.

My steps chase the images of us—of the promising future we would have had in different circumstances. As our footsteps stop outside of The Marmotte's door, I lean into her warmth. I'm the window, she's the sun—remember?

"Dean?" she asks, blinking three times.

Haven't quite figured out why she always does things in threes. Wish I had the time to.

"One stop."

Confused on the street, she stares at me as I wink and climb the steps. As confident as ever, I tug on the door. Except, it doesn't budge.

"They're closed for the holiday, Dean. Let's just go to the party."

Pull again, harder this time, and nothing.

My phone dings, undoubtedly a text from Matt or Hudson apologizing for the hiccup, but checking my phone might give me away. We discussed the details for months, there was very little room for misinterpretation.

Alright, shake it off. Can't let her see me sweat. Tonight has to be perfect.

Before I get too stressed, the lock turns. It's a shame we lent the Polaroid camera to Marlowe, because the look on Hallee's face is priceless.

"What's going on?" she nervously asks.

Surprises aren't her cup of tea, but this is my final grand gesture to remind her of how much she means to me, and how much my life has been changed because of her.

"I called in a few favors from Lea. Apparently no one else has taken the time to learn her name this year. Even the smallest moments matter. *You* have taught me that."

There's this long pause, like we're suspended in time. Like if we don't move, life won't change, but if I linger any longer she'll cry. Reaching out my hand, I bow. "Our personal infinity awaits, milady."

Milady, seriously? Since when do I talk like an 1800s prince when I'm nervous? Luckily, she giggles and gives me my favorite expression—eyes nearly shut because her nose scrunches up, her cheeks raised high on her face. There aren't enough hours left for me to paint it into my brain.

Her hand comes home to mine as I help her up the stairs. The Marmotte's bell dings and, for the first time, she doesn't startle. Will she next year?

The warm air brushes over our faces. This place has always comforted us from the cold.

Taking her coat, I hang it on one of the pegs. She won't want to be wearing it once she walks in. It's one of the little things I have the luxury of knowing about her as her best friend *and* lover. Pretty rare to have both, don't you think? I think so. Makes us extraordinary. Our memories have built us a castle that will withstand the test of time. It has to.

"Oh. My. Gosh." Hallee gasps, covering her face immediately at the sight of the room.

I rush to settle her shaky shoulders and her forehead falls on my chest, in love and in defeat. For a few moments, I hold her as her authentic self. Lord knows we've worked so hard to get to the place where she believes she matters. I wouldn't dare trample over that now.

My gleaming eyes glance around to keep from tearing up. Hudson's staring back at me, his face a bit broken. His eyes are reflection pools, waiting to overflow.

"*Wow*," I mouth.

Lifting his hands, he gestures, *I don't know.*

Of course he knows, but I sure don't. I have absolutely zero idea the hoops our friends jumped through for us to ensure we have this last perfect evening. It's beyond anything I could've ever imagined.

It's whimsical, it's magical, and it's everything happy. They've built a time capsule of our every emotion—of everything I love about my girl.

It is the best of us, without the looming storm cloud of worry. Together, they've transformed our place into a safe haven where only beautiful things exist. A world where there is no pain, anxiety, or loss. Where even the minor details are remembered. Where beautiful light shines, and sunflowers are returned home to their sun.

They've built a momentary wonderland where forever exists and dreams really do come true.

Hallee

The candlelight grabbed my attention first. The whole room looked yellow, as if it was on fire, but then I saw them.

The sunflowers.

Dean crashed into me before I could fall, holding me up because this life isn't real. If I don't move, we don't exist. If we don't exist, then we can't go away. We can stay here forever and cease to exist together, right? Please, tell me I'm right.

He's done it.

He has completed the impossible task of slowing me down—of anchoring me to this moment. My restless hunger for hurry has been curbed, and even my mind has finally halted on its endless spiral to nowhere. Safe in his arms, I squeeze him tightly and breathe in his scent. After all this time, it has remained the unfailing antidote for my anxiety.

Our place. It's shining in the moonlight for us.

Candles line the edges of an aisle leading to our table. Somewhere along the course of the year, the middle went from the scariest to the best place to be. The middle of the room, the middle of the bed, the middle in the group of our friends. Who would've thought?

The rest of the tables are gone, replaced by an endless sea of yellow. He turned our sanctuary into a sunflower field for me.

A *click* comes from the corner of the room, and a few chuckles respond to my small jump. I know those chuckles . . .

Marlowe and Avery.

There they are, waving at me from the corner with Hudson and Matt. Their tuxedos of confidence are paired with their infamous devilish grins. Please, let me remember those grins.

"I had to recruit backup, but—" Dean whispers, pausing when my eyes catch his. "Every sunflower within a seventy-five mile radius has officially been returned home to its sun."

This has to be a joke. He can't be serious. My open jaw begs for the punchline, but why is he just staring at me?

He's actually serious?

"Dean," I breathe, unsure if he can even hear it. He's so sweet, and this life is so great, and this life is about to change.

Hudson whistles from the corner, and as Marlowe pushes play on the music, Dean lifts his arm for me to spin under like a princess at a ball.

Chill bumps cover my arms as lyrics of first looks, dark rooms, and time moving way too fast fill our place. The song Marlowe and Avery originally used to tease me, now a song to celebrate us. Dean's presence washes away all of my insecurities. There are no clouds in my sky when he's with me. Laying his hand on my lower back, he draws me in for a dance.

"Welcome to our underground wedding, Sunshine."

Click.

Marlowe captures my shock.

I can't believe he actually did it.

We are our very own secret society of sunflowers, defying the government in the most pure way—in pursuit of light and love. The realest and truest form of it. To have and to hold for whatever eternity is to come. *This* is our very own little infinity.

"But—it won't be recorded. It won't matter aft—"

"It matters." Dean's strong voice cuts through my doubt. "It matters. It's never foolish to do things that make you happy, regardless of if it's valued by others. You asked earlier this year if there were many ways to matter. My answer is yes, and this—*us*—matters. We matter. Separately and together we are great, but let it be together. Please, let it be together."

His eyes hold my heart while it splinters at the desperation lining his face.

"Dean, I—" can't breathe as he drops to one knee.

"Marry me, Hallee. Let me love you with reckless abandon. Be my wife."

Wife.

The word replays in my mind, searching for a memory associated with it. All I can recall is our conversation about the possibility of this in a different life. Never has he gone this far.

I've never married him.

"How could I ever say no to those eyes?"

Cheers erupt from our friends, fading to the background as he sweeps me off my feet in a passionate kiss. Could be seconds, could be minutes, before Matt clears his throat. We *did* just agree to marry each other. Now is probably the time to do it, because well, tick-tock.

Hopping over to us, Hudson sifts through the sunflower field.

"Congratulations." His voice cracks, absent of its usual hint of humor as he hugs me. A tear falls from his face as he pulls away.

"Hallee, there's no good way to ask this, but would you allow me the honor of walking you down the aisle?"

Gesturing to the candlelit walkway, he flinches at my wavering breath.

"I totally don't have to! No hard feelings at all. We just thought that after everything we've been through, maybe you wouldn't want to be alone."

It's the first time I've heard nerves in his voice. He's completely unaware that my tears are an outpouring of gratitude for his offer. Matt would've been wonderful too, but Hudson, the chronically unserious friend, wanting to escort me doubles the impact of the intention.

"I would love that," I blubber between sobs.

"Then if you would come with me, milady."

"Seriously, milady?" I accidentally laugh in his face. We really have impacted each other, even down to our shared vocabulary.

"I'll see you up there," Dean whispers, pressing a quick kiss to my forehead and skipping away.

"Pulse check. You nervous?" Hudson asks, leading me back to the claustrophobic entrance of The Marmotte.

"I'm always nervous."

"Excited?"

Yes.

Can't say it though, or I'll cry. He knows it, too. Reaches out and gently brushes my hand before pinching the same pressure point that Dean does, in between my pinky and ring finger.

"How did you know that calms me down?"

"Lucky guess."

"You're the closest I'll ever get to having a brother," I admit.

Do I have one out there?

Dean's right. There are many ways to matter, and I'm not sure that any single way is greater than the other. My soul craves friendship as much as it longs for a deeply romantic love. My heart thrives on the days when I feel so carefree I could almost float away, but I wouldn't know the value of those days without the ones where anxiety paralyzes me. The days where I feel trapped in a shrinking box of my own thoughts matter just as much as tonight does, because without the darkness I would never appreciate the light.

Maybe the importance of something is not about being ranked on a vertical scale where one thing comes out victorious. Maybe it's a horizontal spectrum for us to travel across over time, constantly reassessing and redefining what we need in that current moment. Life is a cluster of significance, with the little moments constantly shaping us into different versions of ourselves.

As a guitar melody plays over the speakers, Hudson glances down at me.

"Love ya, sis."

"Love you too."

"Shall we?"

Squeezing his arm three times, I reply, "Don't let me fall."

Too bad, I already have.

- 43 -

December 31, 2045

Dean (3 hours until Midnight)

Do you think Hallee realizes now why Marlowe forced her to wear white tonight? My woman put up an excellent fight, insisting that white on New Year's is socially unacceptable. I've never known her to back down from a belief, but against all odds, she was convinced.

Hallee's been asking Avery for weeks why she suddenly had to work late. Avery somehow successfully swerved her questions, hiding that she'd been meticulously practicing sunflower arrangements to create the perfect bouquet. Hal's heart would explode at the dedication our friends have shown to celebrate us.

As Hallee walks home to me, the moonlight dances across the sequins of her dress and shimmers on her tear-soaked cheeks. The veil between heaven and earth is torn, and for a moment we get to feel eternal. Heaven has descended to earth, I swear it.

Stopping before me, she unlinks her arm from Hudson's.

"Thanks for taking care of her, sir. You raised a good one," I joke, firmly shaking his hand.

"Take care of her." He smiles, drawing a few chuckles from Avery and Marlowe. Even Hallee spares a giggle. As she steps forward, the smell of her perfume brings along an unexpected clash of emotion.

This is the happiest day of my life.

This is the saddest day of my life.

Today we gain and we lose, and I'm not ready. Don't think I'd ever be.

The paradox of emotions is almost too much to bear as Matt opens our wedding ceremony. "Good evening. We gather here together to celebrate the extraordinary display of love that continuously pours out of these two wonderful individuals."

Wow, he's being formal. The air of respect, of honor, for how far we've come is nothing that I expected but everything I needed.

"Dean and Hallee, you have redefined what it means to love your neighbor. Individually, you have brightened the lives of your friends, but together you have been an unwavering force of hope for us all. You are our reason to believe that good things can continue to flourish in devastating circumstances."

As she meets my gaze, I search for the pages of emotion I'm used to reading. All I see is joy. Pure joy—for what we were, are, and will be.

"Dean, you wanted to say a few things?"

"Yes, I did. I mean, I do."

"Not time for the I dos yet, Dean," Matt mumbles out of the side of his mouth.

Hallee's face falls a bit as she admits, "Dean, I didn't prepare anything. I didn't know."

"I know, Hal. I don't want anything other than your unfiltered, unapologetic self. You're the one who is good with words, remember? It was me who needed to practice for this."

And I have—practiced. In the quiet moments after she falls asleep, in the shower, at the station, waiting for coffee, I've trained my mind to love her better in this way.

"Do me a favor?"

"Of course."

"Just listen and accept everything I say to you. Can you do that for me?"

Swallowing down her tears, she takes a wavering breath.

"Of course," she sighs.

The words I can offer are not a vow of promises to keep, but a eulogy to honor the love we have held so close.

"My stubborn, complex, essential Hallee. You are so incredibly easy to love, and my only regret is not telling you sooner. All of my best qualities have been strengthened by you, and my worst have shrunk substantially because of your light." Pride swells in my chest that she doesn't shake her head no. I knew she'd feel different after a year with me.

"In our free fall down to see how deep our love could span, you have captivated me. The way you've protected your ability to see the world with compassion. The bravery you exude in daring to dream beyond the constructs of this life. The kindness you show in acknowledging every single stranger you pass. The way your nose crinkles when you giggle. The way you've never given up on your quest to get me to read. The blush that floods your cheeks when you burn dinner. The hamster wheel of thoughts running wild in your beautiful mind—they are all part of the infinite reasons why I love you and am *forever* changed because of it. My heart is tattooed with the language of our love, and somehow, somewhere, someday, I will remember you. To put it simply, I love you more than you love an organized schedule, twinkly lights, painted sunsets, a takeout vanilla latte, and listening to Taylor Swift. And *that* . . ." I pause, reaching up to cradle the side of her face, "that is an immeasurable amount of love."

My words taking her breath away is the most tangible example of how much better I am because of being loved by her. Her tears rain onto my hand as she cradles it on the side of her face. If we stayed like this through midnight, would we still forget?

"My gentle, loving, kind, Dean."

Another wave of pride rushes through my chest because it's true—I'm all hers. It's the best thing I'll ever be.

"What a gift it has been to know a timeless love. Your selfless, patient, steady, and consistent pursuit of me has been the most exceptional display of love in its purest form. You have challenged each of my insecurities and re-framed them in a positive manner. Where shame once ruled, love has won. I'm kinder to myself, and to others, because of the confidence I've built, just by being loved by you. I will never forget—" Her voice breaks and grip tightens as she closes her eyes for a moment before meeting mine again. "I will never forget the way you smirk seconds before teasing me, the way your head tips back when you are laughing extra hard, the butterflies in my stomach when I look into your eyes and the desire in them as you hold me, the words you have said to me, or the way my world is a million times lighter with you in it. You are the buoy that holds me above the crashing tide, reminding me of goodness, of hope, and of joy. Rewriting the law of the land, you've built me a reality where my wildest dreams have come to life. It has been the great joy of my life to love you and to be loved by you."

Inhaling quickly, her breath is shaky as she continues, "Because of you, I finally know peace. I will love every part of you, forever. You are, and always will be, my favorite reason."

The devastation behind her *never forget* echoes off the walls of my chest. Makes me want to cry a bit. Makes me want to die a bit. If we die, can this be our reality? Is there an afterlife where we can exist together?

The beautiful fragility behind her trusting stare strengthens me. I've never loved her more than I do right now, and I'll only love her more with each second until midnight. I'll love her after midnight, too. Won't remember her, though.

Leaning down and resting my forehead onto hers, I cup the sides of her face and lace my fingers into her hair as if it will tie her to me.

"Can you promise me one thing?" I whisper.

Her silent stare answers for her. *No, I can't.*

No one can promise anything anymore, yet I find the courage to ask.

"Will you paint me a sunset someday?"

Hallee

Our falling tears water the sunflowers as our hearts are pulled apart by the contradiction of holding on tightly and letting go. I chose my words carefully, acknowledging the best things that I *will* remember about him, and refusing to speak about us as something being washed into the past.

Hudson's holding Marlowe and Avery together through the sadness creeping in. There's not a dry eye in the room as they watch the assumed conclusion of our love story. However, this can't be the end for me. This will just be a carriage ride back to the beginning of our next life together. There's no estimated time stamp on the loneliness that awaits, but I will be warmed by the fire of hope that has set up camp in my bones.

My fingers cling to the ghost of Dean's hand as he reaches into his pocket, pulling out two identical gold bands.

"Have you been planning this since the park?"

"Consider your theory confirmed, Hal. There's always an ulterior motive when a man buys jewelry."

"I knew it." I giggle through a sob.

"I'm sorry it's nothing extravagant, but I thought that it'd be best if they didn't draw any unnecessary attention. We can wear them into next year so when it comes down to it, I'll always carry your love with me, and you mine."

"It's perfect, Dean."

He's as gentle with the rings as he's been with me, delicately twisting them in his fingers while standing and staring. After nearly a year of us, he is still just Mr. Stand and Stare. With his help, I have picked up my pieces and created a mosaic worthy of his attention. I am finally the work of art he once suggested I was, custom-made to hang in the home of his heart.

Glancing at him with all of the warmth I have left, I lift my left hand. Matt begins his final speech as Dean's trembling hands slide the ring onto my finger, and I do the same for him.

"With these rings as a symbol of your undying love, you are committing to carry a piece of each other with you, always. Dean, is this a commitment you are able to uphold? If so, now is the time for the damn *I do*."

"I do," he says, laughing like he can't believe this is happening.

"Hallee, is this a commitment you are able to uphold? If so, please say I do."

"I do," I whisper, barely able to speak.

"With the approval and final authority of The Sexy Six, I now pronounce you husband and wife. Dean, you may kiss your bride."

His eyes roam over my body before he pulls me in for a kiss. Beginning softly and building with passion, he dips me down in the safety of his arms as our favorite fans cheer. None of this would have been as exceptional without them.

"It is my greatest honor to announce as a couple, Mr. and Mrs. Dean . . . uh . . ." Matt tries to stifle his laugh because none of us know our last names.

"Mr. and Mrs. Dean!"

Hysterical laughter overpowers the pain. Even in sadness, there is joy.

"Time to party!" Marlowe cheers, sprinting behind the coffee counter. Dipping down, she lifts a beautifully decorated cake.

"It took awhile, but I finally perfected the Peter method. Turns out I *can* be good at listening," she quips.

"Ah, the Peter method. How could I forget?"

Dean's eyes squint suspiciously as we cut into the cake. "Come here, Hal."

"Absolutely not."

"Why? You afraid of a little cake?"

"You wouldn't dare." My eyes flare as he pretends to shove it in my face.

"Right as always, Sunshine."

Marlowe pops champagne as we feed each other the first bite.

"Shit," she mumbles as it bubbles over her hand and onto the floor. "Lea's only request was to not make any major messes."

"What will they think about the sunflower field sitting in their table space?" Avery asks.

"Yeah, they're beautiful, but wouldn't leave a very good tip," Hudson jokes.

"I can't take all of them with me, can I?" I ask. Maybe someone will think the display was for them and feel special on the first day of the year.

"I've got it handled. The Marmotte will be restored to working order by opening day," Dean answers. Even now, he calms my obsessive need for control.

"One final order of business," Avery says, winking and joining Marlowe behind the counter. "The official, Top Secret, Marriage License of Dean and Hallee."

"Are we actually doing this?" I ask as Dean and I look from each other to the paper.

"We're doing this," he says with a single nod.

Happiness and sadness go head-to-head in the boxing ring as he grabs the pen. Happiness is starting to win, throwing an uppercut as he proudly signs his name—including a last.

"Did you make that up?" I ask, and the fire of hope flares. *Please say no*, I blink.

"I did."

Sadness takes a knockout punch.

"I love it." The words choke out as I kiss his cheek.

Picking up the pen, I sign my name—first and last.

"That settles it. You two are officially *Most Likely to Elope*," Matt jokes.

This year's title is my favorite so far. Wait, does he—?

"Hudson is *Life of the Party*," Avery murmurs.

"Avery is *Best Dressed*, for sure," I say, holding Matt's intrigued gaze. "Her closet really is impeccable."

"Flawless taste, truly," Marlowe says as every single one of us nods. "Matt is *Most Musical*."

"Marlowe is *Best Laugh*," Matt responds.

It's true. I'm glad I won't have to miss it tomorrow. Matt's eyes fall because he'll have to.

"Okay, okay, you all got individual ones," Dean says. "We do too. Hallee is *Most Likely to Change the World*."

My shoulders tense. Does he know?

Will he ever know?

"Dean—" I swallow. Am I about to do what I'm about to do? "Dean is *Most Likely to Be Remembered*."

Life ceases to exist. Even the ground shudders at the strength of my final arrow aimed at The Gift. Is the room spinning? The air is getting thicker . . .

"I think a toast is in order!" Marlowe interrupts, sparing us from the approaching mental breakdown.

Raising his glass, Hudson starts us off. "To doing things that matter to us."

"To creating pockets of joy," Avery sounds off.

"To a year of a life well lived," Matt joins, raising his glass with the others.

"To the most bold and reckless display of affection," Marlowe chimes in, smirking at Dean.

"To finding each other again," I whisper.

"To *forever*," Dean closes the toast.

This time, there's no uncomfortable energy shift as there had been the first time I spoke of *forever*. There's a charged silent agreement between the six of us—we will not be diminished down to a stunted future. Tomorrow, they will be scattered pieces of fabric waiting to be stitched together, and I will be the seamstress.

My memory will reunite us all.

- 44 -

December 31, 2045

Hallee (1.5 hours until Midnight)

Walking down the front steps of The Marmotte felt like walking away from everything good in the world. No one dared to take a step away as the door slammed shut behind us. Marlowe was the one to try and ease the devastating reality of goodbye.

"We'll see you tomorrow," she said, staring into my widely terrified eyes.

"Tomorrow," I replied, and the devastation in her glassy eyes as they flicked to Matt made it that much harder to breathe.

Glancing to Marlowe and Avery, Dean's voice broke as he said, "Take care of each other. Please, take care of my wife."

"We will," Avery whispered, choking back a cry as Hudson pulled me into the world's tightest hug.

"You be good, you hear me? In here," Hudson paused, gently tapping my chest. I inhaled deeply, breathing in his final moments of kindness as his hand raised. Staring into my soul and tapping my forehead three times, he added, "And in here, yeah?"

My face shattered with my heart as I nodded and Matt pulled me close, holding my head tightly as if he could hold my mind together. "You heard him," he whispered, kissing my forehead. "Hold the line, Hal."

"I love you," I cried, clinging to their hands as if a tight grip would embed the words in their skin, and that was it. Whatever we'd been ended as quickly as it had begun. Everyone else chose to go to the party, drowning themselves in alcohol and leaving us to drown in each other before time burns us away.

The door closes behind us as Dean lifts me, pressing me up against it. Holding tight to the back of my thighs, his kisses trail up my neck to my ear. Exhaling the last of my nerves, my fluttering breath makes him freeze. One hint of discomfort moving forward, and he'd stop. No questions asked. There would be no waiting until I finally had the courage to say no . . . if I ever did. His continued dedication to leading with the highest level of respect is the entire reason I trust him enough to cross this line. To give him all of me.

Lowering my feet to the floor, his hands trail up my body and tilt my chin up. Brushing his thumb over my lower lip, his eyes lock onto mine.

"Have you ever?" he asks, eyes gleaming with desire.

"I can't remember."

Without repeating history, the final answer is still held captive by my mind's trigger guard.

"Neither can I," he admits, chuckling through the sadness of that statement.

The consequence of uncomfortably running into a past lover has been erased, but the potential of a sacred, loyal love has been stolen.

"Hallee, this is the only time I'll ask you—"

This plane is going down. How dare he quote me from our first date?

"Do you want this?"

I can't speak. If I speak, my voice will break, and I'll hear the sound, and the sound will remind me of all the times his voice has broken for me. All the times his heart has, too.

"You wanted to be defined by a great love, Hal. Whether we do this or not, we have achieved that. We have known and been marked by an undeniably great love."

My head nods, shaking tears free as his lips fall to my forehead. There is no greater act of love, even if it's our departing gift to one another.

We had taken it so slow, building our emotional connection and holding back the physical one. Should we have done it differently? The time was ticking past us, regardless of how hard we tried to stop it. Maybe in another life we will understand how a government could do this—how they could be so careless with their people.

For now, we are left to weather the brunt of their cruelty. Excuses of good intentions don't erase the need for accountability. Someone should pay for the damage they've done, but our souls didn't purchase the extra insurance coverage.

"Where'd my Sunshine go?" Dean's words pull me from my thoughts, and my eyes return to his gravity. "There she is."

He's my whole world. We have reached the final descent of our fall together, and I couldn't be more thankful for the leap we took from that very first date.

"I need to hear you say it, Hal."

Smiling, I recall the words he'd said to me in the midst of my fear.

"I've got you, Dean. Let's fall."

Unleashing our caged passion, our bodies collide. His jacket hits the floor, and the sound echoes through my mind as I hear it from years past. As he lifts his shirt over his head, I watch his shoulders rise and fall. The pace of his expanding chest matches my pounding pulse.

Slowly, and delicately, he strips away the final barriers between us, revealing all of me to him. Hesitating for a moment, his eyes travel over my body. As I reach to nervously twist my hair, his hand catches mine midair.

"Stop," he pleads. "Let me look at you."

I laugh to cover how odd it feels to have someone know me this intimately. Nervous habit strikes again and I reach up, but he softly grabs my wrists.

"You are astonishing," he whispers into my neck, laying me down gently.

Chills slide down my body with his hands. They're slow but sure, engraving every inch of me into his mind. My hands match his pace, tracing my very own constellation onto him. This is love, this is trust, this is passion, and as our kiss deepens, the bow that held me together unties. Releasing the rest of me to him, I dissolve into his touch. Our bodies unite and travel to our very own galaxy where time is infinite and we are too.

We are too. We are too. We are too.

He is my moon and I am his sun, burning brightly until the stars appear and guide us back into the earth's cold hands. Holding tightly to him, I silently beg his body to stay, now and forever.

"I love you," he whispers as he softly kisses my lips.

"I love you."

Tears soak the pillows as we hold each other. The high of surrendering to our great love, consumed by the reality that tonight is the final nail in our coffin. Each hammer down steals more air.

When morning comes, we will be on two separate sides of the fault line, relying on my scar tissue map to guide me home to its keeper.

There's nothing to say in this intense joy, and intense sadness. No words will grant us the justice we deserve. No words will hold us together, so he upholds his promise from our very first date, holding me all night. My final request leaves my lips as I drift to sleep.

"Remember me happy, Dean."

I'll remember you happy, I promise.

Dean (Forty-Three minutes until Midnight)

Remember me happy, Hal.

Forty-three minutes until the new year demolishes our safe haven, and steady tears flow down my face as I hold her until I forget.

They promised it was a gift, allowing us to live a wonderfully wild life.

I bought into the sale of our souls, blindly following their promises and excitement about erasing the damage caused by generations before us.

I believed it was better to forget than dwell on past lives I had lived, people I had loved, friends I had lost. Their freedom seemed like the better option at the time. Now it feels like murder committed in the name of freedom.

How dare they make me forget the smile that stops time and shines happiness onto anyone in the room. The way her eyes light up when she smells fresh flowers at the market. The adorable way she sips coffee even when she knows it's too hot. The way she feels like the past, present, and future all at once. The way her body fits in mine, perfectly in every way, and the way I could've loved her for a lifetime. Longer, even, and probably will, regardless of our circumstances. My mind will never know a love like this again, but my heart will hold onto it. Maybe it'll even flare next year, beating faster to tell me she's close to me.

The memories of our year cascade through my mind like a collage of photos that I can't bear to lose. Pictures of the future, the life we would've lived, join in to enhance the sting. Riding bikes in the park, teaching her to cook, a perfectly pink sunset. A heart in ink on my arm, paint as blue as the night sky, laughter that feels like home.

Laying here is like watching us fall from the sky. For a while, we were floating. When did it change? We've been distracted enough that we're past the point of parachute release. Nothing is going to stop our fall, and trying to get to her is like trying to move in zero gravity.

When she first realized we were falling, she thrashed around. Took almost a year for her to soak in all my peace. Now she's frozen, hand outstretched, and it's almost worse this way. Looks like a statue that will permanently shatter when she hits the ground.

My arm hurts from reaching. Even out of its socket, I'd come up short. I'm only an inch away. Would it be better if I was further?

Here in my arms, she's peaceful. Deadweight. But our home's about to break, and I'm not ready. Never would be.

I'll take this love to the grave.

- 45 -

January 1, 2046

Hallee

The morning sun pierces the curtains, shining through my eyelids and alerting me that it's January 1st.

It's January 1st, and the light has done this before, this bed has held me before, this smell has calmed me before.

I remember.

Miles's mother was right—it was possible all along.

My eyes stay shut, avoiding being the ones to call the time of death on our love. Dean should be asleep next to me, but my back is too cold. He always keeps me warm. My hands work up the courage, reaching over to barely touch where he should be. Every ounce of composure leaves my body as wrinkled bed sheets meet my fingertips.

"Oh shit, you're awake!" his voice rings in my ears.

My eyes fly open, and there he is. The love of my life, standing and staring. I don't dare to even breathe.

"I'm sorry—"

No. Don't apologize because then it's true, and it can't be true because if it's true then I'm alone. Wasn't I always, though? Love did a good job of hiding it, but I think I always was.

"It's okay," I breathe out.

No it's not, but it's not his crime to apologize for. His eyes fall, like how they do when he's disappointed in himself, and it throws a knife at my chest. Hitting me full speed, it tears apart my ribcage to get to my heart. Must've made it, because this immediate hollow ache—this has to be death.

I'm going to be sick.

Shoving Dean to the side feels like breaking the law, but I barely make it to the sink before emptying my stomach, over and over.

His hands write the language of our love onto my back, replacing the ghost of his fingers from the night before. Even now, he's my greatest comforter.

"There's no way to explain that I'm not usually this type of guy without sounding totally like that type of guy," he explains, awkwardly chuckling in the silence.

You're not, my wide eyes blink, but his strained eyes have forgotten our secret language.

We're both at a loss of words for very different reasons, and the expanse between our souls has me dry heaving for the next five minutes. Dean disappears, probably innocently fleeing from his own apartment because of the books in his room. He always thought it was a girlie hobby, never even picked one up. Not a single book all year.

"I didn't know what you'd like, so I grabbed it all," he says, walking through the doorway holding every drink he can, and another wave of nausea crashes into me. He looks like he did the first time I stayed over.

He does know what I like, or at least, he did. My Dean knows everything about me. This Dean is a shell of him. Still mine, though. How can that be? To belong to someone as you were, and still belong to them after you aren't what you were?

Love umbrellas over change, I guess.

Denial overtakes me as I stare into his galaxy eyes. It pushes me right into him, and my arms hug tightly around his waist. The longer he hesitates, the tighter I squeeze, because there has to be a point when the pressure will click and restore what was lost.

Please, Dean, hold me like you used to. His mind forgot. Did his body forget me, too? I have to get out of here, I can't breathe.

Setting the drinks on the counter, his arms finally fall into place. It's exactly where they used to, but it's still not the same. This timid, forced, and empty touch feels like needles pricking my skin. Death would've been better than enduring this kind of loss. Fuck them for doing this to us.

How could they do this to us?

"Thank you," I mutter.

"No big deal," he replies.

It is, in fact, the biggest deal, but he thinks the thank you is for the help today. A part of it is, but most of it's not. The truth is, I never thanked him for loving me. Why didn't I do it when I could?

He made me believe I was easy to love. Do you know how hard it is to convince me of something? Even the most critical part of me believed it by the end. Did he know how thankful I was before he forgot? I need to know, but he won't know, and I don't either, so I never will. I do know that my love was enough for him, always, and his love will get me through this.

Avoiding eye contact, I grab the Sprite and walk out of the room. Is this the last time I'll be able to look into his eyes?

Hudson's voice talking to Matt punches me in the gut. "What's your favorite color?" he asks.

Doubling over, I drop to the floor with my drink. How did I forget I'd see them too? Please, someone help me breathe. I can't breathe. I can't *breathe.*

"Don't have a favorite, but red makes my skin crawl. Not sure why," Matt answers.

Losing his first victim will remind him that red reminds him of fire.

"I like blue, I think. Can't quite remember, but blue seems right," Hudson replies, laughing as if this is funny.

He's always laughing. Except last night, when he wasn't. Did he laugh with Avery before the year ended?

He's wrong. Blue used to be his favorite, but it changed to green because of her. *Green reminds me of a fairy*, he used to say. His favorite person reminded him of one too.

I never figured out what they were. Don't even know if they figured it out, but it doesn't matter now. I couldn't even save my own fairytale. There's no way I could have saved theirs too.

"Ah, a fuck and flight!" Hudson jokes, tapping Matt's arm and side-eyeing me. "Where ya going, sweetheart? Why don't you stick around?"

Apparently, friends can break your heart too. The shattering of being reduced down to a fuck and flight blurs my vision.

We used to joke about how those days were in the past for us, clinging together as if we were the only six people on the planet. The ultimate ride or dies—friends until death separates us. Careless, to not take into account the death of our souls.

"Wait!" Dean calls as I run to the front door.

Instinctively, my hand freezes on the doorknob. Tapping it three times with my pinky gives me the strength to turn. My face is a river, a natural flowing stream, and he's staring while standing on the edge.

"I'm sorry about them, I—" Confusion lines his face as he does a double take of his best friends. He doesn't know how to apologize for them because he doesn't know who they are. Doesn't know how to say goodbye to me, either, but he was never supposed to have to.

Rubbing the back of his neck, he closes his eyes and shakes his head. "I'm sorry, I don't remember."

Someone, end this.

"What is your name?"

Please, finish me off.

"I'd love to see you again. You're absolutely radiant."

Sunshine.

The missing nickname snaps my bones. Broken by my favorite person in the world, how cruel is that?

Tension thickens the air, attempting to revive our history. For him, this is the beginning of what could be. For me, this is the excruciating breakup of what already was.

As my stomach rolls again, I swallow down vomit and the pain of his silence. Begging for him to ask me to stay, my soul digs its claws down my rib cage. Each scratch is a deeper and deeper plea. *Please, ask me*, I blink. His blank stare splits my spine.

I'm so sorry, I blink.

"Goodbye, Dean. I like your books."

Slamming the apartment door behind me, I place my hand on the outside. "I love you," I breathe.

One.

Two.

Three.

My soul exits my body, watching as I float to the elevator. Did it sound like home to him? Hearing his name on my lips.

As the elevator carries me away from the battlefield, I finally sink to the floor. Does anyone know a surgeon? There's a Dean-shaped hole in my heart. Please, stitch him back into me before it concaves and crushes off my blood flow.

Dean

"Good lay, man," one of the guys calls out, but I'm frozen, imagining her hand on the doorknob. Am I crazy, or did her pinky tap it three times? Nothing makes sense anymore.

Open it. Open it. Open it, my heart demands. Could she still be there?

"Come sit," the other guy insists, patting the couch beside him.

Each step over replays the devastation in her eyes as I asked her name. How could I have treated that beautiful, radiant woman like she was dispensable?

Who have I become?

I woke up before her, and immediately felt guilty for not recognizing the body sleeping so peacefully in my shirt. She looked as if she'd done it so many times before. Honestly, I wanted to stay there with her, but the longer I lay there, the more the implication of the situation set in, and I couldn't take it anymore.

She didn't even stir when I carefully moved her off me as if I could break her. Assuming a shower would jog my memory, I tip-toed and started the water. Instead of walking me down the steps of how I'd gotten here, it rained down confirmation that I have no recollection of last night.

Or the night before last.

Or the night before that.

Turning off the shower, I stepped into the fog-filled room and wiped a circle on the mirror. For a few seconds, I stood there staring and pleading for my mind to toss out a name that fit my reflection. Instead, there was silence and the bizarre realization that I don't know who I am.

Or I hadn't, until she said it.

Dean.

The sound of that name on her lips awoke all of my senses, shaking me out of my confusion and filling the air with the comforting smell of sweet vanilla. It was almost familiar, that vanilla.

"She called you Dean, so that rules out one of the three," the one with the black hair says, pointing at the three binders sitting on the coffee table.

Reading the spines, I glance at Hudson and Matt. Which is which?

The one with the buzz cut tosses mine into my lap and urges, "Open the damn thing."

"We sure?" I ask, trembling.

"Do it," the other one insists.

Leaning in around me, the guys and I read about the world we live in. The first page is marked with basic identifying information, followed by an explanation of our situation.

The Gift of Forgetting.

A deep sigh leaves my lungs. It's a brief description, but enough information to reassure us that this happens every year. We are safe, apparently.

"I need a minute," I say, politely excusing myself.

The lightweight door slams behind me way harder than I intended.

"Sorry!" I yell, turning to take in the room that is allegedly my own.

The shining sun highlights the wrinkled sheets where two bodies lay last night. Makes a lump form in my throat, so I swallow it down and crawl back onto the right side. My heartbeat echoes off the walls of my chest. Why does it feel like I just lost something great?

What the—

The light catches a gold band on my finger as I place it on the pillow she slept on. Flipping my hand back and forth, I check for any unique qualities to it. Anything at all to explain why I have this.

An image of the woman reaching for the doorknob freezes in my mind like a paused movie. Her pinky tapped it three times, didn't it? And next to her pinky . . . she had one too.

The vision dissolves into a figment of my imagination as I blink. Frustrated with my fickle memory, I wrestle with it for an hour. She had one. She didn't. She did. She didn't. She did.

Chills cover my arms as I remember the feeling of her all over me this morning. The way she fit perfectly in the nape of my neck, how tightly she hugged me, how long she held on, how devastated she looked saying goodbye. She knew my name, and it was familiar coming off of her lips.

Sliding the ring off, I hold it between my fingertips and raise it to the sun. The hollow ache in my chest grows as I read an engravement, hidden only for me to see.

She's the one who looks like sunshine.

My hand flies to my chest, trying to calm my pounding heart. Even in her despair, the woman was radiant. A living, breathing light, and she had a matching ring.

Who was I before this morning?

Her voice is the first to talk to me, repeating over and over,

Goodbye, Dean. I like your books.

What a strange thing to leave me with. My eyes flick to the bookshelves lining the walls. Should I—?

No.

Well?

Anticipation shoots adrenaline through my fingers as my feet answer for me, carrying me to the books.

She was devastated. She knew my name.

- 46 -

January 1, 2046

Hallee

I like your books.

Not, I love you. Not, you love me. My last words, a final battle for us. Yesterday, our hands recognized each other, holding on tight as we braced for the impact of the fall.

Let me go, I asked him on that blanket in the park.

I've got you, he assured, and we plummeted over the cliffside, never looking back. Not once did he falter in his promise to me.

Until now.

His mind failed him and his body followed, leaving me alone to shatter on the ground. Here I lie, utterly broken without his peace to fight off the swelling darkness.

Don't let me go, I pleaded last night. Isn't it funny how time changes things?

This morning, I could've told him. Could've explained that against all odds, we've found each other time and time again and fallen in love in a hundred different ways. I could've begged and pleaded for him to remember the life we've built over the last four years. Could've screamed that he's a proud firefighter, he likes his coffee hot but never finishes the last sip because it's too lukewarm, can't sleep unless his feet are under the covers, feels happiest in the sun, avoids Main Street because of the cracked sidewalk. Could've reminded him that he's superstitious, has never questioned the circle of life, has a scar on his left side, and promised to hold me forever through the trap of this life.

For hours, I could've desperately clung to our past lives and laid my heart on the chopping block. Would it have been worth it?

Words wouldn't collect his emotions and restore his mind of the love we share. They'd only fall flat coming from a stranger.

That is all I am to him now.

A radiant stranger.

He would've misunderstood, and that would've been the worst part, so I accepted his first, second, and third apologies for not remembering his one-night stand. He tried to comfort me as I fell apart in front of him, but I felt his discomfort when he shifted. Clinging to him so tightly was inexplicable. He let go of a stranger, but I let go of my whole heart.

As I was forced to settle with the ghost of him holding me, the invisible tether joining his soul to mine stretched until it hurt. Not the good kind of hurt, where the stretch is helping, but the bad kind, where it could snap your hamstring and your life would never be the same.

Will my life ever be the same?

Without him, my entire world caved in, and I averted my watering eyes as the imbalance of our emotions hung in the air. There was no sane explanation for such a drastic reaction to a one-night stand. There was no sane explanation for any of this mess.

The game has been reset, and it's an impossible one to win. With everything else I've remembered, I've forgotten how to pretend.

Years and years of the cat-and-mouse game have all led to the same outcome—me loving him deeply. The evidence is written all over my scarred heart.

As his gaze held mine, he cocked his head to the side. Our silent communication shouldn't come for at least another three dates, so I stared and acted as if I didn't understand that he was asking me if I was okay.

Mrs. Stand and Stare, at your service.

I waited for his eyes to flicker with a sense of knowing, for him to break the silence. I waited . . .

And waited . . .

And waited . . .

I will love every part of you, forever, I vowed.

Including the part that forgets.

This dance we've been in of losing and finding, falling and loving, mending and breaking, has swept me away, and I'll never stop spinning in the hope that he'll remember me. For the rest of my life, I will find him again. I'll fight for us, delicately weaving our paths back together in a natural cadence—building us a story that will withstand the hardship of this life. He will fall in love time and time again like the tides of the sea, and I will follow his rise and fall by meeting him where he is each year.

I will smile at him in passing and introduce myself like a stranger. *Recognize me, please*, my eyes will beg. I'll playfully flirt as if it's the very first time, shyly agree to a date like it's our first, and when he dares to hold my hand, I'll act as if his body isn't already my safest place. I'll desperately hold onto the highs of summer to carry me through the lows of the repeating new year. My love for him will not fade, will not falter, and I will never find another.

His ghost is walking with me as I visit our very own cemetery. Headstones mark our memories laid to rest.

Here lies the park . . . the wildflowers . . . The Marmotte.

Here lies the apartment . . . the rooftop . . . the wedding.

The secret society of sunflowers—that one hurts the most. The fresh dirt blows into my eyes and blinds me to the rest of the visions, like Dean was blinded to us.

Useless, a degrading voice swarms my grief, dragging me down to the bottom of the ocean. I think I'll die down here. It'll be good if I do.

Foolish.

Wait, was that voice—me?

It's been so long since I've heard it, it sounds like a foreign language. Dean talked to me kindly, so I talked to me kindly too, but without his protective presence, my light has been blown out. Maybe I'm not the sunshine, but the fragile flame of a candle.

Months of silence have prepared the meanest part of me for its return attack, launched at my most vulnerable point. Foolish is right. I was so foolish to assume that healing could come from anywhere except myself.

What am I now?

Arrows fly through the sky, aimed at my deepest insecurities. The faster I walk, the more it looks like the sun has set the pine needles on fire. Where is my firefighter? Don't pine needles burn the fastest? I guess I burn the fastest too.

What did my love amount to?

It's nothing, and *I* am nothing. I'm worthless, insignificant.

I've failed. I've failed. I've failed.

The brutal words whip into my skin. How could I be so stupid? Nothing I've done has made a difference. Even my greatest efforts didn't change our heartbreaking end. Wanting something enough doesn't mean it will happen.

Dean's compassionate words echo in my mind, racing to the front line for me. *There are many ways to matter*, he'd said. *You matter.*

If I mattered, he would've remembered me.

My mind fights against his comfort and is met step for step. Our contrasting statements clash like bone striking bone.

I know you, Hal.

I'm a stranger to him.

I love you.

I'm not enough, not enough, not enough.

Come on, Sunshine. You carry all of the light you need.

His words lift my chin like his hands used to as his love surrounds me like a shadow, emphasizing the power of my light. Can it hold me up while I fight against the rising tide?

You be good, you hear me? Hudson's voice sails directly for me, carrying Matt's along with it. *Hold the line, Hal.*

Yes—hold the line.

This cruel melody is not the tune that will play over me. My forehead tenses, recalling and longing for the familiar touch of my friends. They will not fight alone on the front line. Dean loved me deeply—they all did—and I'm better because of it. The Gift doesn't get to take me, too. It doesn't get to reset my love for myself. It's true, all I have left is me, but waging battle is worth it to save the girl brave enough to dream. I will not be diminished into a broken reverie. I am worth fighting for.

You matter, Dean had said.

I matter. Didn't believe him then, but I do now. My own words become powerful weapons and I load the next shot, aiming it directly at the darkness.

I haven't failed. The reverberations of my love will still be felt.

Pull back, and release.

He has known a great love because of me.

Release.

My friends have been loved deeply because of me.

Release.

My walking pace quickens as my mental strength builds. Resistance has turned the tides of the battle.

I have a purpose.

Release.

I will recover what was lost.

I am loved. Unbreakable. Significant.

Release. Release. Release.

I am enough.

That's my girl.

I am not alone.

I've got you. I've got you. I've got you, Hal.

Dean's voice surrounds me, replacing my guards of self-defense.

"I love you," I whisper to the wind.

I love you.

His words are my only companion as I walk home to introduce myself to Marlowe and Avery.

- 47 -

January 1, 2046

Dean

Reach up, grab the book. It's very simple, but I've been standing in front of this bookshelf for five minutes trying to force my shaky hands to work. The longer I wait, the more the anticipation builds. The anticipation is the worst part, right?

I can't decide if one option or two hundred options is more overwhelming. One is what it is, but two hundred is whatever I choose. A comforting neon teal cover catches my eyes the most. Probably the best one to start with.

Breathe in comfort, exhale nerves. Breathe in comfort, exhale nerves. Breathe in comfort, and pull—down falls a small rectangle, not much bigger than the palm of my hand.

The noise it made landing on the hardwood plays on a loop in my mind as I pick it up and sit on the edge of my bed. For one second, I hesitate, bracing for the impact of whatever is to come.

One.

There she is, covered in paint, and laying against my chest. She's smiling at the camera, and I'm smiling at her with an admiration as deep as the blue paint strokes on my face. Dark as the night sky, that paint.

As if it remembers holding her, my heart pounds harder, transporting me back into the melody of her laughter. *I want to recreate one of my favorite book scenes*, she'd said, mischief twinkling in her eyes. *Whatever makes you happy*, I'd agreed. We'd used each other as canvases until the sunset faded and the stars came out to play.

Open it, I can almost hear her say, and the room begins to sway as I immediately obey.

August 2043
My Dean,

The words ignite in my chest—I belong to someone. She was devastated. She knew my name. Inhaling deeply, I start again.

August 2043
My Dean,
Thanks for reminding me that it's good to do things that matter to us, and for helping me turn this day into a work of art. I'm so glad the stars heard us. I'll be yours to stare at today, and forever.
Love,
Your Sunshine—Hallee

Hallee, I whisper, as if it's a secret I'm not supposed to know. Frantically jumping off my bed, I rush to the shelves and pull off as many books as I can hold. Unable to wait any longer, I sink to the floor and open the next cover.

There's a picture of us in the kitchen, and it comes alive in my head. She's spinning behind me while I stir the pot on the stove. Leans in for a kiss, and the oven timer cuts us off.

She was devastated. She knew my name.

October 2044

My Dean,

I love cooking with you. Well, watching while you try to teach me to cook. We both know everything I make is inedible, but I'll spend forever spinning in the kitchen with you.

Love,

Your Sunshine—Hallee

Closing my eyes, endless memories project to the beat of my pulse. Me, carrying her out of a smoke-filled apartment. Her, crying because she burned dinner again. Pumpkins smashed on the apartment floor. Wishing on shooting stars.

Two Polaroids fall onto my lap as I open the next book—one of her smiling, and one of me. *You better take the sunflower with you*, I'd said that day. *It belongs in the sun.* To test the validity of these returning memories, I close the book. The cover should be—a sunflower field. Exactly as I remembered.

She was devastated. She knew my name.

March 2045

My Dean,

An old woman at the bookstore surprised me with this today. She saw me looking at it in the romance section, and it felt like a sign from the universe. You should read it. It reminds me of us.

Love,

Your Sunshine—Hallee

Tears soak the pages as I thumb through every single book on the shelf. There are *years* of memories, pictures, and letters that have all been hidden in plain sight—protected by the secrecy of my room.

I spend hours puzzling together our timeline, reflecting and rebuilding the stained glass window of our relationship with her scattered pieces of sun. More and more comes back to me as a tsunami demolishes the constructs of our government's *gift*. It couldn't withstand the aftershock of the earthquake her love started, but I could.

She started this. All this time, she'd been building our very own library love story to pull me back into her orbit.

I hope if it was important to me, I'll find my way back to that passion somehow, I told her once. Can't exactly remember when, but the words voice over the picture of her in my head. Why were her eyes so sad?

No wonder I never wanted to read a book. They were never important to me. The passion for me to find my way back to is *her*.

Surrounded by four years of love, I grab the final book on the shelf. Seems like an old classic—leather-bound, with a small flame on the spine but no other significant markings. There isn't even a title engraved on the front but, just like the others, it has a picture in it.

She was devastated. She knew my name.

November 18, 2045

My Dean,

Our love story goes back further than I ever imagined. December 31, 2040, to be exact. It didn't take long for me to connect the dots of how interwoven our lives have been once I learned our deepest fears manifest through nearly identical nightmares. For years, I believed it to be oblivion I could feel approaching, relentless in its search for me. Really, it was you.

It was always you, coming to save me from it all.

We were so young then, barely eighteen. It had to have been your first year as a firefighter. Despite it being New Year's Eve, you all arrived quickly. I was barely holding onto consciousness when I heard you and forced out my final plea for help. I thought you'd left, and started counting the seconds until death collected me. As I made it to second fourteen, you risked it all.

You came back for me.

That's where my memory of the night ends. It took two wandering years until you found me again in this life. For the last four, our lives have collided. Each passing New Year's Eve has only been a pause in our timeless love.

This was my fourteenth second. My Hail Mary to the gods that you will finally pick up a book, and at least one of these will release an avalanche of memories reminding you of the life we've built.

Maybe it didn't work, and you still don't remember me. If that's the case, I need you to know it's not your fault. Maybe you never found these at all. Either way, I will never give up hope that somehow, somewhere, someday, you will come home to me.

I love you enough for the both of us.

Love,

Your Sunshine—Hallee

My rainfall of emotion smudges her beautiful handwriting as I struggle to breathe. The memory has been transported into my bedroom, filling my lungs with invisible smoke. Her helpless whimper reverberates through my head.

She's right. It was only my first year; I could've easily missed her. Almost did, but something made me wait. That one extra second changed my entire world.

The walls close in as the face of the girl I carried out finally comes into focus. My Sunshine was the fourteenth life I had saved.

. . . the only peace for my soul is that our memory of this will be wiped clean in an hour.

It was my favorite gift, to forget. Now, I want nothing more than to remember every second of this beautifully broken life.

- 48 -

January 2046

Hallee

The anticipation of a caffeine rush is the only reason my heavy bones finally rolled out of bed. Grief has been my sole companion, muting the world around me. It's worn many hats over the past week, but the greatest trick it played was convincing me it was a friend rather than my captor.

At first it was cathartic, warming me with a flame that melted the days together into one. Each hour, I assumed I'd reached the bottom of the trench, yet I still haven't. Isn't it astounding, how much your heart can break?

There should be a sedative for this. Without his body next to me, I can't sleep. My mind is still convinced he's dead if I'm not touching him. Would my heart feel it if he was?

My bed is perfectly placed under a storm cloud on my ceiling. It's darkened with each passing day, and I've sunk into the cold sheets as ice chips rain down, pelting me with thoughts trying to convince me it wasn't real.

How could it have been? It was so easily erased, and any proof I had, I left behind for him to find. Remember when I hoped his books would belong to me one day? Excruciating, how funny that is now. As I placed the first one on the shelf last year, I recalled how long I've been silently fighting The Gift. Just as Dean has, the idea came back to me every year. It seems I'm bolder than I originally thought, using books as my own small act of defiance.

The hailstorm started slowly, releasing a few pieces that fell and bounced off my skin. Then, the clouds poured out ice like weapons, each one pelting me harder than the last and leaving me battered beyond repair.

So, yes, at first grief was a friend.

Now it's my cynical captor, torturing me with what could've been, and I finally made my great escape to uphold our morning coffee tradition. I lost track of which day my tears had washed away the smell of Dean from his sweatshirt, but I still can't bring myself to take it off. Didn't even risk brushing my hair, only putting on pants and shoes. Probably should've tried a little harder, but I didn't expect The Marmotte to be so busy only one week into the new year.

Last year's regulars are already becoming this year's regulars. Jack is reading the newspaper at his usual table, and Lea's taking orders as the same light streams through the floor-to-ceiling windows. Misery is worn exclusively by me, but of course the others look light as a feather—they are blissfully unaware of everything they've lost. They're blissfully unaware of the grief connected to missing someone deeply. A bitch, that grief. Pain like I've never known. Is this place named The Marmotte because it's just a regular stop in the melancholy groundhog day that is our lives?

I pity the other morning regulars for their oblivion and pity myself for the lifetime of pain I'm chained to as the only civilian who remembers what it feels like to be loved and to lose it, repeatedly.

Inhaling sharply, I force my attention to our table in the center of the room. There—

I can't do this. How am I supposed to do this?

Pushing off seeing his eyes, I glance at his shoes first. He wore those in the park the day we learned you actually *can* forget how to ride a bike. For a moment, I'm back there listening to him laugh with his head tipped back. Will I ever hear him laugh again?

No air is enough to ease the asphyxiation aching my lungs. A rainstorm falls from my eyes, blurring my vision. It's not a loud, attention-seeking cry, but a calm, controlled, acceptance of devastation, because his jeans are next. The dark wash I'd bought him in the fall. We spent hours trying to get the mud stains out after I'd tackled him in the corn maze. I'm pretty sure he ended up secretly buying a new pair because he knew they were my favorite, but I'd never asked. Will I ever find out?

One hand's in his lap, and one's holding his coffee like it used to hold me. Inhaling, I miss the taste of peppermint. Yes, even peppermint, because it's another thing that makes me feel close to him. It's what's in his cup right now. Don't even have to ask, because I know him.

I know him. I know him. I know him.

Can the inside of your body bruise? My soul is pounding, fighting to return to its homeland, but my feet are cemented in the permanent exile of remembering and being forgotten.

Impatient customers shuffle around, cutting me in line as nausea overwhelms me like an addict on the comedown from a bad batch. I never wanted to detox, and now I'm counting the days until I can relapse into his love.

To ease the ache, I whisper out an edge of my devastation.

I miss you.

If my eyes glaze over enough, will they reflect pain instead of absorb it?

His sweatshirt is a twin to the one he gave me the day he'd ruined my crewneck. A twin to the one that's become my emotional support item in his absence, and to the one I'm wearing now.

The block letters complement his rosy cheeks. I could almost swear they're glimmering in the light. As a stranger bumps into me, my gaze shifts to his hat. Really, backwards? Substantially shocked, I finally look into the eyes with a gravity strong enough to defy the odds. The eyes I can't say no to—they've been staring at me, too.

I force the kindest smile I can as my heart waves at him. There's a lot to be lost in a bad first impression, and it's definitely not my best work. Did I just lose him again?

He returns my weak attempt with the smirk that drives me crazy. The one he wears when he teases me, or is about to surprise me, or is thinking about things we did the night before. The smirk I recognize as love, a response to my empty smile he should recognize as devastation. I'd give everything in the world to have even our worst day again.

His mind may not remember me, but he's still human. His heart is the same, and it will remember.

It will remember. It will remember. It will remember.

Is the floor getting closer to my face? The ringing in my ears is all I hear, as the loss of my life gestures to Lea. My feet turn on auto-pilot, flying me to the pickup counter before I crash and burn. Lea sets down a drink just as I walk up.

"Hallee, your vanilla latte is at the bar."

"Did you just say—?" I gasp as she cuts me off.

"Hallee!"

Her smile detonates the grenade. Hello, MedFlight? We've got a soldier down!

Hope floods in with the drink's familiar smell, patching the pieces of me back together. It's dangerous, this hope. This cruel, unusual joke from the universe will be my final breaking point. Is this my punishment for my resistance to The Gift?

The ringing in my ears returns as I look around frantically for another Hallee.

I never even ordered.

As if I could scare him away, I carefully glance back to our table. The rainstorm has returned, blurring my vision, but I think he just gestured to me?

Who, me? I blink.

It's crazy, but as he blinks back I swear his eyes say, *yes, you.*

After three fear-filled steps, he spins his coffee, revealing a note written in his handwriting.

My sweatshirt looks good on you, Hal.

His arms wrap around me as I crumble in the middle of The Marmotte. *Always and forever*, his hands will catch my fall.

Dean

After days of consideration, I decided there's no place more special to reveal that her clever mind has restored my favorite part of me than the place where I made her my wife. In the true spirit of Hallee, I planned two backups.

The first: showing up to Happy Bookday. She'd go to work eventually; being a reliable employee is important to her.

The second: banging on the door of her apartment like a madman. Both were acceptable options, but my woman deserves the best, and this plan is my very best.

Of course, it did hinge entirely on her addiction to takeout coffee, but I knew she couldn't resist.

My heartbeat's so connected to hers that it quickened moments before she walked in. My soul responds exclusively to hers, now and forever.

Forever. Her toast resounds through my mind, as many of her flare signals from the previous years have over the last few days. At what point did she start to hope, and how was she strong enough to hold onto it as we went down with our sinking ship?

The Marmotte lightened when she walked through the door, even as anguish clouded her like an early morning fog. Her empty eyes blatantly ignored every person in her path, and it took all of my strength to stay seated—to wait for the right moment.

The desperation in her eyes as she whispered *I miss you* released a faucet of sympathy tears from mine. Holding her gaze like a lover in the night, I covered my joy with the best smirk I could, and spun the gold ring on my finger.

She's the one who looks like sunshine.

There's a future where we are not victims of our circumstance. Our love has not been buried in the grave of second best, but is alive, breathing, and pulling us back together like two separated magnets.

As Lea called her order, I snapped my favorite Polaroid of them all—her reaction to hearing her name. Hope ignited in those empty eyes, and I couldn't wait anymore.

Only waited two seconds after turning the cup to rush to catch her fall. I promised I always would, and she's always done things in threes.

"I've got you, Hal," I whisper, leaning into her sweet vanilla scent.

"Thank you," she cries.

"There you go again, surprising me."

"I never told you thank you for loving me, and helping me love myself. Thank you. I love you. I love you. I love you."

"Enough for the both of us?"

"Immeasurably."

The word sends us back to our sacred, little infinity—standing hand in hand, sliding matching gold bands on our fingers. At the time, I'd had nothing to promise, only memories to lay to rest. She'd promised me, though. *I will always remember,* she'd said.

She meant it.

Taking her hand in mine, I gently remove the gold band on her finger.

"I promise . . ." I swallow down the rising lump in my throat. She's fought so hard to hear this.

"I promise to never forget. To hold you through the nights you can't sleep. To scratch your back like it's a full-time job. To laugh at all of your cheesy jokes. I promise to provide an endless wardrobe of sweatshirts that smell like me, cook every meal we don't eat out, and read all of the books on the shelf. I promise to spend forever reminding you of your worth and carrying you through the dark days. More than anything, I promise to never forget you. I'll always be your snow globe, raining down peace when the world shakes us up."

"Shut up!" she squeals. "You remember I love snow globes!"

"I do—I know you."

"You know me."

"Meet me at The Marmotte," I say, tears pouring from my eyes as I wink.

Her bottom lip quivers as she holds out her hand, silently requesting for me to solidify the promises I've made.

"I love you, Hal."

"He's the one who feels like peace," she whispers as I slide the ring on her finger.

"You found it."

"I did, and I love you too."

"You were never alone in the fight."

Pride swells as her shoulders relax. Peace—I've already fulfilled that part of the promise by loving her with everything I have. Our love and serenity go hand in hand.

- 49 -

January 2046

Hallee

Happy Bookday hasn't changed at all over the course of my many first days here—seven, to be exact. This is my seventh first day of work, and my body still remembers my nerves from the very first one.

It never got easier, like I assumed it would. I assumed over time my body would grow tired of living in a constant state of fight or flight. Assumed that after years of blisters from the friction of forcing myself to fit their mold, my heart would callous over. Instead, I bled out.

The first two years, my greatest wish was, *let me lose myself completely.* All my nights were spent screaming back and forth between who I was becoming and who I always dreamed I'd be. Eventually, the former drowned out the latter, and I wilted away like a fragile flower in the winter. There was not enough antiseptic in the world to prevent the infection that flatlined my soul.

I needed a miracle, and then he came along.

Dean was the resuscitation paddles that gave purpose to my pulse, shocking me over and over until the best parts of me came back to life and the worst parts laid to rest. After that first revival, he became a crucial part of me. In his absence, I was constantly struggling to find my way back to him, but in his presence the stars aligned into a map, leading me to achieve all of the dreams I had wished away.

He celebrates the wildest parts of me and values the ones the world convinced me were a waste of time. All of my scattered pieces were gathered together by the gentle consistency in how he cared for me. *This is art*, and we're a masterpiece—beautifully broken but cemented together by our love. Together, we are priceless. So, as he asks me for the fourth time if I'm ready, I'm able to nod confidently. The world isn't so scary with his hand in mine.

The bell in Happy Bookday dings, and I don't startle at its loud jingle.

"Happy New Year!" Miles cheers, shuffling around the fantasy aisle.

He's shelving. That would've been the second thing he trained me on, after we did our initial walk-through of the store. Back to front, front to back—remember?

Books block his view as he turns the corner to meet me . . . again. Peering around them, his eyes fall on Dean's hand holding mine. The shield of his calm facade is stripped away as the books cascade to the floor. With each crash, his face blanches more.

Letting go of Dean's hand, I walk toward Miles, arms open wide in invitation for him to receive the hug he desperately needs. Timidly, he accepts.

"Hello, Miles," I whisper.

"Hello, Hallee," he responds, crying as I hug him a little tighter. It's the least I can offer my friend who has spent so many years in social isolation, patiently and graciously keeping me company throughout my journey while I regularly abandoned him on his. It wasn't my fault, but I still wish it had been different.

"You actually did it. You remember. Both of you?" His trembling hands grip my forearms.

"We do."

"It's conclusive," he breathes. "How did you—"

"We're not exactly sure, but it all started with your mother and her balloon."

His sigh of relief could blow over a town.

"I promised I'd remember her, and I keep my promises."

"The greatest gift you could've ever given me." His eyes squint as he smiles, and tears pour down his face.

"I could never forget the woman who was the catalyst for change. *She* reunited *me* with the greatest gift—the gift of remembering."

A sob escapes him as he recalls his late mother.

"Miles, I have to know. What was her name?"

Standing tall, he proudly replies, "Laelynn, and my father's name is Jack."

Chills snake up my spine as I recall the man from The Marmotte. "L" was for Laelynn all along. Jack was lost, and now he's been found.

"Would you tell us about her?" Dean softly asks, and unashamed joy pours out of Miles as he wipes away his tears.

"Where would you like me to start?"

For the entire day, we sit in the children's reading nook, listening to stories about his mom. He speaks of his childhood, all the way to her final years where he was merely her favorite book salesman. We hold space for his grief and cherish his vulnerability. We laugh until we cry, and cry until we laugh again. This is the irreplaceable heartbeat of life—the ability to connect with one another.

Laelynn must've stopped time for us to have this intentional conversation, because not a single customer came in all day. She's taking care of her son, even now. The setting sun is our only cue that the day has passed us by.

While we finish stocking the shelves, golden light streams in through the windows. With the three of us, it only takes about fifteen minutes before we walk out together. Miles fumbles with the keys, and a familiar push begs me to ask, "Do you know what her name meant? Your mother."

"Actually, yes!" Again, the joy in his voice has returned. "Laelynn is of English origin, meaning *flower of hope*."

"What a fitting name," I say with a smile. My voice cracks as emotions pour over me, and I blink away the tears pooling in my eyes.

"Do you know what your name means?" he asks.

No, I shake my head.

The world stops spinning as we turn and behold the sunset painted before us. It's a sea of colorful dots surrounded with wisps of clouds. Pink and yellow are mixed together in this absolutely stunning arrangement. It's unprecedented in beauty, really. Some might even say it looks like—

I can't believe it; Laelynn painted us a sunset. A beautiful bouquet of balloons.

Standing and staring at me with tear-filled admiration, Dean answers Miles's question.

"Heroine, Hal. Your name means heroine." He hesitates, reaching up to cup my cheek. "In other words—a very brave woman."

- 50 -
May 2096

The History of Psychology 2335

"For our final lecture, we have a very special guest," Mr. Holiday says, beginning class right on time.

He looks different today, lighter somehow, and is way overdressed. The tuxedo shoes click just like his other ones, but he's holding his head a little higher. He's never come across as a prideful man but he almost looks proud—confident in how much we've grown over the semester.

It seemed hopeless for us at the beginning, our values blurred between living an unattached life and planting roots to impact generations. It's important to let go, but when the party lights fade and we're left alone in the company of ourselves, are we happy with who we are and how we've treated people? Are we happy with the legacy we'll leave behind?

I never thought I would be, but somehow this class has changed that. It's made me love myself more.

"As you know by now, The Experiment was conclusive."

Cheers erupt from the frat pack in the third row, and a few claps resound from the back row bandits. Mr. Holiday's lectures have captured the heart of the entire room, and every single student was invested in the outcome by the end.

Our final reading assignment was The Experiment report, revealing the conclusion we have all been waiting for:

Yes, we are permanently marked by the people and experiences of our lives.

The evidence is written throughout the entire textbook, in the personal accounts of the civilians. All it took was one to prove it.

One balloon of hope.

One woman.

One great love.

At admission of their memory, The Experiment was concluded and the inhumane testing ceased. Their courage to dream changed the world, making it possible to rebuild a better one from ground zero, and Mr. Holiday has dedicated his entire life to ensuring history doesn't repeat itself. I hope I dedicate my life to something so important.

"I'm sure you're wondering about the civilians we've studied. As much as I would love to share how their lives have unfolded, it's not my story to tell." Turning his body toward the double doors, he extends out a hand. "It is my greatest joy to introduce you to the very brave woman whose light freed us all, Mrs. Hallee Holiday."

The sound of her clicking walker enters first, followed by a single yellow balloon, marking her every movement as she shuffles across the floor into the warm embrace of her husband. Matching gold bands shine brightly on their fingers, and gasps of shock cascade through the crowd as each student finishes their mental game of connect-the-dots.

Standing before us is the great love we have spent the entire semester studying, learning from, and cheering for. The great love of Dean and Hallee Holiday redefined *forever*.

The freshman stands first, starting the most genuine ovation I've ever participated in. No one makes an effort to end it. It's only when Mr. Holiday holds up a hand that we find our seats again, sniffling to regain our composure.

"Sunshine, the floor is yours."

Pride is in every syllable. The first time this semester he has appeared proud, and it's all because of his wife.

"What are you going to do, stand there and stare at me?" she asks.

"What more would you expect?" He smiles as her eyes roll.

"Forgive my shaky hands. Being the center of attention has never been my favorite thing," she says, her nose scrunching up as she giggles.

"My Dean has told me so much about you. Mostly how bright you all are, and how eager you are to learn. I'm here to offer any closure that I can. What questions do you have?"

Hands shoot up all around the room, including those of students who have never participated, and identical smirks form on Mr. and Mrs. Holiday's faces as they exchange an enthusiastic glance.

Questions sound off one after the other, and she answers every single one with a deep intentionality, taking pauses if necessary to choose her words carefully. She handles each one with the same level of care, acknowledging its importance, and we sit completely still, holding onto her wisdom like a lifeline. There's a quality about her so warm, that even when she doesn't have the answers, her vulnerability is comforting.

Despite that, there's this nagging pressure building inside my chest, urging me to get involved. Fidgeting my fingers, I try to push it down, but it only strengthens with each attempt. Mrs. Holiday takes notice of my uncomfortable movement in the sea of statue bodies and gives me a familiar smirk of curiosity.

Wait—does she recognize me?

Looking down at her balloon, I find the courage to raise my hand and untie my tongue when she calls on me.

"Go ahead, Rayne," she encourages, nailing the pronunciation just as Mr. Holiday had.

"How did you choose your last name?"

Their eyebrows raise in unison as Mr. Holiday hobbles to her side. Giving me his signature nod of approval and laying his arm around her, he answers for them both.

"Every day with my Sunshine is my favorite day. Life with her is an infinite holiday."

The very first question we'd asked him echoes in my mind, *What's your favorite holiday, Mr. Holiday?*

"Groundhog Day," I mutter.

"Come on, Rayne, use your voice," Mrs. Holiday pushes. "Rainy days aren't for everyone, but they do serve their purpose."

The rest of the class turns to me, confused as can be, but I know exactly what she means. She does recognize me. What a gift my grandparents have had in the friendship of the Holidays.

"You said your favorite holiday was Groundhog Day, because—"

"Because it reminds me to look at the light," Mr. Holiday says, tipping his head slightly to the right.

Reaching out and grabbing Hallee's hand, he stares at his wife with tear-filled admiration.

". . . and what a beautiful light she is."

- epilogue -

4 years post-experiment

Hallee

"You did good, Hal."

"We did good, Dean."

"You know, we do eventually have to name her."

"Really? I had no clue! The nurse has only reminded us every ten seconds when she comes in!"

"It's been two days since we had her, Hal. She needs a name."

"I know, I know, but it has to be right!"

We'd had a name planned, but when she arrived, it wasn't as fitting as it should've been. It wasn't right. So, as the days have blurred into nights, the question still remains. What is her name?

"Knock, knock!" Avery's voice whispers around the cracked door. I've been counting down the hours until our friends would be able to come meet her.

"Come on in, she's sleeping!"

Avery creeps in slowly, dragging Hudson in behind her with their intertwined hands. *Best Dressed* and *Life of The Party* still ring true to this day. Matt and Marlowe follow, swinging their hands like they're young and in love. *Most Likely to Surprise You* is more fitting for them.

We were right to be nervous about our friends getting together. It hasn't always been a steady path, but the bumps and bruises along the way have strengthened us beyond belief. We've carried one another through the challenges of rebuilding a life—a family. It's lonely being the first ones, but the times have changed, and this time we remember.

"Oh, Hallee! She's radiant," Marlowe squeals, as quietly as possible. "Just like her mother."

Tears stream down Avery's face as she lays a hand atop her growing belly—her and Hudson are not far behind us.

"You okay, Avery?" I ask. Hormones can be a wild ride.

"Yes." She sniffles as Hudson gently rubs her shoulder. "I'm just speechless. What a wonderful little miracle."

"Hi baby girl, I'm your Uncle Hudson," he whispers, gently tickling her cheek. "No matter what anyone says, I am *definitely* the one you come to for advice. Do you hear me?"

Hudson's eyes well with tears as she lets out a little squeak. *Life of the Party* has been a crier these days. Romantic movies, talking about babies, hugging Avery. Time has caught up with him, and he doesn't quite know what to do with the weight of everything he's thankful for.

"You did good, sis," he says, leaning over and planting a kiss on my forehead.

"That's what I said." Dean laughs.

"Ew, you called her sis?" Marlowe quips, and my heart bursts. These are the days I'd wished for.

Matt is silent, as he usually is when he's emotional, but his face is glowing with pride. One exchanged look is all I need to understand what he's feeling—pure love.

"What is her name?" Marlowe asks.

"We were just narrowing it down, actually, be—"

A knock on the door interrupts my explanation, and a bouquet of colorful balloons floats in. Hesitating respectfully before entering, Miles peeks his head into the room.

"Is now an okay time?" he asks. "I can always come back."

"Miles!" our friends cheer.

"Now is a fantastic time to meet your granddaughter," Dean says, welcoming him with a warm hug.

He's not technically her grandfather, but this family is a unique one. Our daughter will be one of the lucky few of her age to call someone by that title.

"How are you, Hallee? Are you good?" he asks, setting the balloons in the corner.

"I'm great." I smile.

"You did good, girl. Look at her!"

The room erupts in near-silent laughter.

"I did really, really, really, good," I say, wheezing between words from laughter. "Would you like to hold her, Miles?"

Awe and wonder flow on his smiling cheeks as he cradles her safely in his arms.

"What do I call her?" he asks.

Dean and I's eyes shift to each other, to the balloons, and back again. Him blinking three times is all the confirmation I need.

"Miles, meet Lae."

"No!" he gasps, shock flashing across his face.

"Yes—Lae Lynn Holiday."

Quiet cheers erupt from our friends.

"It's perfect," Avery cries.

Giving a big stretch, little Lae yawns as her tiny hands grab onto Miles's pinky finger.

"Welcome to the world, Lae," he whispers, brushing his thumb over her hand. "I'm so excited for all of the memories we will make."

- acknowledgments -

First and foremost, if you're here, that probably means you've read my book. Thank you for taking the time to experience *I'll Paint You a Sunset Someday*. I hope you felt seen, represented, understood, or less alone because of this story.

My favorite person, my biggest fan, and my best friend—the man who has me 100% convinced that the invisible string theory is real—my heart is permanently marked by your gentle, understanding, kind, and patient love. Thank you for your unconditional support in any and all of my creative endeavors, your patience as I hyperfixate until a project is finished, and for loving all of my traits the world swore were faults. You help me hold the line. I love our joke that we are Jim and Pam, but I love the most that we are just *us*.

Our sweet daughter, who inspires me every single day to notice and appreciate the little things—even at three years old, you are the wisest of us. Right now your favorite thing to say is that you'll always be our little caterpillar, and I want to remember that. I'll spend my entire life learning to paint sunsets so that when it counts, I'll paint you the prettiest one you'll ever see.

My Heavenly Father, who answered my life's longest question by giving me these characters, thank you for providing me a newfound peace and trust, and for the abundance of joy that flooded my life as you laid the stepping stones for each step of this process.

Abby: this entire project from start to finish is a celebration of the safe space you have built, allowing me to drown out fear with joy. Thank you for the years' worth of patience you've shown as I've obsessed over the themes in this book, for shepherding me toward Jesus, and for reminding me that love and light always prevail.

My copyeditor and proofreader, Laura Brock, who has been my loudest cheerleader, fiercest advocate, gentlest educator, and most trustworthy advisor for the writing, editing, and publishing process, this book would not exist in its greatest form without you. Thank you for patiently sharing your extensive knowledge with me, for going above and beyond to ensure I never doubted your belief in this story, and for the dedication and flexibility you've exhibited in caring for my story at every level it's existed in. It's one of my biggest honors to say—we did it!

Mom and Dad: thank you for doing your best, for raising us to be brave enough to try new things, and for working diligently to provide us with fun experiences, resources, and a superb education. I'm so thankful to know love in a multitude of capacities because of you, and to know the great blessing it is to have a friendship with your parents. "Shake It Off" and "Long Live" forever and ever. I love you.

My extended family, who are scattered all around Michigan: I love you and think of you often. No amount of distance or years could ever stop the legacy of the Wolverines. Go Blue!

My first reader, Natalie: this book would not be here today if my life lacked your gentle and consistent belief in my ideas. Your unmatched wisdom has deeply impacted my courage to trust my instincts, to choose to see the good, and to believe beyond anything else that love, in all its forms, is the grand magnetic center star that will change the world. I'm infinitely grateful for every season we've walked through together as friends and thank the stars (who *obviously* listen) for each memory we have and the memories we will make.

My dear friend, Sarah, who gave me my "Nick Miller" moment and who inspires me every day to continue to show up for myself and create—you will always be my favorite artist. (Unless my child decides to be an artist. Then, I guess by default, you'd be second place.) (Just trying to keep you humble.) I'm so proud to be your friend and to finally understand why people say they love girlhood. I'm convinced it's because they have friends as good as you. Thank you for creating my first-ever fan art and for sticking around through all of my "big ones."

My soul sister, Jennifer: you love this story with a passion that matches my own (and that is a nearly impossible task to accomplish). When I think about the lowest points of this process, I'm instantly reminded that I was never alone because you were right there. As each task snowballed into something new, you walked with me, and it was the greatest kindness you could've offered. I wholeheartedly believe God smiles every day because of the friend you are to me.

Rachel: you are a perfect example of living life with a contagious vibrance that challenges others to live for more. You were the light at the end of the tunnel, guiding me to finish what I'd started, and the friend who would run the marathon with me to the finish. Thank you for leading with kindness and for living bravely, boldly, and unapologetically.

Madeleine and Harper, it's a blessing to know you, to learn from you, and to celebrate the beauty of creativity alongside you. Thank you for continuously reminding me *why* I'm doing this, and for believing in me when I didn't believe in myself. You inspire me just by being you. Keep shimmering!

My phenomenal friends and beta readers, Lauren, Chelsea, Bri, Audrey, Lynzee, Jess, Sarah, Katie, and Mariah: you surprised me the most. As insecurity started to pour in, you superglued those cracks shut. You took this book under your wing and dedicated your time, heart, and energy to me and these characters. Thank you for your constructive feedback, your questions, comments, highlights, and your kindness through every step of this process. I hope, with this final version, I've taken the best of what you loved and only made it greater.

My bookstagram family, who have watched online as I've transformed into an author: you have done for me what the inner circle did for Feyre. Thank you for your interactions, positivity, excitement, and support as I've navigated changing seasons and chasing a dream. If you're reading this at 3 a.m., this is your sign that it's time to go to bed!

The staff at Summer Moon, I promise I did not intentionally name my characters after you, but you can imagine my surprise as I slowly realized the place I write best has been surrounded by people with the same, or similar, names as some of my characters. Thank you for learning my name, and my daughter's, and for giving us a place that finally feels like home in a city we've lived in for years. It's always been less about the coffee and more about being known.

To the many brave, creative women taking risks to create something beautiful, I'm deeply inspired by your courage, curiosity, and vulnerability. I've felt less alone because of you, and hope that somehow in reading this story, you feel inspired too.

Taylor Swift, if by some bizarre happenstance the planets ever align and bring this story to you, thank you for allowing us to grow up with you. I've been a fan since *Debut*, and it has been such a gift to continue to be inspired by your different Eras. My life is significantly happier because you've been woven into it. I've had the time of my life with you!

To the younger versions of me that dreamed of where I'd be someday—it all works out the way it's supposed to, and you're more capable than you ever dreamed.

About the Author

Bex Alexander is a romance author from Tulsa, Oklahoma. She prides herself in writing wholesome stories—with accurate mental health representation—that capture the entire emotional spectrum of the human experience. She hopes to ignite further conversations about love, life, and love of life while also giving readers relationships to root for!

www.bexalexander.com

Instagram: @bexwritesbooks

www.ingramcontent.com/pod-product-compliance
Lightning Source LLC
Chambersburg PA
CBHW031834310726
48972CB00005B/1278